Skulduggery Pleasant

RESURRECTION

DEREK LANDY

HarperCollins *Children's Books*

First published in Great Britain by
HarperCollins *Children's Books* in 2017
Published in this edition 2018
HarperCollins *Children's Books* is a division of HarperCollins*Publishers* Ltd,
HarperCollins Publishers
1 London Bridge Street
London SE1 9GF

The HarperCollins website address is
www.harpercollins.co.uk
1

ISBN 978–0–00–821960–4

Typeset in Baskerville MT by Palimpsest Book Production Limited,
Falkirk, Stirlingshire
Printed and bound in Great Britain by CPI Group (UK) Ltd, Croydon CR0 4YY

This book is dedicated to Yve.

Yve, our friendship is like a fine wine: it improves with age, is fragrant and ebullient, and it has aromas of mulberries and pencil lead and...

No. No, that's not it.

Our friendship is less like wine and more like a journey. It has twists and turns and sometimes you lose the signal for the radio and find yourself driving around in circles thanks to the cheap sat nav you bought from that guy with the...

No, that's not it either.

Our friendship is less like wine, and less like a journey, and more like a... a...

Listen, Yve, they're going to print in the morning and I have to get this dedication done in the next few minutes but I really can't think of anything that adequately describes our friendship so it'd be much easier if we just weren't friends any more.

Really sorry.

*In the nothing before the beginning
there was a thought. And the thought
became the beginning.*

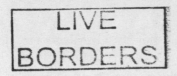

1

A new beginning.

That's what this was. A fresh start. He was going to deliver this one piece of information and then leave. He could go home, back to New York, or maybe Chicago, or Philly. Ireland didn't suit him any more. He was done with it – and it, apparently, was done with him. He was OK with that. He'd had some good times here. He'd had some fun. He'd made some friends. But a new day was about to dawn. All Temper Fray had to do was survive the night.

The wall up ahead cracked. By the light of the streetlamps, the cracks spider-webbed. Any last vestige of hope that he'd just be able to walk out of here vanished with those cracks. Temper had seen this trick before. A redneck psycho called Billy-Ray Sanguine used to jump out at people as they passed, kill them before they blinked. Temper had met Sanguine once. For a hillbilly hitman, he'd been all right. Whoever this guy was, he was no Billy-Ray.

The wall spat out a skinny little runt who came at him with a big knife and a bigger snarl. Temper ignored the snarl for the moment, focused on the knife, batting it away and slamming an elbow into the runt's mouth, dealing with the snarl almost by default. The runt went down, all flailing limbs and broken teeth, and Temper hurried on.

1

Yep. Things were going badly. But of course they were. Nothing ever went well for Temper Fray.

A motorbike came round the corner ahead of him, its single headlight sweeping the storefronts, and slowed almost immediately. Temper kept walking, keeping his head down, his hands swinging loosely by his sides. The guy on the motorbike wasn't wearing a helmet, and he wasn't looking at Temper. He was focused on the road, keeping his head straight. Just a guy on his bike, that's all, going about his business. As he drew parallel, his right hand drifted into his jacket.

Temper lunged, shoving him as he passed, and the bike toppled and the driver cried out as he fell. Temper kicked the consciousness right out of him and the guy flattened out. Bending over him, Temper reached into his jacket, found the gun and pulled it free. He checked it was loaded, then flicked off the safety. His own gun was on the kitchen table in the house he'd been staying in, alongside his phone. He'd have traded all the guns in the world for his phone right now. What he wouldn't give for a chance to call in reinforcements.

What he wouldn't give to call in Skulduggery Pleasant.

He hurried down a side street. There was a woman walking towards him, silhouetted by the lights, her shadow stretching long and thin over the cobbles. He couldn't see her face. It could be Quibble or, worse still, Razzia, or it could just be another citizen of Roarhaven going for a late-night stroll through the city. Temper held the gun behind his back and kept walking.

They drew closer. The gun felt slippery in his grip. He went left and so did she, and it was only when they passed each other that he glimpsed a face he didn't recognise. She gave him a courteous nod and he returned it, and they walked on and he breathed in relief.

"Excuse me," the woman said behind him, and he turned just as a shadow detached itself from their surroundings and snapped the woman's neck. She crumpled and Razzia stepped over her body.

"Thirteen," Razzia said in her broad Australian accent. "Thirteen innocent bystanders. I'm not saying I'm breaking any records, but you gotta admit that's impressive." She looked up, smiling brightly. Beautiful, blonde, always dressed in tuxedos, Razzia was also completely and utterly insane. "You have been a naughty boy."

Her hand flashed up and Temper ducked, hearing tiny teeth snapping beside his ear. He glimpsed the black tendril retracting into Razzia's palm like a nightmarish tape measure and fired at her, but she was already sliding back into the shadows. There was someone behind her, striding up. A bald woman with a gun. Quibble.

She opened fire and he kicked a door open and fell inside, more bullets peppering the doorframe after him. Inside there was a man leaping off a couch and a woman with two mugs of coffee in her hands, staring at him in shock as he barged past her. Temper ran into the next room, saw two men through the window and turned back, took the stairs. The couple shouted and raced after him, and now he could hear a baby starting to cry. He ignored it, hurried to the master bedroom, and through the wide-open curtains glimpsed a young man on the rooftop opposite. Thin, with shockingly platinum hair. Nero. Temper blinked and the young man was gone.

"Dammit," Temper muttered.

He sprinted to the window and then Nero was beside him, sticking his foot out, and Temper tripped and collided with the wall. He twisted, bringing the gun up, but Nero was suddenly right next to him, snatching the weapon from Temper's hand before vanishing again.

Temper had a full second to get to his knees before Nero teleported back into the room, gun aimed squarely at Temper's chest. This time he'd brought a friend, dressed in black, a

3

uniform of rubber and leather. The mask he wore covered his whole head. Not even his eyes were visible behind those tinted lenses.

"Hey, Lethe," said Temper, slumping back and offering a feeble wave. "What's going on?"

Lethe observed him for a long few seconds. When he spoke, his voice was that familiar hollowed whisper that picked over every word with undisguised relish. "I knew you were never *truly* one of us."

Temper shrugged. "Easy to say with hindsight..."

"I could see it in your *eyes*," Lethe said. "Despite your protestations, despite your *wild claims*, you didn't hate the mortals *nearly* enough."

"Well," Temper said, resting his back against the wall and crossing his legs at the ankles, "I've always had trouble hating people because they're different than me. It's a black thing; you wouldn't understand. Or maybe you would. Could there be a brother hiding beneath that freaky mask of yours?"

There was movement out on the landing, and Lethe stepped aside as Razzia sidled in. Memphis and Quibble shoved the young couple into the room behind her.

"Look who we found downstairs," Razzia said. "More innocent bystanders."

"Please," the guy said. "I... I don't know what's going on, but we're not a threat to you, I swear we're not. I'm – listen to me, we're both Arborkinetics. We have a child in the other room, please let us—"

"What's an Arborkinetic?" Memphis asked, his lip curling while he pressed his gun against the young woman's head.

"Plants," said Quibble. "He talks to plants. Makes them grow."

Memphis laughed and said, "Man, that's dumb," which was rich coming from a guy who dressed like Elvis.

"Plants," said the young man. "Exactly. We can't hurt you. If you let us go, we'll—"

Quibble raised her gun to shoot him in the head, but Lethe held up a hand. "Ah-*ah*," he said. "They may talk to plants, but they're still *sorcerers*. They're still part of the *family*. We don't kill family unless we absolutely *have to*."

"Thank you," the guy said. "Thank you so much."

"*Hey*," Lethe said, "we're all on the same *side*." The baby started crying again, and Lethe glanced at Quibble. "Kill the *child*."

The young couple immediately tried to break free, but Razzia hit the guy so hard his legs gave out and then grabbed the girl, held her in a choke.

Lethe didn't take his gaze off Quibble. "You're still standing here. The child is *annoying* me. *Kill* it."

Quibble had now gone quite pale.

"I'll do it," Razzia said happily, but Lethe shook his head.

"No," he said. "I instructed *Quibble* to do it, so Quibble *will* do it."

Quibble didn't want to do it. "Please," she said, her voice soft. "It's just a baby."

Lethe observed her through the tinted lenses of his mask. "I see."

Tears in her eyes. "Lethe... come on, please..."

"You, ah, are refusing to *obey*, Quibble?" Lethe asked.

Memphis glanced away, refusing to meet Quibble's eyes. Nero looked bored, while Razzia watched with growing enjoyment, completely oblivious to the fact that the young woman she was choking had passed out.

"I can't kill a kid," Quibble said quietly.

Lethe took a moment. "Oh, dear."

She was dead. She knew it. Temper had seen that look before, that doomed expression on a slackening face. In his experience, there were only three possible options open to her at this point. The first was to run, but Lethe had a Teleporter on his side, which kind of ruled that out. The second was to give up: to accept what was coming or start begging. But begging wasn't Quibble's style. Quibble was an Option Three kind of girl.

She raised the gun, aimed it straight at Lethe's face. Immediately, Memphis raised his, pressing the muzzle to Quibble's temple.

"Don't," Memphis whispered. "Don't you do it."

"This is exciting," Razzia said, and clapped her hands. The young woman slumped to the floor, unconscious.

"This is *unfortunate*," said Lethe. "Very, hugely, *unfortunate*."

"I can't murder a baby," Quibble said.

"Babies are just people who haven't grown up yet. You've killed *loads* of people. *Loads*."

"So let's wait eighteen years and I'll kill this one," said Quibble.

"Oh," said Lethe. "Oh, this is one of those... *principle* things, isn't it? That's... that's *sad*. I'm *sad* now. You've made me *sad*. Because now I'll have to kill you, Quibble, and... and I would prefer *not to*."

His hands flashed, stripping the gun from Quibble's grip and turning it back on her, pulling the trigger before she knew what was happening.

Her body toppled backwards. The wailing from the other room got louder, and Lethe handed the gun to Razzia. She looked at it like it was a piece of rotting fruit, and tossed it away.

"I'm sorry," Lethe said to Memphis. "I know you were *close*."

"She was my sister," Memphis said.

"Oh," said Lethe. "Didn't know you were *that* close. I feel I have to *ask*, though, Memphis, and please, try not to take *offence*. Are you going to try and *kill me* for this? To exact *revenge*?"

Memphis looked down at Quibble's body. "No, I guess I'm not," he said at last.

"Good," said Lethe. "That's good. It's best, after a *family tragedy*, that everyone tries to *move on*, and put the past where it belongs. In the *past*."

"Do you want me to kill the baby?" Razzia asked hopefully.

"What baby?" Lethe said, and turned back to Temper. "You're coming with *us*, Mr Fray. We have *questions* to ask."

Another man entered the room, a guy with a braided goatee. Temper tried to keep him away but one touch was all it took, and all the bad thoughts Temper had ever had swirled and swarmed and swamped his mind.

2

When the bad thoughts crept up on her, and they did, they came slowly and quietly, slipping in unbidden to the back of her mind, and there they waited, patiently, for her to notice them.

She viewed them as if from the corner of her eye, hesitant to acknowledge their arrival and powerless to make them leave. They stayed like unwelcome guests, filling the space they occupied and spreading outwards. They slowed her down. They dragged on her, made her heavy. When she walked, her feet clumped. When she sat, her body collapsed. It was hard getting out of bed most days. Some days she didn't even try. She knew what was coming.

She was going to die. And she was going to be on her knees when it happened.

She couldn't see her death, but she could feel it. Kneeling down to change a car tyre, she had felt it. Kneeling down to clean up after she'd dropped a plate, she had felt it. Kneeling down to play with the dog, she had felt it.

This is how I'm going to die, she'd realised. *On my knees.*

And always, always, after this had occurred to her there came another thought, the thought that it had already happened, that she was already dead, that her body was growing colder and her blood wasn't pumping any more. She experienced moments of pure terror when she believed, believed with everything she had, that she was trapped in her own corpse, that nothing worked and that no one could hear her screaming.

And then she moved, or she breathed, or she blinked, and with each new act of living she clawed her way back to the realisation that no, she wasn't dead. Not yet.

It was mid-afternoon, and it was cold. The cold meant something. It was the last bite of the beast called winter, a beast that had stayed too long already. She could feel it on her face, on her ears; she could feel it seeping through her clothes. It meant she still had a spark of life flickering inside her. That was good. She needed that. But it also signalled a loss of focus, as she found it increasingly difficult to summon the crackling white lightning to her fingertips.

Eventually, she just sat on the tree stump on which she'd placed the tin cans she'd been using as targets. Three of them were scorched. Two were brazenly untouched. Still, three out of five meant that at least her aim was improving.

She hugged herself. It was an old hoody, but she liked well-worn clothes. Her jeans were a state, and she'd forgotten what colour her trainers had once been, but they were comfortable, and more importantly they were *her*. Lately she'd needed reminding of just who that was.

She looked at the trees. Looked at the sky. Got her mind away from her thoughts. Her thoughts weren't kind to her. They hadn't been for quite some time now. She looked at the twigs on the ground. They were dry. It hadn't rained in two weeks. A rarity for an Ireland still locked in winter's jaws. She watched a beetle scurry beneath a leaf, caught up in its own little life. To the beetle, she must be a vast, unknowable *thing*, a hazard to be avoided but not overly concerned about. If a god is going to step on you, it's going to step on you. You're not going to waste your little beetle-life worrying about something you have no control over.

She looked up, half expecting to see a giant foot descending, but the sky was blue and clear and free of gods. She waited, nonetheless.

Then she stood, and took the trail back through the trees. She used to walk this path as a child, side by side with her uncle. They talked about nature and history and family and he told her stories and she did likewise. They competed as to who had the goriest imagination, but even when he conceded defeat, with a look of mock-horror on his face, she knew he was holding back. Of course he was. Gordon was the writer of the family.

She remembered walking through this woodland with him. She could recall, quite distinctly, as if looking at a photograph, the angle at which she'd seen him. She was small and he was a grown-up, and his hair was brown and thinning where hers was long and black, but they had the same eyes, the same brown eyes, and when he laughed he had a single dimple, just like she did. It had been twelve years since Gordon had been murdered, twelve years since she'd tumbled into this twilight world of sorcerers and monsters and magic. She'd been twelve when it happened, not even a teenager when she'd started her training. The years, they had thundered by, heavy and unstoppable, a boulder rolling downhill. Bruises and broken bones and bloody knuckles and screams and laughs and tears. A lot of tears. Too many tears.

The house Gordon had left her sat on the hill, visible through the trees ahead. Even after it had officially passed into her ownership, she had been unable to think of it as anything other than Gordon's house. Every room, and there were many, reminded her of him. Every Gothic painting on the walls, and they were plentiful, brought to mind some comment or other he had once made about it. Every brick and piece of furniture and bookcase and floorboard. It was Gordon's house, and it would always be Gordon's house.

Then she'd gone away. Five years she'd spent on a sprawling farm on the outskirts of a small town in Colorado. She had a dog for company, and occasionally company of the human variety, but she kept that to a minimum. She didn't want to be alone with her thoughts, but she deserved to be. She deserved a lot of horrible things.

And then she'd come home to Ireland, and realised that in those intervening years Gordon's house had changed, somewhere in her thoughts. Now it was just a house, and so she called it by its name, for names were important. Gordon's house became Grimwood House, just as Stephanie Edgley had once become Valkyrie Cain.

She started up the hill, stopped halfway to turn and look beyond her land, to the farms that spread across North County Dublin like a patchwork quilt of different shades of green and yellow. Here and there the patchwork failed, replaced by neighbourhoods of new families and the roads that linked them. There was talk of a shopping mall being built on the other side of the stream that acted as a border to her property – a stream that Gordon liked to call a creek and that Valkyrie liked to call a moat. Maybe she'd get a drawbridge installed.

She climbed the rest of the hill, approaching the house from the rear. Xena saw her coming and perked up, came trotting over to greet her. With her fingers scratching the German shepherd behind the ears, Valkyrie unlocked the back door and let the dog go in ahead of her. She closed the door once she was inside. Locked it again.

Her phone was on the kitchen table. She had three missed calls. One message. She played the message. It was from her mother.

"Hey, Steph, just calling to let you know that I'm doing a roast chicken for Sunday, if you want me to make enough for you. I know it's only Tuesday right now, but I'm planning ahead and, well, it'd be good to see you. Alice is always asking where her big sister is." She introduced a little levity into her voice there, to pass it off as no big thing. "OK, that's all. Give me a call when you can. We know you're busy. Love you. And please stay safe."

The call ended, and Valkyrie checked who the other calls were from, though she needn't have bothered. They were both from him.

She left the phone where it was and showered, and when she came back downstairs the phone was ringing again. She answered.

"Hey," she said.

His voice, smooth and rich, like velvet. "Good afternoon, Valkyrie. Are you busy?"

She was standing barefoot in the warm kitchen, her hair still wet and water trickling down the back of her T-shirt. "Kinda," she said.

"Would you be able to spare some time? I could do with your help."

She didn't answer for a bit.

"Valkyrie?"

"I don't know," she said. "I don't know if I'm ready. Give me a few weeks. In a few weeks, I'll have myself sorted out and then I'll be able to lend a hand."

"I see."

"Listen, I have to go. I've got things to do and I haven't charged my phone so it's going to die at any moment."

"You'll be ready in a few weeks, you say?"

She nodded to the refrigerator like it was he himself standing there. "Yep. Give me another call then and we'll meet up."

"I'm afraid things are a bit more urgent than that."

She bit her lip. "How urgent?"

"Me-driving-through-your-gate-right-now urgent."

Valkyrie went to the hall and looked out of the window, watching as the gleaming black car came up the long, long driveway. She sighed, and hung up.

She stayed where she was for a moment, then unlocked the front door. It took a few seconds, as she had installed many new locks, and she pulled it open just as the 1954 Bentley R-Type Continental rolled to a stop outside. He got out. Tall and slim, wearing a charcoal three-piece suit, black shirt and grey tie. He didn't feel the cold so didn't bother with a coat. His hair was swept back from his forehead, but his hair didn't matter. His eyes were sparkling blue, but his eyes didn't matter. His skin was pale and unlined and clean-shaven, but his skin, that didn't matter, either. His hands were gloved, and as he set his fedora upon his head – charcoal, like his suit, with a black hatband, like his shirt – his hair and his eyes and his skin flowed off his skull, vanishing beneath the crisp collar of his crisp shirt, and Skulduggery Pleasant, the Skeleton Detective, turned his head towards her and they looked at each other in the cold sunlight.

Valkyrie walked back into the house. Skulduggery followed.

Xena had taken up her usual spot on the couch in the living room, but when she saw Skulduggery she jumped down and ran over. He crouched, ruffling her fur, allowing her to lick his jaw.

"I always feel vaguely threatened when she does this," he muttered, but let it continue until Valkyrie called her away. He straightened, brushing some imagined dust from his knee. "You're looking well," he said. "Strong."

Valkyrie folded her arms, the fingertips of her right hand tapping gently against the edge of the tattoo that peeked out from the short sleeve of the T-shirt. "Gordon had his own personal gym installed in one of the rooms on the second floor."

Skulduggery tilted his head. "Really? I've never been in there."

"Neither had Gordon, from what I can see. The equipment was never used. It's pretty good, though. State of the art twenty years ago. I had similar stuff in Colorado."

"So that's how you're spending your time?" Skulduggery asked, walking over to the bookcases. "Lifting weights and punching bags? What about the magic? Have you been practising?"

"Just stopped for the day, actually."

"And how's that going?"

She hesitated. "Fine."

"Do you have any more control over it?"

"Some."

"You don't sound overly enthused."

13

"I'm just rusty, that's all. And it's not like I can ask anyone for advice. I'm the only one with this particular set of abilities."

"The curse of the truly unique. But yes, you're absolutely right. We don't even know the limits to what you can do yet. If you'd like me to work with you, I'd be happy to do so."

"Ah, I'm grand for now," she said, watching him examine the books. "Why are you here?"

He looked round.

"Sorry," she said quickly. "I didn't mean to sound so... unwelcoming. You said there was trouble."

"I did. Temper Fray has gone missing."

"OK," she said, and waited.

"That's, uh, that's the trouble I mentioned."

"Temper's a big boy," Valkyrie told him. "I'm sure he knows what he's doing."

"Barely."

"Well, he seemed really competent to me."

"You met him *once*."

"And during that meeting he struck me as someone you don't have to worry about."

"I sent him undercover. I think they might have figured out that he's not on their side."

Valkyrie sat beside Xena, whose ears perked up, expecting a cuddle. "I can't do this, Skulduggery. I'm not ready to go back."

"You're already back," he countered. "You made the decision to return, didn't you?"

"I thought it'd be easier than it has been. I thought it'd be like I'd never left. But I can't. So much has changed, and not only with me. After Devastation Day, after the Night of Knives... so many of our friends are dead and I don't understand how things are now. I just need more time."

Skulduggery sat in the chair opposite, elbows on his knees and hat in his hands. "You're freezing up," he said. "I've seen it happen. In war. In conflict. Soldiers see things; they do things... I don't have to tell you about the horrors of combat, of taking lives, of people trying to take yours. With that kind of trauma, there is no easy fix. There's no one-size-fits-all solution. You get past it however you can.

"But one thing I do know, from my own experience, is that the longer you leave it, the harder it gets. Fear is cold water rushing through your veins – if you don't start moving, that water will turn to ice."

"How do you even know I can still do this?" Valkyrie asked. "Physically?"

"You proved that you could when Cadaverous Gant and Jeremiah Wallow went after you."

"That was five months ago," she responded.

"I'm not worried about the physical," he said. "Your instincts will come back to you. Your training will kick in."

She looked at him, her eyes to his eye sockets. "Then what about the mental? I've been through a lot. Might not take much more to break me."

"Alternatively, as you've been through a lot, there might not be much more that *could* break you," Skulduggery said "I'm going to need you with me on this, Valkyrie. I'm a better detective with you as my partner, and I'm a better person with you as my friend. The world is a lot different to the one you walked out on. The Sanctuary system has changed, Roarhaven has changed... sorcerers have changed. There are very few people I can trust any more, and there's something coming. Something big and something bad. I can feel it."

"There's always something big and something bad coming," Valkyrie said. "Sometimes it's you. Sometimes it's me."

"And sometimes you and me are the only people who can stand against it. You're not meant to hide away here, Valkyrie. You're not built for it. You're built to be out there helping people, doing what you can because you don't trust anyone else not to mess it up."

"That was the old me. These days I can quite happily leave the big jobs to others."

"Prove it," Skulduggery said, getting to his feet and holding out his hand. "Come with me for twenty-four hours. If you can walk away after that, I'll let you go and won't ask you again until you tell me you're ready."

She hesitated, then sighed. "OK. But I'm not taking your hand. It's silly and I'd feel stupid doing it."

Skulduggery nodded. "See? You're already making me a better person. Grab your coat, Valkyrie – Roarhaven awaits."

3

The city passed beneath him, and he landed on the lower rooftop, stumbling slightly. He turned, his black coat whipping around him. No one there. No one chasing him.

He breathed out slowly, hearing the slight rattle the mask made. He was going to have to get used to that sound. The mask was snug, and covered his whole head, and it was heavy. The carved beak weighed the whole thing down. He took off his wide-brimmed hat, examined it. He looked equal parts ridiculous and intimidating – but he didn't mind that. Throughout history, plague doctors had always looked strange.

It was a clear day, cold, with only a few clouds in the sky, and below him Roarhaven's streets were alive with people. They talked and laughed and shopped and complained and went about their business. He'd forgotten that, sometimes, this could actually be a nice city in which to live. Funny how violence and terror and death could taint your opinion of a place.

He'd lost friends here. He'd seen them die, seen the life leave their eyes while he held them in his arms. He'd seen destruction on an almost unimaginable scale. The screams had burned their way into his memory. The images had seared themselves into his thoughts.

But that was why he was here. That was his mission. Sebastian Tao put his hat on. He wanted to find Darquesse. He *needed* to. In a world gone mad, bringing her back was the only sane thing to do.

4

Devastation Day, that's what they were calling it now, the day Darquesse had stormed through Roarhaven, levelling its buildings, murdering its inhabitants: 1,351 people had died in those few hours at the hands of an almost-god wearing Valkyrie's face.

Not just her face, of course. Before the murder and the mayhem, Darquesse had been a part of her. Her true name, the source of her magic made flesh. And now Valkyrie was going back there. Because of course she was.

They joined the M1, then the M50, then turned south-east and drove for half an hour, leaving motorways and service stations behind them. Xena lay on the back seat of the Bentley with her head resting on her paws.

"German shepherds shed their coats," Skulduggery said. "Is she shedding now?"

"She's always shedding," Valkyrie replied.

"Your dog is the only dog that has ever been in this car, you know."

"She's honoured."

"It was meant as a complaint."

Valkyrie shrugged. "You have me for twenty-four hours. She can't go twenty-four hours without being fed."

"We could have left her with your parents."

"She doesn't know them."

A pause.

She could feel him watching her. She kept her eyes on the road ahead.

"When was the last time you were in Haggard?" he asked.

She didn't answer. She could feel the sharpness coming on.

"You've been back in the country for five months. How many times have you seen your sister? Three?"

"Let's not talk about this right now, OK?" she said. "I'm not in a sharing mood."

Skulduggery nodded, and Valkyrie felt bad, but she was used to that feeling.

They passed a few signs warning of a flood ahead, then drove by some announcing LOCAL ACCESS ONLY, then about half a dozen PRIVATE PROPERTY signs, before turning on to a long, narrow road that led into the empty distance. An elderly farmer opened a rusted gate and allowed them through, muttering into his lapel as they went. The road seemed to be pockmarked with potholes, some wide enough to swallow a wheel, but the Bentley sped over them without even a rumble. Just another illusion to keep the mortals out.

Advancements in cloaking technology meant that not only were magical elements within the cloaked area rendered undetectable, but what passed for a normal image could also be extrapolated and projected in real time. Skulduggery had explained all this on her first trip back. He'd talked about the marvels of what had been achieved and what was now possible for the future. Valkyrie hadn't paid attention. Her focus then, as now, was to try to spot the shimmering air of the cloaking field before they passed through it. But now, as then, she failed miserably, and Roarhaven appeared before her in an instant – a vast, walled city exploding into being where a moment ago there had been nothing but dead trees and lifeless scrub.

They slowed as they neared Shudder's Gate. Named after a friend of theirs who had lost his life to a traitor whose name

Valkyrie refused to say aloud, the gate was supposedly the only way in and out of the city – although Valkyrie had her doubts about that. The Supreme Mage was a woman who understood the merits of a good secret entrance, after all. Or, at the very least, a good escape route.

The Bentley prowled forward, reflected in the visored helmets of the grey-suited Cleavers who stood guard, and they joined the traffic that flowed through the city streets like blood through the veins of a giant. Here, on the outskirts, the streets formed a tightly packed grid, and the traffic moved easily. But the closer they got to the centre, the more erratic the design became, and the slower they travelled. They were closing in on what had become known as Oldtown: Roarhaven in its original incarnation, with its narrow streets and narrow houses. The city around it had been constructed in a parallel dimension, then dropped here, on top of and around the original. It was a masterpiece of design by its architect, Creyfon Signate, and a testament to his genius, if not his choice of associates. A lot of bad people were involved in the evolution of Roarhaven. Most of them were dead now.

The city had changed a lot since Valkyrie had been away, rebuilt after the battle with Darquesse. The eastern quarter had been obliterated in the fighting, but fortunately it had been mostly uninhabited at the time. It was still largely uninhabited, though, even with brand-new buildings and roads. Those who had to live there, because of the massive influx of residents over the last five years, reported crippling psychic stresses and traumatic dreams. Those sorcerers whose abilities lay on the Sensitive spectrum couldn't go any further east than Testament Road, for fear of permanent neurological damage.

Just one more thing for Valkyrie to feel guilty about.

Roarhaven's population had surged in the last few years. There were magical communities all around the world – some consisting of nothing more than a single street, and some as big as a mid-sized town. There were even three Mystical Cities that only appeared on earth every few decades, places of wonder and absolute freedom. But Roarhaven... Roarhaven was not only the biggest sorcerer city there ever was, it was the first to become part of the landscape. Mages came with their families, and they suddenly didn't have to hide who they were or what they could do. Those who didn't find jobs immediately worked at creating them. It may have been a city of mages, but it was still a city, and like any city it ran on its businesses. It had its shops and its stores and its restaurants and cafés, and it had cinemas and theatres and libraries and swimming pools. It had its own financial sector, albeit a small one, and it was all linked to – and dependent on – the mortal world beyond the wall. The highest salaries went to the people who integrated Roarhaven's activities with the rest of the world without mortal accountants or lawyers or politicians noticing anything amiss. Roarhaven: the Invisible City.

Once they were through Oldtown, the traffic eased up. Travel here was mainly by silent trams that hovered centimetres off the ground, as any cars other than those with Sanctuary tags were forbidden to enter the Circle zone.

In the middle of the Circle stood the High Sanctuary, a palace by any other name, raised thirteen marble steps above street level. Its walls were thick, formidable, and its towers and steeples stretched for the sky as if rejoicing in their own splendour. Twelve years ago, the Sanctuary had been located beneath a waxworks museum in Dublin. When that had been destroyed, it had moved to a flat, unimpressive circular slab of a building that had once stood here.

Now, that slab was hidden deep within this majestic structure, an imperfection to be painted over and forgotten about.

A cathedral reared up on the east side of the Circle. This was new, and it worried Valkyrie. Black and grey, it had wide shoulders, and its towers were almost as tall as the High Sanctuary's. In exchange for various concessions, including a vow of non-violence, the Church of the Faceless had been granted legitimacy before Valkyrie had left for America. Disciples of the Faceless Ones had been allowed to worship openly from that point on.

For centuries, the Faceless Ones had been regarded as little more than sadistic fairy tales – insane gods banished from this reality aeons ago by the Ancients, the first sorcerers – but Valkyrie herself had witnessed their attempts to regain a foothold in this reality. Their existence confirmed, sorcerers flocked to their teachings, and Church numbers had exploded. Otherwise good people attended this cathedral and the other churches throughout the city – and the world – and prayed to cruel gods whose very appearance would have driven them insane. Valkyrie didn't understand it, but then she didn't understand most religions. Faith, she had learned, just wasn't for her.

The Bentley slowed to allow a tram to pass, then moved on to the entrance to the High Sanctuary's underground car park. A City Guard, flanked by Cleavers, held up his hand, and they rolled to a stop. He came forward, eyes on the Bentley, an unimpressed curl to his upper lip. The dark blue uniform struggled to contain his gut, and the badge on his chest glinted in the sun. He had two stripes circling his shoulder, indicating his rank, and his thick belt, on which hung his gun and sword, was polished black leather. The City Guards hadn't existed when Valkyrie had left. There had been a sheriff's position and the Cleavers, of course, but they had been all that were needed to safeguard the streets. Apparently, those days were gone.

Skulduggery rolled down his window. "Corporal Yonder," he said, "how are you this fine morning?"

"Identification, please," the City Guard responded, hooking his thumbs into that belt of his.

Valkyrie frowned. "Being a living skeleton isn't identification enough?"

"Corporal Yonder has always been a stickler for the little rules that make life worth living," Skulduggery said, taking a wallet from his jacket and handing it over. "Though not so keen on the bigger rules, are you, Corporal?"

Yonder didn't answer, just glared at them both before opening up the wallet and examining the credentials within. "State your business," he said at last.

"We've come to pick up an ID just like that one, which has been delivered here for collection," Skulduggery said. "My partner has finally agreed to accompany me on an investigation. It is truly a momentous day."

Yonder closed the wallet with a flick of his wrist, but held on to it. "It doesn't feel momentous to me," he said. "It feels like a Tuesday. You can't use the car park."

Skulduggery's tone was amused. "I can't?"

"The car park is for Sanctuary staff only."

"I have jurisdiction here, do I not?"

"The way it's been explained to me," Yonder said, "is that while you may technically have jurisdiction, we are not obligated to assist you in any way. So you can't use the car park. It's staff only. Also, there are no pets allowed."

"Well," said Skulduggery, "that's quite rude. I mean, I wouldn't call Valkyrie a *pet* so much as a—"

Valkyrie sighed. "He meant the dog."

"Oh," Skulduggery said. "Yes, the dog. I can assure you, Corporal Yonder, that the dog will be staying in the car."

Yonder opened his mouth to argue, then turned, somewhat sharply, and Valkyrie watched a City Guard with three stripes around his shoulder striding towards them. Valkyrie recognised him from his time as a Sanctuary operative. His name was... dammit, what was it? Larrup? She was pretty sure it was Larrup. He was saying something she couldn't hear, but it made Yonder flush a deep red. Yonder stepped back, jaw clenched, as Larrup reached them.

"Detective Pleasant," Larrup said, snatching the wallet out of Yonder's hand, "my apologies for the delay. You have business inside?"

"Yes, we do," said Skulduggery.

"Go right in, sir." Larrup returned Skulduggery's ID to him, then waved for the Cleavers to stand aside. He bent down, looked in at Valkyrie. "Detective Cain," he said. "Good to have you back."

"I'm not back," said Valkyrie. "I'm visiting."

"Yes, ma'am," said Larrup. "Good to have you back, nonetheless."

He gave them a quick salute and the Bentley moved forward smoothly, and took the ramp down, into the High Sanctuary.

5

"Explain," Valkyrie said, a moment later.

Skulduggery steered them between the aisles of cars. "Explain what?"

"Why did the idiot think he could stop us parking here? You do still work for the Sanctuary, don't you?"

"Yes," Skulduggery said. "Well, no, not really."

"But didn't you tell me that you'd been made Commander of those morons?"

"I did, and I was, though they prefer the term *City Guard*, if I remember correctly..."

"So what happened?"

"I quit." The Bentley swerved into an empty space and Skulduggery turned off the engine. "I felt I would be better suited operating outside the system, as it were, and it just so happened that there was a job opening for exactly that position." They got out of the car. Xena barely stirred on the back seat.

"So, if you're not City Guard Commander or a Sanctuary Detective, what are you?" Valkyrie asked as they started walking.

"Centuries ago," Skulduggery said, "before the Sanctuaries were formed and each territory had its own Council of Elders, magical communities were bound together by way of a loose, international agreement of sorts. *We'll help you if you need it, providing you help us if we need it* – that kind of thing. During this time there were certain sorcerers, much like the Marshal Service in the Old West, who delivered justice around the world and enforced the recognised law. They were called Arbiters. When the Sanctuaries came along, Arbiters weren't needed, but the institution was never actually disbanded."

"So the new Supreme Mage in all her majesty made you an Arbiter?" Valkyrie said.

"Actually, it was a lowly Grand Mage who bestowed that honour upon me," Skulduggery said. "Grand Mage Naila. The African Sanctuary has troubles of its own right now, but they've been keeping an eye on how things have been going over here. As Arbiter, I now have jurisdiction all around the world and I'm free to investigate whatever I choose."

"And who's your boss?"

"Technically, I don't have one."

"How do you get paid?"

"I don't do what I do for money."

There was a low buzzing in Valkyrie's ears that she tried to ignore. "But you do get paid, right? Who pays you?"

He sighed. "Each Sanctuary contributes a proportional amount in order to fund the Arbiter Corps."

"And how many people are in the Arbiter Corps?"

"Including me and you? Two."

"I'm not a part of it."

"Your credentials were approved two hours ago."

"By who?"

"Me."

The buzzing got louder until it filled her head, and then her vision blurred for a moment, then came sharply into focus like a new lens being attached to a camera. The world suddenly burst with colour, a glorious red that overlaid Skulduggery's body, and Valkyrie staggered.

"Valkyrie?" he asked. "Are you OK?"

She nodded, aware that she was blinking madly. "I'm just... I can see your aura."

He tilted his head. "I didn't know it was showing."

"Give me a moment. It'll go away."

"Take your time," he said, but even before he'd got the words out her vision had already snapped back to normal.

She straightened. "I'm good."

"You're sure?"

"I am. Really. It's happened plenty of times before." She squeezed her eyes shut, then opened them. "I call it my aura-vision. I really need a better name for it, but whatever. If you're interested, your aura is a vibrant red."

"Ah, excellent," he responded. "Is red a good colour for one's aura to be?"

"I have no idea. Most auras I see are orange. I think you're different because... you're different."

He nodded. "That would make sense."

They walked on towards the far wall, where the concrete ground gave way to highly polished tiles. Skulduggery stood on one, making sure to keep his feet in the centre. Valkyrie did the same on the neighbouring tile.

"Skulduggery," she said, "do you really think that you being your own boss is wise? You're an incredibly irresponsible person."

He nodded. "That did worry me at first, yes, but the more I thought about it, the more accustomed I became to the idea. I think I'll be a wonderful boss, actually, and I certainly intend to lead by example."

The tiles lifted off the ground, and Valkyrie had a moment to steady herself before shooting upwards to the squares of light in the darkness above. She still didn't know what was so wrong with the regular old elevators just a little bit further on. At least you weren't in danger of falling off one of them. This was, in her quiet opinion, needlessly magical.

Skulduggery swerved in front of her and her tile darted around him, twirling as it ascended. They passed through the empty squares above, the tiles clicking into place, and Valkyrie stepped off, a little dizzily, into the obsidian and marble foyer of the High Sanctuary.

The Cleavers standing guard remained impassive, but there were some curious glances from the people hurrying by. After a moment, Valkyrie realised they weren't looking at Skulduggery – they were looking at her. It was like they'd never seen a pair of ripped jeans before.

Administrator Tipstaff came over. A narrow man with a neat haircut, he held a stack of folders under his arm and looked like he hadn't slept for days.

"Detective Pleasant," he said, "Detective Cain, thank you for being on time."

"We're on time?" Skulduggery asked, sounding surprised.

"I truly appreciate it," said Tipstaff, "as I am incredibly busy today. While I do acknowledge the magnitude of Detective Cain's appointment to the Arbiter Corps, I'm afraid we'll have to dispense with the usual pomp."

Skulduggery tilted his head. "There's pomp usually? I wasn't shown any pomp when I collected my badge. There was a smidgen of circumstance, but no pomp. I feel quite let down."

Tipstaff ignored him, and handed Valkyrie a wallet. "Detective Cain, I have been instructed to tell you that even though the Supreme Mage had no say in approving your appointment, she supports you one hundred per cent and welcomes you back into the fold."

"I'm not back," said Valkyrie, opening the wallet. Beside her name and photograph there was a sigil made of silver, half the size of her palm. She slipped the wallet into her back pocket.

"May I enquire as to what case you are working on?" Tipstaff asked. "Of particular interest would be any potentially catastrophic global events. Our early-warning system in this regard has been quite limited ever since the Night of Knives."

The Night of Knives had taken place two years earlier. At precisely the same time in four European countries, assassins unknown had slit the throats of eleven psychics as they slept. How the assassins had plotted against and then killed people who could literally see the future remained a mystery, almost two years on.

"If you are investigating something of appropriate seriousness," Tipstaff continued, "the Supreme Mage has extended to you our full co-operation."

"*Supreme* Mage," Valkyrie echoed. "Grand Mage just wasn't enough for her. She had to go all Supreme on us."

Tipstaff gave a quick, polite smile. "Her duties are immense, as you are probably aware. There were no objections, however, when she claimed her new title."

Valkyrie gave him a small smile back. "Lack of response isn't exactly a glowing endorsement."

"Perhaps not," said Tipstaff. "But the case you are working on...?"

"Probably nothing," said Skulduggery. "I thought I'd bring Valkyrie in on something nice and gentle, just to ease her back into things. But I assure you, if the potential for catastrophe increases by any significant margin, we'll let you know."

"That would be much appreciated," Tipstaff said, and glanced at his watch. "And now I must depart. Good luck, Detectives."

Valkyrie nodded to him as he spun on his heel and hurried away, and in that moment she caught another person glancing at her. She glared and the man looked away quickly.

"People keep staring at me," she said.

"I'm sure it's just your imagination," Skulduggery responded, heading for the exit.

Valkyrie followed him as the doors opened into the sunshine. People strolled across the Circle and a few even braved the cold to eat lunch at the fountain and the base of the clock monument. Beyond them, the Dark Cathedral loomed.

"I don't like it," she said.

Skulduggery didn't even have to ask what she was referring to. "It is quite an imposing structure, if one were to be imposed by structures."

She folded her arms. "I don't like where it is. It looks like it's challenging the Sanctuary's authority. I bet Eliza loves that."

Skulduggery adjusted his cufflinks. "Actually, Eliza Scorn is no longer leader of the Church. I don't even think she's in the city any more."

"How awful," said Valkyrie. "I'm really going to miss her."

"She *was* quite charming."

"I think I'll get over it, though."

"The rest of us have."

"So who's in charge now?"

"That's where things get decidedly less fun," Skulduggery said. "A man named Creed is to take over. Quite a pious fellow. Likes the rulebook. Is fond of self-flagellation."

"Ah," Valkyrie said dismissively, "who doesn't like to self-flagellate every now and then?"

"During the war, he denounced Mevolent as having strayed too far from the teachings of the Faceless Ones."

"He thought Mevolent was too soft?" Valkyrie asked. "Mevolent? The guy who tried to take over the world and kill all mortals?"

"Ah-*ah*. He never said he wanted to kill them *all*, just that he wanted to kill *some* of them and enslave the *rest*."

"And this new guy denounced him. He sounds lovely."

"You're going to like him, I just know it."

They watched the people go by.

"You didn't tell Tipstaff what you're working on," she said.

"No, I didn't."

"Any particular reason?"

Skulduggery shrugged. "I don't have to. I don't report to anyone here. If they're smart, they'll keep out of my way and let me do my job. Sometimes that happens. Sometimes it doesn't."

The monument in the Circle, across from the fountain, was a

huge, three-sided clock, its inner workings exposed to the elements. The clocks were each stopped at different times, representing different stages of Devastation Day. The first clock was frozen at the moment Darquesse broke through the energy barrier protecting the city, the second clock was trapped at the moment she set off that devastating explosion in the eastern quarter, and the hands of the third clock were eternally stuck at the moment Darquesse left this reality, believing she had destroyed everything worth destroying.

It appeared, however, that a clock wouldn't be a clock, even one as symbolic as this, without the ability to tell the actual time, so within every face there were the shadows of hands that weren't there. This, Skulduggery had explained to Valkyrie upon her return, was a metaphor for life carrying on after catastrophe. They were also pretty accurate, which was a plus.

Checking the time, Valkyrie waited until no one was within earshot. "You've got me for twenty-two hours and thirty-three minutes," she said, "and Temper Fray is still missing. What's the plan?"

"We're going to need someone to go undercover, I'm afraid. Nothing dangerous, I assure you. At least, it shouldn't be. I presume it won't be dangerous in the slightest, but it might be just a little bit dangerous, if we're unlucky. Which we usually are, let's be honest."

She looked away so he wouldn't see the doubt in her eyes, but it was too late.

"Everything all right?" he asked.

"I can't do it," she said softly.

"Can't do what?"

She cleared her throat. "Can't go undercover, Skulduggery. I just can't. I'm not... I'm not at my best and I'm not ready for it. I don't even want to be here, for God's sake. I'm sorry, I don't want to let you down, but surely there's someone else we can send. There has to be."

His head tilted. "There is."

She frowned. "Really?"

"I wasn't going to send *you*, Valkyrie. You're far too conspicuous, especially in Roarhaven. No, this will have to be somebody new. Somebody totally unconnected to either of us. Somebody no one would ever suspect of doing anything remotely adventurous. Luckily, I have just the boy in mind."

6

The prophecy told of the first-born son of Caddock Sirroco and Emmeline Darkly, a boy of intelligence and strength with a courageous heart who, in his seventeenth year, would face the King of the Darklands in a battle that would decide the fate of humanity.

Omen Darkly was not that boy. Omen Darkly was the *second*-born son of Caddock Sirroco and Emmeline Darkly, albeit only by a few minutes, and, as such, he got all the leftovers.

Auger, the first-born, was tall and good-looking. Omen had yet to really start growing, and he was worried about a new rash of pimples that had appeared on his chin overnight. Auger's dark hair looked styled even when messy, but Omen's hair, the colour of wet sand, looked messy even when styled.

There were other problems, too. His waist, for example. Yes, it was wider than he'd have liked, but more troubling was that the way it was shaped made it impossible for shirts to stay tucked in. There were possibly some issues with his feet, too, as shoelaces stubbornly refused to remain tied. But, even beyond the physical, Omen struggled in comparison to his brother. Auger would have come top of his class even if he didn't work hard, but work hard he did. Omen had never mastered working. Given the choice between studying a textbook or daydreaming, he'd choose daydreaming every time. He liked some subjects well enough, in particular the languages of magic, but he just didn't have the drive that his twin possessed. He didn't have the focus. And he certainly didn't have the natural talent.

But he wasn't jealous. For all Omen's faults, and he recognised that he had many, he at least didn't blame his twin for his own shortcomings. His brother was a good guy. His brother was a great guy. His brother was the greatest guy alive, in fact, because in three years' time he'd turn seventeen and fulfil the Darkly Prophecy and fight to save the world. Can't get any greater than that.

So Omen didn't mind being constantly overlooked. He was used to it at home, and he was used to it in school. Everyone wanted to hang around the Chosen One. Nobody wanted to hang around the Chosen One's brother.

Sometimes, in his quieter moments, Omen would fleetingly wonder what life would have been like if he had been born first. He bet it would have rocked.

But again no jealousy. No bitterness. Just easily quashed curiosity. He didn't mind.

He watched Auger pass in the hall. A First Year kid tripped and dropped his books, and Auger helped him pick them up. He joked with the kid and the kid flushed with happiness and walked away with his books in his arms and a new confidence in his step. The Chosen One had that effect on people.

Omen kept watching, as a boy with bronze hair and a girl with a wide smile joined his brother. Auger's friends were almost as cool as Auger himself, having earned their place at his side by not giving a damn about his celebrity status. Omen knew that Auger, in fact, would have sought them out once they'd satisfied his mysterious checklist. It took a lot to be Auger Darkly's friend, and Kase and Mahala had passed that test without ever knowing they'd taken it.

Omen closed his locker and slung his bag over his shoulder, then headed off to his next class.

This was his third year at Corrival Academy, deep within the heart of Roarhaven's cultural district. Protected from the surrounding streets by four massive walls with a massive tower at each corner, the school would have been the biggest structure in the city were it not for the Dark Cathedral and, of course, the High Sanctuary. Within those massive walls of the school stood the main building of stone and staircases and balustrades and balconies, and another half-dozen adjunct buildings dotted around the campus and courtyards.

Omen liked the place well enough, and liked Roarhaven, too. It was a lot better than where he'd grown up. The magical community in his hometown near Galway was small and suspicious of their mortal neighbours. His parents, in particular, were guilty of harbouring a deep and abiding distrust of anyone born without magic. Of course, they distrusted most people born *with* magic, too, so he had been glad to leave it all behind and come here, to the most exclusive school in the world. The fact that he had only been invited to attend because of the Darkly Prophecy did not matter to him one little bit.

Omen even liked the uniform. He said he didn't, claimed he hated it to anyone who would listen, but it was actually pretty cool, all things considered. Black blazer worn with black trousers or skirt, white shirt and tie. Each of the Years, from First to Sixth, had a different colour, starting with yellow and ending with black. As a Third Year, Omen's tie and the piping on his blazer were both purple. The school crest, a dragon and three burning towers, was captured in a patch worn on the left breast, and the uniforms looked cool no matter the size or weight of the student. Omen may not have won any Student of the Year prizes (they usually went to Auger), and he wished he could fit into a uniform a size or two smaller, but he definitely felt that all-too-rare sensation of pride whenever he donned those clothes.

Now he joined a line of smartly dressed students as they filed into class. He did his best to tuck in his shirt, then sat at his desk and pulled a book out of his bag.

"Where'd you get to?"

Omen looked up. Never's ash-brown hair was tied back today, which meant he was identifying as male. This was unusual for a Tuesday. Normally he was a she by this stage of the week, although Omen knew by now that to assume anything of Never was a mistake. Back in First Year, she had stood up in class and declared loudly that he would not be held to anyone's expectations but her own. He sat next to Omen in most of their classes together.

"I had a study period," said Omen. "Where were you?"

"Maths," said Never. "Where you should have been."

"We have maths next class."

"No, we had maths last class. Peccant has you down as ditching."

"Aw, man."

"You should really look at your timetable every once in a while."

"He hates me so much."

"You're not his favourite, it has to be said."

The door at the front of the class swung open and Miss Wicked walked in. Immediately, the chatter died. Miss Wicked was one of those teachers who demanded obedience from even the unruliest of students. In his three years of attendance, Omen had never seen her angry, had never heard her raise her voice, and yet she somehow remained intimidating despite this calm demeanour.

She was tall and brilliant and blonde and slender, and she had a tongue as sharp as her cheekbones and always wore pencil skirts and high heels. Omen was a little bit in love with her.

"Today we are going to be discussing Necromancy," Miss Wicked said in that precise way of hers, where every word was perfectly formed. "Can anyone tell me the names of some prominent Necromancers of the past?"

Hands went up, Omen's included.

"Axelia," Miss Wicked said.

Omen almost sighed. Axelia Lukt was the prettiest girl in school, with hair almost as blonde as Miss Wicked's and big blue eyes and the cutest Icelandic accent Omen had ever heard. Omen had had many conversations with Axelia, conversations where he'd joked and laughed and made incisive comments about world events. He'd been charming, funny and considerate, and the fact that she hadn't yet fallen in love with him was a puzzle he just couldn't solve. Maybe the fact that all of these conversations had taken place entirely in his head had something to do with it, or perhaps it was because he had yet to engage her in an actual, physical, *real* way. Whatever the reason, girls remained a mystery to him, but he was determined to figure it out.

He'd started practising in the mirror.

"Morwenna Crow," Axelia said, answering the question while simultaneously proving that a better volunteer could not have been chosen. "Melancholia St Clair. Lord Vile."

Miss Wicked nodded. "Lord Vile. The most notorious. Can you tell me the object into which he poured his power?"

"His armour," said Axelia. She was so smart.

"Very good. Necromancy is death magic. Shadow magic. As such, it is a lot more volatile than Elemental magic, or even most Adept disciplines. Necromancers store a good portion of their power in an object that they either wear or carry around with them."

"Necromancers are sad little lunatics," said Jenan Ispolin, his lanky frame lounging back in his chair. "My father rounded them all up years ago, dragged them out of their little temple and kicked them out of our country." Jenan's father was the Bulgarian Grand Mage, and his smirking son rarely let anyone forget it. Like Omen, Jenan belonged to a Legacy family, where everyone was encouraged to take on the same surname – but, whereas the Darkly name had somewhat positive connotations, the Ispolin name brought to mind brutality under the auspices of law. "That's what you do to people like that."

Miss Wicked observed him. "People like what, Jenan?"

Jenan sat up a little straighter, and cleared his throat. "Uh, Necromancers, miss."

"Necromancers are sorcerers, the same as you or I. Are you going to condemn them for their chosen discipline?"

"No, miss," Jenan said, flushing red. "I just meant... when the Death Bringer was around, she—"

"Her name, please?"

"Melancholia, miss. When Melancholia was around, she tried to kill billions of people. That was the Necromancer plan all along. My father said they were all murderers and he didn't want them in our country so he... he kicked them out."

"And what if some of your classmates harbour a desire to join a temple and study Necromancy?" Miss Wicked asked. "How do you think they feel right now, to hear you speak of them this way?"

Jenan shrugged. "Dunno, miss. Don't care."

"We have a Necromancer on our teaching staff, here at the Academy. Are you calling her a murderer, too, Jenan?"

He shrugged again. Defiant this time.

Miss Wicked nodded, like she had reached a conclusion she had no intention of sharing. "I see," she said.

There was a knock on the door and a blushing First Year came in. He hurried up to Miss Wicked, passed her a note, and hurried out as fast as his little legs could carry him. Miss Wicked glanced at the piece of paper, then looked up.

"Omen," she said.

Omen sat straighter. "Yes, miss?"

"Your presence is required elsewhere."

A creeping dread came over him. Peccant must really be on the warpath if he was taking Omen out of class. "Do I really have to go?"

Miss Wicked gave a half-smile, and a part of him, beyond the dread, delighted in being able to amuse her. "Yes, you do. Take your bag and report to the South Tower."

Omen frowned. "Mr Peccant isn't going to throw me off, is he?"

"I have no more information than that, I'm afraid. You'll have to take your chances. Off you go."

Omen glanced at Never and got a sympathetic look in reply. He stuffed his book into his bag, headed for the door and tripped over Jenan's outstretched foot. Omen went stumbling and the class erupted into laughter that was immediately curtailed by Miss Wicked's arched eyebrow.

Omen left the room and dragged himself to the South Tower. Peccant may have been an excellent teacher, but he was also a terrifying man with an explosive temper, and Omen had always got the impression that teaching was just the wrong vocation for him. Maybe something like State Executioner would have been more suited to his personality. Or Puppy-Killer.

Despite his reluctance to arrive, Omen walked a little faster. To keep Peccant waiting when the teacher was already in a bad mood would not have been wise. Omen took the main stairs up and cut through the Combat Arts block. Not every Corrival graduate was going to work for a Sanctuary, but it was still generally acknowledged that being able to defend yourself was a good thing, and should be encouraged. In this block, they devoted equal time to the physical and magical sides of self-defence. Auger, of course, was the star pupil.

When Omen reached his destination, there was nobody waiting for him. He walked out on to the covered balcony that circled the tower. The wind was pretty stiff up here. He looked out over Roarhaven. From where he was standing, he could see the High Sanctuary and the Dark Cathedral, challenging each other across the Circle zone. Below him, people walked over the bridge that spanned Black Lake. He thought he saw movement beneath the water and he peered closer. The Sea Maiden had her home down there, somewhere in that sparkling darkness. A beautiful woman with long dark hair, Omen had only glimpsed her once, but that had been enough to enthral him. Below the waist she may have been a serpent, but above the waist she was divine.

"Mr Darkly," a man said from behind. Right before he turned, Omen thought it was Peccant speaking, but it wasn't.

It was Skulduggery Pleasant. Skulduggery Pleasant was standing there, speaking. Beside Skulduggery Pleasant stood Valkyrie Cain. Valkyrie Cain stood beside Skulduggery Pleasant, and they stood there, looking at Omen, and Omen stood there, looking at them and trying his very best not to geek out.

7

"I'm your biggest fan," Omen said before he could stop himself.

Skulduggery Pleasant's head tilted. "Thank you," he said. He was wearing the coolest suit Omen had ever seen, and he was a skeleton. Omen had known this, of course he had, but there was a world of difference between knowing there existed a living skeleton and actually seeing him in front of you. There were no wires or strings keeping the bones together, at least none that Omen could see. He was tall, and the brim of his hat dipped low over his eye sockets.

Valkyrie Cain – *the* Valkyrie Cain – was almost as tall as Skulduggery, and prettier than she appeared in the photographs he'd seen – and she appeared plenty pretty in the photographs. Her black hair was a little longer. She was bigger, too. Slim, but beneath her jacket her shoulders were wide. It was weird seeing her in jeans. Like she was out of uniform.

"My name is Skulduggery Pleasant. This is my associate, Valkyrie Cain."

"Hello," Omen said. He sounded reasonably calm, which surprised him. His voice didn't break, which delighted him. This was a good start, but he could feel the excitement bubbling up from his chest. He hiccuped. "Excuse me," he said.

"Your name was given to us by one of your teachers," Skulduggery continued. "Apparently, you are someone we could possibly trust with sensitive information. We need your help, quite frankly."

Omen nodded. Then frowned. Then tried to smile. Then looked confused.

"This world faces a threat," Skulduggery went on, "and we think you may be able to help us stop it."

"Oh," said Omen, it all suddenly making sense. "No, sorry, you've got the wrong brother. I'm *Omen* Darkly. You want *Auger* Darkly – he's the Chosen One."

"We haven't made a mistake, Omen. It's you we want."

A frown creased Omen's forehead once more. "Why?"

"Your brother would draw too much attention," Valkyrie said. "From what I've heard, people notice when he walks by. We need someone who disappears in a crowd."

Omen smiled widely. "That does sound like me."

"What we're about to ask you to do shouldn't be dangerous," Skulduggery said, "but, if it turns out that way, your skills could come in useful."

My skills? Omen thought.

"My skills?" Omen said.

"Your brother has received the best combat training available anywhere since he was four years old. You help prepare him, don't you?"

"I've... I've trained with him since we were kids, yes. What's this about, please?"

They came forward. Omen had to resist the urge to step back.

"There is an organisation," Skulduggery said, "which doesn't have a name. We've been hearing rumours about it for years, an anti-Sanctuary, designed to sow the seeds of chaos and discord around the world and, ultimately, force a war between sorcerers and mortals – a war that sorcerers, presumably, would win, though not without heavy cost. We don't know who's in charge. We don't know where it's based. We don't know how many agents it has or how powerful it may be. What we do know is that it's been working behind the scenes for decades. We have had run-ins with only three people who we suspect were directly connected to it. The first was a man called Bubba Moon, who claimed to have been visited by a 'being of wonderment and awe', demanding blood sacrifice. The next two were a couple of killers with a mission to complete – Cadaverous Gant and Jeremiah Wallow."

"What was their mission?" Omen asked.

"To kill me," said Valkyrie.

"Oh."

"Out of those three individuals," Skulduggery continued, "all were American, and only Gant is alive and at large. Whether their nationality is a coincidence or means something more, I can't say yet. In the last three years, however, the rumours I've been hearing have intensified. Apparently, the anti-Sanctuary is now operating out of Roarhaven."

"OK." Omen tried smiling again. "I still don't know what you want with me, though."

"An associate of mine went undercover," Skulduggery said. "Temper Fray. He infiltrated a group of sorcerers who talk about mortals like they're vermin. He befriended them, and started giving me names. Melior. Smoke. Lethe. Then he disappeared."

Omen stared. "Is he dead?"

Skulduggery tilted his head. "Hopefully not. Before he vanished, Temper became convinced that the anti-Sanctuary had someone inside Corrival Academy recruiting young and impressionable students."

"Oh my God," said Omen. "You want me to go undercover."

"Yes."

"Even though the last person you sent undercover got killed."

"Temper might still be alive," Skulduggery said, sounding irritated.

"Oh, right, yes, of course. Sorry. But you do want me to go undercover, yes?"

"That's correct."

Omen looked at them both, and completely failed to stop the stupid grin from crawling across his face.

"Dear God," Skulduggery said. "You look demented."

"I'm just really excited."

"It's getting freaky," said Valkyrie. "Quit it."

"I can't. I don't know how."

"We're not asking you to take any risks," Skulduggery said. "We're asking you to keep your eyes and ears open. Are any of your fellow students acting suspiciously? Are they congregating at unusual times, in unusual places? Your teachers – are they acting normally? Do any of them seem unusually angry?"

"Mr Peccant is usually unusually angry," Omen said at once. "Usually at me."

"I'll investigate Mr Peccant, don't worry," Skulduggery said, "but I'll need you to focus here, OK? Any behaviour that strikes you as out of the ordinary. That's what you need to be looking for."

"And then what?"

"Then you tell us," said Valkyrie.

Omen nodded. "OK, yeah. And then what?"

Skulduggery and Valkyrie looked at each other.

"I don't understand," said Skulduggery.

"Like, do I come with you, then?" Omen asked. "Do I still have to go to school, or will you give me a note to get out of classes or something? I mean, I'd use my reflection, but the teachers can always tell, and little alarms go off sometimes."

Valkyrie held up her hand. "Wait, hold on. We're asking you to snoop around this school. That's it. That's all we're asking, and that's all you're going to be doing."

"But... but you might need me. For stuff after."

"Doubtful."

Omen looked at Skulduggery. "But sir... I read all about you. All about the both of you. You took Valkyrie on as a partner when she was twelve. *I'm* fourteen."

44

"This is true," Skulduggery said slowly. "But, as it was pointed out to me only an hour ago, I am a very irresponsible person. I'm trying to change that, truly I am, so unfortunately I am not taking on any more partners. Ever."

"Then I'll... I'll be your protégé."

"I'm not taking on protégés, either."

Omen looked at Valkyrie. "Could I be *your* protégé?"

She looked horrified. "What? No. I don't have protégés. I'm too young to have protégés. I'm only twenty-four, for God's sake. I barely know what a protégé is. I'm still the kid here. I'm still the... Skulduggery, tell him. I'm the young one in this whole dynamic."

Skulduggery nodded. "You definitely are the young one. Though technically he *is* younger."

"But he's not a protégé! Or a partner! He's a schoolboy! I'm the partner, I'm the young partner. I still have learning to do. I'm still..." She trailed off, then glared at Omen. "I'm the young one here."

"OK," he said. "Sorry."

"I feel like we've strayed a little off topic," Skulduggery said, "so allow me to pull things back to our original question. I realise this is a lot to take in, but we have to know – Omen Darkly, will you help us save the world?"

8

Cadaverous Gant was of the opinion that this world was not worth saving.

It was peopled with savages who revelled in their own ignorance, who splashed about in the mud and the mire like children. This was a Truth he had glimpsed even before his Great Awakening, a Truth that had stained his hands red, that had left bodies in his wake, and it was a Truth that would rend flesh and shatter bones for years to come. Cadaverous would be there to see it happen. This he had been promised.

Sorcerers called them *mortals*. Cadaverous preferred to call them what they were: *cattle*. Dead-eyed and unthinking. Bags of meat and fountains of blood, unimaginative animals awaiting slaughter. In the end, they all sounded the same. They all wept the same tears, prayed to the same gods, offered the same feeble entreaties. And they all died the same. Every single one of them.

And there had been many. The methods he had used may have varied, but the deaths were identical. Once they'd got past the terror, once they'd realised their fate was inevitable, they were still surprised by the very act of dying, as if they hadn't truly believed it could happen to them.

In his mortal youth, he had gloried in the hunt. They ran, screaming and sobbing, the perfect prey, and he pursued, calm and determined, the perfect predator. When his muscles were strong and his legs were quick, their deaths were explosions of brutal violence. When his muscles weakened and his legs grew tired, their deaths were splendid blueprints of meticulous planning. His house was his weapon, his traps mere extensions of his will.

And then his heart attack, and the voice, the woman's voice, that whispered to him and led him to his Great Awakening.

Charles. Charles, open your eyes. Open your eyes, Charles. You are mine. You will come to me.

And so he left his mortal life behind and opened his eyes to the lights of the operating room and the sounds of the machines and the doctors and the nurses and the clink of scalpels on trays and the squeak of the wheels of gurneys and the faraway voices and the chatter and that soft whispering in his mind that said, *Charles, welcome back, we have work to do.*

She had brought him magic in those moments of death. He was an old man, but his magic made him new again. He was strong, and quick, with a new appetite for killing and a new mission. The war they were to bring about. The things they were to do.

There had been missteps. There had been failures. He had suffered defeat and suffered loss. The boy he had mentored, the boy to whom he had bequeathed his knowledge and his insight and his philosophy, who had grown to be a man of sterling character and dark potential, had been delivered a meaningless death at the hands of a mewling, pathetic young woman, a woman just like all the others except for that crackling, cackling power that she held in her fingertips.

Cadaverous had wanted immediate vengeance, but the voice in his head commanded him to wait. *Soon*, she said. *Soon you will have her life in your hands. Free me, and you will have both your reward and your revenge.*

And it was almost here.

*

He stood on the clifftop, looking out to sea, the cold wind snagging at his coat. The others stood beside him but not with him. He was apart from them. He was special.

"I can't see it," said Nero. His voice had adopted the annoying whine that irritated Cadaverous so much.

"Of course you can't," Smoke said. "It's got a cloaking shield around it."

"But if I can't see it then I can't teleport on to it, can I?"

"You *can* and you *will*," said Lethe. "We know *exactly* where it'll be in three minutes, so, in three minutes' time, you're going to teleport out *there*." He pointed directly in front of them. "It's *perfectly* safe."

"What if you're wrong?" Nero asked.

"We're *not*. We have its *schedule*."

Nero hugged himself against the cold. "What if the schedule's wrong? We're going to be teleporting into empty space."

"It won't be empty."

"But what if it is?"

"Then you'll start *falling*, and you'll teleport yourself to *safety*."

Nero's eyes narrowed. "Wait, what? No one's coming *with* me?"

"It's too risky."

"You just said it was safe."

"It *is* safe. But it's too risky for *all of us* to go at once. You go, *confirm* it's there, then come back for us."

"Sounds pretty easy to me," Razzia said, nodding with confidence.

"OK," said Nero, "so what if it *is* there, but I 'port right into the middle of a group of Cleavers?"

"Then extricate yourself from the situation," Smoke said, like he was talking to a four-year-old.

Nero shook his head. "Everyone here seems to have this idea that I'm just a mode of transport. Listen to me: I'm not a car, OK? I'm not a car or a train or a plane. I'm a person. Teleporting somewhere blind is a sure way to get myself killed."

"*Trust* in the *plan*," said Lethe.

"If I get caught or get killed, there *is* no plan," Nero countered. "I want someone to come with me."

Razzia stuck her hand in the air. "I'll go with him!"

"Not her," Nero said immediately.

Razzia frowned. "Why not me? What's wrong with me?"

Nero looked around for help. With none forthcoming, he swallowed thickly. "Uh... you're just... You're not very stealthy."

"Bull dust! I take off these heels and I barely make a sound when I walk. My feet are tiny. Look at them. It's amazing I don't fall over more often."

"Well, it's not really the stealth that's the problem," Nero said. "You just, in certain circumstances, you tend to go a little... crazy."

Her eyes narrowed. "What?"

"At times."

"Crazy?"

"A little."

"I go crazy?"

"No," Nero said. "No, you don't. At all."

She snarled. "Then you'll let me go with you?"

Nero paled. "Of course."

"Yay!" Razzia said, happy again.

Lethe held up a hand. "Nero may have a *point*, Razzia. This infiltration requires a certain *deft touch* that you may be lacking."

Razzia bit her lower lip while she pondered. "Well," she said, "I suppose I do go a little crazy sometimes."

"I'll take Memphis," said Nero, but Memphis shook his head. "Hell, no, I ain't going."

Nero looked dismayed. "Why not?"

"You might get it wrong, man," Memphis said, running a comb through his hair. "Or you might teleport us into a group of Cleavers. I'll stay here until I know the coast is clear, thank you very much."

Cadaverous sighed. "I'll go with him."

Nero scowled. "I don't want *him* to come."

"You've already turned down one and been rejected by another," Cadaverous said. "It's me or it's no one. I'm sick of listening to you complain about not being appreciated for who you are or what you contribute to the team. That's all I've heard from you for the last few weeks. If you're too scared to go alone, then I shall hold your hand. Is that acceptable to you, Mr Nero?"

"I don't like the way you're talking to me."

"I somehow fail to care."

"Gentlemen, *gentlemen*," Lethe said, holding up his hands, "there's no need for *hostility*. Cadaverous has made a *kind-hearted* offer. Nero, will you accept?"

"Sure," Nero said grudgingly.

"*Beautiful*," Lethe said. "Razzia: what is the time?"

Razzia nodded. "Time is a social construct designed to derive order from chaos."

"Well put, Razzia. And do you *have* the time?"

"Oh," she said. "No, I don't wear a watch. I don't believe in them. Time's never done me any favours, and that's fair dinkum."

"I see. Smoke?"

"It's twelve oh four," Smoke said. "Twenty seconds to go."

Lethe rolled his shoulders. "Nero, Cadaverous, *prepare* yourselves. The rest of us will *stand ready*."

Cadaverous took hold of Nero's wrist.

"We don't need to be touching," Nero complained.

Cadaverous gave him a smile. "I'm just making sure you don't forget about me in all the excitement."

Nero took a moment to roll his eyes before looking straight ahead, at the patch of thin air he was aiming to arrive at. As the seconds ticked away, Cadaverous used his tongue to pick a piece of meat from between his teeth. He spat it out.

"Go," said Smoke.

Suddenly they were 1,100 metres off the coast and falling towards the churning, freezing sea. Cadaverous's body released a bolt of adrenaline. Nero tried to snatch back his arm. He was about to panic, about to teleport away. Cadaverous tightened his grip.

And then his feet vanished.

The rest of him followed, almost too quick to register – his knees, thighs, hips, chest – and then they had dropped through the cloaking shield and Coldheart Prison burst into existence beneath them, a floating island of rock on which sat the walls, the fences, the watchtowers and the prison buildings themselves.

They teleported lower and flipped, so that their momentum took them upwards and then cancelled out. When they stopped rising, Nero teleported them once more, straight down to solid ground. They landed gently and crouched, waiting for the alerts to be called. When they heard no shouts, heard no alarms, they dared to raise their heads.

They were on the very edge of the island, perched on the slippery rocks. Before them was a fence. Beyond that, another fence. Towers, manned by Cleavers, stood at regular intervals – eight towers to a side. Walls and more fences separated the yard into sections for prisoner recreation and sections for staff. The buildings were big and blocky and imposing. Small windows and few of them. Solid doors.

The main prison building was a massive tower with broad shoulders. Slanted windows at the very top gave it its scowl. The inmates called this building the Brute.

"Fetch the others," Cadaverous said, the wind whipping away his words. Nero vanished.

As irritating as Nero could be, he was also the key to taking this prison. So long as his enemies were within a certain range, he could teleport them away without having to lay a finger on them. The sigils and safeguards that kept out others of his ilk had no effect on him. He was, to all intents and purposes, virtually unstoppable. That reason, and that reason alone, was enough to keep him alive.

He arrived back with Lethe and the others.

"Cleavers in every tower," Cadaverous told them. "Electrified fences. Cameras covering the yard. Just as we were warned."

"And we're not yet fighting for our *lives*," said Lethe, "which means we are *indeed* in the one blind spot the island offers."

"Our information was correct," Smoke said.

Lethe looked at him. "You doubted it?"

"I don't like spies," he said, pulling at the braids in his goatee. "Theirs or ours."

"Well," Lethe said, "I for one am *grateful* for our spy. It bodes well for what is to come. You all know what to *do*. You all know where to *go*. We want the Cleavers and all Sanctuary personnel *dead* or *gone*. This is to be a clean sweep. Ignore the convicts. They'll beg you to open their cells, but we're not here for *them*. We're here for *her*. We're here to find the *box*."

"And while we're all risking our lives," Nero said, "what are you going to be doing?"

Lethe nodded towards the Brute's slanted windows. "I'm going to be in the *control room*," he said. "Someone's got to *steer* this thing, after all."

9

Skulduggery and Valkyrie watched as Omen Darkly, his schoolbag slung over his shoulder, failed utterly to take his leave with anything resembling dignity. He tried two locked doors before finding the one that led off the balcony and into the tower. He waved, blushing madly, and disappeared.

"Interesting boy," Skulduggery said. "Not what I would call especially impressive, but an interesting boy, nonetheless."

"I don't know about this," Valkyrie said. She was getting cold. "He's a kid, Skulduggery. We shouldn't be involving him in this stuff."

"Perhaps," Skulduggery said, "but he did make a valid point. I involved you in 'this stuff' when you were even younger."

"That's different."

"How so?"

"That was me," she said. "I could handle it."

"I think Omen will surprise you."

"He forgot which door he literally just came through."

"So it'll be an even bigger surprise."

She peered over the railing, down on to an empty courtyard. "He's not going to get the chance, though, is he? He keeps an eye out for this recruiter person and that's it, he goes home."

"This is a boarding school."

"You know what I mean."

"That's all we'll need him to do, yes. But there's a stubbornness in his eyes that I've really only seen once before."

"I was never stubborn," Valkyrie said, climbing over the railing. "I just happened to be right."

She let go and plummeted. The South Tower was six storeys high and she was halfway to the hard ground before the air began to slow her descent. Skulduggery drifted down beside her, wrapping his arm around her waist.

"I do wish you'd tell me before you jump," he said, "especially if you aren't even going to *attempt* to use your powers."

"I can't fly," she reminded him.

"You've flown before."

"I've *hovered*."

"Hovering is the first step to flying," he said as they touched down gently in the empty courtyard. He released her. "That's what I tell people who ask for tips."

"Do many ask?"

"More and more," he said. "Apparently, there's been a resurgence in people choosing Elemental magic as their discipline, all because they want to learn to soar above the clouds."

The wind had messed up her hair, so she tied it back into a ponytail. "Even though none of their Elemental teachers can fly? This doesn't suggest to them that maybe flying is harder to master than it would appear?"

"They don't care," Skulduggery said. "They just want to emulate their heroes."

"You mean you."

"As the only Elemental who can actually fly, yes, I mean me. Don't you miss it?"

"Flying? The only times I've *properly* flown, Darquesse had taken over. The memory's a little tainted."

"I suppose," he said, then took his pocket watch from his waistcoat and glanced at it. "There's someone I need to talk to before we leave. Will I meet you back at the car?"

"Ah," she said, "I kinda want to explore a little, see what's what."

"Oh. OK. And you're sure you don't want to head back to the car and wait for me there?"

"You're worried that my dog will have peed on your seats, aren't you?"

"The thought has occurred to me."

"Xena will still be asleep, believe me, and she doesn't pee in cars. You go talk to whoever you have to talk to, I'll have a walk around and I'll meet you out front in, what, twenty minutes?"

They split up, and she passed through the nearest door, found herself in a corridor just as the bell rang and students swarmed out, filling the spaces and jostling Valkyrie as they squeezed by. She sighed with irritation, kept her elbows down and didn't hit anyone. After another few seconds, the crowd started to thin and she could walk without tripping over anyone.

Four kids with green ties stood in a group ahead of her. They started whispering. Valkyrie kept her head down and her eyes on the floor as she passed them. Out of the corner of her eye she saw them glance her way, and when they were behind her the whispering picked up again.

Valkyrie turned to face them. "What?" she snapped. "What is it that's so fascinating about me? *What?*"

The kids froze. They actually looked scared. One of them snapped out of it, hurried away, and the others quickly followed. Valkyrie glared at them until they had disappeared round the corner. Then she started to feel stupid for overreacting.

She turned again, just as a young woman dressed all in black strode up to her with an arm outstretched.

"Hello!" the young woman said, and Valkyrie was shaking her hand before she knew what was happening. "It's very good to meet you! I've heard so much about you, naturally, but it's so good to finally meet you in the flesh!"

She was Scottish, had long red hair, a few freckles and the brightest smile Valkyrie had seen in a long time.

"You'll have to forgive the students," the woman said, lowering her voice slightly. "It's not often they meet someone famous."

Valkyrie took her hand back. Gently. "I'm not famous."

"Ah, well, *infamous*, then."

Valkyrie took a moment to work it out, then she sagged. "Oh, right. Darquesse."

"They've seen all the pictures," the redhead said, "all the videos. And there are plenty of videos of Darquesse tearing the place up. They don't mean anything by staring, really they don't."

"It's fine," Valkyrie replied. "Amazingly, I kind of forgot that people would associate me with her, even though we shared the same face. Just another thing to feel bad about, I suppose."

"Mmm," said the redhead, because she obviously couldn't think of a way to salvage this topic of conversation. Then she brightened again. "I'm Militsa Gnosis. I teach Magic Theory."

"You're a Necromancer?"

"Guilty as charged," Militsa said, and then suddenly stopped smiling. "Which is probably not the best phrase to use when most of your Order plotted to kill billions of people. If it makes any difference, though, I didn't know anything about the Passage or what the Clerics were planning."

"So you're a *good* Necromancer?"

"Yes," Militsa said, beaming once again. "I was going to store my magic in a ring like you did, but I didn't want you to think I was copying you, even though I so would have been, so I keep it in this instead." She pulled back her sleeve, revealing a thick bracelet. "It's pretty cool, I think."

"Yeah."

Militsa's smile faltered. "Oh, no."

"What?"

"I'm being lame, aren't I?"

"Sorry?"

"I'm being so lame right now," Militsa said, her chin dropping. "You think I'm a complete idiot, don't you?"

"Do I?"

"You must."

"I don't think so."

"But I'm babbling. I'm just a babbling idiot that ran up to you and started babbling. This is so embarrassing. Why do I have to be so lame?"

"I... I don't think you're lame."

"That's just because you're a nice person."

"I'm not that nice," Valkyrie said. "Really, I'm not. I'm quite rude."

"You're not rude."

"I am," Valkyrie insisted. "Before this conversation is done, I bet I'll have been rude to you by accident."

Militsa looked up. Her eyes were huge. "You mean it?"

"I do. And you're not lame and you're not an idiot. You're just being friendly. You're a friendly Necromancer, which is kind of unique."

"We're not known for being friendly, I'd have to agree," Militsa said, brightening.

"So you're a teacher here?"

"Yep. I guide students through their options, as far as choosing a discipline goes. I never meant to be a teacher, to be honest. It's not something I ever saw myself doing, but it combines two of my favourite things – talking about magic and... and, well, *reading* about magic, I suppose. I don't have a very wide range of interests."

"Maybe you should get out more."

"That's what my mum says, but then she's three hundred years old. I think she has unrealistic expectations when it comes to me. I'm just a normal girl. Give me a good book and a sofa and I'm happy, you know?"

"Can't beat a book and a sofa."

"If I wasn't a teacher, I'd probably be a researcher, maybe be a part of Project Torchlight. Have you heard of it?"

"I haven't, I'm afraid."

"Ah, no matter. My point being, I specialise in the Source – which is another reason I'm so pumped to be meeting you." Militsa hesitated, her eyes sparkling. "Could I see your magic? Could I see what you can do?"

"Uh..."

"Just a little bit, I swear. You're incredible to me, that's all. You're connected to the Source of all magic like nobody else. Your magic is... it's pure. Unfiltered."

"I'm not very good at controlling it," Valkyrie confessed.

"I'm not surprised," said Militsa. "I've got theories about it, if you'd like to hear them."

"Uh, maybe. I'm a little busy right now..."

"Oh, of course," Militsa said, laughing at her own stupidity. "Of course you're busy, you're Valkyrie Cain! But if ever you wanted to talk about it, just knock on my door. I will literally drop everything to talk to you. Literally. Everything." She brushed her hands together. "Dropped."

"OK," said Valkyrie. "Well, I might do that."

"Or if you just want to hang out," Militsa said. "You haven't been to Roarhaven much, have you? Again, I'm not a stalker, I just... I'd have heard if you were in town a lot. I could show you around. There's actually a pretty good arts scene here. Bizarre, I know, but there you go. Might be fun, if you're into that kind of thing. Or we could go for a coffee. Or a drink. Or dinner. Would you like to go to dinner?"

"No thank you."

"Right, of course, you're busy, I get it."

"It's not that I'm busy," said Valkyrie. "It's just that I don't want to."

Militsa blinked. "Oh. Well, I mean, OK. That's cool."

Valkyrie's face soured. "And now I'm being rude, just like I knew I would."

"You're not rude, no."

"It's just I'm not looking for a friend right now."

Militsa blinked. "Ohh. OK."

"I'm sorry. I don't want to offend you, but I'm trying to stay away from people until I get my head straight."

"Gotcha," Militsa said. "No explanation needed. You've been through a lot and the last thing you need is someone to talk to."

"When you say it like that," Valkyrie said, "it sounds stupid."

"Not at all. This is totally my fault – I just feel like I know you already. I've asked Fletcher so many questions."

Valkyrie raised an eyebrow. "You know Fletcher Renn?"

Militsa looked surprised. "Well, of course. He's a teacher here."

Valkyrie couldn't help it – she grinned. "Fletcher? Seriously? What does he teach? What does he know well enough *to* teach?"

Militsa grinned with her. "Teleportation. He's only got three students, and only one of them can actually teleport, but he's pretty good. I think you'd be impressed."

"That's hilarious," said Valkyrie. "Is he all strict and stuff?"

"Very. He has a teacher voice."

"Oh, wow."

Valkyrie's phone buzzed with a message from Skulduggery, saying he'd be delayed another ten minutes. As she slipped it back into her jeans, she noticed Militsa glancing at her watch.

"You probably have work to do," Valkyrie said.

Militsa nodded. "I'm supposed to be teaching a class right now. If this was a mortal school, the kids'd be tearing up the place, but Corrival students tend to be so boringly well behaved that they're probably cleaning the windows. The coffee offer will remain open, by the way, for as long as you need it to be. Or, you know, dinner. Whatever."

"Thank you. Really. I appreciate the gesture."

"No problem," Militsa said, and beamed another smile. "It

was so nice to meet you, Valkyrie. I hope we *can* get to know each other better."

Valkyrie smiled back, and Militsa turned with a swirl of her cloak and walked off. She wore a cloak. Valkyrie hadn't known very many people who wore cloaks. Not even Skulduggery wore a cloak. What an odd girl. Valkyrie liked her.

She left the school, with its magnificent arches and grand staircases, and walked the wide streets. Plenty of time to double back and meet Skulduggery. There was a guy on the corner, barefoot and dressed in sackcloth, holding a sign that warned her that the end was nigh. To reinforce the point he was making, he shouted it at anyone who was passing.

"The end is nigh!" he screeched to Valkyrie, shaking the cardboard sign. "The end is nigh!"

"Isn't it always?" she asked, and left him shaking the sign resentfully.

She made a note of the street names as she went by. Gorgon Street. Titan Street. Bellower Road. She crossed Meritorious Square and took the narrower streets now, away from the staring, whispering people. She walked down Blood-drenched Lane, took a right on to Decapitation Row. At least they were easy to remember.

She smelled food and her tummy rumbled, so she followed the smell and then abruptly lost it in a dead end that went by the charming name of Putrid Road. She turned, and stopped.

Three people stood there – two men and one woman – staring at her with a special kind of look in their eyes. Valkyrie had seen that look before. She was well used to that look.

That look meant that, at some point in the next few minutes, they were going to try to kill her.

10

Sebastian watched it all from the rooftop.

He watched the three of them follow her away from the crowds, away from anyone who might step in. He would have expected more from Valkyrie Cain. He would have expected her to be a lot more alert. But there she was, in jeans and a T-shirt instead of her usual black, walking like a zombie, just going where the streets took her, like she had a thousand different things on her mind and she didn't want to think of a single one of them. He watched her reach the dead end and turn, and freeze.

He crouched low, and bit his lip beneath his mask. He had his mission. He shouldn't be wasting his time on things like this.

Below him, Valkyrie waited for the three people to say something. When they didn't, she spoke. "I'm not Darquesse."

Sebastian's ears were covered, but he heard her perfectly.

"You look like Darquesse," said the woman. "You look the way she did when she killed my family. Except you're not smiling. Darquesse was smiling."

Valkyrie hesitated. "I'm not her."

The man on the left was packing some extra weight, but he looked strong, like those clenched fists would hurt. "Darquesse killed my daughter," he said. "Burned her to nothing. I doubt she even noticed she'd done it."

"My brother tried to fight her," the second man said. "I begged him not to, but he thought if he could sneak up behind her, while the Skeleton Detective and everyone was distracting her, he could snap her neck before she knew what was happening. My brother, who had never snapped a neck in his life. He never even got close."

"I'm sorry for your pain," Valkyrie said slowly. "I'm sorry for what you've been through, and for what your loved ones went through. But I'm not Darquesse."

"We know," the woman said. "We know you're Valkyrie Cain. We know all about you. We know Darquesse was your true name, and we know she inhabited the body of your reflection. We know all this. Everyone does. Everyone knows that none of it would have happened if it weren't for *you*."

"Sensitives had dreams about her for years before she showed up," the second guy said. "They warned you. All that time, you knew what would happen if you kept going. But you didn't want to go back to a mortal life, did you? You wanted to be one of us. A sorcerer."

"So you let it happen," the first man said. "You allowed it to happen just like the Sensitives predicted it would, because you were having too good a time going off on all your adventures."

"Nothing to say?" the woman asked, walking forward. Sebastian tensed. "For a girl with a reputation for being a smart-mouth, you're awfully quiet."

"Leave me alone," Valkyrie said.

"You shouldn't have come back."

"Leave me alone. Please. I don't want any trouble."

The woman sneered. "Begging didn't save my family. It's not going to save you."

The woman slapped her. Hard. Sebastian's own cheek tingled in sympathy, but Valkyrie just stood there.

Obviously of the opinion that a simple slap wasn't going to do the job, the first man stepped up and swung a punch that sent Valkyrie spinning to the ground. Sebastian readied himself to jump in the moment Valkyrie retaliated – but she just stayed down, propped on her elbow, holding a hand to her face. The woman kicked her in the shin, ended up hurting herself as much as she hurt Valkyrie.

Slowly, Valkyrie stood back up.

The first man looked at the second, who hesitated, then nodded and clenched his fists also. These were not warriors, Sebastian saw. These were just ordinary sorcerers. Ordinary, angry sorcerers.

The second man hit Valkyrie, a light punch to the shoulder.

"Come on!" said the first guy. "Harder!"

The second man stared at Valkyrie, his lips curling as he cultivated his anger, and he hit her again, this time in the face. Valkyrie took a few steps back before she regained her balance. Blood dripped from her bottom lip. Still she did nothing.

The punch was followed by another, and another, fists fuelled by pent-up rage, by loss and love and hate, all that pain finally finding an outlet in the infliction of pain on another. Valkyrie was doubled over by a shot to the belly and then sent to the ground again. A low, tortured moan escaped her as she struggled to breathe.

And, once more, she got to her feet.

The woman pushed her way to the front, clicking her fingers and summoning a ball of flame into her hand. This changed things. Valkyrie shifted her balance slightly as she watched the woman, waiting to see what she would do. Waiting to see if she'd cross the line.

For a moment, the woman seemed to reconsider. Sebastian had a good view of her face, and he saw the conflict there. The emotion. The flames dimmed, looked like they were about to go out.

But then something – a memory, an urge, a flash of ruthlessness – flared the flames in her hand and she moved her arm back, preparing to throw, and Valkyrie leaped at her, smacking her hand down and driving her elbow into the woman's jaw. The woman crumpled and the fire went out.

The first man snapped his palm against the air and the space rippled, but Valkyrie was already lunging at the other guy. She rolled under his punch and grabbed him, twisted him, threw him over her leg and he went tumbling.

The first guy charged, too angry to use magic. Valkyrie met him head-on. She crashed into him, using her elbows as a battering ram. He staggered back, clutching his chest, trying to get his breath back. She let him fall to one knee, gasping, and turned to the smaller man as he rose. Again, she closed the space between them, refusing to give him a chance to throw a punch or use his magic. She slapped him so hard Sebastian winced, and wrapped her arm around his throat as he spun. She kicked out his leg and crouched with him, tightening her stranglehold. He struggled, tried to pull her hair, but she stayed calm and just kept squeezing.

The first guy was getting his breath back, and he was attempting to stand, clicking his fingers at the same time. Any moment now his hands would be filled with fire.

Sebastian leaped, crashing into him from above. The big guy went down as the other guy lost his battle to stay awake. Valkyrie laid him on his side, turned and observed Sebastian as he stood there.

For a long, long moment, nothing was said. Sebastian allowed himself to think that maybe Valkyrie was overawed. Maybe she was intimidated.

"You look so dumb," she said.

"Do I?"

"Did you fly, or jump?"

"Oh," he said. "I jumped. I was up there." He pointed above him. "And now I'm, you know... down here."

"That's a good story," Valkyrie said.

"I, uh, I feel like I haven't made the best first impression."

"How could you possibly think such a thing, wearing a mask as ridiculous as that? Do you have a name?"

Sebastian smiled beneath his mask. "Names," he said, "are power."

"Fine," she said, wiping blood from her lip. "I'll call you Mr Beakface."

He stopped smiling. "No, don't call me Mr Beakface. Call me the Plague Doctor."

"Mr Beakface is easier to remember."

"Please don't call me that."

She peered closer. "Are you an actual doctor?"

"I'm here to fix things."

"So no."

He sighed. "Not a doctor as such."

"And why are you wearing a mask?"

"It came with the suit."

"It makes your voice sound funny."

He frowned. "Does it?"

"You don't hear that? It echoes."

"Oh," he said. "I don't know. I didn't know it echoed."

She stepped over the unconscious body at her feet. "What do you want?"

"Like I said, I'm here to help."

"By arriving at the last minute when the fight is just about done? You're handy."

"I mean, from now on," Sebastian said. "I'm here to help from now on."

"What are you going to help with? Has the Black Death come back?"

"Well, no. But bad things are coming."

"Why do people keep saying that like it's a surprise?"

"I'm a friend, OK? That's all you need to know."

She looked at him. "I've just had this conversation with someone else. I'm not looking for any more friends. Do yourself a favour and stay out of my life."

She walked by. For a moment, he thought she was going to lunge at him, to tear off his mask and reveal his face... but she passed him like she couldn't be bothered with anything any more.

"Valkyrie," he said.

She turned. Waited.

"Why did you let them hurt you?"

"They caught me by surprise," she said.

"No, they didn't."

"Believe what you want. I don't care."

"One other thing? I, uh, I would appreciate it if you didn't tell anyone about this."

She frowned. "Sorry?"

"Skulduggery," Sebastian said. "Anyone else. It would be better if they didn't know about me. Not yet."

"Why?"

"I can't tell you. Please, for now, keep this between me and you."

She put her hands on her hips and looked down, like she was counting to ten. She raised her head. "Listen, Mr Beakface—"

"Plague Doctor."

"—I'm not comfortable keeping any secrets from Skulduggery, even the important ones. I wouldn't view meeting you as important."

"Valkyrie, please. When I can explain myself, I will. I know it's asking a lot, but... trust me."

She sighed. "Fine," she said, and walked away.

11

Two minutes later, the Bentley pulled up by the side of the road and Valkyrie got in.

"A guy in a stupid mask asked me not to tell you he exists," she said, reaching back to pet Xena.

Skulduggery nodded. "Fair enough."

12

They drove east through the city, parked and went walking. Xena, on a leash but without a muzzle, investigated every stray scent. Valkyrie hadn't been to this part of Roarhaven since it had been rebuilt. The apartment blocks were big – the apartments within them small. The streets, though new, had already developed potholes. Mostly uninhabited, with little in the way of shops, the few people they passed there either stared at Valkyrie in shock or actually crossed to the other side to avoid her.

"This is not doing my self-esteem any good whatsoever," she muttered.

"Maybe they're afraid of the dog," Skulduggery said.

"They're afraid of something."

Skulduggery took off his hat and placed it on her head. "Is that better?"

"I look stupid."

"Not everyone can pull off a hat like this, it's true."

She tugged the brim low, shielding her face as they approached a mother and small child. The kid pointed at Skulduggery, ignoring Valkyrie and Xena altogether. She kept the hat on.

"Where are we going?" she asked.

"There's a bar somewhere around here," Skulduggery answered. "From what I've heard, it's rife with anti-mortal sentiment."

"You think the bad guys drink there? What's it called?"

"The Mage's Lament."

"What's he lamenting," she asked, wincing slightly, "not ruling the world? Bit of a long shot, isn't it, checking out a bar the bad guys *might* frequent?"

"I am merely aware that my twenty-four hours with you are slipping away, so I thought we may as well try a few long shots while we're together. Are you feeling OK? You've gone quite pale."

"I'm fine," she said. "Just have a headache starting up."

"Probably from all the punching you've recently undergone."

She shrugged. "People don't like me here. I have to get used to it."

"So you're not going to alert the City Guard, have these people arrested?"

"They attacked; I defended. It's over. Besides, it's not like the City Guard would take me seriously. They're probably looking for any excuse to slap the shackles on me."

"Perhaps you're right. I suppose I should just be thankful that this mysterious stranger showed up in time to rescue you."

"He literally landed on the guy's head. He didn't rescue anyone. Stop saying that."

"I just find it amusing that you'd need to be rescued."

"First of all, I didn't need anything of the sort. Second, what are you talking about? You used to rescue me all the time."

"That was different. That was the natural flow of events. I'd rescue you, you'd rescue me, it's how we worked. It's how we work still. We're there for each other, aren't we? Until the end?"

"I suppose."

Xena stopped walking, started whining. Valkyrie crouched, ruffling her fur. "What's wrong with you, huh? What's wrong with my baby?"

Skulduggery looked around. "I think we're going the wrong way," he said, and turned. Valkyrie followed as he walked back the way they came, Xena trotting happily ahead of her.

"It's not like you to get lost," Valkyrie said.

"I have many things on my mind. And, judging by the long periods of silence you sink into, so do you."

"I don't have to be talking every moment we're together, do I?"

"No," he said. "But that's never stopped you before."

She shrugged. "The world is a scary place, and it's only getting scarier. The American president is a narcissistic psychopath. Fascism, racism, misogyny and homophobia are all on the rise. We've ruined the environment. Animals are going extinct faster than I can name them. Bullying is everywhere. Nobody talks to anyone who doesn't share their views. Everyone hates. Everyone shouts. Everyone cries. There is literally no escape for the human race unless someone steps in and *orders them* to be better. But the only people who could do that are sorcerers, and that would bring about the war with the mortals that Cadaverous Gant and these anti-Sanctuary nutjobs so desperately want. So... y'know. Rock and a hard place."

"You think cheery thoughts, don't you?"

"Can't help it. I'm a naturally optimistic person."

They reached the Bentley and it unlocked with a beep.

"How's the headache?" Skulduggery asked.

"Fading," Valkyrie said. "Are we not sticking around? I thought we had to find The Mage's Lament."

"I've decided that I don't like long shots. They're annoying, and rarely work out. Besides, it's the middle of the day – I doubt there's anyone interesting there right now. A better use of our time might be to take a drive up to Cassandra Pharos's cottage."

Xena jumped in the car and Valkyrie got in after her. "You really want to take a detour?"

"You never got a chance to say goodbye when you left for America," Skulduggery said, shutting the door and starting the engine. "Maybe some of your reluctance about committing to coming back stems from a lack of closure."

"Wow."

"What?"

"*Closure.* Wow."

They pulled out on to the road and started driving. "Closure is important," he said. "You moved to Colorado and assumed that people like Cassandra and Finbar would be here when you got back. You never said goodbye."

"You think I feel guilt about that?"

"You don't?"

"No," Valkyrie said, giving him back his hat. "And the only people who should are the people who killed them."

The morning after the Night of Knives, Skulduggery had called Valkyrie in Colorado to let her know what had happened. She'd spoken to him while wrapped in a towel. The house was quiet apart from the faint splashes coming from the shower. By the time she'd hung up, the water had been turned off and the shower door was opening. She sat on the edge of her bed, tears in her eyes. She didn't go to the funerals.

They rolled up to Cassandra's cottage a little after 2 pm. Valkyrie had mixed feelings about the place. On the one hand, Cassandra had always reminded her of the grandmothers she'd lost when she was a kid. She'd been warm, and funny, and fascinating. She'd had stories to tell about each and every facet of her life. Just to be in her company had brought a glorious feeling of being welcome. Of coming home.

But the cottage had a cellar, and in that cellar there was a floor that was a metal grille over a bed of coals. And when the steam swirled and Cassandra played her visions out in 3D, like holograms, the warmth vanished, despite the rising heat, replaced by the cold dread of the horrors to come. It was in those steam clouds that Valkyrie had first seen the rubble of Roarhaven during Devastation Day, and her own face, mere moments before she went on to kill her baby sister.

Valkyrie let Xena roam, and eyed the cottage. "Why are we really here?" she asked.

"I have a theory that needs to be tested," said Skulduggery. "No more questions. I don't want to spoil the surprise."

He found the key beneath an old pot and opened the front door, and Valkyrie took a dry leaf from the battered packet she kept in her jeans, popping it into her mouth as she stepped through. The cottage was just as she remembered – the comfy sofa, the faded rug, the guitar on a stand in the corner – but the dream whisperers which had hung from the rafters were gone. Valkyrie was glad. They were creepy little things.

"Are you OK?" Skulduggery asked.

The leaf had started to dissolve on her tongue, but she chewed the rest to get rid of it faster. They were great for numbing pain, be it from a broken leg, a gunshot wound, or a mere headache, but no one had yet bothered to make the damn things taste better. "Another headache," she said as she wandered over to the guitar. "Nothing to worry about." She picked it up.

Skulduggery's head tilted. "Perhaps."

She strummed. Badly. "Perhaps what? It's a headache. People get headaches all the time. Especially after they've been punched in the face."

Skulduggery took a small bag of rainbow dust from his pocket, held out his hand and let it sprinkle through his gloved fingers. It fell as golden particles. "Do you remember what gold means?"

"Gold means psychic. Which is to be expected, right? Even though Cassandra's been dead for two years?". She played the first few bars of 'Stairway to Heaven', got it wrong and tried again.

"You are quite correct," he responded, sealing the bag and putting it away. "This cottage contains an abundance of residual psychic energy, enough so that anyone with Sensitive tendencies would be vulnerable to their influence."

"OK. So?"

"We were nearing Testament Road when you got the headache earlier," he said. "The part of town where Sensitives can't go."

Valkyrie laughed. "Oh, wow. This is your theory? You think I'm a Sensitive?"

"I think it's a possibility. The full range of your abilities has yet to be explored. Most sorcerers are restricted to one discipline – I'm one of the rare exceptions, being both an Elemental *and* a Necromancer. But you? You might be something else entirely."

"I think I'd know if I was a psychic, though."

"Would you?" Skulduggery asked, and took the guitar from her hands. He walked away from her, playing 'Heroes' by Bowie. "Tell me something – have you experienced anything unusual recently?"

"You mean apart from you? Listen, I don't have clairvoyance. I can't read people's minds or see into the future." She faltered on the last word, then shook her head. "This is silly. I'm not a Sensitive."

"You don't know what you are," he said, turning and starting to sing.

Xena wandered in and he sang to her while she sat, head cocked to one side, and when he was done he twirled the guitar and thrust it away from him, and it floated back to the corner to settle into its stand. The show over, Xena got up, wandered back outside.

"I didn't know you played," Valkyrie said.

"Cassandra taught me," he responded, and looked around like he'd just realised she wasn't here any more.

Valkyrie let the silence continue for a bit, then broke it. "So we're here," she said. "Remembering Cassandra. Singing. She really would have liked that. What's next? We head back to Dublin and get matching tattoos in honour of Finbar?"

"If you like," he said. "But, since we're here, we may as well go downstairs."

"Why would we want to do that?"

But he was already opening the narrow door beside the cupboard. "Come on," he said, and went down.

Valkyrie hesitated a long moment before following.

It was dark down there. Cold. Old pipes ran up the bare walls. A straight-backed chair stood in the middle of the metal floor.

"I'm not sure what you're hoping to achieve with all this," she said.

He clicked his fingers, summoning flame into his hand. "Your, what do you call it, your 'aura-vision' is a psychic ability. How do you know that it doesn't go deeper? Indulge me this once."

"I'm always indulging you."

"Then indulge me once more." He dropped the ball of fire to the floor. The flames lit the coals beneath and heat immediately started to rise.

"What do you think is going to happen here?" she asked. "I'm suddenly going to have a vision? I don't have visions."

"Not yet, but the energy all around you could trigger something, and, if it does, we'll be able to see it played out in the steam."

"Or we'll just be standing here getting a cheap sauna that will wrinkle your suit and ruin my hair."

"Nothing will wrinkle this suit," said Skulduggery. "Ghastly made sure of it."

"We saw *him* in Cassandra's vision," Valkyrie pointed out. "We saw Ghastly with Tanith. We saw them kiss on Devastation Day – only he died before that could happen. Even if I did have a vision, so what? Ghastly's death proves that visions of the future mean nothing."

"No," Skulduggery replied, taking a yellow umbrella from a hook on the wall and passing it to her. "His death proves that the future can be changed if you know what's coming. And we have *no* idea what's coming. We don't even know who we're up against, not really, so we don't know what we have to avoid. Try, Valkyrie. At least try."

She sighed, then sat in the chair. It was quickly turning hot in here. When the first bead of perspiration formed on her temple, she opened the umbrella as Skulduggery turned the red wheel.

Water rushed through the pipes, gurgling like the belly of a ravenous beast. The sprinklers started up, tapping a growing applause on the umbrella. Steam rose, getting thicker, becoming mist, becoming fog. She lost sight of Skulduggery, but heard the wheel turn again, and the water cut off. She collapsed the umbrella, shook it and laid it on the floor before standing.

"Now what?" she asked.

"Now focus," Skulduggery said. "Or don't focus. Empty your mind, or maybe fill it."

"You're a great help."

"I don't really know how this works."

"Hush," she said.

She stood there, eyes fixed on the empty space in front of her. She tried to relax her thoughts, but they were in as big a jumble as ever. Her head buzzed. The headache was coming back.

"I don't think this is working," she said.

And then something moved ahead of her.

13

A shadow in the billowing steam. Valkyrie narrowed her eyes. "Did you see that?"

"I saw something," Skulduggery said.

"What was it? It looked like—"

Something flared in the distance, a sudden fire or explosion. Valkyrie walked towards it.

"Careful," said Skulduggery, but he sounded so far away. "There's a wall in front of you."

She knew that. Behind the steam and the shadows, she knew there was a solid wall. She knew she was still in the cellar. She knew what was real and what wasn't.

Only there was no wall. Frowning, she kept walking, hands out in front, and with each step she expected to come into contact with the wall and yet each step brought her deeper and deeper into the steam. She turned, looked back.

"Skulduggery?" she called.

He didn't answer. She couldn't see him.

She heard something, though. Someone whistling a tune. A familiar tune. Something old. Sweet yet sad. 'Dream a Little Dream of Me.' It moved from right to left. She went to investigate, but something about the tune made her pause, and she realised she didn't want to know who the whistler was. She stayed still, listening to the tune fade.

A line of people trudged out of the nothingness, walking right into her, dissipating upon contact. She watched them, their heads down, their footsteps heavy. Men and women and children, bags on their backs, bags in their hands. Faces tired and anxious. Scared, even. A continuous line. So many of them.

The steam stole the people away, and she turned and there were flames all around her. A town was burning. Screams mixed with car alarms. Before her, two figures, side by side. She recognised Omen Darkly, his face older, and bleeding. Beside him, a handsome boy, clutching his injured shoulder. She became aware of figures behind her and she turned, saw their forms without faces, felt their anger, their hatred, their aggression. Omen and the other boy, his brother perhaps, clicked their fingers and summoned fire into their hands.

"You actually think you're going to win?" somebody asked, and she turned, saw the Plague Doctor a moment before the steam stole him away. She looked back and the burning town was gone and Saracen Rue was dead on the ground, his throat torn open.

Valkyrie held her hand over her mouth. "Skulduggery!" she called. "Skulduggery, where are you?"

Cadaverous Gant emerged from the steam, holding a rag doll in his left hand, a rag doll in a blue dress. He walked so quickly that she put out a hand to stop him and his image broke apart, and beyond him she saw Tanith Low, her blonde hair cut to above her shoulders, backing away from something, fear in her eyes.

She turned, the clouds swirling, and she glimpsed China Sorrows lying in a field of broken glass, blood drenching her blouse, her eyes open and unseeing. Valkyrie turned away to shouts, to jeers, and saw a stream of energy blast through the chest of a girl, saw her fall back, hair covering her face, and when Valkyrie went to catch her the images swirled away and Valkyrie could see herself, on her knees, tears running down her face. Defeated. Alone.

And she knew she was watching her own death.

Valkyrie's legs gave out and she collapsed. She didn't try to get up again. She stayed where she was, her eyes tightly shut, hands over her ears.

"Make it stop," she muttered. "Make it stop."

A fingertip, under her chin.

This was real. This reassured her. Valkyrie breathed, calming, and opened her eyes, but it wasn't Skulduggery crouching before her, it was a woman with silver hair, and Valkyrie jerked away, fell back, and the woman laughed.

"All this pain," the woman said. "All this death and destruction. It's because of you, my dear. All because of you."

"You're... you're not real."

"I will be," the woman said, and smiled. "You will make me real. I know who you are. I know your secret." The woman stood. "I am the Princess of the Darklands, and I'm coming for all of you."

Her image drifted away on the thinning steam, and Skulduggery plunged through, scattering it completely.

"Did you see that?" Valkyrie asked.

"Some of it," he said, helping her up. "Not all."

"Her, I mean. Did you see her? The woman with the silver hair?"

"I'm afraid I didn't," he said, guiding Valkyrie to the chair.

She slumped down on to it, her limbs leaden. "She spoke to me."

"To a future version of you."

"No, Skulduggery – to *me*. She was speaking to me, now, just a few seconds ago. She touched my chin. I could feel it."

"That's not possible."

"I know that. But I'm telling you it happened. She said she knew my secret. What secret? Do I even have any secrets? She said she was the Princess of the Darklands and that she's coming for all of us. You didn't see her? Hear her?"

"All I saw were the lines of people, the fire, Saracen, and then China. You're sure she touched you?"

"Yes," she said. "I mean... I'm pretty sure. I could feel – or at least I think I could feel..." She sighed. "I don't know. The whole thing was kind of overwhelming."

"What else did you see?"

"Tanith. She was fighting someone – big surprise. I saw Cadaverous Gant, that Plague Doctor guy, and Omen and another boy – I think it was his brother. You know what that means, don't you? Omen stays involved. We can't let that happen. Asking him to keep an eye out for suspicious behaviour is one thing, but actually mixing him up in this stuff is just too much. He thinks this is all a grand adventure, but we're going to get him killed."

"Did you see him die?"

"No, but that's hardly the point, is it? We can't endanger the lives of two innocent boys."

"I'm afraid we might not have a choice with Auger. The Darkly Prophecy relates directly to a King of the Darklands – obviously a relation to the woman you saw. He's already involved, and it's got nothing to do with us."

"But Omen isn't. There's nothing in that stupid prophecy about Omen, right? Skulduggery, promise me you'll fix this."

"I'll speak to him," Skulduggery said.

"You need to make sure he stops. He has to understand that we don't want his help any more."

"I'll pay him a visit."

"Let him down gently, though, OK? He seems... I don't know. Fragile."

Skulduggery tilted his head. "Does he?"

"You don't think so?"

"No, actually. He doesn't have your strength, but I detected a certain durability about him."

"He can be durable on his own time, then, because I don't want him to take one step further into this thing."

"Very well."

He watched her take the packet of leaves from her jeans.

"Are you sure you want another of those?"

"My head is splitting."

"I'm not surprised. But an over-reliance on painkillers is not something you want to develop."

She folded one, put it in her mouth. "They're leaves, Skulduggery. I'm not exactly going to get addicted to leaves, am I? It's not like they make me feel good. They just stop my head from exploding."

"Non-exploding heads is something we want to encourage," he admitted, and helped Valkyrie up.

By the time she'd climbed the stairs, her strength had come back to her. She stepped outside and the cold air froze her through her damp clothes. She hurried to the Bentley, let Xena in and got in after her.

Skulduggery slipped behind the wheel. "Congratulations," he said, starting the engine. "You have looked into the future. You are a bona-fide psychic."

"Yay," she said without joy. "I'm not going to start reading people's minds, am I? I find it unbearable enough reading their faces."

"I don't know," he answered. "I've never seen such a range of abilities in one person before. We don't know your limits yet. We don't even know if you have any. This is actually quite exciting."

"Then you can be quite excited and I'll just sit here and worry."

He turned his head to her slightly. "Did you see anything else?"

"I saw enough," she said, and looked out of the window.

14

The First Years were playing basketball on the outside court. Omen could see them from his desk. No magic was allowed, though, so it looked like a pretty dull game. He watched Rubic and Duenna walk across the small courtyard, deep in discussion. Not an unusual sight, the principal and vice-principal talking and walking, and certainly not enough to arouse Omen's suspicions – but what better recruiters could the anti-Sanctuary have than the leaders of the school?

Omen sat back in his chair. The last class of the day was geography. The teacher's name was Valance. He was an Adept, though Omen didn't know which discipline he'd specialised in. So far, there didn't seem to be anything suspicious about Valance's behaviour. He just talked about geography a lot.

Omen cast a surreptitious eye over his classmates. They all looked pretty normal – bored and impatient for the lesson to be over. Apart from Chocolate, but then Chocolate loved geography. She was weird like that.

He smiled to himself. He liked this. Having a secret. Having a mission. Skulduggery Pleasant and Valkyrie Cain had come to *him*. Not to Auger, not to anyone else. To *him*. That meant something. A moment like that, he reckoned, a moment that singles a person out, validates their entire existence, gives their life meaning... Well. Something like that could be the start of something amazing.

"Omen."

Omen looked up. "Wuh?"

"Did you get all that, Omen?" Valance asked, clearly aware that Omen had not. "Could you repeat it back to me?"

"Uh..."

"I don't believe that's a part of it."

"No, sir," said Omen. "What I meant was... I didn't actually catch it, sir."

Valance nodded. "I see. Which part?"

"Sir?"

"Which part didn't you catch? Or, to put it another way, what's the last part you *did* catch?"

Omen wished he didn't blush so easily. "Uh..."

"Yes, Omen? Was it the volcanic ash part, or the igneous rock part?"

"Volcanic ash, sir."

"Ah," said Valance, and Omen knew instantly that it had been a trap. "Even though I've spent the entire class talking about the history of the European Union, the last thing you heard was me talking about volcanic ash, which you would have learned about in First Year. What Year are you in now, Omen?"

"Um, Third, sir."

"So for the last two years you haven't caught anything I've said?"

Omen lowered his head. "I wasn't paying attention."

"Sorry, Omen, what was that?"

"I wasn't paying attention," Omen repeated, louder this time.

"I am shocked," Valance said. "Shocked and appalled. Could you do me a favour, Omen? Could you try to pay attention? Could you do that for me? Or, at the very least, could you try not to be so obvious when your attention wanders? I am a very sensitive educator, and this will not have done my confidence any good whatsoever."

Everyone else was enjoying this immensely. Omen kept his eyes on his desk. "Yes, sir."

"Thank you," Valance said, and went back to teaching.

Omen copied down the notes and did his best to listen and look attentive, until the bell rang and he joined the others in filing out into the corridor. He dumped his bag in his locker and went walking, hands in his pockets, head down but eyes up.

Searching for the recruiter.

He passed the main gate, glanced at the street beyond. Only Sixth Years were allowed out after the school day had ended. They could spend their afternoons in Roarhaven and only had to be back for Evening Study. Omen, like everyone else, was stuck in here all day, five days a week. Of course, with his parents being the kind of parents they were, he rarely got to go home on the weekends, either. Not that this was necessarily a bad thing. He much preferred walking the school's empty corridors on a Saturday and Sunday evening than sitting in his bedroom being criticised by his mum and dad.

He wandered for hours, spying. He passed the staffroom where the faculty watched the Global Link on TV, catching up on news of all things magical from around the world. He followed students, listening in to snippets of conversation, and trailed after various teachers, veering off when they started to notice. He enjoyed trailing after Miss Wicked the most. Of course, she was also the quickest to sense him, and his face burned with the heat of a thousand suns as he panicked and turned abruptly left. He walked into a wall and stayed there, like he'd meant to do it all along.

He got to the fourth floor without uncovering any evidence of enemy conspiracies. He saw Peccant coming the opposite way and dived round the corner. He waited there, back pressed flat against the wall. Students passed, ignoring him. He didn't care about them. All he cared about was that Peccant should pass by, too.

Peccant turned the corner, stopped suddenly and glared. "Mr Darkly." His voice was deep, his eyes narrow, his face lined. His hair was grey and his suit was tweed. "I've been looking for you."

Omen stepped away from the wall, and tried smiling. "Yes, sir?"

"Where were you this morning, Mr Darkly? You were supposed to be in my class, were you not?"

"I got mixed up, sir."

"Mixed up?"

"I got my timetable mixed up, sir. I'm really sorry."

Peccant loomed over him. "And where were you?"

"In a study class, sir."

"Supervised by whom?"

"Miss Ether."

"And do you usually have a study class supervised by Miss Ether on a Tuesday?"

Omen swallowed. "No, sir."

"Who usually supervises your Tuesday study class?"

"Uh... you do, sir."

"And did it not strike you as odd, Mr Darkly, that I was not supervising this study class? Did it not occur to you that, maybe, you had got your timetable 'mixed up'? Or did you think that I had suddenly become younger, and a woman?"

"No, sir."

"None of that struck you as odd?"

"No, I mean, yes, I mean... I didn't think, sir."

Peccant leaned down. "There we have it. The crux of the problem. You *didn't think*. That's how you operate, after all, is it not? That's how you work your way through life."

Omen swallowed. "Yes, sir."

"Yes, sir," said Peccant, mocking his voice. "So polite. So benign. I find it hard to believe you share even the flimsiest strand of DNA with your brother. Even when he's caught breaking the rules, at least he does it with gusto. There's no gusto with you, is there?"

"No, sir."

Peccant took another moment to glare at him, then straightened up. "You have detention tomorrow. Be there on time or you get double."

Peccant strode away and Omen stood with shoulders slumped.

"He hates you."

Omen looked up as Filament Sclavi strolled over, hands in his pockets and an amused smile on his face.

"I have seen him take a dislike to people before," Filament said, "but that was... what is the word, for the thing? That was *malicious*. It was as if he were gaining personal satisfaction from it."

Omen didn't know what to say, so he just said, "Yeah."

"You are Omen, yes? Auger's brother? My name is Filament. How is it going?"

"Going fine," said Omen without thinking. "Well, I mean, apart from the detention I just got."

"That does suck, yes," Filament said. He was only a Fourth Year, but he looked older, about eighteen. He was tall and strong and handsome, like an Italian version of Omen's brother. The only other thing Omen knew about him was that he was a member of the Eternity Institute, a self-help organisation that had posters up all over the school. "Do you play any sports, Omen?"

"Me?" Omen asked, even though it was obvious that it was him Filament was talking to. "No, I don't. Never really understood it."

"You have, um, never understood any sport in particular, or just sports in general?"

"In general," said Omen. "Could never wrap my head around the, y'know, the point."

Filament grinned. "So, if I suggested that maybe you try to join the rugby team, you would have no interest?"

Omen frowned. "I'd get squashed."

Filament laughed. "You would not get *squashed*."

"I would, though. Those guys are all huge."

"Not all of them. Not even most of them, actually. I am not huge, am I? Yet I play rugby. There are some positions, in fact, where being a smaller player is an advantage."

"Yeah," said Omen, "for the opposite team. So you can squash them. I don't think, if I did take up a sport, that rugby would be it, to be honest."

"Ah, very well," said Filament. "We play against mortals. We pretend to be like them, pretend to be a normal school, and we are not allowed to use magic, obviously... and sometimes we do well, and sometimes we get our asses kicked. I just thought that having a Darkly on the team would boost morale."

"I'm really not the Darkly you want. Maybe if you ask Auger...?"

"I have," said Filament, laughing. "He was really nice about it, but there was no way he would ever say yes. He is probably too busy having his adventures, yes? Hey, is it true, what he did last year? He stopped that human sacrifice guy?"

"It's true," said Omen. "At least, I think it's true. He doesn't really talk about that stuff, not even to me."

Filament shook his head admiringly. "It must be some life to live, huh?"

"Must be."

"And it must be a lot to live up to, as the twin brother."

"You'd imagine so," Omen said, "but I try not to try too hard. I'd hate to disappoint anyone."

"That is probably wise, Omen." There was a shout from down the corridor, and Filament waved, then turned back. "So hey, it was very good to meet you. I have passed you loads of times, but never had a reason to say hi. So... hi."

"Hi."

"And if you ever change your mind about the rugby..."

"The only way that'd happen is after a concussion *playing* rugby, so..."

Filament laughed. "Very well. I will see you around, then, Omen."

The dinner bell rang, and Omen took one of the smaller staircases down. Never was sitting with his other friends, so Omen sat alone and watched people as they ate in their groups. The Sixth Year boys scared him, so he didn't spend too long looking at them. The Sixth Year girls intimidated him, so he didn't spend too long looking at them, either. The Fifth Year girls intimidated him, too, and so did the Fourth Years, so he pretty much stayed away from the girls completely.

His eyes settled on Jenan and his friends. They sat at the table at the far side of the hall, smirking to each other because that's what they did – they smirked and felt superior. It was their favourite pastime.

It wasn't a big deal, slagging off mortals. Omen didn't like it, but it was everywhere, it happened in every part of the school, all the way up through the Years. Even some of the teachers indulged in it for a cheap joke and an easy laugh. But Jenan and his friends – Lapse and Gall, Sabre and Disdain – their comments were made of harder stuff, of sharper words. Their jokes were jagged, edged in bitterness. If a recruiter was to start recruiting in Corrival, Jenan Ispolin would be the obvious place to start.

And they were all part of a history study group, Arcanum's Scholars, formed by Mr Lilt – a passionate teacher who, now that Omen thought about it, never had a good word to say about any mortal. Lilt sat at the staff table, chatting happily to one of the Combat Arts instructors.

Parthenios Lilt. Omen's first suspect.

Excitement flared in his belly, as the idea registered with him that he might actually be good at this.

15

"I'm terrible at this," Valkyrie said, closing the fridge door. Xena cocked her head quizzically. "Doing my own grocery shopping," Valkyrie explained. "Human is no good at being human."

Xena offered a whine of agreement.

"Don't worry," Valkyrie told her. "I've got plenty of food for you. That's all you care about, isn't it? As long as you're fed, that's all that matters." She opened a pouch of dog food and emptied it into the bowl on the floor. "Unless I can microwave myself some of yours. It doesn't look *that* bad..."

Xena didn't seem impressed with that notion. She crowded her bowl, shielding it from view as she ate.

"Fine," Valkyrie said, shrugging into her coat. "I'll be back in a few minutes. Protect the place while I'm gone, OK? And no parties."

Xena ignored her.

Valkyrie got in the car and drove the fifteen minutes to the Super Saver in Haggard. She picked up the essentials, loaded in a treat or two and took it to the till. As she was waiting to pay, she saw her mother perusing the shelves. Valkyrie stayed very still.

Her mother looked around, eyes low, smiling as Alice came into view. Little Alice, with those dimples and that ever-present smile, showing her mum which box of cereal she'd like. Valkyrie handed over cash, didn't bother with the change, just grabbed her grocery bags and walked quickly out of the store. To be spotted was to be hugged, was to be showered with love she didn't deserve. To be spotted was to see the excitement and love in Alice's eyes – eyes she had seen flutter closed five years earlier, when Valkyrie had killed her in a misguided attempt to save the world. The fact that she had clumsily managed to revive her moments later didn't change the fact. Killing was killing. Murder was murder.

Valkyrie loaded the bags into the back of the car and got out of there.

She was halfway home when the phone rang. It made her jump. She pressed Answer and Skulduggery's voice filled the car.

"We have a name," he said.

"Sorry? A name for what?"

There was a pause from the other end. "You sound like you're in a bad mood."

She sighed. "I'm just hungry. I haven't eaten since breakfast. And the fact that I now have visions has made me hugely grumpy. I don't want to see the future, Skulduggery, especially if the future looks like that. I'm barely holding it together as it is."

"What do you mean?"

Her hands tightened on the wheel. "I mean the stress."

"You're sure?"

"Yes. The stress. You know this. I talked about this."

"You did. But for a moment it sounded like you've been going through more than you've been letting on."

"No. Just the stress. So this name you're talking about – a name for what?"

"For a suspect."

"Wait, we have a name for whoever's been recruiting from Corrival Academy?"

"We *may* have."

Her eyes narrowed. "And where did we get this name,

Skulduggery? Who gave us the name? It was Omen, wasn't it? It was. For God's sake, I thought we agreed on this."

"We do," Skulduggery said quickly, "and I was planning on talking to him in the morning, breaking it to him in person, and then a short while ago I received his text message. I didn't expect him to come up with a name so quickly, to be honest. I mean, it's probably nothing."

"It's undoubtedly nothing," said Valkyrie. "He's had half a day of being undercover and he has a name for us already? Either Omen is imagining things or he's the greatest undercover agent in the history of the world."

"You may be right."

"So who is it?"

"Who is what?"

"The name."

"Oh. Parthenios Lilt, a history teacher."

"And why does our super-spy think the history teacher is a recruiter for the anti-Sanctuary?"

"The history teacher doesn't like mortals, for one thing."

"I don't like mortals."

"You don't like anybody."

"That doesn't make me the recruiter."

"Parthenios Lilt leads a study group called Arcanum's Scholars, a reference to Rebus Arcanum, a supposedly long-dead explorer into Realms Unknown. That's what he called them. With capital letters and everything."

Valkyrie stopped at a crossroads as a huge tractor, festooned with lights, rumbled by. "Why is he *supposedly* long dead and not *actually* long dead?"

"We never found the body."

"And what does he have to do with this Lilt guy?"

"Nothing as far as I can see," Skulduggery said. "That's just what Lilt calls his study group. Six boys, three girls in all. Omen doubts they do any actual studying – he says they're just not the type – so the question then becomes what is Parthenios Lilt teaching those students?"

The tractor trundling away, Valkyrie eased out over the crossroads and continued on. "And Omen thinks he's recruiting them for the anti-Sanctuary."

"Yes, he does," said Skulduggery. "I've looked into Mr Lilt. I've just had a few minutes, but already I'm finding things that lead me to believe he's led a varied life."

"He's a sorcerer. That shouldn't surprise you."

"He authored a report for the French Sanctuary on Neoteric sorcerers, nearly forty years ago. He actually coined the term."

"Then he should have done a better job because it means nothing to me."

"Neoterics are mages without recognised disciplines," Skulduggery said.

"Like Warlocks."

"Not *really*. Usually, they're people brought up outside the magical community. They don't know the rules, so they make their own, and their magic adapts to their personality."

"So sorcerers who didn't know they were sorcerers," Valkyrie said.

"I suppose that's a fair assessment. From what you've told me, Cadaverous Gant is probably a Neoteric. When his magic manifested, it fitted itself around his warped sensibilities and resulted in his unique power. They are relatively rare, thankfully, but usually unstable, unfortunately, so we keep an eye out for them. Most incursions occur because a Neoteric sorcerer has lost control and a mortal is right there to witness it."

"Jeremiah Wallow was probably a Neoteric, too," she said, the car going over the humpback bridge on the way to her house.

"Very likely, and Lilt may have had contact with them both. Valkyrie?"

"I'm here."

"Did you hear what I said?"

"Yeah. He may have had contact. So Omen might be right."

"It's a possibility. I'm heading back to Roarhaven. The High Sanctuary has a copy of the Neoteric Report and I want to reacquaint myself with it. Can you meet me there tomorrow?"

"Sure," she said, if the nightmares that she knew were coming didn't drag her down. If she could get out of bed in the morning. If she could even convince herself that she wasn't dead.

"Is everything OK?" Skulduggery asked. "You sound... distracted."

"I'm fine." *I'm not.* "Just hungry." *Just nuts.* "See you in Roarhaven."

She ended the call, passed the heavy gates and drove up to her front door. She got out, breathed in the cold air and leaned against the car for a moment with her eyes closed. She wasn't going nuts. She wasn't insane. She was as healthy as ever. Everything was perfectly normal.

When she opened her eyes again, Darquesse was sitting on her front step. "You're late," she said.

16

"Surprise," said Never, taking the seat beside Omen in the Dining Hall and flicking the hair out of her eyes. "Someone is actually sitting beside you for breakfast. Wonders – will they never cease?"

Omen frowned. "People sit beside me all the time."

"Rarely by choice, though. Admit it, Omen, you're delighted to have someone to talk to this early in the morning, aren't you?"

Omen didn't answer. But he was.

"However, the truly amazing thing," Never continued, "is that I'm sitting beside you even though you've been avoiding me all day."

"It's... first thing in the morning."

"Don't deny it, Omen. When you deny a truth, a kitten dies."

The din in the hall – chattering voices, clinking utensils, the heavy tread of feet and the tortured scrape of chairs – had not yet reached deafening proportions, so, when Never leaned in and lowered her voice, Omen could hear her perfectly.

"You better tell me what's going on and you better not lie. You're a terrible liar. I always know when you're lying because your ears go red. Are you going to eat that?"

"It's my breakfast," said Omen.

"I know. Are you going to eat it?"

"I'm eating it now."

Never sighed. "Then are you going to finish it?"

"Probably. Where's your breakfast?"

"In my stomach, where all breakfasts belong. Can I have that sausage?"

"The one on the end of my fork? No. It's mine. Look." Omen took a bite. "See?"

Never turned her head, so she was looking at Omen out of the corner of her eyes. "You're definitely acting weird."

"No, I'm not," said Omen. "I'm acting normal because I *am* normal."

Never flicked her hair again. She liked flicking her hair. It was one of her things. "You couldn't be normal if you tried. Not with your family."

"Well, I don't know what you want me to say. But I'm not acting weird."

"You were walking around yesterday, peering at everyone and trying to listen in to their conversations."

"No, I wasn't."

"Whatever." She used the air to lift a bread roll from the basket. Even though teleportation was her natural gift, and she was the only one in Mr Renn's class who could *actually* teleport, Never was pretty good at everything, Elemental magic included. She was definitely better at it than Omen.

Omen hesitated. "Do you, uh, do you think they noticed?"

"Who?"

"Everyone."

"That you were spying on them? Naw." She dropped the bread roll back. "People tend to ignore you. It's a gift you have. So what were you up to?"

"I can't tell you."

Never glared. "Since when do we keep secrets from each other?"

"We keep loads of secrets from each other," Omen said, frowning. "Literally, loads."

She shrugged. "We should stop that. A friendship like ours is a friendship that relies on one hundred per cent honesty at all times."

"Then is it true what I heard about you and Rasure Cross?"

"One hundred per cent honesty *from this moment on*," said Never, smoothing down her skirt. "Hey, did you hear? Skulduggery Pleasant was here yesterday."

Omen stuffed some egg into his mouth. "Yeah?"

"Chocolate said she was in French and she happened to glance out the window and there he was."

"That's cool."

"She said Valkyrie Cain was with him."

"Right."

Never's face had already soured. "I thought they'd split up."

"I, uh, I don't think they were ever together in that way..."

"You know what I mean. I thought she'd gone off to live out her life in America. That's what I was hoping. She probably missed the limelight too much, had to come back to get everyone talking about her again."

"OK."

"Chocolate said that she looked *just* like Darquesse."

"Well, obviously."

"Yeah, I know. I just expected her to look a *little* different from all the videos, you know? You'd think she'd have dyed her hair a different colour or something. It's like she's proud of what she did."

"Ah... I don't think that's fair..."

"She's walking around the same city she half *destroyed*, Omen. What else would you call it? And why are you defending her?"

"Because it wasn't her, was it? It was Darquesse."

Never had that look on her face.

"Stop," Omen said quickly. "We're not talking about this again. We have different opinions and I know how angry you get when we talk about it, so let's not, OK? Not today. I have too much on my mind."

She stared at him. "You have what?"

He blushed. "I, uh, I have a lot to think about."

Never laughed. "You have too much on your mind? Oh my God."

"Please forget I said that."

"I will never, ever forget you said that. Oh my God, you sound just like my mother."

He sagged. "You're not going to let this go, are you?"

"No. I'm not. At all. Mum."

Omen sighed, and swallowed the last mouthful of his breakfast before putting his knife and fork on his empty plate. "I'm going to go get ready for class now, because at least in class no one laughs at me quite as much as you do."

Never grinned. "Bet you don't even know what class we have."

"Actually, I do," said Omen. "We have history, with Mr Lilt."

"A man gets in his car," said Parthenios Lilt, perched on the edge of his desk. "It's night. The drive home is going to take him an hour. His favourite TV show starts in forty minutes. He starts driving. He goes a little faster than he really should. It starts to rain. His windscreen wipers aren't that great. The road is slippery. He's tired. He hasn't slept well. He's thinking about an argument he's had with his boss. He gets to a sharp bend. He skids and crashes. What caused the accident?"

The class was silent. Lilt looked around, eyebrow raised expectantly. After a few moments, Megan Epithet put up her hand.

"He's never heard of the Internet?"

Lilt frowned. "Sorry?"

"He can watch his show online whenever he wants," Megan said. "He doesn't have to hurry."

"Ah," said Lilt. "No, I think you're missing the point a little."

"The sharp bend," said Never. "If it'd been a straight road, he wouldn't have had to turn and he wouldn't have crashed."

"But he's taken that bend every day for twenty years and he hasn't crashed before tonight. Can you really say the bend is the problem?"

"The rain," said someone else.

"The speed," said another.

Lilt held up his hand. "I'll put you all out of your misery. There is no *one* thing that caused the accident. It's a combination of things. Each factor, on its own, didn't make him crash. But put together... the crash looks inevitable. And so it was for World War Two. Reparations. The rise of nationalism. Appeasement. Europe's reluctance to—"

The door opened and Jenan stepped in. Lilt glanced at the clock.

"Three minutes left of class, Mr Ispolin."

"Yeah."

"'Yeah'?"

Jenan straightened. "Yes. Sir."

"Are you going to tell me where you've been?"

"I was called in to the Principal's Office."

Lilt sighed. "Misbehaving again, Jenan? What did you do this time?"

Jenan scowled. "Didn't do anything."

"I'm sure you didn't. I'm sure Mr Rubic invited you in for a friendly chat about the weather." Lilt waved him to his seat. "Go on, you may as well sit down. Try not to cause any more disruption."

Jenan went to his desk and Lilt chewed his lip. "Where was I?"

"World War Two," said Megan.

"Yes, thank you. And what were the Sanctuaries doing during all this escalating tension? Were we getting involved? No? Why not?"

"The Scandza Accord," Jenan said as he slouched into his chair.

Lilt nodded. "You are on your way to redeeming yourself already, Jenan."

The thought occurred to Omen that naming Lilt as a suspect

was one thing, but if he really wanted Skulduggery and Valkyrie's approval he'd be better off getting some actual proof. He smiled, liking that idea immensely.

"Can someone remind me what the Scandza Accord is?" Lilt asked. "Omen?"

God, no. Not again. Omen sat up a little straighter in his chair. He knew the answer. He knew he did. It was there, in the clutter of his mind. He just had to find it. "It's the, uh, the thing."

A few people laughed.

"The thing, Omen?"

"The agreement," Omen said, blushing. "The agreement that Sanctuaries would never interfere in mortal affairs."

"The *official* agreement," Lilt corrected. "It was unofficial policy for centuries before the Elder Councils of the world thought it'd be a good idea to put it down on paper. So, if we weren't to get involved and prevent a war and a Holocaust that killed millions, what *were* we to do? Anyone?"

"Observe and protect the mortals from magical threats," said Never.

"That's right."

"Babysit," Jenan muttered. That got a few laughs.

"Let's not be mean," Lilt said, barely suppressing a smile.

The bell went. Lilt stood.

"No homework tonight," he said, "but you still have the essay on Archduke Ferdinand to hand in tomorrow. No less than six pages. I want some effort put into this one."

Omen and Never squeezed out of the room, joining the throng of students in the corridor. "Do you know how to join Arcanum's Scholars?" Omen asked, trying his best to sound casual.

Never frowned at him. "Why?"

"My mum has been on at me to do better," Omen said. A Fifth Year barged into him on his way past, nearly spun him round. He winced, rubbing his shoulder. "I thought a study group might be a good way to get ahead."

"A study group is a great way to get ahead," said Never, brushing a strand of hair behind her ear, "but not that one. You know who's in it, right? Ispolin and his cronies. Why the hell would you want to join them?"

"Ah, they can't be all bad."

"I'm sure they have their good points," she said, "but being decent people is not one of them. Omen, you're a great guy. Why would you ever want to be part of something they're involved in?"

"I just... Jenan missed nearly the whole class and Lilt didn't even bat an eyelid. I could really do with having a teacher on my side like that."

Never stopped walking and turned to him. "Is this because of Peccant? Omen, Lilt isn't going to stand up to Peccant for you. Nobody stands up to Peccant. Except maybe Miss Wicked."

"Still, though..."

"And you've seen what they have to wear. You've seen how dumb they look, with their little masks."

"The secret society Arcanum was part of, they wore those masks."

"I know the history, Omen. Unlike you, I actually pay attention in class. But even that annoys me. Wearing the masks implies a grand old tradition, right? This school is less than five years old. It has no traditions. This isn't Yale. They aren't the Skull and Bones Society."

"The what?"

"My point is: do you really want to wear the stupid mask and go to their secret meetings?"

"Secret?"

"Secret," said Never. "As in behind-closed-doors secret."

"I thought they met in the West Library."

"Not for ages. I swear, do you pay attention to *anything*? These days they meet in one of the back rooms of the fifth-floor library."

"Huh," said Omen. "And they close the doors?"

"Yes, they do."

"Ever wonder what they talk about?"

"Oh, I *know* what they talk about."

"You do? What?"

Never rolled her eyes. "History, Omen. They talk about history."

"Oh," he said. "Oh, yeah."

High heels clacked behind them, and Omen only realised that the corridor had emptied as they turned.

"Where are you two supposed to be?" Miss Wicked asked.

"Chemistry," said Never.

"I'm not sure," said Omen.

"Never, run off to chemistry, there's a good girl. Omen, find out where you're going and go there."

"Yes, miss."

She moved on, and Omen smelled her perfume as she went.

"Catch you on the flip-flop," said Never, and sauntered away, her skirt swishing.

"What class do I have now?" Omen called after her.

"Look up your timetable," she called back.

"Where's my timetable?"

"In your bag."

Omen frowned at his empty hands. "Where's my bag?"

"You left it in history," Never said, and disappeared round the corner.

"Dammit," said Omen.

17

"Crap," said Valkyrie, the coffee spilling onto her sleeve. The guy who had bumped into her glowered like he was expecting an argument, but Valkyrie just turned away, took some napkins and left the café without saying anything else. A few years ago her words would have sliced through him until he apologised, maybe started crying, but that particular fire wasn't burning inside her anymore. She didn't know if it'd ever come back.

She got to her car, put the cup in the holder and dried herself off as best she could, then drove to the High Sanctuary. She showed her badge to the Cleaver and he allowed her into the car park. She picked a spot beside the Bentley and got out, zipping up her coat. It was another cold day.

Taking her coffee with her, she rode the elevator up, ignored the looks she got and made her way to the Records Department. Skulduggery was the only person here at this hour of the morning. He was wearing another three-piece suit – darkest blue this time, with a white shirt and blue tie. His hat was off and he tapped at a computer. A thick file lay open beside him, spiral-bound. Entire lines were blacked out.

"This it?" she asked, flicking through the pages.

"That's the Neoteric Report," he said, still looking at the screen.

"What's with the black lines?"

"Sensitive information, too secret for the likes of us."

She sat, took a sip of coffee. It was her first from a Roarhaven café, and it was amazing. She wasn't surprised. Of course the coffee would be amazing here. Sorcerers loved doing things better than the mortals. "So tell me," she said.

Skulduggery tapped a little more, then turned in his swivel chair. "I think we have our suspect."

She frowned. "Omen was right?"

"He may have good instincts for this kind of thing."

"But we don't care how good his instincts are, do we? Because we're cutting him loose, right?"

"Absolutely," Skulduggery said. "But I thought it'd be nice if I could tell him that his hunch was right before I essentially fire the boy."

Valkyrie shrugged. "Suppose that is a nice thing to do. What have you found?"

"The names of some of these Neoteric sorcerers Parthenios Lilt dealt with are the same names that Temper Fray passed on to me as anti-Sanctuary operatives. Two in particular stand out – Richard Melior and Azzedine Smoke. Much of the information about these two has been classified, but, from what I can gather, Melior is something of a Vitakinetic and Smoke has the ability to corrupt those he touches."

"What do you mean by corrupt?"

"Control," said Skulduggery. "According to this, if he touches you, you essentially become a psychopath, and you're compelled to obey whatever order he gives you."

She frowned. "That's a dangerous skill to have."

"Yes, it is. The corruption lasts for approximately forty-eight hours, but a lot of damage can be done in two days. As we both know."

"So if we're going up against someone who could basically brainwash us and turn us against each other..."

"We'd better not let him touch us," Skulduggery finished. "Or you'd better. I don't have a brain to wash, as it were."

Valkyrie grunted. "And the healer?"

"Doctor Richard Melior," said Skulduggery. "A practising surgeon in a mortal hospital – Johns Hopkins in Baltimore, in case you're interested—"

"I'm not."

"—whose power goes beyond that of regular Vitakinetics – though in what way, I don't know. We might have a lead on him. Smoke would appear to live up to his namesake. I can't find a trace of him in the database. But Melior divides his time between Baltimore and his modest house right here in Roarhaven. I say we drop by, see if he's home and ask him where they're keeping Temper."

"Uh-huh."

"You have a query?"

She didn't know how to put this gently. "You *have* taken into account the possibility that Temper Fray might be dead, right? They might have killed him when they caught him and just disposed of the body."

"I have taken that into account," said Skulduggery, "but I'm not overly fond of the possibility so I'm choosing to pretend it doesn't exist. It's a remarkably cheering solution to an otherwise depressing situation."

"Pretending something doesn't exist is a practical outlook, is it?"

"I never said it was practical, just that it cheered me up."

"And this Melior guy... We've both seen Vitas use the same energy to hurt people as well as to heal them. Can this guy hurt us?"

"If you're asking if things could get dangerous... that's always a possibility. I see you're still not wearing the armoured clothes Ghastly designed for you."

"They were getting a little snug around the shoulders."

"Snug or not, they've saved your life on more than one occasion."

"If I decide to come back full time, I'll wear the black, I promise."

His head tilted. "I haven't persuaded you yet?"

"Not yet," said Valkyrie. "But your twenty-four hours aren't up for another—" she checked her watch "—hundred and fifty-seven minutes."

"Ah," he said, "plenty of time."

"So will we be going after Melior with an army of Cleavers or what?"

"Not really, I'm afraid. That would mean handing over authority to the City Guard, and we want to stay as far away from them as possible."

"So we're going in alone?"

"Don't say it like that."

"How should I say it?"

"I don't know." He stood. "Say it with a little more enthusiasm."

"So we're going in alone," she said. "Yay."

Skulduggery put on his hat. "Much better."

18

They took the Bentley to the Narrows, in the South-East District. The buildings along the wall were smaller than those in the middle of the city, and here the streets were thin and winding. Skulduggery parked and he and Valkyrie went walking. The shade cast by the tightly packed buildings robbed them of their shadows. Only at midday did sunlight ever have a chance to warm the paving stones.

They passed a mother and her children, all of whom stared at Skulduggery as they passed, and ignored Valkyrie. It was a nice change.

They got to Richard Melior's house. The upper bay window was open. Without breaking stride, Skulduggery wrapped an arm round Valkyrie's waist and took them both off their feet. They drifted up and through the window, touching down in the bedroom. The bed was unmade. The door to the ensuite was open. From inside, the sound of someone brushing their teeth.

Spitting. A tap running. The clink as a toothbrush went back into its holder.

A man came out, dressed in jogging bottoms and a T-shirt. His feet were bare. His black hair was short, his haircut expensive. His beard was trimmed close. He stared at them.

"Doctor Melior," Skulduggery said. "Good morning. I'm going to have to ask you not to make any sudden moves."

Melior darted for the door, but Valkyrie shoved him towards

Skulduggery who grabbed him, spun him around and sent him stumbling to the wall.

"That would count as a sudden move," Skulduggery said. "My name is Skulduggery Pleasant. This is Valkyrie Cain. We'd like to ask you a few questions, if you have the time. We're looking for a friend of ours. Male, about your height, African-American. His name is Temper Fray. I believe you know him?"

Melior licked his lips. "You... you can't be here." He was American.

"We won't be long."

"You can't just... you can't just come into my house. You need a warrant or a—"

"You're thinking of mortals," said Valkyrie. "You're thinking of cops. We're neither."

"Get out," Melior said, shaking his head. "I'm telling you to leave. Leave now."

Skulduggery picked up a framed photograph by the bed, of Melior and a man with a remarkably square jaw. "This is nice," he said. "Your husband? Savant Vega, isn't it? Is he in? Could we speak to him?"

Melior's eyes narrowed. "I told you to leave."

"Calm down, Richard."

"They'll know. They know you're here now. You've got to leave."

"Not until you tell us what you know of the anti-Sanctuary," Valkyrie said.

Melior pressed the heels of his hands into his temples and screwed his eyes shut. His face was red and he was muttering.

"What's that, Richard?" Skulduggery asked. "We can't hear you."

Valkyrie frowned. It wasn't only Melior's face that was going red. It was his neck and his arms and his feet, too. His whole body was flushed and trembling. He was *burning from within*.

"Skulduggery..." Valkyrie murmured, suddenly wishing that

she was at home with the dog, having a nice quiet morning, far away from people who wanted to do her harm.

"Let's not resort to violence, Doctor," Skulduggery said. "If we feel we are about to be attacked, I must warn you that we *will* defend ourselves."

Melior's eyes snapped open. "You brought this on yourselves," he growled.

Skulduggery grabbed Valkyrie, pulled her behind him as he raised a hand. There was a *whump*, like a sudden explosion of flames, and a wave of energy hit Skulduggery's shield of air and threw them both backwards. Valkyrie tumbled out through the window, the world tilting crazily, and then all too suddenly the ground crunched into her shoulder. She would have cried out if she'd had any breath left in her body. She turned over, trying to suck in air as she clutched her left arm.

Skulduggery sat up beside her. "Are you OK?"

She shook her head, and managed to draw in a single breath. He helped her to her feet.

She did her best to ignore the rising pain. "Didn't think... Vitas could attack like that..."

"This one appears to be special."

Melior's door opened and Melior stormed out. He was wearing trainers now, the laces not yet tied, and was shrugging into a jacket.

Skulduggery drew his gun. "Stay right there, Richard."

Melior barked out a mirthless laugh, and six people appeared around him.

At first, Valkyrie thought they were all Teleporters – they'd arrived at the same instant and none of them had been touching – but that notion fell apart the moment one of them, the woman in the tuxedo, extended her right arm. Her palm opened and a black tendril shot out, its barbed teeth closing round Skulduggery's gun, yanking it from his grip. She smiled widely, her tongue between her teeth.

The man beside her had a black, braided goatee. The guy next to him had an Elvis haircut and wore a purple suit.

To Melior's right were three men. The one furthest away was dressed in an ill-fitting suit and he wrung his hands nervously. Beside him was a handsome young man with shockingly bleached hair. He looked like a washed-out supermodel with a rock-star sneer. Valkyrie just *knew* he was the Teleporter.

The sixth member of the group was dressed head to foot in black rubber.

"Mr Lethe," Skulduggery said, brushing dust from his jacket. "Good to finally meet you."

The masked man held up a finger. "Just Lethe will do," he said, his voice distorted. "It's very good to meet you, too, Detective. I've heard so many *stories*. So many *wild tales*. You've had quite the life of *adventure*, haven't you?"

"It's not over yet," Skulduggery said.

Lethe chuckled. "I fear it may be, actually. And beside you the Swathe of Destruction herself, *Valkyrie Cain*. Now *your* death, Valkyrie... *your* death will be *special*."

Valkyrie stayed quiet. Her shoulder was dislocated and the pain was making her sweat, and she couldn't be bothered engaging with this creep.

"Let's not get ahead of ourselves," said Skulduggery. "We only came here to chat to Richard. We've lost a friend, you see, and we were—"

"Oh," Lethe interrupted. "You mean Temper. Yes, we *know* Temper. He's alive, in case you were wondering. We haven't *killed him* yet, or anything like that. We're all sorcerers of *some description*, after all. We're *family*. Not *monsters*."

"That's good to hear."

"And, if we kill family, we like it to be an *occasion*. We want it to be *memorable*. To *stick in the mind*. We're not going to kill him just because he's an enemy, or because he *betrayed* us. He was probably only obeying orders, right? Infiltrate the group. Gain our trust. Lead to our downfall. That sort of thing."

Skulduggery nodded. "That sort of thing. Exactly."

"Was it you?" Lethe asked. "Did you send him in, Detective? I'm sorry, can I call you Skulduggery?"

"Of course."

"Did you send him in, *Skulduggery*? Did you send him in to *spy* on us?"

"I did."

"That was *sneaky* of you."

"We were only returning the favour. You and your group have been pretty sneaky yourselves, what with—"

"No," said Lethe.

Skulduggery tilted his head. "I'm sorry?"

"You don't get to steer the *conversation*, Skulduggery. You're not in charge here. *We are*."

"Very well. It's all yours."

"How *gracious* of you," Lethe said. "You've taken a risk coming here. A *big* risk. A big *mistake*. Skulduggery, I know you've been Commander of the Supreme Mage's personal *Gestapo* here in Roarhaven for the last few years, and the stories I've heard about the things you've *done* in that time... *Shocking*. Simply *shocking*. But I fear you may have lost your edge now that you're back as the *Dynamic Duo*. Things have... well, they've *changed* since you've been away. The *world* has changed. It's sharper. It's nastier. It's *cut-throat*. I would have loved nothing more than to have watched you both embark on more adventures, to watch you both fight to preserve the status quo yet again... but I'm afraid I can't allow it."

"You have your plans," said Skulduggery. "It's understandable."

"Not *my* plans," said Lethe. "I'm just a pawn. We're all just *pawns* in the great game."

"And the objective of the game?"

Lethe shook his head again.

"What *is* the anti-Sanctuary?" Skulduggery asked. "What is it really?"

"It's *beyond* you, I'm afraid. I doubt you could *fathom* how we see the world. We're not like you. We're not... *content*. You're scared of us and *of course* you're scared. We are something you don't understand. We are the *future*."

"Can I talk now? You've had your say, I think it's only fair that I have mine."

Lethe walked forward. "There's nothing *fair* about this world, Skulduggery. We don't always get what we *want*, do we? For example, I bet you want to walk away from this encounter, isn't that right? I bet you want to *live*, yes? But you're not going to."

Skulduggery observed him. "Seven against two," he said. "And, as you can undoubtedly tell, Valkyrie injured herself in the fall."

"It's not *seven* against *two*," said Lethe. "It's *right* against *wrong*. It's *me* against *you*. If you win, you walk away. If you lose, you *die*, and we take Valkyrie here."

"I see," Skulduggery said. "Well, that seems reasonable." He took off his hat, handed it to Valkyrie. She stepped back.

"Before we begin," Skulduggery said, "can I ask what your magical ability might be?"

Lethe chuckled again. "You can *ask*."

19

Lethe went at him and Skulduggery let him come.

He started with a kick that Skulduggery swayed away from. He spun with a back fist that got nowhere near. Next he sprang, twirling in the air like a Cleaver, and Skulduggery dodged back.

Valkyrie's left shoulder was on fire. She glanced away from the fight, to Lethe's friends. All of them, apart from Melior and the guy in the ill-fitting suit, were grinning, enjoying the spectacle as Lethe leaped and lashed out and Skulduggery just kept out of his way. It looked like it would only be a matter of time before one of Lethe's attacks landed. They were anticipating it. This was sport to them.

But Valkyrie knew better.

Lethe was good, of that there was no doubt. As quick and agile as a Cleaver, he threw in a load of extra moves that almost caught Skulduggery out. But Skulduggery kept out of reach, watching him, observing him. Understanding him.

And then, once he'd absorbed enough information, Skulduggery acted.

He stepped inside a wild hook and flipped Lethe over his hip.

Lethe hit the ground and rolled, came up to his feet in one smooth motion. He bounced on his toes like a boxer for a moment, and moved back in again.

Skulduggery stayed where he was.

Lethe spun with a kick and Skulduggery stepped forward, tripped him, and Lethe executed a one-handed cartwheel to avoid hitting the ground a second time.

His friends cheered and clapped. They had no idea what was about to come.

Lethe changed tactics. He stopped with the spinning and the whirling, and came in straight and strong. His hands flashed. Skulduggery covered up, didn't even try to block the strikes, but when he got close enough he reached out, grabbed Lethe and pulled him in to an elbow to the jaw.

Lethe stumbled away. His friends laughed.

A quick shake of the head and Lethe returned to the fray. He punched and Skulduggery grabbed him again, headbutted him, kicked his knee and slammed him to the ground. Lethe thrashed and squirmed, managed to roll away. He tumbled backwards to his feet.

Now it was Skulduggery's turn to move in. A left jab and a right hook sent Lethe staggering. When Lethe threw a punch in return, Skulduggery grabbed his wrist, wrenched it, and only Lethe's agility allowed him to spin out and free himself.

Skulduggery hit him again, and again. Lethe wobbled and dropped to one knee. Valkyrie expected the others to rush in at this point, but they stayed where they were. The cheering had died down, but they were still grinning.

Skulduggery stood over Lethe. "Where's Temper?"

Lethe held up a hand for Skulduggery to wait, like he wanted to catch his breath.

"*That*," he said at last, "was a good one."

He stood up slowly, groaning as he did so, then he dropped low, slamming a fist into Skulduggery's ribs.

Skulduggery grunted and stumbled back, and Lethe straightened.

"So it's true," said Lethe. "Even without *flesh*, even without *nerve endings*, you do feel *pain*. That's interesting. I don't think I've ever killed someone as interesting as *you*, Skulduggery."

Lethe stepped in with what looked like a kick. Valkyrie was fooled. So was Skulduggery. He went to move inside the arc of the kick, but Lethe was ready for him. The kick was nothing but a feint, and Skulduggery slid straight into the elbow that knocked him back. Lethe followed it up by grabbing Skulduggery and hitting him three times before flipping him to the ground.

Valkyrie stared, her entire body cold.

Skulduggery caught a boot to the face that sent him sprawling. He got to one knee and snapped his palm out. The air rippled, but Lethe had already moved up beside him. He grabbed Skulduggery's wrist and brought his elbow down and Skulduggery's forearm broke.

Skulduggery cried out in pain and fell back. His gloved hand hit the street, bones spilling. Lethe kicked it away.

Valkyrie started forward, but the woman in the tuxedo intercepted her, slapping her dislocated shoulder. She cried out and the woman smiled at her.

"We're giving them a fair go, remember? One on one. To the death." She was Australian. "Things are always more exciting when they're to the death, don't you reckon? Hopscotch – to the death. Dance-off – to the death. Fight to the death – to the death." She shrugged happily. "It's *fun*."

Clutching his flapping sleeve, Skulduggery tried getting up. Lethe leaped, spun in the air and came down on top of him, pinning him in place.

"Can you lose consciousness?" Lethe asked, hitting him. "You've got no brain to concuss, so maybe not. But it's fun trying, isn't it?"

Lethe hit him again, then reached down, forcing a hand into Skulduggery's mouth, taking a grip. "I told you," he said. "The world is a different place."

Lethe wrenched and Skulduggery screamed as Lethe pulled his jawbone off.

Valkyrie grabbed the Australian and sent white lightning

coursing through her, and she shot back off her feet and Valkyrie spun, raising her arm to Lethe.

But everything was moving so fast. Lethe blurred and her lightning was too slow. She tried whipping the lightning after him, but he blurred back, ducking under it. Impossible. Nobody was that fast, not even with magic.

And then Lethe was moving at normal speed again and Valkyrie stepped back, trying to work out what the hell had just happened. Suddenly the guy with the bleached hair was standing right in front of her. He hit her, square on the chin, and her head rocked back and her legs gave out and she was on the ground, looking up at the cloudless sky.

"You shouldn't have come," the Teleporter was saying. "Should've found somewhere else to hide. Now we've got you." He grinned down at her. "Bet today isn't turning out how you hoped, huh?"

"Don't *gloat*, Nero," said Lethe. "It's not cool." He looked down at Skulduggery, who was sitting up, his broken arm curled against him, his good hand clutching at his damaged skull. "I've *damaged* you. Richard could put you back together quite *easily*, I imagine. He might even be able to do *more*, given time. That's why we have him, after all. To breathe *life* into the *lifeless*. But as interested as I would be in seeing that, from a purely *academic* point of view, I'm afraid I cannot allow it. You are the *enemy*. You must *die*. Richard, can you *kill* him?"

Melior hesitated. "Yes," he said. "Probably."

Lethe beckoned him over with Skulduggery's jawbone. "Then, by all means, have at it." He tossed the jawbone away.

Melior hesitated, but with a nudge from the goateed man he started walking over. Valkyrie tried getting up, but Nero stomped on her shoulder and she screamed and fell back.

And then Fletcher Renn appeared in the middle of it all.

Even through tear-filled eyes, Valkyrie recognised him. Tall. Good-looking. Blond hair still ridiculous.

Fletcher turned, taking in the scene. For the first time, Lethe and the others didn't seem so confident. Fletcher winked at Valkyrie.

"I don't know exactly what is going on here," he said. "All I do know is that two dozen Cleavers are on their way. You can try to leave if you want. I don't care. But I'm taking Valkyrie and Skulduggery. If I were you, I wouldn't try—"

He stopped talking.

Valkyrie sat up. At first, she thought Fletcher was frozen, but no, he was still moving. Just very slowly. Incredibly slowly. The nervous guy in the ill-fitting suit had his hands raised and his eyes were narrowed. He was doing this. She'd seen it before, or something like it. Jeremiah Wallow had been able to slow time whenever he attacked, so as to prolong the pleasure of the kill. It seemed to her to be the perfect power for serial killers everywhere.

"Nero," said Lethe, "I think it's only fitting that one Teleporter should kill another."

"As you command," Nero said, taking a long knife from his jacket and walking up behind Fletcher.

Hissing with the pain, Valkyrie got to her knees and let loose a stream of lightning. She missed the guy in the ill-fitting suit, but did make him duck away.

"—to stop me," Fletcher said, moving normally again.

"Behind you!" Valkyrie called, and Fletcher vanished just as Nero went to stab him in the back, appearing beside him an instant later and slugging him across the jaw.

Nero stumbled and Fletcher teleported to Skulduggery's side and they both disappeared. A moment later, he was pulling Valkyrie to her feet and then they were indoors, in a hospital, and Fletcher let go of her and teleported again.

Two orderlies were helping Skulduggery on to a bed. Another one came for Valkyrie. Reverie Synecdoche hurried in from another room, eyes wide in alarm. Fletcher reappeared, his hands full of Skulduggery's discarded bones.

"Here's the rest," he said, and Nero appeared behind him.

"No!" Valkyrie cried, and Fletcher turned and Nero plunged the knife into his belly.

20

"Ouch," said Omen, sticking his thumb into his mouth and sucking it.

Never didn't even look up from her textbook. "What'd you do?"

"Paper cut," said Omen.

"I'm sure you'll survive."

The detention hall was empty except for them. It would have been empty except for Omen if Never hadn't decided to keep him company at the last minute.

"You're hiding from someone," Omen said.

"No, I'm not," Never replied. "I just thought I'd make a start on my homework, that's all. How far are you through Peccant's punishment?"

Omen checked. "Almost halfway."

"You'd want to get a move on."

"It's really difficult."

"That's why it's called a punishment and not a treat."

Omen checked what he had left to do, then looked up. "Never..."

Never didn't answer.

"Never..."

"What?"

"Can you do it for me?"

Never turned the page, kept reading. "No."

"But you're so much better at maths than I am."

"My cat is better at maths than you are."

"But it'll only take you a few minutes to get through the rest of this."

Never sighed. "Omen, I hate sounding like a teacher, or a parent, or just a general adult, but if you don't do it yourself you'll never learn."

"It's maths, though," said Omen. "I'm not going to need maths when I leave school."

Never closed her book, and raised her eyes. "What are you going to be?"

"When I'm done with school? I don't know."

"Then how do you know you won't need maths?"

"Because whatever I'm going to be, it won't be a mathematician or an accountant or, y'know, someone who does a lot of sums. I know how to add and subtract and divide... that's all I need to know. What else is there? What else is important? Is calculating the angle of something really going to be that necessary in my everyday life? Is it?"

"I'm not doing your work for you."

Omen lowered his head to the desk. "But I hate it."

"You remember back in First Year, when we became friends? You remember how that happened?"

"Of course. We started talking, and we just got along."

"No, that's not how it happened at all. I was chatty, amusing and effervescent and you barely said a word to anyone. I was incredibly popular – do you remember that? I had just made a stirring, inspiring speech about my own particular rules that I wanted people to follow regarding my gender-fluidity. I listed the pronouns I was prepared to accept and the times at which I was prepared to accept them. I let people know that everyone was different and that my rules might not be the same as their rules. I was interesting. I was engaging. From that moment on, I had my pick of friends. Do you remember all that? Do you?"

"I remember you talking..."

"But, even though I had my pick of friends, I'd watch you in class and think to myself, *This Omen kid might be cool.* You were always on time, you never took your eyes off the teacher, you always worked so hard... How did *that* guy become *this* guy?"

Omen didn't say anything.

"That wasn't a rhetorical question," said Never.

"It sounded like one."

"What happened to you, Omen?"

"I don't know what you want me to say, Never."

"Is it a parent thing, or...?"

"I dunno. I mean... I don't really examine why I do things."

"Obviously."

"But you know how they are. Mum only calls when she's wondering why Auger isn't answering his phone. Dad... well, Dad never calls. I... I suppose when I started here I thought I could become someone new. Like, someone they'd approve of."

"And?"

Omen shrugged. "I realised I couldn't do it. I tried working hard, but nothing changed. I wasn't suddenly the smartest kid in the class. I was still me."

"How hard did you work, though? I mean, how long did you give it?"

"Ages," Omen insisted.

"And why did you stop?"

"Well, like, it was *really* difficult."

Never sighed, and looked away for a moment, gathering her thoughts. "There's nothing actually wrong with you. I mean, you know that, right? Your parents are obsessed with making sure Auger is ready to fight the King of the Darklands, whoever the hell he is. So yeah, you get ignored. But you're still a worthwhile person. You're decent, you can occasionally be funny and you have a good heart. It's why people like you."

Omen's eyes widened. "People like me?"

"Probably, yeah."

"Wow. Do you know who?"

"No. We don't have a club. We don't have badges or go to meetings. I'm just assuming other people like you because, well, because I can*not* be the only one, I swear to God."

"Thanks, Never. You're cool, too."

She frowned at him. "I know."

The door opened, and Auger stepped in, smiling when he saw Omen looking up.

"What'd you do this time?" Auger asked. "Hey, Never."

"Hi, Auger," Never said, giving a little wave.

"I missed a class," Omen said. "By accident. Don't tell Mum and Dad."

"Dude, if I told them half the stuff you got in trouble for, you'd never be able to leave the house. I thought Miss Ether supervised on Wednesdays."

"I'm the only one in detention," Omen said, "so she told me to get on with it and then she left."

"Never, what are you doing here?"

Never shrugged. "Keeping him company."

Auger smiled another one of his dazzling smiles. "You're a class act, you know that?"

"Yes, I do."

"Why do you want Miss Ether?" Omen asked.

Auger gave a quick one-shouldered shrug. "Nothing important. Just have to check something with her. Homework stuff. Anyway, try and stay out of trouble, you two."

And then he was gone.

Never looked at Omen. "What do you think's going on?"

"I bet he's on another adventure," Omen said.

"Me too. Like the time with the substitute teacher who turned out to be a serial killer, or all that possession stuff last year. Hey, you think he'll ever invite the two of us along? I mean, you *are* his brother, and we *are* best friends."

"Are we?"

"Aren't we?"

"Well," said Omen, "you're *my* best friend, but am I *your* best friend?"

Never thought about it. "Probably not," she admitted. "But you're up there. Top four."

"Four?"

"I'm very popular with a lot of diverse groups," Never explained.

"Four, though."

"Maybe five."

"Ah, for God's sake."

"One of these days," said Never, "the Chosen One will ask for our help, and we will prove ourselves and then we'll be part of his gang. Wouldn't that be something? You, me, Kase, Mahala and Auger, saving the school, saving the city, saving the world."

"Ah, I don't know," Omen said, slouching.

Never arched an eyebrow. "What's wrong with that?"

"Nothing. It's just... I've seen him save the school and save the city, and in a few years I'll see him save the world... and it's not really that glamorous. He gets hurt. Like, *seriously* hurt. A lot. Last year he almost died."

"I heard about that."

"I don't know. Having adventures is fine and everything, but I've been around this stuff my whole life. It starts to wear thin after a while."

"Yeah," Never said, "maybe. Or maybe it wears thin when you're watching it. Maybe if you were having those adventures yourself, it wouldn't seem quite as bad."

"Yeah," Omen said quietly. "Maybe."

Never's phone beeped and she checked it, then slid her book into her bag and stood up. "OK, I'm off."

Omen frowned. "Who was that?"

"Who was what?" she asked, walking to the door.

"Who was that messaging you?"

"I don't know what you're talking about. You're talking crazy. Stop talking crazy now, you hear? All that crazy talk will land you in the crazy house, you crazy biscuit." And then she was gone.

Omen stayed in his seat for another ten minutes, spectacularly failing to complete the work that Peccant had set for him. Once the allotted time was up, he hurried to his locker, dumped his bag and climbed the stairs to the fifth floor.

He slipped into the library. Lounging around in the seating area, Jenan Ispolin and his friends congregated and chatted – loudly. The librarian, a bald old man with an astonishingly white beard, like a skinny Santa Claus, was asleep behind his desk.

Omen darted behind the bookcases as more Arcanum's Scholars joined the group. He got into a position where he could peek without being seen.

"Did you hear?" Colleen Stint said, talking in her usual breathless fashion. "Did you hear what happened?"

Jenan took his time looking at her. Everyone knew Colleen fancied him like mad, and Omen was sure that Jenan despised her for it.

"What happened to what?" Jenan asked, like he couldn't be bothered hearing the answer.

"What happened to Skulduggery Pleasant and Valkyrie Cain," Colleen said.

Omen crept a little closer, making sure he caught all of it.

"They were in the Narrows," Colleen continued. "Went to arrest someone. Just the two of them, like. No Cleavers or back-up or nothing."

Jenan sat straighter. "They dead?"

"No," said Colleen, "but close to it. They got the crap kicked out of them."

"Everyone's talking about it," said Byron Grace. "There was

123

a Teleporter and a man in black, and he went up against Pleasant and—"

"Kicked the crap out of him!" Colleen finished, shooting a glare at Byron for daring to interrupt. "Like, threw him about the place. I heard he pulled the skeleton's head off."

Jenan sat forward. "Seriously?"

Colleen folded her arms. "That's what I heard."

Jenan took a moment to absorb the news. "Well now," he said, "looks like we chose the winning team."

A few of them laughed at this. Omen's frown deepened.

"You think it's them?" Lapse asked, too stupid to put things together by himself.

"Of course it is," said Jenan. "We've been told for ages that they're a force to be reckoned with, right? Who else could do something like that? This is it, boys and girls. This is where it all kicks off."

"About time," muttered Gall.

Byron took a seat, like he was exhausted, his bag spilling open on the ground beside him. "We don't know for sure," he said.

Jenan shot him a look that boiled with hostility. "What did I just say? There's no one else who could do something like that. The guy in black? I bet that was Lethe himself."

"Yeah," said Byron, "maybe."

Jenan stood. "What the hell is wrong with you, Grace? You going soft all of a sudden?"

Byron paled. "No."

"You're full of the big talk when all we're doing is planning," Jenan said, "but the moment it turns real your spine turns to jelly. Is that what's happening?"

Byron shook his head, but didn't answer.

"Everyone, listen up," Jenan said, looking round. "These aren't games we've been playing. This isn't dress-up. This is real life, baby. The plan has been set in motion. We have *all* been set in motion. We were told they had big plans for us. Well, this is where it starts. If you're having doubts now, at this stage... I'm sorry to tell you that you've missed your chance to back out. You're here now, and that means you're in. No excuses. Does everyone, and I mean *everyone*, understand that?"

Nods all round. Even Byron.

Jenan retook his seat. "Good."

The librarian snorted and woke, raising his head. "Quiet down there!"

"Sorry," said Jenan without even looking at him.

The librarian went back to sleep.

Omen's gaze fell upon Byron's open bag, and the golden mask that peeked out.

He wished his brother was here. Auger would not only know what to do, but he'd also be able to do it. And, if it went wrong, he'd be able to get out of it. Omen, though, was the screw-up of the family. Omen's efforts were doomed to failure. He knew this.

And yet, if what Colleen had said was true, the stakes were high. And high stakes meant chances needed to be taken, no matter how ill-advised they might be. And this chance was *incredibly* ill-advised.

Omen crouched, held out his hand and touched the air.

He visualised interlocking blocks from his fingertips to the bag. Pushing was easier. He could have pushed the bag over without even trying. But pulling... that was where things got tricky. He'd done it before, though. Not in class, and not in exams. He'd done it at home. Auger had taken him through it. Omen had been calm, then. He tried to be calm now.

So he ignored the rapid beat of his heart, and the jagged spikes of adrenaline that made his hand tremble, and he focused on the imaginary blocks... and the mask moved.

Jenan and the others kept talking. No one noticed the mask lifting itself out of the bag.

Omen laid it gently on the carpet and left it there for a moment while he shook out his hand. He took a deep breath, reached out again, focused on hooking his fingers into the air just right and pulled.

The mask moved slowly across the ground.

Bit by bit, it got closer. For a terrifying few seconds, it was out in the open, and Omen lost his grip. He'd allowed his mind to wander, to imagine what Jenan and the others would do if they caught him. Would they kill him? It seemed ridiculous, that a bunch of his classmates would actually try to kill him, but, if they really were involved with this anti-Sanctuary thing, killing a witness might not be something they would baulk at. Certainly Jenan wouldn't hesitate to throw Omen off the balcony. That'd be something he'd probably enjoy.

Omen pushed such thoughts from his mind, reached out again and pulled the mask closer. Now it was under a small table, blocked from the view of the others. It was going well. It was actually going well. It was actually going to work. Omen smiled, and his fingers moved with too much enthusiasm and the mask shot off the ground. He snatched it from the air as it sped past his face, falling backwards and lying there, eyes wide, waiting to hear the shouts of alarm.

But Jenan and the others kept talking, and Omen let himself breathe again.

Someone new came in and Omen got up.

"Good, good," he heard Parthenios Lilt say, "everyone's here. Let us move to less salubrious surroundings. Ceremonial masks on."

Omen stayed hidden, clutching the mask with both hands.

"Uh," he heard Byron say.

"Is there a problem, Mr Grace?" Lilt asked.

"My... my mask isn't in my bag, sir."

The library went very quiet.

"Mr Grace..." Lilt said.

"I put it in there, sir," said Byron. "I know I did. It must have fallen out or..."

"Mr Grace, these masks are a symbol. These masks mean something. They meant something to Rebus Arcanum and they mean something to us."

"Yes, sir," said Byron.

Lilt sighed. "I have a spare in my office, on the shelf near the window. Go and fetch it."

"Yes, sir," said Byron. "Thank you."

Omen heard him hurry out.

"We'll probably have to kill poor Byron before too long," Lilt said sadly. Then his tone brightened. "OK, everyone, into the back room. We have much to discuss."

21

Cadaverous preferred the silence. The others – Lethe and his gang of misfits – hadn't returned to the prison yet, so he didn't have to suffer through the banality of their conversation. There was no one there to engage with, anyway, no true discussions to be had. Debate with people so limited was a pointless exercise. He didn't even hear the convicts, tucked away in their cells, as they begged for freedom. He was not their jailer and he would not be their saviour. He was just an old man listening to the voice in his head.

You are close, Cadaverous. Come to me.

Cadaverous enjoyed this time alone. He wandered the prison corridors and searched the offices, stepping over discarded scythes and fallen automatic weapons while he checked for hidden passages.

Two hours after beginning his search of the prison's lower area, he found rough-hewn steps leading downwards, and downwards he went, feeling the cold and the damp seep into his bones. His flashlight was new, its bulb powerful, but the darkness ate up the beam, swallowed it, as if there were no walls for it to hit, no features for it to catch.

There was just the dark down here. The dark and the voice.

You will be rewarded.

He licked his dry lips. There was only one reward he was

interested in, something he had possessed once, all too briefly, before it had been snatched away from him. He hadn't known what he'd had. He hadn't known the value of it until it was gone.

Free me, said the voice, *and I will make you young again.*

The walls closed in and the beam swept over the cold stones, which were wet to the touch. The walls brought a new sharpness to his footfall. The reflected light illuminated his frozen breath. He slipped on the steps, almost went tumbling, had to jam his hand against the wall to save himself, opening a cut along his palm. He examined it under the light, watching the blood trickle. He wiped it on his shirt. He couldn't feel the pain.

At the bottom of the steps there was a steel door the colour of storm clouds. He took out the set of keys that he'd found in the control room and looked at each key in turn. He found the one most likely to fit and eased it into the lock. It turned smoothly, with a deep and satisfying clunk, and he pushed the door open.

It was a small room. Circular. No light. No ornamentation. In the middle of the room, there was a metal box on a pedestal.

Cadaverous approached. The hair on his arms, on the back of his neck, stood on end. The ring held a small key, much smaller than the others. He found it by touch, unable to take his eyes off the box.

The key turned in the lock. The lid opened ever so slightly.

Cadaverous pocketed the keys and reached out with trembling hands. He hesitated only a moment, then raised the lid fully. It was surprisingly heavy.

In the box, there was a heart.

In his head, there was a voice.

It said, *Good.*

22

Bad things happen all the time.

That's the number-one lesson Valkyrie had learned in the last twelve years. Bad things happen, and they generally happen to good people. Innocent people. Passers-by, caught in the crossfire, consumed by the madness. Like Fletcher.

She stood by his bed in Reverie Synecdoche's private medical practice, a three-storey building in one of the more affluent parts of town, and watched him. He didn't move. A machine helped him breathe.

She reached out, touched his arm.

"I'm so sorry," she whispered. "We were stupid and you saved us. It's our fault you're here." She leaned down. Spoke softer. "I don't think I can do this. I don't think I'm able to do this any more. I don't know what to do. I don't know how to tell him."

Voices reached her – Reverie talking to a nurse passing in the corridor outside. Valkyrie squeezed Fletcher's hand. "Please get better," she said.

Reverie walked in and Valkyrie turned.

"He's stable," Reverie told her. "We've stopped the bleeding. There is some nerve damage that we're correcting. It's a slow process, repairing nerves always is, but he's going to be fine. Would you like to stay? I can have a chair brought in for you."

"Thank you," said Valkyrie, "but no. The Supreme Mage has requested a meeting. How's Skulduggery?"

"We're putting him back together. Again. His jaw has been reattached, so he just has to wait for his arm to set. He'll be out within the hour."

"Thank you, Reverie. Sincerely."

"It's what we do. I'll let you know if there's any change to Fletcher's condition."

Valkyrie thanked her again and left the clinic, taking a tram to the High Sanctuary. For a fleeting moment, she entertained the idea that maybe she'd skip the meeting, get in her car and drive home. She quite liked the thought of forgetting about all of this and just living a normal life, her and her dog. The twenty-four hours she'd promised Skulduggery had ended that morning, after all. She didn't owe it to him to do this. She didn't owe it to anyone.

But she flashed her badge at the door to the High Sanctuary and walked in, leaving the sounds of the city behind her, along with fanciful notions of a quiet life.

The Room of Prisms had changed since she'd been here last. There were still those slivers of angled glass that dropped from the ceiling and rose from the floor like stalactites and stalagmites. Some of them met in the middle, forming thin pillars she had to slip between. The change had come at the far end of the room, where the steps rose to the ornate throne on which sat the Supreme Mage.

Another image from the vision blossomed in Valkyrie's mind, this time of China Sorrows lying on the ground, blood staining a blouse that looked remarkably similar to the one she was wearing now, the one that went so well with the black, high-waisted trousers. Over that blouse she wore her chain of office, fitted with three glittering jewels. Her hair was black. Her face was perfect. Her eyes were closed.

Two bodyguards flanked her, standing to attention. On China's left, a woman with a mask covering everything but her eyes. Her arms were bare and muscled, skin like dark chocolate. A weapon of some sort was strapped to her back.

To China's right stood a man in an identical uniform – a sleeveless robe, belted at the waist. His head was uncovered, however. He was a handsome man, looked Indian. He had two metal discs hanging from his belt.

There was movement reflected in the angled glass, but Valkyrie had to look around a bit before she pinpointed the source. Tipstaff worked his way over to her.

"Detective Cain," he said, keeping his voice low, "it's good to see you. How are your injuries?"

Valkyrie's shoulder throbbed dully. "Fine," she said. "I got off lightly."

Tipstaff nodded, looking suitably concerned, then he motioned to the throne. "You'll have to forgive the Supreme Mage," he said. "She will be with you in a matter of moments."

Valkyrie looked up the steps. "What's she doing?" she asked. "Power nap?"

The briefest of smiles on Tipstaff's lips. "Ha. No. She is accessing the Whispering. A recent development, inspired by your travels in alternate dimensions, actually."

She looked at him, waiting for an explanation.

"When you reported back on the city controlled by the alternate version of Mevolent," Tipstaff said, "you mentioned the World Well. The Supreme Mage was intrigued by the idea of what is essentially a psychic Internet, and so has had her best people working on one for Roarhaven. We call it the Whispering – a way to connect people and share information. It should be ready to be released to the citizenry in less than a year. Right now, the Supreme Mage is the only one with access. It is a much more efficient way of taking the pulse of the city than endless hours of briefings."

"All the information is downloaded directly into her mind?"

Tipstaff nodded, then shrugged. "We're trying to find a better term for it than *downloaded*, though."

"Something that sounds more magicky?"

Another smile. "I suppose. Yes."

"Just because it's a mortal term doesn't mean sorcerers can't use it," Valkyrie said. "Isn't it one of the purposes of the Sanctuaries to remind us that we're not above them?"

"Indeed it is," Tipstaff said. "Although it's hard not to feel superior when they have people like Martin Flanery as American president."

"Flanery's an idiot," Valkyrie admitted, "but, as far as I know, he hasn't tried to take over the world or kill everyone in it. Can I ask you something, in the spirit of sharing potentially catastrophic global events? Have you guys had any encounters with, or warnings of, a woman with silver hair?"

"Not that I'm aware of," said Tipstaff. "Do you have a name I could check for?"

It would have been so easy to tell him, to mention the Princess of the Darklands, but something stopped her. Maybe it was Skulduggery's newfound caution with information, or maybe it was simply the fact that she didn't work for the Sanctuary any more. Whatever the reason, she gave a weak shrug and a weaker smile. "I'm afraid not."

"I'll check our records," Tipstaff said, "see if anyone with silver hair has raised a flag lately."

"Thanks."

"Anything to help the Arbiter Corps." Tipstaff looked at his watch. "The Supreme Mage should be surfacing any moment now..."

Valkyrie looked up as China's pale blue eyes fluttered open.

"I'll leave you to it," Tipstaff said softly, and left.

"Valkyrie," China said, taking a moment to get orientated. "What's Skulduggery's condition?"

"He's fine," said Valkyrie. "Annoyed, but fine."

China sat forward, focusing fully on Valkyrie. "And Fletcher?"

Valkyrie hesitated. "They don't know. There have been complications."

China shook her head. "He's become invaluable to me, that boy. He's a teacher, did you know that? Single-handedly training up the next generation of Teleporters. He's found his vocation."

"Reverie is hopeful."

"I was wondering about that," said China. "Is there any particular reason you chose to go to Doctor Synecdoche over the medical team here at the High Sanctuary?"

"I didn't choose anything. I didn't even know she'd opened her own clinic. That was all Fletcher. I think he just brought us to her on instinct."

"I see," said China. "Yes. I'm sure that was it." She sat back, allowing herself a smile. "How are you, Valkyrie? It's been far too long."

"I'm good, thanks."

"You seem hesitant. Is something wrong?"

"Your chair," said Valkyrie. "From down here, it looks a lot like a throne."

"Is there anything wrong with that?"

Valkyrie shrugged. "I don't know. Sitting in a throne all day might make it easy to forget that you're an elected official and not, you know... a queen. Or an empress."

China observed her, then stood and came down the steps, her bodyguards accompanying her. "There. Is that better?"

"Much," said Valkyrie.

China got to the bottom, and embraced Valkyrie. "It's good to see you again," she said softly.

"It's good to be here," Valkyrie lied.

China stepped back. "The reports I've been hearing on what happened... they lack certain details, such as why on earth you went to the Narrows without Cleaver support. Obviously, as Arbiters, you have the authority to go where you like. But I have to ask, in light of what happened... was that wise?"

"In hindsight," said Valkyrie, "no."

China hooked her arm through Valkyrie's and started walking. The bodyguards stayed behind them. "Who was it? Who attacked you?"

"I don't know all of them," Valkyrie said. "A man named Lethe. Another named Richard Melior. A Teleporter named Nero."

"And you think they're connected to this anti-Sanctuary?" China asked. "Oh, yes, Skulduggery told me all about his suspicions. I wasn't sold on the idea, I have to admit. An organisation working behind the scenes for centuries without us knowing about it? It seemed preposterous." She sighed. "It doesn't seem so preposterous any more."

"I'm assuming the Cleavers found no trace of them when they arrived?"

"None at all," said China. "The City Guards conducted a thorough search of the area – I'm afraid we have no idea where this Melior man may have gone."

"Why did Skulduggery quit?"

China frowned. "I'm sorry?"

"Being City Guard Commander. Why did he quit?"

"It was always going to be temporary," said China. "I knew that when he took the job. Skulduggery wants to be out there, in the thick of the action. Being the Commander meant he was stuck behind a desk for most of his time here. He got it up and running, though, which is what I needed him for. When he left, there were no hard feelings."

"That's it?"

"Yes. Why, did he say any different?"

"He didn't say anything. Which made me wonder."

China smiled again. "You know him well."

She removed her arm from Valkyrie's, and tapped the edge of her wrist. A tattoo glowed briefly, and the wall ahead of them turned transparent, revealing the city of Roarhaven below. "So what do you think of the place?" China asked. "Has it changed much since you've been away?"

Valkyrie nodded to their left. "The Cathedral is new."

"Yes," said China. "An impressive, if foreboding, structure, is it not? But it's important to let the people have their faith. It rewards them. Keeps them happy."

"Keeps them obedient?"

"Oh, Valkyrie... when did you become so cynical? But the Dark Cathedral is only *one* of our new additions."

"I visited Corrival Academy."

"Isn't it wonderful?"

Valkyrie nodded. "That's the kind of school I could have done with, growing up."

"Which is exactly why it's there," China said. "Before, our children went to mortal schools and learned what they could about magic from a variety of sometimes unsuitable sources. But the Academy will give the next generation all the advantages they could possibly need. Teaching everyone the same rules, the same values..."

"Get them thinking the same way."

An eyebrow arched. "You *are* cynical."

"And so many students," Valkyrie said.

"Yes. From all over the world. The best and brightest, all under one roof."

"The children of the most powerful sorcerers, from every single Sanctuary on the planet... It's some achievement. And hey, at least you know that it'll keep their parents in line, right? No one's going to want to go to war with Roarhaven when you have their kids under lock and key."

China looked at her. "You make it sound like they're prisoners."

"Do I?"

China pointed straight ahead. "There we have the Fangs. Have you visited? Three square kilometres where the vampires have taken up residence. People told me it was a mistake to let them live among us, but do you know how many vampire attacks there have been in the last five years? Not a one. It's been yet another great success – testament to what can be achieved when different people, different *species*, work together."

"You sound like you're angling for my vote," said Valkyrie.

China laughed. "I'm just proud of what we've accomplished here, and I don't want to see it threatened by a few angry young sorcerers. I've got Commander Hoc investigating the attack personally. He won't be long finding those responsible."

"That's good of you," said Valkyrie. "I doubt Skulduggery's going to want to abandon his own investigation just yet, though."

"Oh, absolutely. The advantage the City Guard have, however, is that they possess all the resources they could ever want – and they never go into a situation without back-up."

"It does sound nice."

"There's always a spot open for you, should you decide to give it a go..."

"Without Skulduggery?"

"He's spent five years without you. I'm sure he got used to it."

Valkyrie shook her head. "Thanks for the offer, but I'm not even sure if I want to come back."

"Oh? This isn't your triumphant return?"

"It's more of a test run, really."

"I see. Does Skulduggery know this?"

"I told him."

"And does he believe you?"

Valkyrie frowned. "He'd better."

China looked out across the city. "Skulduggery is a frightfully intelligent man, but, like all frightfully intelligent people, he assumes certain things. I think your return to his side would be one of those things he would assume to be a foregone conclusion." She glanced at Valkyrie. "You may well have to remind him that it isn't."

*

Valkyrie returned to Reverie's clinic. She got to Skulduggery's room and stopped in the open doorway. He stood with his back to her. He didn't have his shirt on. She watched his bones move as he examined his reattached forearm. Those bones were nicked and scratched with scars they'd picked up over the years. He flexed his fingers. Valkyrie didn't say anything.

Skulduggery put on his shirt. It hung off him as he did up his tie, like it was still draped over the back of the chair. Suddenly it filled out, as if the man underneath was flesh and blood. Skulduggery tucked it in and reached for his waistcoat.

Valkyrie hesitated, then walked away.

23

His footsteps were lonely.

Odd that the word would occur to him like that. 'Lonely.' Up here, though, on the rooftop, his footsteps couldn't be anything *but* lonely. He didn't have anyone to talk to. Didn't have anyone to wait with. It was just Sebastian up here, his coat flapping in the breeze, and being alone was a feeling he was just going to have to get used to.

Looking back, in the years to come, he didn't think he was going to like this period of his life.

He walked to the open skylight and looked down into the dark bowels of the building. The ground was littered with rubble and debris, like a thin, flaky scab covering a wound. Sebastian didn't like being perched on a roof while there were life-and-death struggles going on below him, but he was here for a reason. He had a mission. A calling. He couldn't afford to get distracted.

A door crashed open somewhere in the shadows below him, and Sebastian dropped to his belly to get a better look. Kathryn Ether, a teacher from the Academy, sprinted into view. A dark shape coalesced before her and she stopped so suddenly her feet flew from under her. The darkness became a shape, a figure, a man. Ether scrambled back, and the man – long-haired, with burning orange eyes, dressed in chain mail – stalked after her.

Sebastian found himself tensing, but fought the urge to jump down. Rule One was *don't get distracted*, and he figured getting horribly killed by a chain-mail-wearing lunatic would be a pretty big distraction, all things considered.

Then Auger ran from cover, holding a thick metal spear, and Sebastian actually sighed with relief. Arriving in the nick of time. Immediately, Auger's friends Kase and Mahala darted from their hiding places, and they sprinted in from three directions. The burning-eyed man saw them coming, and roared. When the distance between them closed to five steps, Auger plunged the spear into the ground. Kase and Mahala did the same.

The spears started glowing. Threads of energy passed between them, trapping the burning-eyed man in a triangle. His roar of rage turned to a roar of panic. Mahala backed off. Kase too. Only Auger stayed where he was, eyes locked.

The spears grew brighter, the threads of energy getting thicker – and then the burning-eyed man arched his back and screamed, and the energy poured into him and turned him to ash.

The spears stopped glowing.

Auger ran to Ether and helped her stand. The others came over. Sebastian couldn't hear what was being said. He had no idea who the burning-eyed man was, no idea why he had been after a teacher, but none of that mattered. Another monster had been stopped. Another threat had been averted.

He watched Mahala and Auger walk away with Ether, leaving Kase to gather up the spears and head in the opposite direction.

Sebastian didn't know an awful lot about Mahala, but he'd done his homework on Kase. The funny one of the group, the one who used jokes to mask his unhappiness, the one who tried to hide the fact that his father had inadvertently formed a cult that worshipped Darquesse.

This made him interesting.

Sebastian followed Kase for a little under ten minutes. It was not easy, travelling across rooftops. It was even less easy to travel across rooftops while keeping track of the turns Kase was making.

Eventually, Kase came to a house on Morwenna Row and sneaked in the back door. When he came out a few minutes later, he wasn't holding the spears. He hurried off in the direction of the school, and Sebastian watched him go. He had arrived at his destination.

He jumped down, went to the back door and tried the handle. It moved easily. The door opened. Sebastian slipped inside.

Kase's kitchen was a mess. Food-encrusted plates were stacked high in the sink. The table was covered in papers and battered notebooks. The floor needed a sweep, and a wash, and possibly a new floor.

Kase's father was in the living room. Bennet Troth sat on the sofa, his head down, the TV on but muted. He had the same dark hair as his son, but like his house it looked like it needed a wash.

Sebastian stepped in. "Hello, Bennet," he said calmly.

Bennet looked up and froze, his eyes wide, his mouth open.

"I'm not here to hurt you," said Sebastian. "I'm here to talk. We have something in common, actually. If it'd be OK with you, I was hoping we could sit and have a chat. What do you say?"

Bennet blinked. His eyes were glassy, his face red. On the table before him was a half-empty bottle of wine.

"Bennet?"

Bennet got to his feet and immediately stumbled, clicking his fingers, throwing sparks and sudden flames, but was too drunk to cultivate them into anything useful.

Sebastian walked forward quickly, hands out. "I won't hurt you, I'm just here to talk, I swear."

Bennet lashed out, a punch that missed without Sebastian even having to duck. "Away from me!" he roared. "Get away!"

Sebastian backed off. "OK, Bennet, OK, whatever you want."

"What I want?" Bennet raged. "What I want? I want my wife back!"

"I'm sorry?"

Bennet charged and Sebastian sidestepped, his coat flapping like a bullfighter's cape, and Bennet hit the wall and spun.

"I think we need to calm down," Sebastian said.

"You kidnapped her! Bring her back!"

"I didn't kidnap anyone."

"I'll kill you, you hear me?"

"If your wife is missing, you should alert the City Guard."

Bennet sneered. "They'd never help me. They laugh at me. They hate me."

"Does Kase know?"

"Didn't tell him," Bennet said, emotion crumpling his face. "Don't want to worry the boy. But you... you're going to tell me where she is."

"I don't know where she is, but if I help you find her, you've got to help me, all right? Do we have a deal?"

"Yes. Yes, anything."

"OK then. Do you know who would want to kidnap her? Do you have any enemies?"

And then it was like all of Bennet's fury abandoned him, and he staggered to the sofa and collapsed on to it. "Too many," he said, tears in his eyes. "Everyone knows. They know about..."

"They know you worship Darquesse?" Sebastian asked gently.

Bennet nodded. "I get rocks through my window. I... I lost my job. People around here, they hate me. My poor Odetta, she doesn't even see Darquesse the way I do, but they still... they still went after her."

Sebastian hesitated, then took a step closer. "What happened?"

Bennet looked up. "Who are you?"

"You can call me the Plague Doctor," said Sebastian. "Like you, I see Darquesse differently from other people."

There was a knock on the front door.

Bennet's eyes widened. "Odetta!" he said, and lunged out of the room. Sebastian watched from cover as Bennet pulled the door open to reveal a pimply-faced boy.

"You Bennet Troth?" the boy asked.

Bennet's shoulders fell. "Yes," he said.

"Got a message for you," said the boy. "It's about your wife. You're never going to see her again so don't bother looking."

Bennet grabbed the boy, shaking him. "Who sent you?" he roared. "Where is she?"

Sebastian ran forward as the kid struggled.

"Let go of me, you spanner!"

Sebastian pulled Bennet back, forcing him to release his hold. "Easy now," he said. "Easy. Let's all just calm down."

The kid stared. "Why are you dressed as a bird?"

"I'm not," Sebastian answered.

"Yes, you are. You have a beak."

"I don't have feathers, do I?"

The boy shrugged. "Some birds don't have feathers."

Beneath his mask, Sebastian frowned. "All birds have feathers. Feathers are what makes them birds."

"What about the duck-billed platypus?" the boy asked. "That doesn't have feathers. It has fur. What kind of duck has fur?"

"The duck-billed platypus isn't a duck. It's a platypus."

"What's a platypus?"

"It's a monotreme," Bennet said miserably. "A mammal that lays eggs."

"Oh," said the boy. He looked back at Sebastian. "Is that what you're dressed as, then? A duck-billed platypus?"

"No," said Sebastian. "I'm the Plague Doctor. You have information about this man's wife? Where is she?"

"Don't know," the boy said. "But if he grabs me again I'm gonna deck him."

Bennet reached for the kid. "Tell me where she is!"

"Get your hands off me, you psycho! I don't know where your stupid wife is! I was paid to knock on this door and give that message to a guy named Bennet Troth, that's all."

"Who paid you?" Sebastian asked.

"Some guy."

"What guy?"

"I don't know who he was," the boy answered. "He was in a big coat and hat. Huge hands. Didn't see his face."

"What did he tell you to say? Exactly?"

The boy sighed again. "He didn't say anything. Two minutes ago I was walking along and he shoved a note and some money into my hands. The note said to tell *this* nutbag that he'll never see his wife again, so to not bother looking. If I'd have known I'd be attacked for delivering a message, I'd have asked for more money."

"Only two minutes? Which way did he go? What direction?"

"I don't know." The boy looked around, then pointed to a street. "He went down there, I think."

"Then we might be able to catch him," Sebastian said. "Bennet – how do I get up on to your roof?"

24

"Where are you taking me?" Valkyrie asked. Xena ignored her, went snuffling through the undergrowth until she'd found a scent she liked, then set off in pursuit. Valkyrie sighed, and walked after her.

The night was cold, and she stuffed her hands into her coat pockets. She was getting to know the land around Grimwood pretty well, and didn't need a torch any more. Pretty soon she'd be able to navigate these trails and paths through the trees without even thinking about it, like she'd been able to do back in Meek Ridge. She thought about Colorado, thought about how much she'd liked it there. She couldn't go back, though. That part of her life was over. If things didn't work out here, she'd go live somewhere new. Maybe even somewhere warm.

"How about it?" she asked the dark shape that was Xena. "How's Australia sound?"

Xena didn't answer.

"Find a nice place on the coast, far away from everyone. We could go swimming every day, what do you think about that?"

Xena bounded in front of her, looked around and bounded off again.

"We don't have to decide now," Valkyrie told her. "Take some time. Think about it."

Her phone rang. Skulduggery. She chewed her lip, then answered on the fourth ring. "Hey," she said.

"Hello. I'm at your front door."

"Ah. I'm close by, just walking the dog."

"A wholesome way to spend your time. May I join you?"

"I'll light the way," Valkyrie said, and hung up. Energy crackled around her hand, but she hesitated a little before letting it loose, straight overhead. It lit up the night for a split second.

Moments later, Skulduggery strode across the sky. He saw her and quickly dipped, keeping pace with her as she walked.

"How are you?" she asked.

"You mean since I got beaten, fair and square?" Skulduggery asked, landing beside her. "I am chastised. Humbled. A better person because of it, I think."

She raised an eyebrow. He shrugged.

"No, you're right. I'm none of those things. I'm angry, and ready for round two."

"That's what I figured," she said. "Any word on Fletcher?"

"He's conscious. Dr Synecdoche is optimistic that he'll make a full recovery. Give him a few days. He'll be fine."

They ducked under a low branch.

"He saved us," she said.

"Yes, he did."

"We shouldn't have gone in there."

"In retrospect, no, we shouldn't have. But we couldn't have foreseen what happened."

"That's the problem," Valkyrie said. "We didn't know what we were going up against. We didn't know who the enemy were. I'm trying to remember if we were always so..."

"Brash?"

She glanced at him. "I was going to say *dumb*."

He shrugged. "We've walked into bad situations before. It's how we find out who the enemies are, so we're better prepared the next time."

146

"If it wasn't for Fletcher—"

"I know," said Skulduggery. "I know."

Xena was somewhere in the dark. Valkyrie had lost track of her.

"I thought you had him," she said, coming to a stop. "Lethe. When it started, and he was bouncing around with all these fancy kicks, I said to myself, this'll be over in a second."

Skulduggery rubbed his arm. "And then he changed tactics. He's better than me, I'll give him that, but he took me by surprise. That won't happen again."

Xena came trotting back. She went right up to Skulduggery, tail wagging, and he crouched, scratching behind her ears.

"The Teleporter," she said, folding her arms to keep herself warm. "Nero. He brought them all in, but they weren't touching. I didn't think that was possible. In order to teleport other people, you need to be touching them – that's the rule, right?"

"As far as I know," Skulduggery said. "But Neoterics don't concern themselves with the rules."

"And he followed Fletcher straight to Reverie. How did he do that? His powers... he can do a lot more than Fletcher – but Fletcher was almost a Neoteric, too, wasn't he? I mean, he's mostly self-taught."

"But then Cameron Light found him," said Skulduggery, straightening up. "And we gave him a book telling him how to harness his power. From that point on, his evolution was directed in the conventional way. If we'd left him alone, maybe he'd be able to do what Nero can do."

"So are Neoterics more powerful than regular sorcerers?"

"Not necessarily. Our training makes us strong. Their unpredictability makes them strong."

"They have a guy who can mess with time," she said. "Any idea who he is?"

"I found no mention of him in the Neoteric Report, so I don't know where Parthenios Lilt found him."

"Lilt," she said. "I'm assuming now is the time to go after him, yes?"

Skulduggery adjusted his hat slightly. "He has already been arrested," he said. "Commander Hoc saw to it personally."

"Have you interviewed him yet?"

"I doubt I'll be able to."

She frowned. "They wouldn't stop you... would they?"

"Hoc is a smart man, and a good investigator, but when I was Commander we had our differences. Now that he's in charge, I feel he would be disinclined to grant an interview request, even to an Arbiter."

"But China would allow it."

"No," he said. "She wouldn't."

"Skulduggery, why did you quit?"

He took a moment before answering. "Politics."

"China said you couldn't handle being stuck behind a desk all day."

"That was part of it."

Valkyrie didn't press it. She wasn't even sure she wanted to know.

"Shall we go back?" he asked. "You look cold."

"Sure," she said. "Come on, girl."

She motioned ahead of them, and Xena ran on.

"So," he said, as they followed the dog, "are you going to redecorate?"

"Sorry?"

"The house. You may have taken ownership, but it looks like Gordon still lives here. All those dramatic paintings. All that Gothic sensibility."

"I like it," she said. "It reminds me of him. I still miss him like crazy. At least I got to say goodbye the second time he died. And I know what you're going to say. I know the Gordon in the Echo Stone was just a recording of his personality, but I don't care."

"I wasn't going to say anything of the sort."

"Oh. Sorry."

"But he left you his house, Valkyrie. I think it's safe to assume that he expected you to update it a little. It might be nice for you to make your own mark."

"Honestly, Skulduggery, I don't even know if I'm staying."

He stopped walking.

She turned to him. "The nightmares came back last night," she said. "I woke up and I couldn't breathe. A panic attack. I haven't had a panic attack in... a while. I thought I was over them. I don't think I can go on with this."

"You said I had twenty-four hours."

"You've *had* twenty-four hours."

"I didn't think you literally *meant* twenty-four hours. I thought it was more of a metaphor than an actual measurement of time."

"Well, I meant twenty-four hours."

"But we're only getting started, Valkyrie. We've just had our first life-or-death encounter. This is how things go. It's how we do what we do. We have a life-or-death encounter, we stay on it, and then at the end we win and walk away triumphant."

"Yeah," she said. "I don't know if that's going to work this time."

"Stay with me. See it through. I need you, Valkyrie. And you need me."

"Do I?"

He stepped closer. "You'd be lost without me."

"I managed fine for five years."

"You were just recharging your batteries. Now you're ready for phase two."

"I don't think that's right."

"You gave me twenty-four hours. Give me another twelve."

"You've actually *had* another twelve."

"I mean give me another twelve starting from tomorrow morning. You can't leave now. We've just had our first breakthrough."

"I'm not up to it any more, Skulduggery. Come on, you must be able to see that. We were outmatched. Lethe pulled your jawbone off, for God's sake."

"Which was painful, but useful."

"How the hell was that useful?"

"When I could no longer speak, he filled the silence. He told us what they were after."

"He did?"

"To breathe life into the lifeless. That's why Melior is so important to them – he's the vital piece of this puzzle. That's how he differs from other Vitakinetics – if I am interpreting Lethe correctly, the good doctor can actually bring someone back from death."

Valkyrie frowned. "You're serious?"

"Deadly."

"So they're... they're going to resurrect someone? Like *actually* resurrect them? Who? This Princess of the Darklands woman?"

"Possibly."

She frowned. "Do you know who she is?"

"No," he said. "I know who she *might* be, but I don't want to say just yet. Trust me on this. For the moment, we need to focus on Richard Melior. He's the key. If we can stop the anti-Sanctuary at this early stage, then their plans for war will never be set in motion."

"And if we find Melior, but Lethe and the others are still with him?"

"We'll run away."

She thought for a moment. "That's honestly the best plan you've ever come up with."

"I thought you'd like it. So you'll stay with me? For just a little while longer? Give me tomorrow."

"You know, you're probably better off on your own."

He tilted his head. "I disagree most vehemently."

She sighed. "Tomorrow, then. One more day."

"Excellent." He swept his arm wide, inviting her to carry on walking. "How is China, by the way?"

"Um..."

"Valkyrie?"

"I'm just trying to find the right word for it. She was... regal."

"Regal?"

"Worryingly regal."

"You think the power may have gone to her head?"

"This is what she's wanted all along, right? She was never satisfied with the other Grand Mages when they were in charge. She was always complaining about how they were blocking her attempts to do this or to do that... Now she's in control. Finally."

"And she doesn't even have a Council of Elders to balance her out."

"She doesn't have a Council? Really?"

"Well," Skulduggery said, "she has what she calls her Council of Advisors – two Grand Mages that she put in power herself, from England and Germany, and the American Grand Mage, who succeeded the old one after he tried to overthrow her."

"So they just agree with whatever she says?"

"Essentially."

"Is there anyone in a position to argue with her?"

"Not really."

"Isn't that hugely, amazingly dangerous? What do we do if she starts abusing her power?"

"We hope her better nature triumphs."

Valkyrie frowned. "Does China *have* a better nature?"

"I suppose we'll find out, won't we?"

25

China Sorrows entered the chamber and immediately the three men rose. Two of them almost knocked their chairs over in their eagerness to offer due respect. The third was decidedly calmer. China took her seat at the north corner of the triangular table and waved at them to sit. The chamber was dark and bare, at odds with the extravagance that defined much of the rest of the High Sanctuary. She had no throne here. No mirrors. This was where the decisions were taken. This was where business was handled.

"The bank," she said, directing the words to Grand Mage Aloysius Vespers of the English Sanctuary. "We're behind schedule."

Vespers, an overfed man with long white hair, gave a combination of a nod and a shrug. "We are, but we're picking up speed. Co-ordinating between the Central Banks of the world was never going to be a straightforward process, yet I am happy to report that we have overcome significant hurdles in the last week alone."

"And how close are we to a bank the citizens of Roarhaven can *actually* use?"

Vespers smiled, like he was delivering good news. "Two years. Maybe eighteen months."

"You've had five years," China said, and she watched Vespers's smile falter. "We have the money – we have more than enough capital – but where has it languished since I first tasked you with this operation?"

"In, uh, in the First Bank of Roarhaven—"

"No," said China. "The First Bank is a building. That's all. It's a building where we keep, relatively speaking, a very small amount of money. Cash for day-to-day requirements. No, Aloysius – I'm talking about the vast amounts of wealth that sorcerers have at their disposal, accrued over centuries. Where is *that* money?"

Vespers reddened. "Mortal banks, Supreme Mage."

"Mortal banks," China repeated. "Where our people risk constant exposure and the magical community at large in no way benefits from all of the investments they make. I asked you for a bank, based in Roarhaven, which all sorcerers around the world could use. A bank that is protected, private, but operates on a global scale. I asked you to *slip it* into existence beside all the other mortal banking institutions. Do you remember me asking you that?"

"Yes, Supreme Mage."

"I didn't want attention drawn to it. I didn't want questions asked. I didn't want opposition mounted. I asked of you impossible things, Aloysius, and what did you say?"

He swallowed. "I... I said I could deliver."

"That's right," said China. "You did."

"I will redouble my efforts."

She pinned him with a look. "It troubles me that your efforts *can* be redoubled."

Vespers shifted in his seat. "I... I only meant that a lot of my time is taken up with leading my own Council. But I will, of course, prioritise the matter from this point on."

China kept her eyes on him until he started to wilt, then turned to the American. "Grand Mage Praetor, how are you faring with President Flanery?"

Gavin Praetor, a trim man with a distinctly feline quality to his movements, inclined his head slightly. "He is a boorish man. Arrogant. Narcissistic. Greedy for money and power. A thug in an expensive suit is how he's being described by certain political commentators. In short, easily controlled and perfect for our needs."

"So long as he gets his second term in the White House," said China.

Praetor nodded. "I don't think we have much to worry about, not with the changes he's made to the election process. The Democrats can't even settle on a candidate to run against him. Every senator, governor or mayor to put their name in the hat takes it out a few weeks later, their reputation in tatters. The media is wondering how Flanery finds out all their secrets."

"So the rumours are true?"

"It would appear so," said Praetor. "We don't know who, yet, but we believe that Flanery has had a sorcerer of some description working for him since before he ran for office. In the past, he's been able to push bills through Congress that ordinarily wouldn't stand a chance. His opponents fall before him. Minds are being read, influenced – if not outright controlled."

"We need to keep an eye on this," China said. "So long as we have him on a leash, he's useful. If he manages to slip that leash, he's dangerous. I want this sorcerer named."

"Of course, Supreme Mage."

"Grand Mage Drang, you mentioned that something was troubling you?"

"Coldheart Prison," said the German Grand Mage, the light catching the single scar that ran from the corner of his eye to the hinge of his jaw. "They have failed to check in."

"So? They've missed reporting in before. It all depends where they are in the world and even what the weather is like."

"With respect, Supreme Mage, I do not think it is that simple in this instance. The last of the safeguards have been removed only last week. For the first time, the prison is vulnerable."

She sighed. "We're all quite aware of your objections to the change in the prison's status, Grand Mage. We've had this debate."

Sturmun Drang raised an eyebrow fractionally. "There was no debate, Supreme Mage. You decided to take sole control of an international prison. You decided to systematically remove the multiple safeguards that nine separate Sanctuaries contributed to make Coldheart absolutely impenetrable."

"It is still impenetrable."

"No, Supreme Mage. Without the international safeguards, the prison's defences have been halved."

"Temporarily. New safeguards – better safeguards – are being implemented as we speak."

"And for those three days, until those safeguards are online, the prison is vulnerable. And it has gone missing."

China regarded him calmly. "I will have my people look into it. I'm sure it's nothing."

"I hope you are right," said Drang. "Otherwise three hundred and twenty-six highly dangerous sorcerers may be on the loose, and we are not doing anything about it."

She looked at Vespers and Praetor. They smiled back, the way people do when they're nervous and unsure and want to calm the waters after a disagreement. China felt no such urge to smile. That was the luxury that absolute power afforded her. "I believe you have someone waiting to meet me," she said.

Vespers stood. "Indeed we do, Supreme Mage. Our apologies for the delays you've endured." Walking quickly, he left the room, the door closing slowly behind him.

China noted the way Drang sighed. He had no time for religion, and even less for religious leaders.

The door burst open.

A large man strode in, dressed in frayed trousers and an old, stained shirt. He was muscled, his head shaven, and reminded China of her brother. This took her by surprise. The last time she'd seen this man he'd had long hair and a filthy beard. His eyes, though, glittered just as brightly as they had that day, decades ago.

Like her brother, Creed's strides were long, and Vespers had to hurry to keep up.

"Supreme Mage," said Praetor, "may we present *Arch-Canon* Damocles Creed."

Creed stopped before her and bowed quickly.

She bowed in return. "Arch-Canon, so very good to see you again. My sincerest congratulations on your appointment."

"If the gods will it, I obey," Creed said. He'd lost his accent since the last time they'd spoken, and his voice was rougher, like he hadn't used it in a long, long time. "Although Eliza Scorn could not have been happy with your ruling."

China nodded sadly. "Unfortunately, I just couldn't allow the Church of the Faceless to be led by someone as flawed as Eliza. In too many instances, she has allowed her personal agenda to interfere with the teachings of the religion I once held so dear to my own heart. If the Church truly is to flourish, then I, and the Grand Mages here with us, firmly believe that it can do so only under the leadership of a new Arch-Canon."

"I have no love for Eliza Scorn," Creed said, "but it's as if she didn't have any choice but to step aside."

"I'm sure she understands, wherever she is. And her decision to leave meant that construction could be completed on the Dark Cathedral. Isn't it a marvel?"

"Its magnificence is only surpassed by the opulence of the High Sanctuary."

"We live in more enlightened times," China said. "Our people can worship who, what and how they want to worship, so long as they do so in peace, and obey our laws."

"A faithful people will always obey the laws of a faithful society," said Creed.

China smiled. "Quite."

"Supreme Mage, you must excuse me. I have travelled far, and

I am tired, and there are already a hundred people standing at the steps of the Cathedral, waiting for guidance."

"Of course," said China. "Your flock needs you."

He bowed again, and strode quickly away. She waited until he was gone.

"You're sure about him?" she asked.

Vespers looked surprised. "Oh, yes, Supreme Mage. Damocles Creed was our ideal candidate from the very start. Devout, respected and strong. There is no one with a voice worth listening to who could possibly object to him replacing Eliza Scorn."

"I seem to recall objecting," Drang said.

Vespers allowed himself a wry smile. "My apologies, Grand Mage. I discounted the atheists among us."

"We've avoided considerable controversy with Creed," Praetor said. "Holding the Cathedral ransom while we forced Scorn out was a risky move, especially with how quickly the Church is growing here."

China ran her tongue slowly along the back of her teeth. Her brother had once told her, during one of the many conversations they'd had about her faith, that religion was a virus. It spread fastest when the conditions were right. Endorsing the Church and building the Dark Cathedral was China's way of controlling that virus, of directing it and containing it. Once she could keep an eye on it, she could stamp it out if needed.

"We're done for the day," she said. "You're dismissed."

Vespers and Praetor offered her their usual gratitude and praise. Drang merely nodded. Then they left the room. Her life consisted of meetings, both long and short, and she was always grateful for the short ones.

She walked to her apartment, and slipped her chain of office on to the blank-faced bust set into the alcove beside the door. A pretty piece of jewellery, and expensive, though completely meaningless. She'd had it made just to have something different from the brooches that other Grand Mages wore. A token of power, that's all it was, but China had learned a long time ago that power perceived is power nonetheless. Tokens were important.

She undressed and slipped her robe on. It was late, and she was tired, but there was still work to be done. The activation of a sigil and the fireplace roared to life. She settled into her favourite armchair, her feet tucked under her, and began to read the topmost file that Tipstaff had left for her. For every advantage that power had brought, it had delivered to her ten times more pressures and responsibilities. The burden of leadership, she had discovered, was a heavy one.

Sleep would have to wait.

26

Omen woke up, and tried to remember his dream.

He could never remember his dreams. They swam immediately out of reach upon surfacing. The glimpses he could snatch came back to him at odd times throughout the day, nonsensical images and feelings of déjà vu. His dreams weren't like Auger's. Auger dreamed of bad people doing bad things. Sometimes his dreams had actually come true. Sometimes he could decipher them, adding this piece to that piece, forming a picture, a crazy jigsaw of future events. Vivid dreams, Omen supposed, were just another part of being the Chosen One, while vague nonsense and logical dead ends were part of being the Chosen One's brother.

The morning light was pale, and lit up the small dorm room without enthusiasm. Outside it was cold. There was a wind, and it pushed at the window – not enough to rattle the pane, but enough to make it flex with a broken rhythm, like a weak heartbeat.

In the bed along the far wall, Gerontius still slept, and in the one nearest the door, Morven snored, the sheets twisted around his lanky body like they'd attacked him during the night. Omen couldn't call either boy a friend, but they were nice enough to him, and he felt obliged to keep out of their way as much as possible. Moving quietly, he got out of bed, tried and failed to find his slippers, and padded out into the hall, the floor cold on his bare feet.

He used the toilet and went to the window, not really expecting to see anything, but his eyes widened when he saw the red ribbon tied around the drainpipe across the way. Suddenly he wasn't sleepy any more. Wishing now that he'd bothered to find his slippers, and *really* wishing he'd put his dressing gown on over his pyjamas, Omen hurried to the end of the boys' block. The door, as promised, had been left unlocked. He sneaked through, hid from Mr Stymie as he passed, the old man muttering to himself like he was asking a question and expecting an answer, and carried on. Finally, he came to another door and knocked once and entered.

Skulduggery Pleasant sat in the store cupboard on an elegant chair he'd undoubtedly taken from somewhere else. He looked up from what he was reading, a file of some sort, and folded it over before slipping it into his jacket.

"I'm here," Omen whispered.

"So I see," Skulduggery said, speaking at a normal volume. "Nice pyjamas."

"Thank you."

"I was joking."

"Oh."

"They're terrible."

"I like the colour."

"It clashes with itself." Skulduggery was wearing a black three-piece suit with a black shirt and tie. His cufflinks were silver. His shoes were polished. It was all so cool. "How are you, Omen? Are you well?"

"I'm fine," said Omen. "Did you check out Mr Lilt?"

"We did," Skulduggery said.

"I've done a little more snooping," Omen said. "I spied on them, on Mr Lilt and the study group. I think Mr Lilt is going to kill Byron."

"Who's Byron?"

"One of the Arcanum's Scholars. Byron Grace. He's all right, actually. He's not that bad."

"Is he part of the group that wants to kill all mortals?"

"Yes," Omen admitted, "but I don't think his heart's really in it. Mr Lilt was saying he'll probably have to kill him. Mr Lilt, that is, killing Byron. Anyway, I was thinking maybe you could take Byron into protective custody? Maybe he's got information we could use. Do we do protective custody, or is that a mortal thing?"

"We do it," said Skulduggery, "but I doubt we'll have to. Parthenios Lilt has been arrested."

Omen blinked. "Because of me?"

A nod. "Directly because of you, Omen. I passed on your suspicions to the City Guard and they wasted no time in kicking down his door. They do so love to kick down doors. Lilt's involvement opened up a fresh list of suspects, and I have a very strong feeling that we'll put a stop to whatever the anti-Sanctuary is planning because of it. We owe you a huge debt of gratitude."

Omen blushed. "It was nothing. I mean, I just... I just kept my eyes open, like you asked."

"What you did was very brave. Never forget that." Skulduggery stood up.

"Are you OK?" Omen asked him.

Skulduggery tilted his head. "Excuse me?"

"I heard you were hurt."

"Ah. Yes, I was, but I'm OK now. It's a dangerous business."

Omen smiled. "I'll try to remember that. So what do I do now?"

"I don't know," said Skulduggery. "Go to breakfast, I'd imagine."

"I mean about the mission."

"I have good news about that, actually. Your mission is over."

Omen's smile faded. "It is?"

"Now you can go back to being normal," Skulduggery said. "Study. Do your homework. Do what you're told. All the things that normal people like doing."

"Normal people don't like any of that."

"They don't?"

"No. Nobody likes doing what they're told."

Skulduggery took a moment to process the information. "Then why do they do it?"

"I don't... I don't know. Maybe they don't know what else to do."

"Huh. Interesting."

"Are you being serious, about the mission being over?" Omen asked. "Because I really think I can be more useful. I have one of their masks, the kind the Scholars wear, and I'm thinking I can get into the room where they hold their meetings."

Skulduggery slipped his gloved hands into his pockets. "Omen, you're a good lad. There's a reason we came to you."

"Yeah," Omen said, "because I'm invisible. Because nobody notices me."

"There is that, obviously, but also because of who you are. You're one of the good guys, Omen. You're one of us. We knew we could trust you, and you've proven us right. But if I can get hurt, and I'm sure you know how wonderful I am, then anyone can get hurt. These people, the anti-Sanctuary, these Arcanum's Scholars – they're dangerous. They're too dangerous to underestimate. I can't risk you because I don't have the right to risk you."

"You risked Valkyrie's life when she was two years younger than me."

Skulduggery nodded. "And it's very hard to argue with that logic, especially when the reason is 'it just felt right'. But it just felt right, Omen. I knew she could handle herself. I knew she'd make it through. I can't explain it, I just knew. But even she, even Valkyrie, has been damaged by this. Damaged by me dragging her into it all. She does her very best not to show it, but I know her too well to be fooled."

"But if you're so damaging to her, why didn't you just leave her alone?"

"Because we're caught in a loop, Valkyrie and I. A very destructive loop. And I'm sorry, but I'm just not going to damage another good person. Not if I can help it."

Skulduggery moved past him, reached for the door handle.

"But I'm nobody," Omen said, and he was surprised to find his eyes blurring with tears. "I don't have anything. There's no purpose to me."

Skulduggery looked back. "There's a purpose to all of us."

"Not to me, and I should know. When you grow up with the Chosen One, all you hear about is destiny, and purpose, and becoming who you were always meant to be. Nobody ever said any of those things to me. Nobody ever asked me what my purpose was, because they knew, they all knew, that I didn't have one. I'm the leftovers."

Skulduggery turned to him slowly. "You don't honestly believe that, do you?"

"Yes," said Omen. "I mean, what else do I have to believe?"

"If you can't believe in yourself, then believe in me. Because I believe in you." Skulduggery held his hand out, and Omen hesitated, then shook it. "Thank you for your help, Omen. We couldn't have come this far without you."

And then he was gone, and Omen was left alone in the cupboard in his stupid pyjamas and his cold, bare feet.

27

The news about Lilt spread through the school in whispers and text messages. History class was supervised by other teachers and the students were told to keep quiet and busy themselves with their work. No one whispered the news to Omen, though. No one cared enough to share.

His moment was gone. His chance at being something, at being somebody, had flowed from his grip like a fistful of water. At break time he sat alone, a ghost, fading slowly back into the furniture. It was what he was good at. It was the only thing he was good at. Any hope he'd ever had of being somebody who'd make any kind of difference had disappeared. What a fool he'd been, to think himself part of the team. Skulduggery Pleasant and Valkyrie Cain and... Omen Darkly? Really? Had he seriously thought that? Had he seriously thought that the two of them, that two *legends* like that, would take him on as an apprentice? What the hell would they need him for? What would *anyone* need him for?

But it had felt so good. That was the really pathetic part. Being a part of it, however briefly, had filled a need within him that he'd never known existed. Up until now he'd been content to be the irrelevant brother. He hadn't minded that everything was about Auger, that nothing was about him. It was how he'd been raised. He'd never known any different.

And then Skulduggery and Valkyrie had come along and told him that he could be a part of something bigger, and it was like a light shining down on him from above. He was singled out. He was special. Not once in his fourteen years had he ever been special. Auger was the first-born. Auger was the Chosen One. From the day of his birth, Omen had been the *other one*. His parents treated him like an annoyance. The people brought in to train Auger treated him like a prop. *See what your brother is doing, Auger? That's the wrong way to do it. Do it like this. Good boy.* And Omen was left in the shadows, always so eager to please, always so compliant. Never complaining. Always grateful for whatever scraps of attention, no matter how meagre, were tossed his way.

And, for two glorious days, it had all changed, and he'd glimpsed what it was like to be important. It had been good. It had been... fulfilling. He'd never been happier. The realisation hit him like heartbreak. He had actually never been happier.

Tears came to his eyes again and he wiped them away, roughly, with the back of his hand. Nobody laughed at him, nobody pointed, because nobody saw, and nobody cared. A sea of black uniforms and coloured ties all around him, ebbing and flowing, and not one of them bothered to even mock him.

Skulduggery was worried about putting Omen's life in danger, but the truth was if Omen had been killed, nobody, apart from Never and Auger, would have cared. He was a ghost in life and he'd be less than a ghost in death.

Did you know that the Chosen One had a brother?

Really? What happened to him?

What happened to who?

Omen had liked being special. It had been a good feeling. A warm feeling. He'd mattered. He wasn't alone. He could see now why brave people did the things they did. Brave things, selfless things... they connected you. They plugged you into the world. He wasn't plugged in any more. He was adrift.

Byron Grace passed, walking quickly like he had somewhere

to be. A few seconds later, Lapse and Gall stalked by, going in the same direction. Heading for the stairs.

Omen stood up from the bench. He tucked in his shirt and watched Colleen Stint, clutching her golden mask, dart through the crowd after them. A meeting. The Arcanum's Scholars had called a meeting without Mr Lilt.

Omen's feet were moving. He was walking – no, running – for his locker. His mind caught up to the decision the rest of him had made, and he took the gold mask and stuck it under his blazer, then ran back, taking the long way to the fifth-floor library. He arrived out of breath, his heart thudding, as Perpetua Darling joined the rest of the Arcanum's Scholars in their usual spot, lounging about on the chairs. Omen spotted the librarian struggling to restock the higher shelves on the other side of the library.

Omen did his best to get his breathing under control, then sneaked behind a fern and crouched down, watching. The Scholars chatted among themselves for a bit, nobody making anything more than small talk. Jenan had his usual seat, just an everyday chair that he managed to make look like a throne.

"What are we even doing here?" asked Isidora Splendour, one of Colleen Stint's best friends. "Mr Lilt's been arrested. They've probably killed him by now."

"They don't kill people they've arrested," said Gall.

"Shows how much you know," Isidora responded. "They killed the American Grand Mage, didn't they? Shot him in his cell."

"That was different."

"How? Exactly how was it different? Cypher plotted against the Sanctuary and they arrested him and murdered him."

"It's different because they killed him after he'd told them everything," said Gall, sounding annoyed that he was being asked to explain himself. "Lilt won't have told them a thing."

"They've got Sensitives, idiot."

"And Lilt's got psychic defences, moron."

Isidora's voice rose. "What did you call me?"

"I called you a moron."

"You take that back!" she screeched. "You take that right back!"

Gall frowned. "You called me an idiot."

"Take it back, Gall," said Colleen, glaring at him while she comforted her friend.

"She called me an idiot first," said Gall.

"You don't call girls morons!" Isidora wailed. Actually wailed. With tears.

"Jesus Christ," Gall said.

Jenan sighed. "Say you're sorry."

Gall's face was a mask of confusion. "But she called me—"

"I know what she called you," Jenan said. "It was ten seconds ago and I was sitting right here. Apologise anyway before she gets any louder."

Gall stared at him, the confusion giving way to resentment, and then he shrugged. "Fine, whatever. Sorry."

"You shouldn't call people that," Isidora said, her voice shaky with emotion.

"Right."

"There are real morons out there and to use the word as a derogatory term is insulting to them, not just to me."

Gall blinked at her. "What?"

"You've just got to think before you yell insults at people. Words hurt, Gall."

Byron sat forward. "So let me get this straight. Calling you a moron, Isidora, is insulting to morons?"

Isidora sighed. "Yes."

Colleen hugged her friend. "Stop talking now, Izzy."

Jenan stood up, bringing an end to the conversation. "We're here because the fact that they grabbed Lilt changes nothing. I got a message last night telling us not to worry. As long as we don't do anything stupid, we're safe. We haven't done anything wrong. We haven't broken any laws. Not yet."

"Who sent the message?" Colleen asked.

"You'll find out in a moment," said Jenan. "OK, it's time to move to less salubrious surroundings. Ceremonial masks on."

The Scholars took out their masks and slipped them on, and Jenan led the way to the back room.

Omen's feet wouldn't budge. His body had frozen. This was a bad idea. This was a supremely bad idea.

His hands moved, slipping the golden mask over his head, fixing it in place, and the moment it was secure his legs woke up. He covered the distance in three seconds, joining the group as they squeezed through the doorway into a room with a large glass door that opened out on to a balcony.

Jenan, the tallest of them, shut the door once they were all in. He didn't glance twice at Omen, and he didn't do a headcount. There was a table in the middle of the room with chairs all around it. If they sat, Omen's ruse would be over before it had truly begun.

One of the Scholars went to sit.

"Don't bother," said Jenan. "You'll want to be standing for this."

"For what?" somebody asked. Sounded like Gall.

Jenan didn't answer. He just took out his phone and checked the time. "Any moment now," he said. "Clear a space there."

There was a little shuffling as everyone crowded into the same side of the small room.

"Somebody close the curtains," Jenan instructed.

People turned their heads, gold masks revolving, but nobody actually moved. Finally, Omen went to do it, and the Scholars looked away. The curtains were heavy, and when they were closed the room darkened considerably. Omen stayed where he was, at the back.

"What are we waiting for?" Byron asked.

"You'll see," said Jenan, and then, like it had all been rehearsed, three people teleported into the room before them.

The masked man in the middle wore an outfit of black rubber. The man to his left had platinum hair and a smile. The woman to his right was drop-dead gorgeous, and wore a tuxedo. Omen didn't have the first idea who they were, but the others certainly did. There was a collective gasp.

"Hello, my friends," said the masked man. His voice was distorted, soft and loud at the same time, like he was whispering into a microphone. "It's an *honour* to finally meet you. Parthenios has told us *so much* about you all."

Jenan spoke up, his own voice tight with excitement. "Mr Lethe, it is a huge honour for us, too. We just want you to know that we are ready, we are so ready, to fight for the cause. Blood has to be spilled and we, all of us here, we are ready to spill that blood for you, sir." Crazily, he saluted.

"Jenan, is it?" Lethe asked, and shook his head. "We don't salute here, Jenan, and there are no *sirs* in our group. I'm not *above* you. I'm not issuing *orders*. I'm a soldier, just like you are. We're partners. *Comrades.*"

"Comrades," repeated Jenan, nodding like this was the greatest word in recorded history.

"I know we've suffered some setbacks," Lethe continued. "Losing *Mr Lilt* to the enemy... that's a loss. I'm not going to stand here and lie to you. Parthenios was a *valued* part of our team, and his arrest... that's a problem for us. But we shall overcome our enemies by *standing together*. I look around this room and I'm filled with... *pride*. With *love*. We're the same. Everyone in here. The same."

Colleen started to say something, but all she could manage was a croak. This drew some nervous laughter from the other Scholars, and the lady in the tuxedo smiled. The smile was unsettlingly wide.

"I'm sorry," said Lethe, "what was that?"

Colleen tried again. "Is it true you beat Skulduggery Pleasant?"

Now the lady chuckled.

"I don't like to *brag*," said Lethe with good humour, "so all I will say is that bones were broken and they weren't exactly *mine*."

The Scholars laughed, and clapped, but kept the claps soft.

"Skulduggery Pleasant is no big deal, though – not really. He feels *pain* like anyone else. I made him feel pain when we met, and I'll make him feel pain *again*. But I'm not the only one who can do that. We can *all* do it. We can all take down their best people. We're all *capable*. We just need to be *smarter* than them, *braver* than them, *better* than them. Everyone in this room can do that. Everyone in this room has the potential to *be* that. And you'll get to prove it very, *very* soon."

A tentative hand rose. "What are we going to do?" asked Gall.

"You're going to *strike*, my friend," said Lethe. "You're going to bring *terror* to the heartland of America and then you're going to watch, you're going to *sit back and watch*, as the mortals tear themselves apart in their *panic* and their *fear*. Mortal society will *crumble*. They'll *hurt* each other, *hunt* each other, *kill* each other and, when they find out about *us*, they're going to turn all their murderous rage *our* way. The Sanctuaries around the world will not have a *choice*. They're going to have *to fight*. We, all of us, are going to start a *war* the mortals can't *win*, and we're going to do it *together*. Mr Lilt, he told us he would trust you all with his *life*. He told us you were *devoted*, just like us. But, now that he's in chains, you're going to need a spokesman."

Jenan stepped forward. "I'll be leader."

The woman laughed. "I like him," she said. "He's certainly bottling his blood's worth."

Lethe nodded. "I have no idea what that *means*, Razzia, but I'm sure you're *right*. He has *ambition*. Ambition is *good*. Leadership is *good*. But our groups don't have leaders. They have *representatives*. They have *spokespeople*."

"Then I'll speak for this group," said Jenan.

"It looks like you already *are*," Lethe said, sounding amused.

"Very well. If nobody has an objection, let Jenan Ispolin speak for *First Wave*."

"First Wave?" Byron echoed.

"Your group," said Lethe. "You need a *name*, don't you? Arcanum's Scholars is a study group. It's for kids, isn't it? But you're not kids. What you *are* is the first wave. You will *strike* first. You will draw first *blood*. When mortals think of sorcerers, they will think of you *first*."

Omen paid attention to the man with the platinum hair when he noticed him frowning. The man's eyes were narrowed, and flicking from one gold mask to the next. He was counting.

Terror seized Omen's chest and he moved slightly, stepping behind the others. He saw the frown deepen, and the count began again.

"We will be in contact with Jenan in a few days," Lethe was saying. "From this moment on, we are *doubling* our precautions. Our *revolution*, which one day will have seemed *inevitable* and *unstoppable*, is still a *fragile* thing. Parthenios's capture serves as a reminder that even the *best* of us can falter. We must be *vigilant*. We must be *ready*."

The man with the platinum hair put his hand on Lethe's arm and spoke to the group. "How many of you are there?" he asked.

"Nine, Mr Nero," said Jenan immediately.

"Then why are there ten gold masks in this room?"

Everyone turned, stepping away from each other and counting for themselves. Except for Omen. Omen just stood there.

The counting faded as the space around him widened.

"And *who*," said Lethe, stepping forward, "might *you* be?"

Omen backed up, face burning under his mask. He felt the thick curtains behind him. Through them, the door handle. He turned it, felt the door open.

Jenan pushed roughly through the Scholars. "Out of the way," he snarled, reaching out. "Who the hell are—?"

Omen surprised himself by shoving Jenan hard in the chest,

171

sending him backwards into the others, and then he barged through the curtains, out on to the balcony, where the wind turned his sweat cold and there was nowhere to go but down. There was a balcony below him, and a balcony below that, and he swung one leg over the side, but his hands gripped the railing and he couldn't go any further. Shapes moved behind the curtain, filling it, too many of his classmates trying to get through at the same time, all of them coming to – what? To push him? To kill him?

Nero teleported on to the balcony and Omen cried out and jerked back, lost his balance, started to fall, but Nero reached out, grabbed his wrist.

Omen hung there, his body committed to the fall, his mouth open, his heart an empty thing in his chest, and all he could feel were Nero's fingers around his wrist.

Nero smiled, and let go.

Omen shrieked as he fell. He was past the first balcony before he even saw it. He reached for the second and banged his arm and kept falling. He saw a face at an open window and Filament Sclavi reached out, tried using the air to stop Omen's descent, but Omen broke through and kept falling, and then there was a strong wind buffeting him closer to the wall and a hand reached down, closed around his wrist.

Omen slammed into the side of the building and hung there for a moment, gasping. He was two floors from the ground, and now he was being pulled upwards to the balcony.

Mr Peccant glared down at him. "Little fool," he growled. "What the hell do you think you're doing?"

Omen didn't answer. The mask had dislodged slightly, obscuring his vision. He did his best to help as Peccant dragged him in and then let go, leaving Omen to tumble through to the floor.

Still, better to tumble to the floor of Peccant's office than to smash to the courtyard below it.

Peccant strode in after him. "Tomfoolery!" he said, the word exploding from his mouth like a curse. Peccant was the only person Omen knew who used words like *tomfoolery*. "What did you think you were playing at? Eh? Take off that bloody mask, for goodness' sake!"

Omen didn't take the mask off.

"This is what happens when children are allowed to lark about unsupervised! This is what happens!"

The office was impeccably neat. The only thing out of place was a black book that had fallen from the desk, presumably when Peccant had leaped to the balcony. Helpfully, Omen picked it up. It was more of a ledger than a book, now that he took a closer look, and there was a crest on the cover, a wolf and a snake.

"Give me that," Peccant snapped, yanking the book from Omen's hands. He threw it into a desk drawer and slammed it shut. "And take off that ridiculous mask! Do you even realise how inaccurate it all is? Rebus Arcanum *despised* the society that wore those masks. For a history teacher, Lilt does like to leave out a lot of little things like details, doesn't he? If he hadn't been arrested for whatever he was arrested for, he should have been arrested for being a damn fool and a bad teacher!"

Omen stood on trembling legs while Peccant went back to the balcony, craning his head upwards. "Where did you fall from? Which window? Is there anyone else being irresponsible up there?"

Omen reached for the door. Opened it. Nobody outside. He stepped out, started walking. Picked up speed. He took off the gold mask and dropped it.

"Hey!" Peccant yelled from inside his office, and Omen ran.

28

"Slow down," Valkyrie muttered, following Skulduggery through twisting alleyways. "You're being conspicuous."

Skulduggery glanced back at her. His façade this morning was of a pale man with arched eyebrows and a widow's peak. He held his hat in his hand, but his black suit was exquisite and he did nothing to hide the confidence he demonstrated in his every step. Try as he might to disguise who he was, he was still drawing stares.

"Much as it wounds my ego," he said, "they're not actually looking at me."

She frowned, turned her attention to the people they passed. He was right. It was *her* face that was widening eyes. It was *her* presence that was generating whispers.

"How much further?" she asked, walking beside him now with her head down.

"A few more turns."

He'd been up all night, but she was the one who was tired. Not for the first time, Valkyrie found herself envying his lack of a need for sleep. She had once loved sleep, had looked forward to being swallowed up by her slumber every night, but now sleep was something she chased. It was a furtive little animal that, even when caught, wriggled and scratched to free itself. And, of course, it brought with it the nightmares.

They arrived at a door like every other door on this small street, and Skulduggery knocked.

A small woman answered, a smile on her well-fed face.

"Lillian Agog?" Skulduggery asked, extending his hand for her to shake. "Skulduggery Pleasant. This is my partner, Valkyrie Cain. We spoke on the phone. How do you do?"

"I'm doing fine, Mr Pleasant," said Lillian. "Come in, the both of you. Please excuse the mess. I've been rushed off my feet lately. Rushed right off them."

Skulduggery stepped in, and Valkyrie stepped in right after him. It was a very tidy house. Lillian led them into the small living room that smelled slightly of must and contentment, and they sat side by side on the couch.

"You must think I'm awful," said Lillian, going straight to the fireplace, "living in squalor like this. Squalor!"

"Not at all," Skulduggery said.

"You're too kind, Mr Pleasant! Too kind!"

Lillian clicked her fingers, summoning fire into her hand, and tossed it on to the bundle of sticks and rolled-up newspaper in the hearth. Once the fire was roaring, she sank into her armchair, her eyes bright. "Now, don't think me rude, but I'd heard you didn't have a face."

"Ah," Skulduggery said, and his façade flowed away, revealing the skull beneath.

"Marvellous," said Lillian, staring in wonder. "Simply marvellous. Do you ever get cold?"

"I'm sorry?"

"You don't have any skin or anything. I'd imagine you'd get very cold this time of year."

"I don't actually feel the cold. It's one of the advantages of being a skeleton."

"Imagine that," Lillian breathed. "You know, I've never spoken to a skeleton before. I've spoken to plenty of people, plenty of them, but never a skeleton. I've talked to tall people, and you're quite tall, but I've talked to taller. And short people. Big people and small people. All kinds. But never someone like you. I bet you get asked all kinds of questions, don't you? About death. About what happens after. Is there a heaven?"

"I'm afraid I don't know. Lillian, we're here to talk to you about Richard Melior."

"Richard, yes," said Lillian. "Lovely man. Just lovely. Oh! My manners! They seem to have abandoned me! Would either of you like some tea?"

"No thank you," said Valkyrie.

"Coffee, then? I'm sure I can make you some coffee."

"I'm fine," Valkyrie said. "We both are. About Richard...?"

"Richard, yes," said Lillian. "Lovely man."

"You got in touch with us," Skulduggery said. "You had someone place a note on the windscreen of my car."

Lillian nodded. "I asked an old family friend who works at the High Sanctuary. I won't give you his name, so you'll have to forgive me, but I don't want to get him into any trouble. Or her! It might be a her! I don't want to get her into any trouble, either. He asked me to keep his name out of this, he's very worried about overstepping marks, and he made me promise, he sat me down and made me promise, to never mention his name. And I said Brian, I said Brian, I'm not going to tell them who you are, you can trust me. He didn't look entirely convinced that I wouldn't let something slip, but I think I've handled it quite well, don't you?"

"Very," Valkyrie said. Her phone buzzed and she glanced at it. A message from her mother. She slid the phone back into her pocket. "So the note, it said you had information on Richard Melior's whereabouts."

"Yes, indeed," said Lillian. "I've known Richard for a long time, him and his husband. Both lovely men. Lovely. I saw him last night – Richard, that is, not Savant – and I sprang into action, is what I did. I asked Brian for a favour, I passed him the note and now you're here."

"And Richard?" Skulduggery prompted.

"I saw him enter an apartment building on Ironfoot Road. A blue door, it was."

"Ironfoot Road," Skulduggery repeated, nodding. "That's very helpful, Lillian. That's exactly what we needed. Thank you."

Lillian waved away the words. "Oh, just doing my civic duty! Now, promise me you won't burst in there and hurt him. He looked quite docile when I saw him. I'm sure he'll come quietly."

"Unfortunately, we don't have that option," Skulduggery said. "He's mixed up with some very bad people, and the last time we went to talk to him we barely made it out. I'm sorry to say that we'll have to use extreme force. Maybe even deadly."

Lillian paled. "I'm sorry?"

Skulduggery stood and put his hat back on. "But thanks for your help."

Lillian sprang to her feet, quite lithely for someone of her size. "Wait a moment! Now, just wait! Richard wouldn't hurt a fly!"

"He already tried to kill us once," said Skulduggery. "He won't get a second chance."

Skulduggery walked for the door, Lillian hurrying after him. Valkyrie got up slowly, watching it unfold.

"He won't hurt you!" Lillian insisted. "Just knock on the door! Tell him who you are! He'll give himself up, I just know he will! Mr Pleasant, please!"

"We'll try to take him alive," Skulduggery said, "but I can't guarantee anything."

Lillian staggered, as if slapped.

Valkyrie passed her. "Thank you for your assistance," she said quietly.

"Stop!" Lillian cried. "He told me to contact you!"

They both turned. "Did he now?" Skulduggery asked.

Lillian clasped her hands to her bosom, as if praying. "He's scared," she said. "You're right, he's mixed up with some bad people. He told me that. He's in a lot of trouble. He said when you went to arrest him, he panicked. He shouldn't have done it, he's sorry, but he's managed to sneak away, and he wants to surrender."

"So he spoke to you," said Valkyrie, "told you to arrange all this, and told you to tell us about Ironfoot Road. Lillian, the moment we read your note, it sounded like we'd be walking into a trap."

She looked horrified. "A trap?"

"How do you even know we're looking for him? It's not common knowledge. The only reason we didn't break down your door is because Skulduggery has been watching you all night. We had been thinking you were in on it, that you were trying to lead us into an ambush."

"No," Lillian said, her eyes wide. "No. Goodness, no. I would never do that, and Richard... Richard is a good man."

"And he's waiting for us at Ironfoot Road?"

She nodded quickly. "Apartment 4. Just him. Nobody else."

"We really want to trust you, Lillian."

"Then trust me! I promise you, this is no trick!"

"Did he say anything else? Anything about some friends of his, about what they're planning?"

"He said if they're not stopped then everything will change. He mentioned a war."

"What war?" Valkyrie asked.

"The war to come," she said. "The war between sorcerers and mortals."

29

Looking back on his life up to the previous night, Sebastian had come to the conclusion that he was, in fact, a pacifist, who just happened to get caught up in extreme acts of violence at regular intervals.

If he'd had his way, the last few years would have contained far less punching, kicking, destruction and death than they had, and he'd be a happier person for it. Then his nights could be spent reading books until his eyes grew tired, after which he'd fall into a comfortable bed and wouldn't stir till morning.

Instead, he had spent the previous night on a rooftop, watching a small house on the edge of the Herbal District. He'd been led here from Bennet Troth's house by the lumbering man in the coat and hat, the same lumbering man who had given that note to the kid, the same one who – Sebastian hoped – knew where Bennet's wife was being kept.

An entire night spent crouched on a rooftop, all so that he could help Bennet so that Bennet, in turn, would help Sebastian.

All for Darquesse.

Now it was halfway through the following day and Sebastian was still here, waiting for something to happen. He really didn't want to have to kick the door down. Kicking the door down would probably lead to violence. Plus, he'd never kicked a door down before and was worried his foot might just bounce off.

A little after noon, he saw Bennet harassing people on the street, waving a photograph under their noses until they snapped at him, in some cases shoving him away. Sebastian tried waving, tried catching the man's attention, but eventually had to resort to shouting Bennet's name to make him look up.

They met in the alley behind the small house.

"I thought I'd hallucinated you," Bennet said. He needed a shave and a shower, but at least he was sober.

"Bennet, you should go home. The man I followed yesterday led me to that building, right there. If Odetta is inside, I'll bring her to you."

"No, I have to be here, I have to do this. She's my wife – don't you understand that? Are you married?"

"I am not, no."

"Then you don't understand. But I can't leave. If she's in there, I have to go in. Now."

"We don't know who else might be waiting," Sebastian said, placing a restraining hand on Bennet's arm. "It's better if we keep an eye on the place, make a note of who comes and goes, formulate a plan, so that when we do go in, we're prepared."

"Has anyone come and gone since you've been on that roof?"

"Well... no."

"Whoever has her, they've obviously no intention of bringing her back to me," said Bennet. "We don't know what's happening in there. We don't know if she's hurt, or how scared she is, and we don't even know why she's been taken. But I cannot stay here while the love of my life is being held captive. I'm going in. Now, I don't know you, but—"

"I'll help," Sebastian said, sighing. "Just please follow my lead, OK?"

"I was hoping you'd say that," Bennet confessed. "I've never been in a fight in my life."

"Yeah, well, I have," Sebastian said. "And I really try to avoid them as much as possible."

With Bennet behind him, Sebastian sneaked up to the small house. He took off his hat, and peered through the window. He counted three men in the gloom. They were big, and seemed to just stand there, stoop-shouldered, not saying anything.

Bennet peeked. "Hollow Men," he whispered.

Sebastian examined what he could in this light. Hollow Men: artificial beings of leathery skin, pumped full of the foulest of gases and used as mindless muscle around the world. The cheaper sort could be dispatched with one slash from a sharp knife – the more expensive kind took a lot more effort. From their vantage point, it was impossible to say which kind these were.

"Do you have any weapons?" Sebastian asked softly.

"Just these," Bennet said, pulling out a knife and handgun.

Sebastian jerked back. "What the hell are you doing with a gun?"

Bennet looked offended. "I'm here to rescue my wife from kidnappers. I figured a gun would be a good idea."

"Do you know how to use it?"

"Of course. It's not rocket science."

"Have you ever shot at anyone before?"

"Hollow Men aren't people," Bennet said. "Shooting them is no different from shooting a target at the range."

"And have you shot targets at the range?"

Bennet faltered. "I kept meaning to get around to it."

"Listen to me," Sebastian said, injecting a little calm into his voice, "I don't feel safe around you when you have a gun. I feel, and I might be way off here, that you can't be trusted with a firearm. If Odetta is in there, I worry you may accidentally shoot her."

"Right."

"Would you say that's an understandable concern?"

"Maybe, yeah."

"So will you put it away and promise not to use it?"

"OK," Bennet said, looking embarrassed as he returned the gun to his pocket. "What about the knife?"

"Actually," Sebastian said, taking it from him, "I'll have that, if it's all the same to you."

"Probably wise," Bennet said, then frowned. "But what am I going to do? I mean... I'm an Elemental. I could throw fireballs. Hollow Men are made of paper – they'd go right up."

"Right, yes, maybe – but is Odetta fireproof?"

"Well, no..."

"Ah," said Sebastian, "then probably not the best idea."

"So what do I do?"

"You come in after me, and you try not to fall over. That sound good?"

Bennet sighed. "Yeah."

"Then that's our plan."

Sebastian sneaked round the corner, and straightened. The knife felt good in his hand. Well-balanced. He took a deep breath. The door looked sturdy. He wondered how much this would hurt.

Before he kicked, a thought struck him, and he reached forward, turned the handle. The door opened.

OK then.

He ran in. The first Hollow Man started to turn and Sebastian slashed it across the arm, then spun, whipping the blade along the next one's back. He flipped the knife in his hand and flung it. It went right through the third one's chest, embedding itself in the wall behind. The Hollow Men staggered, not even attempting to stop the gas from escaping. Protected by his mask, Sebastian watched them deflate through a fog of green.

"Odetta!" Bennet called, hurrying in behind him. He immediately started coughing, his eyes streaming. "Is she here? I can't see her! I can't see anything!"

"I'll check," Sebastian said, guiding him back to fresh air. "Stay here."

He had finished the search in less than thirty seconds, and joined Bennet outside.

"She's not here," he said.

Bennet was on his knees, blinking madly. "As soon as her kidnappers find out someone's been here, they'll kill her. They're going to kill her and there's nothing we can do about it."

"Hold on a second," Sebastian said. "Whoever's been storing those Hollow Men here, they have to be the ones behind this. You're a connected guy, Bennet – who do you know who can find out who owns this house?"

"None of my old connections will speak to me any more."

"Surely there's someone? Surely you still have friends who could check around for you?"

Bennet stopped snivelling. "Maybe," he said. "Maybe I know someone who can help." He took out his phone.

While he made some calls, Sebastian gave the small house another search. He found plates in the kitchen cupboard, and a single cup. There was a small amount of food – enough for one person.

"I might have something," Bennet said when Sebastian stepped out. "This house is being rented by someone. I can't find out the name, but whoever it is is renting a second house here, somewhere in Roarhaven. Maybe Odetta is there?"

"Maybe," said Sebastian.

"We'll have to wait a few hours before I can get the address, but you'll help me? When I have it, you'll help me?"

"Of course," said Sebastian. "That was our deal, right? I help you, and then you help me."

"Thank you," Bennet said, grabbing Sebastian's hand and shaking it. "Thank you so much for all of this. I've got such a good feeling. We're going to get her back. I just know we are."

30

Omen's hands were shaking.

This was normal, he supposed, in the aftermath of a near-death experience – that and the chattering teeth were to be expected. He'd had a dose of adrenaline dumped into his system and now what was left of it was sloshing around in his bloodstream, causing all kinds of tics.

Someone had tried to kill him. Someone had actually tried to kill him.

A few younger boys came into the bathroom, chatting and calling each other names. One of them tried Omen's cubicle. The lock rattled in its bracket and the kid said, "Sorry," and went into the next one. Omen waited until they were all gone before holding up his hand again.

Yep, still shaking. That was probably going to last a while.

His knee hurt. It throbbed, actually. He must have injured it when he'd slammed into the wall under Peccant's balcony.

Peccant had saved him. Wow. Peccant, of all people. Of course, Omen had been wearing a mask, so Peccant didn't know who it was he was saving. If he'd known, he probably wouldn't have bothered.

But that raised a question. Did the others know? Did Jenan, or any of the Arcanum's Scholars, figure out who he was in the short few seconds he'd been in their sights? Probably not. No, definitely not. All they had to go on was hair colour, height and the fact that he was a Third Year. Omen was suddenly grateful that the school had a uniform and that he hadn't been born a redhead. He figured redheads would have a harder time getting away with stuff.

He was safe. He was pretty sure he was safe. Now all he had to do was act natural. Jenan and his friends would be on the lookout for someone behaving suspiciously around them. He could act normally. He'd been doing it all his life. The knack wasn't about to abandon him now.

Omen left the bathroom. He glimpsed Jenan passing in the corridor ahead and he forgot how to walk properly. He frowned as he wobbled. One foot in *front* of the other, right? Wasn't that it? He leaned on the wall for support, then kind of slid sideways to the floor.

"What are you doing?" Chocolate asked, walking by.

"Resting," he answered, like it was perfectly normal.

"You're weird," said Chocolate, and left him there.

He had to tell someone. Skulduggery and Valkyrie – they were the obvious choice. They were the only ones who'd understand, after all, and probably the only ones who'd actually believe him. But, of course, it was Skulduggery who'd fired him, precisely to prevent something like this from happening. He wondered if Skulduggery would be mad. Probably, he decided.

But if not those two then who? Auger? It'd definitely be the smart move... but then everything would change. Omen could see just how it'd happen. Auger would make sure Omen was safe and then he'd talk to Skulduggery and then they'd all go and take care of it together, and Omen would become the insignificant brother again. He couldn't go back to that. Not yet. This was his first taste of something different, of something more. He wasn't ready to give that up.

"Get off the floor, Omen," said Miss Ether as she passed.

"Yes, miss," Omen said, and got up slowly. His legs didn't buckle. That was promising.

The bell rang, signalling the end of break time and the start of the next class – a class that'd have half the Scholars in it, Jenan included. This would be Omen's first real test. He just needed to be normal. He just needed to blend in.

It's what he was good at, after all.

Omen sat with his eyes closed, his legs folded under him and his hands resting on his knees.

"Breathe," said Miss Gnosis. "In through the nose, out through the mouth."

Omen breathed. He was pretty good at breathing. Certainly as good as anyone else in the room. Top marks for breathing.

"Let your body relax," Miss Gnosis said in that Scottish accent Omen loved so much. "Listen to my voice. My voice is the only voice. My words are the only words. Let them fill you, like water fills a jug. Let them fill you like magic. Magic is like water, is it not? It ebbs and it flows. It nourishes. It destroys. It is all things."

Omen could hear his classmates around him. One of them made a whistling noise when they breathed in. It was faintly distracting, but Omen did his best to push it from his mind. He was actually getting relaxed now. The adrenaline was gone from his system. His teeth no longer chattered. His hands no longer trembled.

Miss Gnosis continued to talk. "It doesn't matter what discipline you decide upon, if you choose Adept or stay Elemental – because magic relies on the same muscles. We draw from the Source and we give back to the Source. You can feel it, can't you? All around us?"

The whistling was getting louder. How come nobody else was getting annoyed by it?

"We're not magic's masters," said Miss Gnosis, "any more than a windmill is master of the wind. But the windmill allows the wind to push it, to move it, to power it. The wind? The wind is indifferent to the windmill, because the wind is something vast and unknowable. The same with magic."

Now Omen was confused. Was magic water or wind?

"It comes to us from the Source and it seeps into our universe," Miss Gnosis said. "How much of our reality has been defined by magic? How much mortal technology is dependent on the energies it produces?"

Omen cracked one eye open. It was Gall. Gall and his musical nostrils preventing Omen from finding his centre or whatever it was he was supposed to be finding. He frowned. Was it his centre he was looking for? Was it something else? Had he missed it? He probably hadn't been paying attention. He was always doing that.

"Once we respect magic," Miss Gnosis was saying, her own eyes closed, "truly respect it and everything it can do... only then can we possibly hope to direct it, however briefly, to our own ends."

Omen looked around. Everyone had their eyes shut. They had weird looks on their faces, like they were close to inner peace. He wondered if they were, or if they were just faking it.

"The Surge that you will experience in four or five years' time – maybe six, maybe three – that's just the beginning of your journey to becoming a true sorcerer." Miss Gnosis smiled gently, though only Omen could see. "You have wonders ahead of you, experiences you have not yet even imagined. But first comes work, and preparation and, most of all, patience. I'm going to count backwards from ten now. The closer I get to one, the more alert you will feel, until you open your eyes and you're fully awake and ready to take on the rest of the day."

She started counting down, and Omen yawned. He swivelled his head as he did so, and found Jenan Ispolin staring straight at him.

Omen snapped his head back round and squeezed his eyes

shut, very possibly the worst, most suspicious thing he could do under the circumstances. He wondered if Jenan was still looking at him. He cracked an eye open, turned slightly.

Yep, still looking. This was not good.

Miss Gnosis reached *one*, and everyone else opened their eyes and started getting to their feet. Omen's left foot had pins and needles that took him by surprise as he stood. He stumbled but Never caught him, steadied him. He shot him a look of thanks and Never sighed and rolled his eyes.

"We all live hectic lives," Miss Gnosis said. "Some of you live more hectic lives than others." At this, everyone chuckled and glanced at Auger, who looked around innocently. "Take a moment out of every day to close your eyes and just... feel. Experience what it is to be you. Experience the moment. Experience happiness. That's where true magic lies."

She clapped her hands gently, signalling the end of class.

Omen tried engaging Never in conversation, but he was already heading out of the door. Out of the corner of his eye, Omen saw Jenan coming for him, fists clenched by his sides. Omen tried smiling. It didn't work.

And then Auger stepped between them.

"Hey, Jenan," he said, and Jenan froze, uncertainty flickering across his features.

"Hi," Jenan responded, like it was a trick question.

"Have you decided?" Auger asked. "What discipline are you going to specialise in? Do you know?"

"Uh..."

"I'm thinking Energy Thrower," Auger said. "Ergokinesis, I mean. I do like exploding things. Or maybe Enhancement, maybe try to be the next Mr Bliss. What about you? Or Omen, how about you?"

"I... don't know," said Omen. "Maybe a... a Signum Linguist? I've always liked the languages."

Auger looked genuinely surprised. "Really? You?"

"They're pretty cool," Omen said defensively. "You can do anything if you master them, like the Supreme Mage."

"Well, yeah," said Auger, "but it probably took her decades to even get the basics down." Auger thought about it some more as Omen started to go red, and then he shrugged. "Although, to be honest, if anyone could do it, Omen, it'd be you. You've always been able to *focus*, you know? Better than I ever could."

Omen tried not to look astonished as Auger turned back to Jenan. "What about you?"

"I haven't decided yet," Jenan said gruffly. "Ergokinetic, maybe. I don't know. I've got a lot of options. My father says I'm gifted."

Auger nodded. "And he should know, right? As a Grand Mage and all, he should know."

"Well, of course," said Jenan, adopting the tone he always adopted when talking about how important his family was. "If there's anyone who has the undisputed experience to spot a gifted sorcerer, it's – excuse me."

He took out his buzzing phone, and his eyes widened when he read the message.

Auger shot a quick glance at Omen. "Jenan? You OK there, buddy?"

"What?" Jenan mumbled, then blinked and pressed his phone into his chest, protecting the screen. "Yes. I'm fine. I have to go."

He walked quickly out, barging into Omen without even meaning to. Now the room was empty save for the Darkly boys.

"What was *that* about?" Auger asked, keeping his voice low.

"Don't know," said Omen. "Did you see who it was from?"

Auger frowned. "Who what was from? I'm talking about Jenan coming over like he was about to rip your head off."

"Oh," said Omen. "I'm not sure. He doesn't really like me."

"I know *that*," said Auger. "Everyone knows *that*. But any particular reason he'd want to rip your head off *today*?"

"It's a Wednesday?"

"Actually, it's Thursday."

189

"Aw, man," said Omen, grabbing his bag. "I'm missing maths again. I have to go."

Auger laughed and waved him away, but, instead of turning right to go to maths class, Omen turned left, following Jenan as he hurried towards the dorms.

He managed to stay unseen − largely because Jenan seemed far too preoccupied to check behind him. He watched Jenan go into his room and sneaked towards the door as voices were raised inside. There was movement and Omen flattened himself against the wall, eyes wide, mouth open, nowhere to hide, as Jenan shoved his room-mate out into the corridor.

"I'm sick!" his room-mate complained, clad in his pyjamas. "The nurse told me to stay in bed!"

"I need privacy," Jenan snapped, pushing him further away as Omen slid along the wall behind him, and slipped into the room. It was bigger than his own, even though it only had two beds. Omen dived to the floor, crawled under the first bed and waited.

Jenan ignored his room-mate's curses and walked back in, slamming the door after him. Omen held his breath as he watched Jenan's feet pace up and down. He heard the tapping of a phone, and, a moment later, someone teleported into the room. Omen peered at stylish shoes.

"Mr Nero," said Jenan. He sounded nervous. Scared. This made Omen happy. "Good to... good to see you again."

"Name's just Nero. No *mister* attached." The Teleporter sounded impatient. Angry, even. "Did anyone notice you sneak off?"

"No. No chance. What, um, what's up?"

A slight silence followed, and Omen risked a peek and saw Jenan blush. He could only imagine the withering look Nero must have been giving him.

"What's up?" Nero echoed, starting to walk around the room. "I'll tell you what's up. You let a spy into our little meeting, Jenan.

190

Those stupid gold masks of yours could end up costing us everything."

Jenan's voice was suddenly thick, like he desperately needed a glass of water. "They were Mr Lilt's idea."

"Well then, Lilt's an idiot, and you're an idiot for going along with it. You need to understand something very simple here. First Wave is only valuable to us if nobody knows about it. Do you get that? Do you?"

"I get it."

"Because I don't think you do."

"I do," Jenan insisted. "I get it. Secrecy is—"

"Everything, Jenan. Secrecy is everything. I'd have thought that you of all people would know this. I'd have thought, out of everyone, that you would be the one person we didn't have to explain this to. Your father understands the need for secrecy, right?"

"My... my father?"

"He's Grand Mage of the Bulgarian Sanctuary, isn't he? Grand Mages have to keep secrets. It's what they do."

"Yes," said Jenan. "Of course."

"So this little spy," Nero said, walking over to the bed and turning, "he obviously didn't go splat when he was supposed to. Have you found out yet who he is?"

Jenan hesitated. "Not yet."

The feet shifted slightly, and the bed creaked as Nero sat, pinning Omen in place. "I don't believe this. I'm going to have to go back and tell Lethe that you're in over your head. Who should take your place, do you think?"

Jenan's voice squeaked. If that had happened in class to anyone else, Jenan would have mocked them mercilessly. "N-no, I can still... I can do it. I can."

"It doesn't look like you can. I have to say, Lethe is going to be so disappointed. He wouldn't shut up about you – can you believe that? *Jenan Ispolin is exactly who we need. Jenan Ispolin will*

191

change everything." Nero's voice was tinged with bitterness. "He's going to be gutted."

Jenan did his best to inject some decisiveness into his voice. "We'll find him," he said. "The spy. We'll find him."

"How?"

"We'll question them," Jenan said. "We'll question them all, every Third Year boy of that height with that hair colour. And I know who we'll start with."

"You have a suspect?"

"I do," Jenan said immediately. "Omen Darkly."

Nero leaped to his feet, furious. "You let the *Chosen One* into the goddamn meeting?"

Omen watched Jenan's feet stumble back. "No, no! That's Auger! That's his brother! Omen Darkly's nobody, I swear to you! Even if he told anyone, they probably wouldn't believe him!"

"What about the Chosen One?" Nero asked. "Would the *Chosen One* believe him?"

Jenan swallowed. "Maybe."

"Jesus..." Nero said. "Of all the people to let in, of all the goddamn people, you let in Auger Darkly's *brother.*"

"It mightn't be him," Jenan said quickly. "It might be someone else. We'll find out, though. I'll interrogate him personally."

"You'd better, Jenan. A lot of people are depending on you."

"You have my word. By my family's crest."

"And if it turns out that it was this Omen Darkly... and if he has told the Chosen One... you know what you have to do, don't you?"

There was a hesitation. "Yes. Yes, of course."

"You kill him," Nero said. "You kill them both."

Jenan nodded. "Yes. I swear."

"We'll be back in touch, Jenan," said Nero. "Don't fail us, you hear me? You really don't want to fail us."

Omen didn't know why he did it. He wasn't planning on it, that was for certain. It wasn't something he'd thought about, lying there under that bed. But the moment he realised Nero was about to leave, he reached out a hand, and his fingertip touched the heel of Nero's stylish shoe, so that when Nero teleported, he took Omen with him.

31

"Where are we?" Valkyrie asked, peering out of the car window. The street was narrow. There was graffiti on the walls, none of it any good. She was surprised at this. She hadn't thought Roarhaven would be tolerant of something so mundane as declarations of lust and crudely drawn genitalia. She'd expected their graffiti standards to be higher.

"We are where we need to be," Skulduggery said, coming to a stop and turning off the engine. "Ironfoot Road is close by."

They got out and he locked the Bentley. Valkyrie zipped up her jacket against the cold and they started walking. She kept her head down and he kept his façade up, but everyone they passed was too busy with their own problems to notice them.

They walked for three minutes before coming to a blue door. Valkyrie stood watch while Skulduggery picked the lock. When he was done, he tapped her and they slipped inside. He drew his gun and they crept upstairs to a quiet corridor. They found Melior's apartment and Skulduggery picked that lock next. When the door was open, he splayed his hand, reading the air, and led the way into the kitchen, where Richard Melior stood with his back to them, watching the window.

Skulduggery walked right up to him without making a sound and pressed his gun into the back of Melior's head.

"Not an inch," Skulduggery said.

Without turning, without looking over his shoulder, Melior said, "I'm... I'm very glad you came."

"You should be glad I haven't pulled the trigger."

"I'm glad about that, too."

"Turn."

Melior turned, saw Valkyrie and tried to smile. "Hello."

"If you even think about blasting us again," she said, "we'll hit you until you're nothing but a puddle of mess on the floor."

"I understand. And I'm really sorry about that. If you're in any pain, I can help you."

"I'm fine," she replied irritably. "We have doctors who specialise in *healing* people."

"Take a seat, Doctor," Skulduggery said. "I want you where we can keep an eye on you."

Melior nodded, and sat in the chair Skulduggery pulled out for him. He didn't object when the shackles were produced. Valkyrie turned on her aura-vision for this next part – she wanted to see what happened when they were put on – but she noticed something as Skulduggery moved in. Like most auras she'd seen, Melior's was orange, but it was a slightly different shade. She didn't know what that meant, didn't know if it meant anything, and then the shackles snapped on and Melior's power dampened, and the aura shrivelled away until Valkyrie could barely see it.

She switched off the aura-vision. She was really going to have to find a better name for it. "What were you looking at?" she asked.

"Sorry?"

"You were looking down at the street. At what?"

"Oh," he said, "no, I wasn't looking at anything. I was waiting for you. You came through the window the first time we met and for some reason I thought you'd come through the window again. I never expected you to come through the door."

"Doors are for people with no imagination," she conceded, "but we like to mix it up a bit around here."

Skulduggery sat opposite Melior and leaned forward, elbows on his knees. "You've got a lot to tell us," he said.

"I do. Anything you want to know."

"Let's start from the top," Valkyrie said. "What is the anti-Sanctuary? What's it really called?"

"It's not called anything," said Melior. "It's easier to hide something when it doesn't have a name, I guess. The anti-Sanctuary, that's as good a name as any. They've been working away behind the scenes for hundreds of years. Assassinations. Disappearances. They've orchestrated *wars* to get their agenda just a little bit further along the line. I know what you're thinking. I thought it, too. How could it even exist? How could an organisation like this be responsible for centuries of murder and upheaval and yet no one knows anything about them? But that's why they mostly recruit Neoterics. They're looking for outsiders, sorcerers with no links to the Sanctuaries. They're careful. They're unbelievably, impossibly careful to not leave any fingerprints that'd lead people like you back to them. Or they were, at least. Their endgame is in sight. They're coming out of the shadows."

"What do they want?"

"War," said Melior. "A proper, full-scale war, at the end of which the mortals will be our slaves. They want sorcerers to rule the world."

"Who's in charge?" she asked. "Smoke? Lethe?"

"Smoke's a lackey. He doesn't have one original thought in his head. Lethe's different. He's smarter. Very talented, very dangerous, very cunning. I've never seen him lose a fight. He plays with them at first, lets them think they've got the upper hand... I think he does it because he's bored."

"Why does he wear the suit?" Valkyrie asked.

"I don't know, but I've never seen him without it."

"What about the Teleporter?"

"Nero," said Melior. "An arrogant little creep. In love with himself. Don't know much about him. Don't know much about most of them, to be honest."

"The guy who slowed time..."

"Ah," said Melior, "Destrier. He's not really part of the team, as far as I can tell. He helps out, but he's got his own thing going on. I get the feeling an arrangement has been reached there. They call what he does temporal manipulation."

"Last person I saw doing that was a serial killer."

"He's a weird one, I can tell you that. I've seen him talking to himself – practically the only person he *does* talk to. I've certainly never spoken to him.

"Then there's Memphis. He's got this thing about Elvis. Apparently, he met him once, when he was a kid. But he's dangerous. His power manifested as some form of hyper-agility. I've seen him flip around like a trapeze artist without the trapeze. He used to have a sister, but Lethe killed her. As far as I know, Memphis doesn't hold a grudge."

"Who's the Australian?" Valkyrie asked.

"Razzia. She's completely off the rails. I never know what she's going to do from one moment to the next. She's got a creature living in her arm, a parasite of some sort. I've asked several times to examine it, but she hasn't let me get close."

"Tell us about Smoke," Skulduggery said.

"All I know about him is what he can do. I've seen him touch people – not even skin-on-skin contact, but through their coat sleeves – and they're corrupted. Ordinary, decent people turned into psychopathic versions of themselves. I've seen it go on for weeks – every two days, Smoke just taps them and it starts all over again. I've seen people under his influence kill their entire families and laugh while they do it."

"We'll stop him," said Skulduggery. "We'll stop all of them. Anyone else we should know about?"

"There are others, though they come and go. But that's the main group."

Skulduggery leaned back in his chair. "I've read a bit about you, Doctor. Your power manifested in medical school, didn't it? Up until that moment you had no idea magic existed."

"That is correct," Melior said, nodding. "I did some haphazard research after it happened, managed to talk to a proper sorcerer and had my eyes opened. After that, I met Savant and fell in love, and... well, never looked back."

"And then Parthenios Lilt talked to you."

Melior's face soured. "Yes. He'd heard about me and came to interview me, to run some tests... The term Neoteric was actually my suggestion. We became friends, or so I thought. This was back in the 1960s. Savant and I were living in San Francisco, because where else would you be living in the sixties? Parthenios introduced us to *his* friends – mostly other Neoterics. For a while, it was fun – we even had our own bowling team, as lame as that sounds now and, in fact, back then. But then we met more of his friends. People like Bubba Moon. Have you heard of him?"

"We have," said Skulduggery.

"That's when the alarm bells really started to ring. This was an insane man sitting at the table with us, talking about the tyranny of mortals, about how we should rise up against them and join with the being who lives beyond our reality."

"We met him," Valkyrie said. "The being beyond our reality, I mean. His name was Balerosh."

Melior blinked. "Moon was telling the truth? He exists?"

Valkyrie shrugged. "Not any more."

"Anyway," Melior said after a moment, "I didn't like the way things were going, and I wanted nothing more to do with any of them. Savant took a little longer to come to the same conclusion, but then he sees the good in everyone. His power is knowledge; he absorbs vast quantities of information at a glance, but he's also a pacifist. He's never hurt a soul in his life. I fell in love with him because of that quality, but it also meant that he couldn't understand the destructive urge that I could see in the people around us."

"But you understood it," Skulduggery said.

"I did. When I was a kid, I hurt people. It's why I became a doctor, to make up for the pain I'd caused. So yeah, I understood it."

"What happened then?"

"Nothing," said Melior. "For a long time, nothing. We moved around a bit – it's very hard to stay working in a hospital when you don't age. We learned to forge new certificates with each passing decade. Eventually, we went back to my hometown, to Baltimore. More time passed. We hadn't even thought of Parthenios or any of them in forty years."

"Where's your husband now, Doctor?"

"They have him. Parthenios Lilt and three others broke into our apartment, beat me half to death and took him away. I went to the Sanctuary, but they didn't do anything. Two months later, I woke up to find Lethe standing over my bed. He told me who he was with, said they'd kill Savant unless I joined them."

"When was this?"

"Five years ago."

Valkyrie frowned. "Savant's been gone five years?"

"Every so often, I'll get a voice message telling me he loves me, telling me to be strong..." Melior's voice cracked.

"Why go to the trouble of kidnapping him, though? Why doesn't Smoke just corrupt you?"

"His touch doesn't work on healers," Melior said. "I don't know why. I think it's something to do with our power, maybe it acts as an immune system to his influence."

"Your aura's different," Valkyrie said. Skulduggery looked at her and she shrugged. "It's a different shade of orange."

"I don't know anything about auras," Melior said, "but, whatever the reason, they needed some other way to control me."

Skulduggery asked, "And Lethe's in charge?"

"No," Melior said. "He does what he's told, same as everyone."

"So who tells him what to do? Is there another Balerosh that we don't know about?"

"Not as far as I'm aware," said Melior, and hesitated. "It's the voice in his head."

"I'm sorry?"

"They all hear it," Melior continued. "It's their leader. I don't know anything about her, I don't know where she is, but I overheard some of them talking and they said a name. Abyssinia."

Skulduggery turned his head slightly.

"You know who that is?" Valkyrie asked.

"I might," he said. "I've only known one Abyssinia in all my years."

"Does she have silver hair?"

Skulduggery looked at her. "She does." He looked back. "Doctor, what were you told about your role in all this? What do they need you to do?"

"Please call me Richard. From what I can gather, I'm to facilitate a resurrection. I've done it before, more or less, on patients who've died on the operating table, but never before on someone long dead. This would be exponentially more difficult."

"It would be," said Skulduggery. "For a start, I would imagine that Abyssinia is the one in need of resurrection, as she's been dead for three hundred years."

Valkyrie looked back at Melior. "Is that possible? Could you do that?"

"I... I guess so. Under the proper circumstances."

"If that is the case, you'd have one further complication," Skulduggery said, "in that all that is left of her is a heart."

"I'm sorry?"

Skulduggery stood. "Richard, would you excuse us for a moment?"

"Uh... of course."

"Thank you. If you try anything sneaky, I'll shoot you. Valkyrie?"

Frowning, she followed him into the bedroom, and he shut the door.

"Right then," she said, "you're acting sufficiently suspicious about this, so who is she? Who is Abyssinia?"

Skulduggery crossed to the window and looked out. He took a moment, and turned. "Abyssinia," he said, "was many things." "Fiercely intelligent, incredibly manipulative, savagely violent. She was a mage and a murderer but also, and this is where things could be said to take a surprising twist, were you inclined to be surprised by twists, she was a..."

"A what?"

"I suppose you could call her, if you had to, if you needed to find a label, even though I'm not fond of them myself, I feel they can be far too restrictive though there are, of course, exceptions, you could possibly call her, if you desperately needed to call her anything at all, an... ex-girlfriend."

Valkyrie stared. "What?"

32

"You probably require an explanation," Skulduggery said.

"I probably do."

"Would you like to sit down?"

"Do I need to?" Valkyrie said. "Yes, I'll sit down. No, I won't. I need to walk around for this. I feel I need to be moving. Tell the story." She started pacing.

"Very well." Skulduggery sat on the bed. "Where to start..."

"Start at the skeleton booty call and move on from there. Oh, wait!" She swung round. "Was she a girlfriend before you were killed, or after?"

"After."

"Oh." Valkyrie resumed her pacing. "Go on."

"It doesn't matter how I met her. It doesn't matter where. What does matter is what state I was in."

"What state were you in?"

"A bad one. The war was never-ending. Friends were dying all around us. Every time I got close to Serpine, he'd slip away again. My anger was growing. My hatred was at its peak. Abyssinia knew this. She saw it. She latched on to me. She told me she loved me. I hadn't had anyone say that to me since my wife died. She influenced me. I didn't even notice it happening. Ghastly did. He warned me, but I didn't listen to him. I listened to her, though. Her words infected me; they weighed me down. Dragged me down. She knew I was... what did I call it once? Magically ambidextrous. She encouraged me to explore other types of magic."

Valkyrie froze. "Wait... was this...?"

"I rediscovered Necromancy," Skulduggery said, "and she gifted me with a very special suit of armour."

"She turned you into Lord Vile?"

"No. I did that. I turned myself into Vile. But she was there. She made sure I stayed on course."

"That... that cow..."

"By this point, I no longer cared about which side I fought on. I just wanted to fight. I just wanted to kill. Meritorious's army had too many rules so I switched. Abyssinia brought me over. With the armour on, nobody knew who I'd once been, and the truth was, I wasn't me any more. I wasn't," Skulduggery tapped his chest, "me. I was him. I was my anger and I was my hatred. I quickly became one of Mevolent's generals. I didn't even mind that I was now fighting alongside the man who had murdered my family."

"And what did Abyssinia do?"

"She was beside me the whole way. She tore the life force from her victims, used it to heal her wounds or get stronger. We slaughtered entire villages together. She had an appetite for bloodshed that I found... fascinating. I'd stop sometimes, just to watch her kill. She was born to it. It came as naturally to her as breathing."

"This is getting weird."

"While I was becoming a general, Abyssinia was integrating herself into the upper echelons of Mevolent's army, which had been her plan all along. China Sorrows herself invited her to join the Diablerie. Abyssinia was as fervent and fanatical as any of them, and was just as dedicated. Or so it appeared."

Valkyrie frowned. "It was an act?"

"Abyssinia was full of surprises. One of the reasons she latched on to me was because she saw something in me, something she could twist. She used me to get close to Mevolent. And she wanted to get close to Mevolent in order to kill him, and take his army for herself."

"Ambitious."

"Yes, she was," said Skulduggery. "But she made a mistake. One single, solitary mistake."

"Which was?"

"Me."

"She underestimated you."

"She trusted me. In whatever sick form it took, she actually believed she loved me. She believed I loved her back, even as Lord Vile. Her mistake was to tell me her plans. She wanted me by her side, you see – king to her queen. She planned to kill Mevolent at a feast he was hosting – she was gambling that a move so ridiculously bold would actually be well received by those in attendance. Kill Mevolent in front of everyone and watch them bend the knee. She was probably right, actually. It probably would have worked."

"What... what happened?"

Skulduggery took off his hat, adjusted the brim. "Mevolent held the feast and, even though China and Serpine and Baron Vengeous were in attendance, it was Abyssinia who was seated at Mevolent's side. She must have felt like all her work had paid off – that she was among his most trusted. Her plan – our plan, or so she thought – was to wait for the toasts. When they were both standing, I would strike, incapacitating him. Then she would take his head.

"The courses were served. I didn't eat, naturally. I didn't drink. I watched them all. They talked and laughed and got full and got drunk. Even Abyssinia drank too much. Overconfidence, I suppose. Mevolent stood up, singing Abyssinia's praises for all to hear. But, when Abyssinia rose to toast him in return, I ran my sword through her back."

Valkyrie didn't say anything.

"Mevolent gave me the opportunity to fight and kill," Skulduggery continued. "Abyssinia would have ended the war far too quickly. There would have been no one left to battle if she took over. The world would burn and she would sit in her throne and laugh. So, before she could recover, I lifted her off her feet, walked to the window and tossed her through. She fell to the rocks. It was a long way down."

"Christ."

"Yes."

"That's... I don't know what to say."

"The story isn't over."

"Oh, God. Maybe I do need to sit down."

Skulduggery stood and she took his place on the edge of the bed. "Carry on," she said.

"Her body wasn't where it should have been," Skulduggery said. "We found a trail of blood leading away and then... nothing. But there was no way she could have survived that. The sword was enough to have killed her, let alone the fall. It was assumed that animals had taken her corpse away, or even cannibals."

"Cannibals?"

"There'd been reports of cannibals in the area. Anyway, the war went on. I killed and butchered old friends and innocent people and I did so without one shred of remorse. And then I had my epiphany."

"Epiphany?"

"My moment of clarity."

"I know what the word means, I just want to know what this particular epiphany was."

"It was not relevant to this story," Skulduggery said, "that's what it was. Anyway, I saw the error of my ways, took off the armour, hid it in a mountain where no one would ever, *ever* find it, and returned to being good old me.

"Then, a few years later, Abyssinia returned. Rather than die a painful death alone in the shadows, she had somehow become vastly more powerful. She attacked both Mevolent's army and ours. She decimated battalions. No one could stand against her. Then a deal was struck."

"Between Abyssinia and Mevolent?"

"Between Mevolent and us."

"Oh my God." Valkyrie shook her head. "I need to sit down."

"You are sitting down."

"I need to sit down more."

"A secret deal," Skulduggery went on. "A few soldiers from our side and a few soldiers from their side. The Dead Men and the Diablerie, working together."

"You're joking," Valkyrie said.

He shrugged. "It made sense. She was an enemy to us both, so we pooled our resources and set off. It was an uneasy alliance, to say the least. As the weeks went by, tensions grew. The only reason we didn't murder each other was because we finally picked up Abyssinia's trail. She was travelling with a boy that turned out to be her son."

"So what happened?"

"Abyssinia led us into a trap we barely survived. It was only when China held a knife to the boy's throat that Abyssinia stopped her attack. We offered her a deal. We would let her son go free if she allowed us to kill her."

The room was quiet. "And did she accept?" Valkyrie asked.

"She didn't have a choice," Skulduggery said. "We killed her and we let the boy walk, then we dismembered her, cut off her head and burned her limbs. But it was only when I carved her heart from her chest that it finally stopped beating."

"Jesus," Valkyrie whispered.

"And that's it. That's the story."

"So wait a second," Valkyrie said. "You betrayed her, threw her out of a window, tracked her down and threatened her son, and she agreed to let you kill her... and at no stage during all this did she tell anyone that you were Lord Vile?"

"As far as I'm aware, she didn't breathe a word of it to anyone."

"Why not?"

"I don't know," Skulduggery said. "I hope I don't get a chance to ask her."

"What happened to the son?"

"No idea."

"Could he be this King of the Darklands guy that Auger is destined to fight?"

"Possibly."

"She ever mention that to you, the fact that she was the Princess of the Darklands?"

"It never came up in conversation."

"Where *are* the Darklands? I mean, is it an actual place or, like, a state of mind or something?"

"I don't know," Skulduggery said.

"I'm just asking because if it's an *actual* place, with people and a royal family and stuff, then your girlfriend was an *actual* princess."

"Ex-girlfriend."

"Yes, because that's the point we need to be focusing on." Valkyrie stood. "OK. OK, that's a lot to take in."

"The fact that my ex-girlfriend was one of the most dangerous people I have ever encountered, or the fact that I had a girlfriend?"

"Both, actually." She nodded. "It'll just take me a while to digest all this. But for now I'm ready to go back in. Unless you have any other bombshells about your past that you'd like to share...?"

"None that I'd like to share, no." He went to the door and opened it. "After you," he said.

33

They rejoined Melior in his kitchen. He frowned at Valkyrie.

"Are you OK?" he asked. "You've gone quite pale."

"It's been an eventful few minutes," she answered, "but here's the upshot. Abyssinia was super-powerful and used other people's life forces to heal her injuries and grow in strength. She was finally defeated and chopped up into little bits. Her heart was cut out. Skulduggery, what happened then?"

"We took the heart back with us," Skulduggery said, "put it in a box, put the box in a room and built a prison around it."

"Coldheart," Valkyrie said.

"Named after its first guest."

"Coldheart Prison," Melior said, straightening. "I heard them talking about that. They have it."

Skulduggery tilted his head. "They have the prison?"

"They overthrew it two days ago. Which means they have the heart."

Valkyrie frowned. "And what about the prisoners?"

"I don't know what they're going to do with them."

"We put away some of those lunatics..."

"Could you do it?" Skulduggery asked. "Could you bring Abyssinia back if you just had her heart?"

"If she has this healing ability you described and I had access to the right type of energy, then... then probably, yes."

An idea exploded behind Valkyrie's eyes. "Could you do that to someone else?" she asked, and glanced at Skulduggery. "What about Ghastly?"

"Ghastly and Anton were cremated," Skulduggery reminded her, and the excitement in her chest died as quickly as it had formed.

Then it sparked again. "What about Gordon? We could bring him back."

"I can't," Melior said. "Resurrecting someone who's died on my operating table – that's one thing. But exhuming a corpse, bringing that back? I'm not prepared to do it, not if I have any choice in the matter. I'm sorry. I'm not here to play God."

"We're not asking you to resurrect *everyone*," said Valkyrie. "Just a few. My uncle was such a good man and he was murdered. How is that fair? If it wasn't right to kill him, then how can it be wrong to bring him back?"

"Valkyrie," Skulduggery said quietly.

"What?" Valkyrie said, speaking too quickly, the words tumbling out of her mouth before she knew what she was saying. "How many people have *you* lost that you would love to see again?"

Skulduggery's head tilted ever so slightly, and Valkyrie felt herself flush.

"There are a few," he said. "But I wouldn't presume to have the right to drag them out of their slumber."

"Yeah," she said. "Sorry."

Skulduggery nodded, and turned to Melior. "The circumstances you would need in order to bring Abyssinia back – what would they be?"

"When I revive people on the operating table," Melior said, "I transfer some of *my* energy to them. It weakens me, but after a few days my life force replenishes and I recover. Something like this, though... I'd need to *take* a life force and transfer it to her remains. More than one, actually. Two, possibly three. I'd need a modified Soul Catcher to harness it all, and life forces from mortals wouldn't be enough. I'd need sorcerers, whose unique energy signatures conform to specific..." He trailed off. "Oh, dear God. They knew I'd need Neoterics. That's why they've been recruiting them."

Skulduggery nodded. "So not only has Abyssinia built up a small army awaiting her return, but she's also been using the process to hunt for donors. Infuriatingly clever." He walked to the window and turned. "But if they took your husband to force you to work for them, and nothing has changed, then why come to us now?"

"Because things *have* changed," said Melior. "They're so close to getting what they want that they wouldn't dare kill him now. They need me too much. So I figure there's an opportunity, right? Now is the time to strike, isn't it? Isn't it?"

Valkyrie looked at Skulduggery.

"You actually have a point," Skulduggery said. "Savant's probably never been safer than he is right now."

"Exactly!" Melior said, clapping his hands. "So we go after him. The three of us. If they're keeping Savant anywhere, they'll be keeping him in that prison, right? That makes sense, doesn't it? Where better to keep a prisoner?"

"How much do you know about Coldheart?" Valkyrie asked gently.

"I know it's pretty much impenetrable," Melior said. "Only two people have ever escaped from it. I'm not saying it'll be easy, but you two have accomplished *miracles* together. I've heard the stories."

"And did you know that it moves?"

"What moves?"

"The prison," Skulduggery said. "It doesn't stay in one place. It's a floating island. It could be anywhere in the world right now."

Melior paled. "No. No, please..."

"Richard, even if we found Coldheart, even if we were able to break in... there's no guarantee that Savant would still be alive."

"I don't accept that and I don't believe it. He's alive. I would know if he wasn't alive."

"It's been five years."

"And if we were mortals that'd mean something. But we're not, are we? Five years apart means nothing to people like us."

Skulduggery looked at Valkyrie, then shrugged, and put on his hat. "So let's go rescue the love of your life."

He led the way out of the apartment and down the stairs. Melior followed, his hands still shackled, and Valkyrie came last. She switched on the aura-vision again, focused on Melior, examining how the shackles dimmed his light. She looked at her own hand as they descended, at the ever-shifting luminescence that refused to be contained by her physical form. Her strength, her magic, her *life* beamed out through her skin. She was like a child's drawing of herself, where the child hadn't bothered to colour inside the lines. And, down below, Skulduggery, with his aura of raging red, unlike any other aura she'd seen.

They emerged on to the street and Smoke was waiting for them. He reached out for Skulduggery and Skulduggery batted his hand away, then grabbed his jacket, moved to take him down. But he stopped suddenly, and Valkyrie watched Smoke's aura, dark grey and crackling with yellow, flow over Skulduggery's.

Skulduggery had been wrong. Smoke didn't need a physical brain to override because he didn't corrupt people's minds – he corrupted their very *essence*. And not even Skulduggery was immune to that.

Melior spun to her. "Run," he said, fear jolting through his eyes, and Valkyrie backed off, climbing the stairs again.

Skulduggery turned, looked up at her and tilted his head. "Yes," he said, amusement in his voice. "*Run.*"

34

Melior's door was locked, and sturdier than it looked. Valkyrie slammed her shoulder against it and bounced off, cursed and went running for the window down the length of corridor. Her hand lit up with lightning and the glass exploded, and she glanced over her shoulder just as Skulduggery reached the top of the stairs.

She jumped through the window.

Fell.

She hit the roof of the Bentley and all the air rushed from her lungs even as she rolled off. She managed to land on her feet – by luck more than design – and pushed herself on, struggling to breathe. She forced her staggered run into a sprint, and veered between parked cars, heading for the first open door she could see.

Once more, she glanced over her shoulder, saw Skulduggery floating out through the broken window, legs crossed beneath him in the lotus position.

Valkyrie dodged right, into a bakery, and slid over the countertop. She passed the startled baker, dashed through the back room that smelled of fresh bread and flour, and then she was out through a narrow door and had the road under her feet again. She ran through traffic, ignoring the shouts and the blaring horns. A cyclist hit her and she fell, spinning, to the pavement, and watched Skulduggery floating gently over the bakery roof. He took out his gun and Valkyrie scrambled up, shoving her way through the people who'd stopped to help her.

She reached the corner, turned on to Horizon Street and ducked under the shutter of a restaurant. Inside, the staff was setting up tables.

"We're not open yet," one of them said to her, frowning and coming forward.

"Call the Cleavers," she said, batting aside his grasping hands. "Tell them it's an emergency."

"You can't go back there, that's for staff—"

"Call the Cleavers!" she snapped, and bolted through to the kitchen. There were some delivery guys here, bringing in crates of fresh food, and she slipped past them, emerged into an alley barely wide enough to fit the van. She squeezed by, stumbling on her last few steps, and checked the empty sky before she broke into a run. She just needed to stay out of sight while she put distance between them. That's all. That's all she needed to do.

She got to the mouth of the alley, sticking to the wall, and then bolted for the adjoining street, into a clothes shop where a woman was arguing with her children. There was a door in here with a bead curtain, and beyond that the interior of another shop. Valkyrie ran through one bead curtain and then the next, shimmying and juking her way around display stands and customers, leaving swaying waterfalls of rattling beads in her wake as she traversed the entire street without having to set foot outside. She got to the final store and left through the back.

But the air snagged her feet, lifted her by the ankles and she flipped, head over heels, into the alley wall. She cracked an elbow when she hit the ground and howled, clutching her arm even as she scrambled up. Then she froze.

Skulduggery dropped slowly out of the sky. "I know what you're thinking," he said, emptying the bullets from his gun and pocketing all but one of them. He touched down. "You're thinking, *Oh,*

God, oh, God, I'm going to die. You're thinking, *How can I stop him? Can he even be stopped? Is this the end of the infamous Valkyrie Cain?*"

She forgot about the pain in her elbow. She just stood there, her back to the wall, watching him slide that single bullet back into the chamber, then spin the cylinder and click it closed.

"I don't have an answer for you, Valkyrie. For today, I'm leaving your fate up to chance." He raised the gun and thumbed back the hammer. "Six chambers, one bullet. Do you want to find out if the universe still loves you?"

He didn't wait for an answer, he just pulled the trigger and Valkyrie flinched, but no shot came.

Skulduggery thumbed back the hammer again. "Have you ever thought about this? What it would be like to go up against each other? I don't mean as Darquesse and Vile – I mean you and me. Do you think you stand a chance?"

She swallowed. "I don't know," she said. "But if you really—"

He pulled the trigger and she cried out, but no shot came.

"Sorry," Skulduggery said, thumbing back the hammer a third time. "What were you saying?"

"You're... you're not going to kill me," she said.

"I'm not?"

"You won't. You can't. I mean too much to you."

His head tilted. "You should understand, Valkyrie, that I really don't care about you any more. In fact, I genuinely want you to die, and I want to be the one to kill you."

Her teeth. They were actually chattering, she was so scared. "You think you do," she said, her voice a trembling mess, "but you've been *corrupted*. Skulduggery, you have to remember."

"Well, of course I remember," Skulduggery said. "And of course I only want to kill you because of Smoke's pesky little power. But that doesn't change the fact that I genuinely want to kill you."

"Please, you've got to fight it."

"No, I don't." His finger tightened and she dodged left, but the gun moved with her as the hammer landed on an empty chamber. "Today really is your lucky day, isn't it? Tell you what – if the next two are empty, for the last one I'll only shoot you in the leg. How about that?"

She held up her hands, the way he'd taught her. "You're being manipulated. Are you OK with that? With someone pulling your strings?"

"I'll deal with all that in my own time, don't you worry."

"Skulduggery, you're my best friend and I love you."

"That," Skulduggery said, the hammer clicking back again, "is so sweet of you to say. Put your hands down, Valkyrie. I'm too far away to hit, and we both know you can't rely on your new powers. They're far too unstable. So are you, for that matter."

She hesitated, then dropped her hands and stood up straight. "Fine," she said.

"Fine?"

"If you're going to kill me, kill me. I'd rather you do it than anyone else."

Skulduggery took a moment. "Oh, I see," he said. "You think I'll stop myself. You're betting your life on it."

"Yes," she said.

"And what if you're wrong? What if, the moment I stop speaking, I put my gun to your head and blow your semi-remarkable brains out? In your final moments, how much are you going to regret these last five years? How much are you going to regret that you've refused to rejoin your family, that you've cut yourself off from so many of the vulnerabilities that make you who you are? Are you going to find yourself wishing, as the bullet pulverises all that grey matter, that you'd let yourself enjoy the life you'd made for yourself? Or are you just going to stand there with a terrified look on your face and hope beyond hope that I don't... stop... speaking?"

Skulduggery stepped to her quickly, pulling the trigger twice and then placing the muzzle against her forehead. She stiffened, her breath caught somewhere in her throat, her hands splayed by her sides.

"Tell me honestly," he said, "are you happy you're back yet?"

He dropped his arm, pressed the gun into her left thigh and pulled the trigger. The shot was deafening and Valkyrie cried out and collapsed, clutching her leg, the cry turning to a wail of pain and panic as she watched the blood pumping through her fingers.

"I should be heading back to my new friends," Skulduggery said, putting his gun away. "I don't know how close they are to resurrecting my ex, but I certainly want to be there when it happens. So hey, if you don't bleed out and die right here, I'll see you soon, OK? Maybe I'll get a chance to introduce you to Abyssinia before I kill you."

He lifted up off the ground, rising high above the rooftops, and then he let the wind take him.

35

Air Force One touched down at Joint Base Andrews a little after two. The stair truck was there immediately to meet it. Six minutes later, President Martin Maynard Flanery emerged, the wind lifting his hair, playing with his tie, flapping his jacket.

He tried keeping the jacket closed over his gut as he descended. He didn't like the wind, and he didn't like stairs. He preferred air conditioning and elevators. There was no one on the ground to greet him, just the usual soldiers and Secret Service agents and the huge, armoured Cadillac they called the Beast. The photographer was there, too, taking snaps from ground level. This irritated the hell out of Flanery, as he knew damn well that every single one of those snaps would add a couple of chins to his jawline.

He reached the bottom of the stairs and got into the Beast without even glancing at the photographer. Wilkes got in after him.

"I want the photographer fired," Flanery said the moment the door was closed. "Get me a new one. A better one. One who knows how to take a good picture."

"Yes, Mr President," Wilkes said, nodding. "Of course." He tapped on the glass partition, and the car started moving. "We have a couple of things to get through, sir, starting with—"

"Hold on," Flanery said, cutting across him. He could feel that

217

old familiar rising tide of anger. "Where's Lilt? You found him yet? Hey? And I don't need any more excuses from you. I've had enough of excuses. Excuses don't get me what I need. Are we understanding each other?"

"Yes, sir," said Wilkes.

"So? You found him?"

"I'm, ah, waiting for a call, sir."

Flanery locked eyes with the wilting man. "You're waiting for a call? You're waiting for a call? Let me tell you something. Let me tell you something because I don't think... What is it, three years? Three years you've been working for me?"

"Yes, sir."

"Three years. You'd think you'd have picked this up after three years. When you wait on a call, I wait on a call. You see that? See how that works? When you wait, I wait, and the President of the United States of America does not wait. I do not wait, Wilkes. I tell you to do something, I tell you to speak to someone, or find someone, or get something, or go somewhere, then you do it. I want it done. I want it done immediately. If I have to ask you to find out why Parthenios Lilt has suddenly gone dark on us, my time is already being wasted. But you know what is unacceptable? What's unacceptable is having to wait on you to get me an answer. I do not accept that."

"I am sorry, Mr President. My contact is checking with—"

Flanery held up a hand. "Details. Details, Wilkes. What have I told you about details?"

"You don't need to—"

"I don't need to hear them. They don't interest me. Results interest me. Answers interest me. Details? I don't give a damn about details."

Wilkes's phone buzzed in his hand, but Wilkes didn't look down. Flanery almost wished he would. Then he'd have something else to get angry about.

"Check your damn phone," he said sharply.

Wilkes did so. A single glance.

"My contact has been in touch," he said. "We've located Lilt."

"He better have a good story," said Flanery. "His story better be great. Better be magnificent. He's missed two calls. Two. No one misses calls with me. Martin Flanery is not the kind of man to call back later. I'm not that kind, Wilkes. Where the hell is he?"

Wilkes hesitated. If there was one thing Flanery hated more than time-wasting, it was hesitation.

"Spit it out, for God's sake."

"Parthenios Lilt has been arrested," said Wilkes.

Flanery froze. "What?"

"Apparently, it happened three days ago, sir."

"Who was it? Us or them? Who was it arrested him, Wilkes? Normal people or freaks?"

"Oh," Wilkes said. "Them, sir. Freaks, sir."

The anger in Flanery's chest was a distant memory. Now Flanery was a volcano. Flanery was the goddamn atom bomb. Upon explosion, Flanery would flatten every town and village in the land.

But he couldn't explode. He had to be calm. Just like his father had taught him.

"What's the charge?" Flanery asked, keeping his voice low.

"Sir?" Wilkes said, leaning closer.

"The charge. What's the charge? What has Lilt been charged with?"

"Oh," said Wilkes. "I don't know, sir."

"Find out. Get on that phone and find out. By the time we reach the White House, I want answers. You hear me? You understand me?"

"I understand, sir. But there are other issues we—"

"Forget about everything else. I don't care. I don't care about policies or regulations or the House or the Senate or anything.

219

Don't care. Only thing I care about is what Lilt is charged with and what impact that has on me. You get that? You understand?"

"Sir, yes, sir."

"Then get it done."

"Yes, sir, Mr President."

36

Idiot.

There was no other word for it, really. Only *idiot* summed up the magnificent stupidity that Omen was capable of displaying at any moment and in any situation. Only he could have hitched a ride from relative safety to absolute jeopardy without actually needing to, at all, in the slightest. He had been *fired*, for God's sake. Skulduggery Pleasant himself had told him to leave all this danger stuff to the professionals. He was no longer involved in whatever the hell was going on.

And yet who had teleported, with a man who had already tried to kill him, moving in the span of an eyeblink from beneath a bed in the dormitories of Corrival Academy to the cold floor of what appeared to be a prison? That would be Omen Darkly, yes, sir, it would. No one else could have managed something like that. The Boy Most Likely to Get Himself Killed.

What had he been thinking? What the hell had possessed him to do something so bloody stupid? He hadn't had anything even remotely *resembling* a plan. He was impossibly lucky that Nero had just walked off when they'd arrived. If he'd looked around, he would have seen Omen lying there on the ground with his hand outstretched. He might have accidentally trodden on him, which would have been a ridiculous way to be discovered.

And, as Nero had walked away, did Omen spring to his feet, stealthy as a ninja? Or did he roll sideways into an empty cell, and then crawl under another bed to hide?

The word repeated itself in his head, just for good measure. *Idiot. Idiot. Idiot.*

He peeked out. The cell was old-fashioned, the kind he'd seen in movies like *The Man in the Iron Mask*. Rough-hewn walls. A door of thick metal bars. The only nods to any kind of civilised living were the toilet and the sink. Omen recognised binding sigils carved into the stone. They were dull, which meant inactive. That was good.

He took out his phone. No signal. Omen, like most other sorcerers on the planet, had boosted it to work anywhere. It was a quick and easy procedure – not even he could have messed it up. But it seemed that prisons operated under different rules. Omen reckoned he was in a considerable amount of trouble now. Trapped, alone and with no way of calling for help, the only things he had to rely on were his own magic and ingenuity.

He was, he realised, totally screwed.

Crawling out from beneath the bed, he did his very best not to hyperventilate. He was suddenly freezing. His hands shook and he looked at the open cell door like it was a mouth waiting to spring shut the moment he passed through.

Slowly, slowly, Omen got to his feet and peeked out. The other cell doors were open, too. Empty. They were empty. For the moment – for the fleeting moment he currently existed in – he was safe. Relatively.

He tucked in his shirt, then walked quietly in the direction Nero had gone. The light out here wasn't good, and he welcomed the cold shadows. All the better to hide in, my dear. He laughed a little, and the laugh died and his eyes widened. His laugh had sounded a lot like panic.

He clamped both hands over his mouth as a high-pitched whine started up from somewhere within him. He shook his head, but the whine kept growing. The more he tried to stop it, the louder it got. He took a deep breath and balled his fists, thumped them against his forehead while he screwed his eyes shut.

He would not panic. He would not panic. Auger wouldn't panic in a situation like this and neither would Omen.

The whine, amazingly, went away.

Omen opened his eyes and let out his breath in a slow, controlled manner. He heard voices coming from one direction and so he went the other way. This was not a bad plan. If he could keep walking away from whoever was close, he'd stay safe and undetected until he found a way out. Of a prison. Which were notoriously difficult to leave.

He came to metal stairs and went up, careful not to make too much noise. He took the tunnel, plunging from greasy yellow light into pitch-black with every third step. He came to a corner and peeked. Across a divide he saw a curved wall of cells, all occupied by prisoners, men and women, in yellow jumpsuits. Almost every single one of them was either sitting or lying on their bunk. They were so quiet in their solitude it was eerie. Omen actually felt sorry for them.

He hurried on.

He found another tunnel, which led to another corridor, which led to a row of open cells.

Except the two cells at the end. Their doors were closed.

Omen bit his lip. Going back would mean passing by all those prisoners again. It would mean risking being seen. There was no way out behind him – but for all he knew there could be an open door just ahead.

He moved forward quietly. The cell on the left was dark, but there was a light on in the cell on the right.

Step by silent step, Omen crept. He saw the bunk. Saw a pair of legs, clad in yellow. One was outstretched. The other bent. Omen craned his neck, saw thick fingers holding a battered paperback.

Omen swayed back, and took a deep breath. Confidence. All he needed was confidence. He was going to stride onwards. If the convict looked up, Omen would nod tersely to him, like he was meant to be here. Like it was all normal. He'd be in view for maybe two seconds, and then gone. He could do this. This could be done.

Omen squared his shoulders, and took his first big step.

"You!" the convict roared, and Omen screamed and his knees went and he stumbled back as the convict leaped to his feet. "Who the hell are you? You're a kid! What are you doing here?"

Omen straightened, squeezing one hand in another, and he did his best to smile politely. "Hello," he said. "I'm sorry, I didn't mean to disturb you."

The convict pressed his face against the bars. He was big, with a shaved head, and looked mean. "What the hell are you wearing?"

"It's, um, it's my uniform," Omen told him. "I attend Corrival Academy."

"What's that?"

"A school," said Omen. "In Roarhaven."

The convict blinked. "You on a – what do they call them? Field trip?"

Omen made himself chuckle. "No, no, sir. To be honest, I'm not really supposed to be here. I should probably just go."

"Come closer."

Omen's mouth went even drier than it already was. "I'm sorry?"

The convict beckoned to him with a huge, hairy hand. "C'mere. Get closer."

"I... I don't think that's wise, sir. I think I'll stay where I am, if you don't mind."

"C'mere," the convict said. His hand was poking out through the bars now, fingers curling. "I want to talk to you, but I don't wanna raise my voice. I got a sore throat. I think I'm coming down with something."

"That's awful," said Omen. "But I don't want to catch it."

"It's not contagious."

"Still, though... Best to be safe."

"Come a little closer," said the convict. "Just a little. I'm not gonna hurt you, for the gods' sake. I just wanna talk. Could you at least do me the courtesy of treating me like a regular human being? Or is that too much to ask?"

Omen swallowed thickly, and took a tentative step forward.

"Do not move one more inch," said a voice from behind.

Omen turned, noticing the figure sitting on his bunk in the darkened cell.

"You stay out of this," said the convict.

The figure ignored him. "You know it's a bad idea," he said to Omen. He was American. "You know he's going to do you harm. He knows you know. But what do you do? You don't wish to offend him, so you step closer. How dumb *are* you, slick?"

Omen stayed quiet. He hoped that was a rhetorical question.

"Don't listen to him," said the convict. "I don't think you're dumb. What does he know? He was thrown into that cell a few days ago. He has no idea what the hell he's talking about."

The man stood up from his bunk and stepped into the light. He was good-looking, unshaven, with dried blood on his shirt.

"You just arrived?" Omen asked.

"Not by choice."

"Um," said Omen, "are you Temper Fray, by any chance?"

"I'm not Temper Fray by any kind of *chance*," the man replied. "I'm Temper Fray by *design*. I'm Temper Fray because nobody else could handle the awesome responsibility of being *me*. But who I am is not the issue right now. The issue is what is a schoolboy doing in this particular prison at this particular time?"

Omen thought about it for a moment. "Well, I... I'm kind of here by accident, but since I *am* here I could, maybe, rescue you, if you'd like...?"

Temper Fray folded his arms. "I wouldn't say no."

"What about me?" the convict asked. "Can you rescue me, too?"

Omen turned to him. "I don't really know you, sir."

"My name's Immolation Joe."

Omen hoped that Immolation Joe could see the conflict on his face. "I'm not sure releasing you would be a good idea, though. You sound, just by your name, like you might be a threat to, you know, people. And, to be honest, also me."

Immolation Joe frowned. "What are you saying?"

"I think you might kill me if I let you out, sir."

"And?"

Omen took a moment, and nodded. "That's a good point."

Temper cleared his throat, loudly, and Omen turned to him again. "How about you ignore the multiple murderer you're talking to and just focus on getting me out of here, how about that?"

"Yes," Omen said at once. "OK. Sorry. Do you have the key?"

"Slick, if I had the key, I wouldn't need to be rescued."

"I mean, do you know where the key is?"

"I do not."

"Then do you know how I can rescue you without it?"

Temper sagged. "My initial excitement is flagging, just to let you know. How did you get here?"

"I teleported," said Omen.

"Ah! My man's a Teleporter!"

"Well, no. I hitched a ride, actually. I know what's going on, though. Skulduggery Pleasant and Valkyrie Cain brought me in to help."

"They brought you in? They didn't find Tanith Low or the Monster Hunters or any spare Dead Men that might be floating around? They brought you in? What age are you?"

"Fourteen."

"What's your name?"

"Omen Darkly."

Temper brightened. "The Chosen One? Well, god*damn*, I take it all back."

"Uh... I'm not actually the Chosen One. I'm the Chosen One's brother."

Temper went quiet for a moment. "I didn't know the Chosen One had a brother."

"He does," Omen answered. "And I'm him." The look on Temper's face didn't change, so Omen kept talking. "You don't have to worry, though. I was there for every step of my brother's training, and I picked up a lot." He wasn't quite sure what he was saying any more. He wished his mouth would stop moving. "You're in good hands. I can totally rescue you." Omen gave another smile while his words caught up with him. Holy crap. He was talking gibberish. There was no way Temper was going to believe the stuff he was saying.

"OK, slick," Temper said. "I believe you. Proceed with the rescuing."

Omen couldn't move for a moment. Then he nodded. When that didn't do anything, he looked around. The solution didn't jump out at him so he chewed his lip.

"Kid?" Temper said.

"Do you think they have a spare key, maybe, hidden somewhere?" Omen asked. "Behind a loose brick or something?"

"Probably not."

"OK. That's unfortunate. I'm not sure how I'm going to rescue you, then."

Temper scratched his stubble. "Listen to me, you don't need to. You just have to call Skulduggery and tell him what's going on."

"My phone doesn't work in here. I'll have to go outside and call him. Do you know where the exit is?"

"You have no idea where we are, do you? We're on a floating island. Going outside here means dropping into the ocean."

"Oh."

Temper worked his jaw back and forth, and Omen could tell he was annoyed. "Slick, you're going to have to find a way to open this door, OK? I might be the one in the cell, but we're *both* trapped here. You get me out, I find a way to get us off this rock. Think you can do that?"

Omen nodded. "No."

Temper frowned. "No?"

"I can't do any of that stuff," Omen blurted. "I can't rescue you. I don't know why I said I could. I just wanted to impress you. You seem cool and I want to be cool, too, so I said it, but I'll make a mess of it. I'm already making a mess of it. My brother does the rescuing, not me. I haven't had the practice. I don't have the mindset. My uncle took me aside once and told me I was the worst. He didn't even specify what I was the worst *at*. I think he just meant in general."

"Your uncle sounds like a piece of work, but you've got to get past that. Is he here right now? No. You are. You are here and you can do this."

"I can do this."

"No, you can't," said Immolation Joe.

"Ignore him," said Temper. "You can do this."

Omen bit his lip. "What if they see me?"

"They'll probably kill you. You ever have someone try to kill you before?"

"Yes, actually. This morning."

"I knew it, just by looking at you. You've stared death in the face. That's good. I have people trying to kill me all the time. Getting captured is actually kind of a luxury. What's your name again?"

"Omen."

Temper nodded. "OK, Omen, find a way to get me out of here. I'm counting on you."

Omen didn't know whether he should salute or not, so he just gave a small wave and hurried round the corner. The first thing he saw was a control panel on the wall. He stepped backwards.

"There's a panel here," he said. "Lots of numbered buttons with little lights, but only two lights are on. You think they open the cells?"

"I knew I could count on you," said Temper. "Get me out of here, Omen."

Grinning, Omen jabbed at one of the buttons and the corresponding light went off as he heard a click. He looked back as the cell door swung open, and Immolation Joe stepped out.

"Aw," said Omen.

Immolation Joe clicked his fingers a few times. Sparks flew. Then his hands burst into flame. "*Yesssss...*" he said, gazing at the fire like he was in love.

"Slick," said Temper.

Omen jabbed at the second button and Temper sprang out of his cell, his knee crashing into Immolation Joe's chest. The convict reeled backwards and Temper slammed the door shut. It clicked and immediately the flames died in Joe's hands.

"I'll kill you!" Immolation Joe screamed, grasping for them between the bars. "I'll kill you both!"

Temper ignored him, his eyes closed, savouring the magic that was flooding back into his system. Then he looked at Omen again and smiled, and held out his hand. "Nice going."

They shook.

"Now, let's get the hell out of here."

Smiling awkwardly at Immolation Joe, Omen followed Temper to a set of metal stairs. They went down. Footsteps approached and they flattened themselves against the wall. A man walked by. Didn't see them. When he was gone, they continued onwards, passing through a heavy door that stood open. Leaving the cellblocks behind them, they jogged to the gate at the far end of an unmanned security checkpoint. There were about a dozen stairs beyond it, concrete, and they climbed them and found themselves in a large chamber with a desk and huge doors – the way out.

Omen's joy was somewhat diminished by the sight of Lethe standing there before them.

37

"I thought we *had* something," Lethe said, strolling forward. "But the first chance you get to escape you just *grab* it with both hands, don't you?"

"It'd never have worked between us," Temper said, backing up and keeping Omen behind him. "I'm too clingy."

Even though he couldn't see Lethe's eyes, Omen knew the man was looking at him.

"And this must be the spy from the school," Lethe said. "Skulduggery Pleasant's *secret weapon*. I confess, I haven't a clue who you *are*, but I don't think it matters. Your career has come to a sharp and sudden *stop*, little spy."

"Really?" Temper asked. "You're going to kill him? The kid doesn't know anything. He doesn't even know where he is right now. Let him go. I'll take you on, I'll give you a fight. But let him go, what do you say?"

"You'll give me a fight if I *allow* it," Lethe said, "which I won't. The only reason we haven't killed you already is that we haven't got around to it. I'm going to *rectify* that in a moment. The little spy can either watch and then die, or get the dying over with *now*. Little spy, which do you choose?"

"I... um... I'll watch Temper die first, please," said Omen.

"Thanks, slick," Temper murmured, then addressed Lethe. "May I suggest we hurry this along? My rescue team will be here shortly."

"You mean to say it hasn't arrived already?"

Temper laughed. "You think the kid here is my rescue team? He's just a cheeky little guy who sneaked out past his curfew. No, no – my rescue team is comprised of people you'll probably have heard of. You want to know who's coming next?"

"I'm all ears."

Temper grinned. "Skulduggery Pleasant, Valkyrie Cain and a whole horde of Cleavers."

"That so?"

"It is. Coming straight here."

"My, my," said Lethe. "Sounds like I'm in *trouble*."

"Now, you're good," Temper said, "I'm not denying that. But Skulduggery? Skulduggery is—"

"*Ours*," said Lethe. "Skulduggery is *ours*, Mr Fray. You've been out of the loop, so I'm going to break this to you *gently*. My colleague, Mr Smoke, came into contact with your skeletal friend. *Physical* contact. And you know what happens once my colleague, Mr Smoke, comes into *physical contact* with someone, don't you? You know that *first-hand*, am I correct?"

Temper's grin faded. "Bull."

"Not *bull*, Mr Fray."

"Smoke turned *me*, but he can't turn Skulduggery. That stuff doesn't work on him. His mind can't be read, his—"

"My colleague's ability has nothing to do with the *mind*, Mr Fray, and it's got *everything* to do with the *soul*. So I am in the unfortunate position of being the one to tell you that not only is your friend no longer *your* friend, but that this fictitious *rescue team* you have imagined coming to free you is... Well, it's just *not*. So I'll give you a moment to let that sink in."

Temper didn't say anything in response.

"Has it sunk in yet?" Lethe asked. "I think it has. By the look on your face, I think it has. Which brings us back to the act of *killing you both*. Now, I forget – little spy, did you say you wanted to die *before* or *after* Mr Fray here?"

"After," Omen said, his mouth dry.

"That's right," said Lethe, clicking his fingers. "That's right. Thank you. I get confused sometimes."

He lunged and Temper grabbed him, turned him, tried to trip him, but Lethe buckled his leg and flipped Temper over his hip. For a moment, Lethe's back was to Omen, and all of a sudden Omen was throwing himself on to him. Everything he'd ever known about fighting flushed from his mind and he hung on, clung on, eyes wide with panic, and then Lethe twisted and hit him and Omen was tumbling down the concrete steps.

He sprawled on to the ground, the right side of his face throbbing numbly. He turned his head. From his vantage point, he could see Lethe and Temper from the chests up. The fight flowed quickly. Temper was not winning.

He heard a woman laugh. "Oh, *oh!*" came Razzia's voice. "Can I have a go? Can I, please?"

Lethe sounded amused. "By *all means*, Razzia. Sharing is *caring*, after all." He wrapped Temper up in a choke, then threw him, and followed him out of sight.

Omen got up. Rubbed his knee and his face. Every atom in his body wanted to hide, but they'd find him. Of course they would. And Temper Fray was on his side. He couldn't abandon him. There was a code about these things. Omen didn't know what it was, exactly, but he knew there was one.

Keeping low, he crept up the stairs. The sounds reminded him of the arena back home, when his brother faced a queue of fighters and wouldn't be allowed to rest until the clock ran out. As a kid, Omen had closed his eyes to most of it, but the sounds had got into his head. Grunts. Cries. Knuckles striking flesh. Bodies going down.

He came level with the top of the stairs, watched Temper fight Razzia. Temper was tired, and she was playing with him. Omen didn't know what magical discipline Temper had studied, but, if he didn't use his magic now, he wasn't going to last much longer.

Lethe circled them both, watching. Nero was there, too, standing with his back to Omen, calling out the occasional bit of advice that Razzia would ignore. Nero wasn't wearing his jacket, which meant the knife, sheathed on his belt, was plainly visible.

There was no other choice. The realisation hit Omen like a slap and his guts turned cold and plummeted somewhere deep and dark, leaving a hollow space where only shivers lived. No other choice but to do something stupid. It was this or never escape. This or die here.

Omen scuttled up the last few steps, counted to three and burst forward.

He slammed into Nero and they went tumbling over each other, Omen going for the knife, his fingertips finding the handle and then losing it again. With his other hand, he kept a tight grip of Nero's shirt. He couldn't let go. If he let go and Nero teleported away, he was lost.

They came to a stop. The knife was in Omen's hand, the blade jammed against Nero's throat.

"Sloppy," said Lethe, but he didn't run in to haul Omen off. He didn't move. Razzia didn't move, either. Temper collapsed.

Omen badly needed some water. His throat was parched and his lips were dry. His tongue felt too heavy to form words.

From beneath him, Nero said calmly, "Don't do anything stupid."

Anger flashed and Omen came up to one knee, digging the knife in a little deeper. He could talk fine now. "You're going to let us go," he said, with a hell of a lot more confidence than he felt. "If anyone tries anything, I'll kill him."

Lethe folded his arms. "You will? *Really?* I don't know. Razzia, what do you think? He look like a *killer* to you?"

Razzia jumped up and down. "Ooh, I hope so! Do it! Do it, kid! It's only Nero! If he carks it, we can grow another one!"

Lethe looked at her. "Actually, we *can't.*"

Razzia stopped jumping. "We didn't grow him in a tube?

Strewth, I thought he was one of those genetic experiments I keep hearing about. With the hair and all." She shrugged. "Kill him anyway, kid. Cut his throat and join the club."

"Hey," Nero said loudly. "Hey! Come on! Let's not antagonise the kid, all right? Let's all be cool here."

"Of course," Lethe said, sauntering forward. "You're right, Nero. Of course you are. Let's be *cool*."

"Stop walking," said Omen.

Lethe ignored him. "We'll *all* be cool. Nobody has to hurt *anybody*. Let's just shake hands and part as *friends*, what do you say?"

Temper groaned, and rolled on to all fours. "He takes another step, you start cutting, you hear me?"

"The boy's not going to *cut*," said Lethe. "He's not a *killer*. He's not a *murderer*."

"I'm scared and I'm trapped and you're gonna kill me," Omen countered. "I will do whatever I have to."

"You don't have to do anything," Nero said quickly, "because Lethe is going to stop walking right goddamn now. Aren't you, Lethe? *Lethe?*"

Lethe's saunter, as calm and unhurried as any saunter Omen had ever seen, came to a slow and reluctant stop. He sighed. "Fine. Look at me. Look at how *still* I'm standing."

"Temper, come over here," Omen said. He was sweating. Perspiration ran down his face, down the back of his collar. He could feel how damp his armpits were. The knife. The knife was slippery; he wasn't sure that it'd stay in his hand if he had to stab, but he dared not adjust his grip.

Temper got up and limped over. It was like he was being slow on purpose. Omen had to bite back harsh words. He could feel the panic beneath his skin. It jittered and bubbled and boiled.

Finally – *finally* – Temper was crouching beside him, one hand on Omen's shoulder, one hand on Nero's arm. "All right then," he said, taking control of the situation, "Nero here is going to teleport us back to Roarhaven. You hear that, Nero? Right into the middle of Meritorious Square. If you try something stupid, like dumping us off the edge of a volcano, Omen here will kill you as his final act, won't you, Omen?"

"Yes, I will," Omen said, trembling so badly that the blade nicked Nero's skin. If the shakes got any worse, the knife was liable to fly out of his hand before he got a chance to use it.

"Meritorious Square," Nero repeated. "All right. Just say when."

"None of this *means* anything," Lethe said. "So you escape – so what? You've already told us everything you *know*, which was a paltry amount to begin with. At this stage, you're *worthless* to us. This escape means nothing."

"First you hurt my body," Temper said. "Then you hurt my feelings. I know which will leave the deeper scar. Nero? Mush."

Bright sun glared from a blue sky with no clouds and the sudden rush of cold air and the noise of Roarhaven all around them and Omen flinched and Nero shoved him away, twisting from Temper's grip and vanishing.

People were glancing at them. Two Cleavers were running over.

"You did good, slick," Temper said, lying on his back and looking up at the sky. "You did good."

Omen looked at the knife for a moment, then dropped it and managed a smile.

His first rescue mission.

38

"This is not my first rescue mission," Sebastian whispered to Bennet as they crouched around the corner from the tiny house. "Let me go in first. I'll clear the room of hostiles. When I give you the all-clear, you come in. Understand?"

Bennet nodded. He was visibly shaking. A quick peek through the dirty window had shown them Odetta sitting at a table, a Hollow Man standing right behind her. They had no idea how many other Hollow Men might be in there with them.

Sebastian patted Bennet on the shoulder. He felt an urge to repeat his instructions, but decided against it. Bennet was a grown man, not a child.

Keeping low, Sebastian jogged to the front door. He took a deep breath to steady himself and then kicked, the wood splintering beneath his boot, the door crashing open, and then Bennet lunged past him, pulling his gun from his pocket. There was a scream. Sebastian ran in, but saw Odetta throwing herself in front of the Hollow Man.

"Don't!" she cried.

Bennet kept shifting his aim. "I can't... Sweetheart, if you don't move out of the way, I can't shoot it."

"He's not an it!" Odetta said. "His name is Conrad!"

Bennet hesitated. "I'm sorry?"

"Excuse me," Sebastian said, satisfied that there were no other

Hollow Men in the building, "but what exactly is going on here?"

"We're in love!" Odetta said.

"Yes, we are," said Bennet.

"Not me and you!" Odetta said, almost angrily. "*We! We* are in love!"

Bennet looked at his wife and the Hollow Man. "I'm missing something here."

"I... I think she's leaving you," said Sebastian. "I think she wants to spend the rest of her life with it. Sorry. Him. What's his name again?"

"Conrad," said Odetta.

Bennet laughed. Then his laugh failed and he lowered the gun. "What?"

"It's true," Odetta said. "I'm so sorry, Bennet. I didn't want you to find out this way, but I didn't know how to tell you. I got scared. I thought just walking away would be the best thing, but then I knew you'd be worrying, so I had one of Conrad's friends deliver that message... I suppose it's good, that you're here. We can finally talk about it."

"You're... in love with... with *that*?"

"With *him*," Sebastian corrected.

"But he's a Hollow Man," Bennet said. "He's made of paper. I don't get how this is remotely possible?" Tears brimmed. The gun fell to the floor. "You're leaving me?"

"I'm so sorry."

"You're leaving me for a man made out of paper?"

Odetta wept. "Please don't be nasty," she said.

"But we're married. Why are you leaving me? You can't leave me – we're married. What about our son?"

"Kase knows. He understands."

"But we were going to have *more* children. We talked about it, about giving Kase a little brother or sister."

"He can still have that. But you won't be the father."

"Odetta, come on," Bennet said, moving forward. "Be reasonable. You can't have children with a Hollow Man."

"He has a name!" Odetta said, her anger rising again.

"This is ridiculous! The only way you could have children with it is if they're on a *paper chain*!"

"How dare you!"

"Is that what you want, Odetta? You want paper-chain children? Is that it? You want origami kids?"

Odetta punched Bennet so hard his knees buckled and he fell.

"Don't say nasty things!" Odetta shouted. "You know why I fell in love with him? Because he listens! You say nasty things whenever you get upset! You're a nasty man! I can't stand it! I can't stand it any more!"

"But... but I love you..." Bennet said, struggling to get up.

"The only person you love is *Darquesse*," Odetta spat. "And that is sick beyond reason! There is something seriously wrong with you if you worship that monster! She murdered over a thousand people! How can you talk about her like she's this majestic, heavenly creature when she's killed so many? You, you and your sick friends, there's something wrong with you all!"

Sebastian hesitated, then helped Bennet to his feet. The man felt like kindling in his hands.

"Odetta..."

"I don't want to hear it," Odetta said. "And I think you should move out. I'll be back on Sunday. You better not be there."

"Can we... can we just talk about it?"

"Talking to you has never got me anywhere," Odetta said. "Go home now, Bennet. The next time I talk to you, I'll be divorcing you."

"No, no, please..."

"I'm going to say this once and once only, so open your ears and listen to it. It's only one word. Even you can absorb one word. Ready? Here it comes."

"No. Don't. Please. Who else will love me?"

She leaned in. "Goodbye."

39

"Hello."

His voice. Deep, and smooth. Like velvet.

Valkyrie sat hunched over on the bed, her phone to her ear. Elsewhere in the clinic, beyond her room, people were talking and machines were beeping, but in here Valkyrie was trembling. Her whole body shook.

"I know you're there," he said. "I can hear you breathing."

She stared at the wall.

"That's OK," he said. "You don't have to talk. I can do the talking for both of us. You're probably feeling very alone right now. This is understandable. You're afraid and you're confused and you're panicking."

"It fades," she managed to say.

"I'm sorry? What was that?"

"Smoke's corruption," she said. "It fades away after forty-eight hours."

"That's what you're hanging on to? That's what you're pinning your hopes to? Valkyrie, whatever makes you think that I would *want* this to wear off?"

"Because you're not yourself."

"This doesn't change who I am. I'm still me, Valkyrie. I'm just a more efficient version of me. I've left behind so many little rules."

She shook her head. "Smoke controls you. You're a slave."

"I could see how you would think that, but I'm afraid you'd be wrong. The only time in my life, such as it is, when I've felt more liberated than I am right now is when I wore armour. You should try this. You should join us. I'm sure you'd be a boon to the anti-Sanctuary."

"Help us," she said. "Lethe... Smoke... they think you're on their side."

"I am on their side."

"I don't... I don't believe that."

"Yes, you do. Can I ask you something? Are you worried about your family? Are you worried that I'm going to kill your dog? Or your sister?"

"No," she said.

"Really? Are you being honest?"

"You won't go after my family or my dog. You don't want me wasting my time worrying about the things I love. You want me focused."

"Yes," said Skulduggery. "*Yes*. You know me well, Valkyrie. I'm going to have fun with you. Your death... it isn't going to be quick. And your life isn't going to be painless. From this point until the end, it's going to be... excruciating."

She hung up.

40

Valkyrie's throat was raw, her mouth haunted by the bitter aftertaste of the dried leaves she'd been given to ease the pain of the gunshot wound. Her leg was stiff, but numb, and already healing. She was so incredibly tired, though – like she'd already burned through a day's worth of energy.

"It's temporary," she said to the room. "It's temporary."

And it was. It was temporary. Smoke's corruption, it hit and overwhelmed and then it faded. She hadn't lost him. Skulduggery wasn't gone. Not forever.

She lowered her hands, looked at them while they trembled. She'd get him back. She didn't give a damn what Lethe or the anti-Sanctuary wanted out of all this, but she was going to stop them and get Skulduggery back, and the corruption would fade and that'd be that. Easy. Simple. Straightforward.

She forced herself to breathe deeply, to calm down. Eventually, her hands stopped trembling.

"Can't leave you alone for a second, can I?" Darquesse said, walking in.

Valkyrie ignored her, and carefully swung her injured leg off the bed.

"It's true, then? He really has turned?" Darquesse asked, and sat on the bed beside her. "You must be terrified. Are you? You must be. You're all alone now."

Valkyrie experimented with putting some weight on to her foot.

"He shot you," said Darquesse. "He actually shot you. Yes, he's under the influence of a bad, bad man, but even so – that has to sting, doesn't it? The fact that he is fully capable of hurting you? You've gone all this time thinking the bond between you was so strong it would survive anything... but he fails at the first real test of your friendship."

"He hasn't failed," said Valkyrie.

"Tell that to your leg."

"And our friendship has been tested before."

Darquesse dismissed the notion with a wave. "You mean when you found out that he was Lord Vile? That's nothing. He sinned. Sins are committed in order to be forgiven. But this... this was a real test."

"Don't you have someone else to haunt?"

Darquesse smiled. "Just you. So do you think he'll go after Alice? Do you think he already has her?"

"He won't. He told me."

"You believe him?"

"Skulduggery wouldn't lie to me."

"So he'd shoot you, but not lie to you? Well, I suppose boundaries are important."

"He doesn't want me distracted," Valkyrie said.

"Who's distracted?" Reverie Synecdoche asked, walking in.

Darquesse moved out of the way and Reverie walked right by her.

"I am," Valkyrie said. "Sorry. Just talking to myself."

"First sign of madness," Reverie said. "Can you stand?"

Valkyrie pushed herself off the bed. Her leg didn't buckle, but Reverie was too busy making notes to notice her grimace.

"The scar should be gone completely in two or three days," she said. "You're lucky the bullet didn't nick an artery, though. It could have been a lot worse."

"Hear that?" Darquesse said. "You're a lucky girl."

Valkyrie stuffed her feet into her trainers and crouched to tie the laces. Her jeans were new. The old ones, bloodstained, with the left leg slit up the middle, were in a plastic bag somewhere, waiting to be thrown out or burned or whatever it was they did with ruined clothes here in Reverie's clinic.

"I don't know why she bothered, though," Darquesse continued. "Wouldn't it have been better to just let you die? I mean, it's not like Skulduggery is *not* going to kill you. Your death is as inevitable as it is imminent."

One of the nurses passed in the corridor and Valkyrie straightened and focused her attention on Reverie. "Clarabelle not working here any more?"

"Fine," Darquesse sighed. "Ignore me."

"Clarabelle?" Reverie said, finally looking up. "No, no. She's busy being the worst bartender in the world. She stares into space half the time and for the other half cannot, for the life of her, remember what anybody ordered."

"Everyone's thinking it," Darquesse said. "I'm just the only one brave enough to say it."

"How are Scapegrace and Thrasher?" Valkyrie asked.

Reverie shrugged. "They come in here two or three times a year and I sew bits of them back on. Thrasher is still besotted, Scapegrace is still oblivious, and Clarabelle loves them both without measure. The pub's quiet, but does OK. Thrasher is surprisingly good at bookkeeping, as it turns out."

"I'm glad," said Valkyrie, pulling on her coat. "I'm glad things are working out for them."

"The doctor raises an interesting point, though," Darquesse said, folding her arms. "About talking to yourself being the first sign of madness. Maybe you *are* mad."

"By the way," said Reverie, "I got a call from the High Sanctuary enquiring as to why you were not availing yourself of their medical facilities. I get the impression that Supreme Mage

Sorrows would rather you spend your time where she can keep a closer eye on you."

"I'm sure she would," Valkyrie responded. "Thank you, Reverie."

"It's what I'm here for," Reverie said, and Valkyrie shook her hand and limped from the room.

"Maybe you should ask her to take a look at your head," Darquesse said, trailing after her. "Perform a brain scan or something. I just don't think you're playing with a full deck of cards, that's all."

Valkyrie limped on. Darquesse stayed right behind her.

"Let's face it, you're not exactly a poster child for mental health, are you? A great big chunk of who you are split off from you and killed 1,351 innocent people. You yourself murdered your own sister. And now look – you're being haunted by the ghost of your own split personality."

"You're not a ghost," Valkyrie muttered.

"No one else can see me, can they? They can't hear me or touch me. So I'm either a ghost or a hallucination. I think it'd be better for you if I were a ghost."

Valkyrie turned to her, glaring into the smirk. "You're not a ghost and you're not a hallucination. I know exactly what you are."

"Oh, really?" Darquesse said. "Well then, what am I?"

"You're a *bit* of her," Valkyrie said. "You're a splinter of the real Darquesse. What, you really think I wouldn't have worked it out? You've been hanging around me for five years."

"You don't know what you're talking about."

"You're a stray thought she left behind," said Valkyrie. "She abandoned you, and you don't have the power to go after her. You barely have the power to *exist*."

"That's a cosy explanation," Darquesse said. "I bet it's more comforting than the idea that you're going insane."

"Maybe I can see you because we're connected, or maybe it's because I can see across the magic spectrum. I don't know. But what I do know is that you're flesh and blood. You're not a figment of my imagination and you're not a symptom of my insanity. You want to know how I know?"

"Dearly."

Valkyrie punched her, snapping her head back, buckling her legs from under her.

"See?" Valkyrie said, looking down at her. "Real."

Valkyrie left her there.

Around the corner and halfway down the next corridor, she pushed open a door and stepped in.

Fletcher lay sleeping, hooked up to an IV and a monitor. He was pale. His hair, distressingly, was sensibly brushed back from his forehead. He looked almost respectable, like someone who hadn't known him had prepared him for his coffin.

Valkyrie realised her hands were shaking. She clenched her fists to stop it.

For five years, she hadn't had to visit anyone in hospital. For five years, she'd been away from beatings and stabbings, from murders and plots. She hadn't missed any of it, and yet she'd come back. She'd walked back into this world of violence and pain and death and suffering, and she'd done so fully aware of what could happen. She couldn't explain why.

"Hey," Fletcher said. He was smiling.

She walked closer. "How're you doing?"

"Good." His voice was weak. "But the knife did a lot of damage, so I have to stay very still for everything to settle back into place. I am so incredibly bored."

"I'd say so."

"How are you? I heard what happened to Skulduggery."

"Yeah," she said. "I'm OK. I'll get him back."

"I don't doubt it. Who was it stabbed me?"

Valkyrie sat on the chair beside his bed. "His name is Nero. A Teleporter. I don't know how he did it, how he followed you. I've never even heard of that before."

"Me either," Fletcher said, "and I've read practically every book written about Teleporters. Not that there are many. There are, like, four."

"You've read four books?"

"I've changed," he said, and smiled again.

"Thanks, by the way," she said. "For coming to get us like you did. You saved our lives."

"I'd blush, but I doubt I have enough blood for it. Besides, I didn't have a choice. The call came in that Skulduggery Pleasant and Valkyrie Cain were in trouble and what was I going to do, ignore it? You were my first love. I had to go charging to the rescue."

"My hero."

"Yeah, I'm awesome. Hey, hope you don't mind me saying this, but you look... sad."

"I'll be fine. Skulduggery being gone... it's temporary. That's all."

"He'll come back to you," said Fletcher. "If anyone can snap him out of whatever it is that's affecting him, it'll be you."

"Yeah."

"How you doing, Val? Really?"

She looked away, then back. "Not good," she said.

41

She said her goodbyes to Fletcher and walked towards the exit. She was almost there when the doors opened ahead of her and Temper Fray and Omen Darkly hurried in from the street. She stared.

"I heard what happened," Temper said, his face still puffy from a recent beating. "What's the plan?"

Valkyrie blinked at him. "What?"

"The plan," he repeated, like he was talking to a four-year-old. "To stop them from resurrecting Abyssinia. What is it?"

"I don't... I don't know what... Temper, how are you still alive?"

"Omen rescued me," Temper said.

"Omen's supposed to be in school."

"I'd never have thought Skulduggery would shoot you," Temper said. "I mean, not *actually* shoot you. Not *you*."

Valkyrie shook her head. "Wait, stop, we're not finished talking about this. I'm glad you're alive and everything, but Omen, Skulduggery told you to stay out of it from now on, didn't he?"

Omen nodded, like the guilty schoolboy he was.

"Again, I'm glad Temper isn't dead, but this isn't a game we're playing."

"I know," Omen murmured.

"I don't think you do. Look at me. Look at the fear in my eyes. You think any of this is fun?"

"No."

"This isn't your fight. It isn't your job to deal with these psychos and it isn't your job to rescue people, as pleased as I am that Temper is alive."

"You keep saying that," Temper said. "I don't think I believe you any more."

"I'm sorry I disobeyed Skulduggery," said Omen, "but I really want to be a part of this. It's my one chance to be someone."

"You're fourteen," Valkyrie said. "You have plenty of time to be someone. You don't belong out here. You belong in school."

"Hey," said Temper, putting an arm round Omen's shoulders, "show my boy here some respect. He saved me, Valkyrie. He hitched a lift with Nero, came into the lion's den, sneaked by all the nutcases, freed me from my prison cell and then saved me from getting my ass kicked. It's because of him that I got back in one piece. He can handle himself, OK? Which is more than either of us have done lately."

"He's a kid."

"So were you."

"And look at me now. Seriously. Look at what all that action and adventure has done to me. I'm a frickin' basket case. My best friend has been taken from me and I'm barely holding it together. I've got parents who worry about me and a little sister I never see because I don't deserve her love. My life is a mess, Omen. For the last five years, I've cried myself to sleep and practically every morning I've woken up screaming. I feel myself dip into these pits of sadness and I can see it coming, but I can't do anything about it, and every time it takes me just a little bit longer to climb back out. Is that what you want? Is this the kind of adventure you're looking for?"

Omen didn't respond.

"Have a normal life," Valkyrie said. "Please. Just walk away. Leave it all behind. Leave magic behind. Live as a mortal. That's what I'd do, if I could do it all over again."

"I don't believe that," said Temper.

"And it's a good thing I don't care what you think."

"We could do with his help, Valkyrie, seeing as how we are so vastly outmatched as it stands."

"Well, why stop there?" she asked. "Why stop with a fourteen-year-old? Why not get a couple of toddlers to draw enemy fire? Why not have an entire brigade of babies and idiots?"

"I'm starting to feel a little insulted," Omen said quietly.

"And where did this *we* business start, anyway?" Valkyrie demanded. "We're not a team, Temper. Skulduggery and me, *we* were a team. But I barely know you, and I hardly trust you."

"Skulduggery trusted me."

"Did he? You sure about that?"

She brushed by them both, heading for the exit. Her leg was getting better, her limp less pronounced.

"Lethe told me that Smoke's power corrupts the soul," Temper said, "not the mind. I couldn't tell the difference, to be honest, but that's how they got Skulduggery, in case you were wondering."

Valkyrie stopped. "He got you, too?"

"Of course," said Temper. "Why torture me for information when they can turn me and just ask? I told them whatever I knew, which wasn't a whole lot, and then they put me in chains."

Valkyrie turned, switching on her aura-vision, taking in the glowing warmth of Temper's aura. "You're clean," she said.

"Sorry?"

Her vision returned to normal. "Smoke's corruption, it's not affecting you any more."

Temper frowned. "I know. It only lasted two days or something. Wait, you can *see* that? You can see my soul?"

"I can see... something," she said. "An aura. It's colour, mostly."

"What colour do you see?"

"Orange."

"Is that good?"

"I don't know if it's good. But it's normal."

Temper came forward. "I'm sorry that you don't trust me, and maybe you're right not to. I've done some pretty questionable things in my life. But I don't need to see auras to know I can trust *you*. I know they're looking to use Doctor Melior to bring back someone called Abyssinia, and I doubt that'd be good news for anyone but her, so I'm here to help however I can."

"I'm here to help, too," said Omen. "I know you think I'm a kid, and I know you want me to go away, but I can be useful. I need to do this. You said your parents are worried about you. Mine barely even notice me, and when they do it's to criticise me and call me names. I've never been a part of something like this. Please, let me continue. I'll stay out of trouble, I swear. I'm not going to get hurt."

"You don't know that," Valkyrie said. "For all you know, this is the first step on a journey that will end with you dying in a street somewhere, in your brother's arms."

Omen swallowed. "If that's my destiny, then that's my destiny. But at least I'll have one."

"You've got our help," Temper said, "whether you want it or not. So what do we do?"

She frowned. "Why are you asking me?"

"You're Valkyrie Cain, aren't you? If Skulduggery Pleasant isn't here, you're in charge. What do you think, Omen? Does that appear to be the hierarchy?"

"It does," Omen said, his voice cracking as he came forward. He blushed, and cleared his throat. "I mean, yes. It does. Skulduggery, then Valkyrie, then you."

Temper nodded. "And then you."

"Me? Really?"

"Of course. You've earned your place as fourth in command."

"Wow." Omen beamed. "Thanks."

"You're fourth in a group of four," Valkyrie pointed out. "You're in charge of no one."

Temper slapped him on the shoulder. "Don't you listen to her, slick. You're in charge of yourself and, in the grand scheme of things, that's the only authority worth having. So, Valkyrie, what's our next move?"

Valkyrie took a deep breath, and let it out. "I don't know. What would Skulduggery do? He'd kick down a few doors until a lead presented itself."

"And where's the first door we kick down?"

"I suppose... San Francisco? Maybe? If we can find out where Richard Melior and Savant Vega lived while they were there, we might find someone who knew them, and knew Lilt, back when they were all friends. If we find a lead to Lilt, we're closer to finding a lead to the anti-Sanctuary."

"Huh," said Temper.

Valkyrie sighed. "It doesn't make any sense, does it?"

"No, it does."

"But it won't work, will it?"

"There's no reason why it shouldn't."

"Listen, if you two have any better ideas, please share them. Any ideas at all. In the slightest. Either of you. But maybe not you, Omen."

"Yeah," Omen said.

"You probably wouldn't have anything useful."

"Probably not."

"Don't want to be rude."

"It's not rude if it's true."

"Temper? Do you have anything?"

Temper shook his head. "Nothing better than what you got. Kicking down doors sounds good to me."

"It's a terrible plan."

"It's our only plan."

"On the bright side," said Valkyrie, "China's people might locate Coldheart Prison any moment now, and when they do they'll storm it and it'll all be over and none of this will matter."

"Exactly!" Temper said. "The fate of the world might *not* be resting on our shoulders. We just have to keep reminding ourselves of that." He looked at them both and smiled. "I don't know about you two, but I am *pumped* for this. Really. I'm not even being sarcastic. Not even a little. At all. In the slightest."

42

Whatever disagreements Skulduggery had with China meant little or nothing now, and Valkyrie sat with the Supreme Mage on the highest balcony overlooking Roarhaven and told her everything. China listened and nodded and asked clarifying questions, and when Valkyrie was finished a silence settled and Valkyrie felt relief. Relief that she had unburdened herself, relief that the problem was shared and relief that someone else could take charge from this point on.

It was raining. From up here, the streets looked slickly smooth, the rooftops polished to a slippery gleam. People hurried, wearing coats or carrying umbrellas or manipulating the rain to divert around them. She could hear the faint splashes of cars driving through puddles. It was wet and cold everywhere but on the balcony – on the balcony it was warm and dry.

"Abyssinia," China said. "I never thought I'd have to speak that name again."

"Skulduggery said you were friends."

China's eyebrow raised a fraction. "That's a strong word. But maybe, yes. How much did he tell you about her?"

"Enough to scare me."

"If you're only scared, he must have left out some of the more unsavoury aspects of her story."

"She was that bad?"

"She was worse."

"Has Lilt said anything about her?"

A flicker of annoyance passed across China's flawless face. "He is proving to be most obstinate," she said. "Our Sensitives are having trouble getting past his defences. He's already sent the City Guards into a booby-trapped apartment – it was a miracle no one was killed. I can arrange for you to see him, if you want. Maybe he'll talk to you."

"You've got trained investigators," Valkyrie replied. "You should stick with them."

"Lilt won't even *talk* to them any more. He knows about Smoke turning Skulduggery. Maybe he'll want to gloat about it. It might be an opening you can use."

"China, I really don't think that's a good idea."

China stood up, walked to the edge of the balcony and looked down, then turned. "What's wrong with you?"

Valkyrie blinked. "I'm sorry?"

China waved a hand at her. "This. You. What's wrong? What happened to turn you from the feisty warrior I knew and loved to the nervous, apologetic woman I see before me?"

"I quit," said Valkyrie. "That's what happened. I walked away."

"Why?"

"How can you ask me that? You know why. You were there. You saw what Darquesse did to this city."

"Yes," China said. "I saw what Darquesse did. Not you. *Darquesse.*"

"Everything she did is on me."

"You don't believe that. You can't. If you believed that, you wouldn't be able to get out of bed in the morning. The guilt would have already hammered you into the ground. Do you bear some responsibility? Yes. But not all of it. Not even most of it."

"Even some of it is enough."

"You're lying."

Valkyrie stood up. "Excuse me?"

"You're lying," China repeated. "What else happened? What did you do that made you walk away?"

"Being responsible for the deaths of over a thousand people whose names and faces I will never know... that isn't enough for you?"

"It isn't."

"Then I don't know what to say to you, China. I don't know how I can—" Her voice caught suddenly, and tears came to her eyes.

China waited.

Valkyrie swallowed and looked away again, feeling the sting in her throat that warned her she was about to cry. She growled instead, and that made China smile.

"That's a little of the old Valkyrie," she said. "You always did hate to show weakness."

But Valkyrie shook her head. "Wasn't weakness I hated," she said. "It was losing control." She swallowed again, took a deep breath and blew it out slowly. "It wasn't the thousand faces I didn't know. It was the one face I did." Valkyrie put her hands through her hair, fixing it, recognising even as she did so what a transparent attempt at nonchalance it was. "I needed the Sceptre of the Ancients to fight Darquesse, but it was bonded to my sister."

"And you couldn't use it until it was bonded to you," China said slowly. "So you..."

"I killed her," Valkyrie said. "She was dead for a few seconds, long enough for the bond to be severed. I used the Sunburst to revive her, the Sceptre bonded with me and I used it against Darquesse. All's well that ends well."

"It must have been an unimaginably difficult thing to do."

"To murder my sister? I've done easier things."

"But you revived her."

"But I murdered her. You can say your part as much as you like – my part will always be louder. That's why I walked away."

"And yet you came back."

"That may have been a mistake."

China folded her arms, her chin dipping to her chest. "What you had to do, for the greater good, was horrible. So, if you've lost your nerve, tell me. Just tell me and get it over with. I'll hug you and send you on your way. I'll give you a squad of Cleavers to protect you until all this is over, and we'll stop them from resurrecting Abyssinia ourselves." She raised her eyes. "Is that what you want, Valkyrie?"

Valkyrie looked away. "Might be for the best."

China shrugged. "If that's true, say the word and it'll be done. Say yes."

Valkyrie opened her mouth, but the word was taking its time to build.

"You mentioned the trained investigators I have on the City Guard," China said, "like they'd notice something you wouldn't. Like they'd be better than you. You seem to have forgotten that you were trained by the best."

"I'm not a detective, China."

"Your badge says differently."

"I can't do this without him. You know that."

"You don't have a choice. Skulduggery Pleasant is your enemy now. You've never faced anyone like him before. But he's never faced anyone like you, either."

"He'll kill me."

"He'll certainly try."

"China, I appreciate the vote of confidence, but I don't stand a chance against him. The moment he decides to end the game, I'm dead."

"You know him better than anyone. You know him better than I ever did. With Skulduggery on their side, the anti-Sanctuary will succeed. Abyssinia will be resurrected and, if she wants war, she'll have war. She'll lay waste to everything. The entire mortal world is in danger. That means your family, Valkyrie. We have one chance to stop them, and that chance is to stop *him*. You're the only one who can do that."

"No, I'm not. Get Saracen Rue and Dexter Vex back here. Find Tanith, wherever the hell she is. Call Gracious and Donegan off whatever adventure they're on right now and put guns in their hands. That's what you need. You need a team."

"We need you," said China. "I'll ask Gracious and Donegan to help you if you need them. I'll try to find Rue and Vex, but the last I heard they weren't on good terms. You don't need Tanith Low, but Roarhaven needs you. I need you, Valkyrie. And Skulduggery definitely needs you. He abandoned his family crest because of the things he'd done during the war, and he's spent the time since looking for redemption. How do you think he'll take it if he kills someone while under Smoke's influence? Do you think he'll forgive himself?"

"China..."

"This is a burden. I understand that. You wish you could just walk away. I understand that, too. I'm offering you that chance right now. Tell me you want to go. Say yes, and you'll get a Cleaver escort home. But, if you can't say yes, then find that girl you once were and be her again. We need *that* Valkyrie Cain. I'm sorry, but we don't need *you*."

The rain got heavier. Valkyrie watched it hit the shield surrounding the balcony, the drops hissing, steam rising. Cleavers wouldn't be able to save her, not if Skulduggery came looking, and there wasn't anywhere she could run that he wouldn't be able to follow. She felt like she was on a sinking boat. Her only hope, as much as it scared her, was to dive into the churning waters before the boat took her down with it.

"I need Richard Melior's old address back in San Francisco," Valkyrie said. "I looked it up in the Neoteric Report, but all contact details have been blacked out."

China nodded. "I'll get it for you."

"And I'm going to need a Teleporter. A healthy one."

"Difficult," said China. "There are only three in the world that I know of, plus this Nero and one of Fletcher's own students. Maybe I can organise something. If not, you'll have access to my jet. You also have the entire City Guard at your disposal if you need them."

Valkyrie shook her head. "Skulduggery didn't trust them. That means I don't, either. No offence."

China hesitated. "Of course."

"But I might need Cleavers. Lots of them. At a moment's notice."

"I can give you a sigil," China said. "It can be both a distress call and a homing device."

Valkyrie hesitated. "Sure," she said. "So long as it can't track me without my knowing."

China tapped her forefinger and it began to glow. "You can activate and deactivate it at will," she said. "It's a small sigil, easily concealable. Where do you want it?"

Valkyrie sat again and leaned back, hooked a thumb into the waistband of her jeans and pulled it down to her hipbone. China got to her knees and pressed her fingernail into Valkyrie's skin. It was hot, very hot, but not entirely unpleasant.

"Why did he really quit as City Guard Commander?" Valkyrie asked as China worked. "What did he do? What did *you* do?"

China focused on the tattoo she was carving and didn't look up. "He felt his time here was at an end. I was sorry to see him go."

Her fingernail curved around and then slashed backwards slightly. A dot here, a cross there. Incredibly intricate markings. No blood.

"You didn't answer my question," Valkyrie said.

"Some questions are not mine to answer." China glanced up at her with those beautiful eyes. "Skulduggery has his reasons, Valkyrie. I might agree with some of them, I might disagree with others, but there's no arguing with him. You know that."

She went back to work. Moments later, she was done.

"It's called an auxilium," China said, straightening up. "It's from a time when all sigils had a Latin name. What a dreary time that was. Anyway, tap it and I'll know you're in trouble and where to send assistance."

The sigil was black and small, maybe a couple of centimetres in circumference. The skin sizzled a little, and a second later the tattoo faded away.

"Thanks," Valkyrie said, and stood.

"Detective Cain of the Arbiter Corps," China said. "Good to have you back."

43

He was going to kill her. He was going to torture her. He'd make Valkyrie Cain scream and cry and beg. He'd draw it out. Make it last. He was going to enjoy it, too. Killing her would be his most enjoyable murder since the first, all those years ago.

Cadaverous sipped from his glass of water. Thoughts like that made his mouth dry and his heart beat faster.

The others talked. They sat around the table, located in Coldheart's only conference room, and chatted – Nero and Memphis and Razzia – but Cadaverous stayed quiet. It wasn't that he couldn't chat – he could chat with the best of them. He was the master of small talk. He'd had to be, back when he'd been mortal, having to go to all those insufferable social engagements. Book launches for stale academic tomes. Office parties. After-work drinks. He'd been pretending the whole time, of course, hiding his hatred behind a smile or a witty remark. That's how he'd blended in. That's how nobody suspected anything – not until the very end.

But these days he just wasn't in the mood to talk, to chat. Not since Valkyrie Cain had killed Jeremiah.

Skulduggery Pleasant walked in, went right up to Nero. "May I?"

Nero laughed, and the chatter died down. "May you what?"

"Sit."

Nero indicated around him. "There are two free chairs."

Pleasant nodded. "And I want your chair. May I?"

Cadaverous watched. Such an obvious alpha-male ploy. If Nero had any sense, he'd call it out for what it was and refuse to budge.

But after a long moment of hesitation Nero got up, and Pleasant sat, leaned back and put his feet up on the table. Nero chose one of the other chairs, blushing impotently.

"Now then," Pleasant said, "you probably dislike me intensely – I can understand that – but let's try to move past it as quickly as possible. Who's in charge here? Anyone? It doesn't matter. Allow me to put my name forward as leader of this anti-Sanctuary of yours. It'll save time and prevent a lot of arguments later on. Really, a lot. All those in agreement say aye."

"Aye!" shouted Razzia.

"Thank you," said Pleasant.

"No worries," Razzia said, grinning. "What were we talking about? I wasn't listening."

"That barely matters," Pleasant said, taking off his hat. "A vote from you, a vote from me, and the rest have abstained out of sheer respect. I thank you all. It has been decided."

"I'd heard you didn't quit talking," said Memphis, in that half-slurred, half-drawl way of his. "I just didn't believe it."

"Ah-*ah*, young man," Pleasant said, wagging his finger, "I hold the Speaking Hat. You may not speak without holding the Speaking Hat. That's one of the new rules I'm introducing as leader."

"You ain't our leader."

"Again – Memphis, is it? – who holds the hat? Who does? Me, that's who. Talking privileges are mine. This way we'll all get a chance to be heard eventually. It's called being civilised, which is something else I'm introducing."

Memphis shook his head. "This is ridiculous."

Cadaverous had to hand it to the skeleton, he had style. He didn't even take his feet down. He used the air to boost himself up to a standing position on the table, whipping his gun out as he did so, and took two steps before pointing the gun right between Memphis's eyes. It all took less time than a hiccup.

There was shouting and roaring and consternation – and much laughter from Razzia – but Memphis remained very still, the colour draining from his face.

Finally, everyone else stopped making idiots of themselves, and things quietened down.

"The only thing ridiculous," Pleasant said softly, "aside from your garish jacket and uneven pompadour, is the blatant disregard for the rules of debate. When I am finished talking, you may retort. Otherwise it ceases to be about the content of our conversation, and becomes little more than a contest in volume. Would you agree?"

Memphis didn't say anything. Pleasant let go of his hat, and it floated slowly down to the table. Memphis swallowed, and picked it up. "Yes," he said.

Pleasant put away his gun. He walked back, jumped down and retook his seat, then indicated to Memphis that he should continue.

Memphis cleared his throat. "Not many folks get to pull a gun on me, man. Most who try end up deader than disco. I'm going to kill you for that, just so you know."

Pleasant nodded.

Memphis cleared his throat and adjusted his position. "What I was saying was that you ain't our leader. We don't even trust you. Smoke can do his thing and compel you to obey and all, but I'm sure someone like you, someone who reckons he's the smartest guy in the room, could find loopholes in his orders. You want a vote? My vote is we take care of business, and kill you *now*."

"I agree," said Cadaverous.

Pleasant flicked his hand, and his hat leaped from Memphis's hands and whirled across the table, landing in Cadaverous's lap. It was a good hat. Expertly made, like the black suit he wore. Cadaverous threw it behind him, aware that it didn't even touch the ground before Pleasant used the air to catch it.

"There are plenty of ways to kill a dead man," Cadaverous said. "Give me a day. I'll figure it out."

"Crush his bones," said Memphis.

"Dump him on the moon," said Nero.

Pleasant shook his head. "I don't know what you're all finding so hard to grasp about the principle of the Speaking Hat."

The door opened and Lethe walked in. He stopped when he saw their new addition. "Ah," he said. "You're here. Welcome."

Pleasant plucked his hat from the air. "Thank you."

"It's an *honour* to have you here," Lethe went on, sitting at the table. "You are a *legend*, Skulduggery. The things you've done, the feats you've *accomplished*... It humbles me. I may have beaten you in single combat, but please know that I am *in awe* of you. You have my *utmost* respect."

"That's nice of you to say."

"You know everyone here, I take it? Small talk has been exchanged?"

"To a degree. So do I get to see it?"

"See what, Skulduggery?"

"The little box," said Pleasant, "with the little heart."

"You'll see it when you've proven yourself. When we can *trust* you. You must understand, Skulduggery... we *know* what you're feeling right now. You're *confused*. You have all these *dark thoughts* in your head."

"I'm used to them."

Lethe laughed. "Maybe you are. Maybe. But not like this. Not... *concentrated* like this. It can be overwhelming. The urge to destroy *just* to destroy... it is a *powerful* urge."

Pleasant tilted his head. "You think I'll turn against you."

"It's possible," said Lethe. "These urges can make people do terribly *destructive* things, not always in our *favour*. And if that happens we'll *kill* you, naturally, but I'm hoping that you'll decide to *join* us. All we want is our rightful place as *kings and queens* of this world. Wouldn't you love to walk through *O'Connell Street* or

Times Square or *Piccadilly Circus* without bothering with your false face? Isn't it time that sorcerers like *you* and Neoterics like *us* stopped hiding away from the *mortals*? Isn't it time we took up our *crowns*? Maybe you don't agree. Maybe you're happy where you are."

"I've never had a problem with the mortals," Pleasant said. "One of my best friends was a mortal."

"So you're *not* going to help us?"

"I didn't say that. Those dark thoughts you mentioned, they're doing quite a number on my morality, such as it is. There are all kinds of people I suddenly want to kill, mortals included. I'll help you, because I like your plan and I'm interested in seeing if it'll work, but I have one condition. More of an unbreakable rule, actually. Valkyrie Cain is mine."

"Ah," said Lethe. "Yes, we *thought* you might bring this up. Valkyrie Cain, *unfortunately*, is already promised to *Cadaverous* here."

"And I'm not letting her go," Cadaverous said.

Pleasant turned his eye sockets to him, and Cadaverous could see the light reflecting on the inside of his skull. "You blame Valkyrie for your friend's death."

"Jeremiah Wallow," Cadaverous said. "He had a name."

"And yet, the way Valkyrie tells it, Mr Wallow fell. She didn't push him. She didn't kill him."

"She's responsible for his death."

"So is gravity, but you're not out to kill gravity, are you? Your friend is dead, you're angry and upset, you want someone to blame. Perfectly understandable, if completely redundant. Your sadly deceased friend's own clumsy incompetence does not guarantee you the right to Valkyrie's life. It just doesn't."

"I've already staked my claim."

"Calling shotgun does not guarantee you a front seat, Cadaverous. We're not children here, are we?"

"Skulduggery," Lethe said, "I'm afraid we *have* already agreed that *Cadaverous* kills Valkyrie."

Pleasant went quiet for a moment, and sat back, steepling his fingers. "I'm trying to decide," he said.

"Decide what?" Lethe asked.

Pleasant stood, and took out his gun. "Which one of you I kill first."

"Sit down," said Smoke, walking into the room, and immediately Pleasant sat. It was a petty joy that leaped into Cadaverous's heart, but it was a joy, nonetheless.

"How's it feel," Nero asked, "to be his puppet?"

"This is an odd sensation," Pleasant muttered.

Smoke sat at the table. "I control you. You do what I tell you. If I instruct you to dance for us, you'll dance for us. If I instruct you to only talk in rhyming couplets, that's what you'll do. You are mine – you understand that? You have no free will when it comes to me."

"This is interesting," Pleasant said. "But I'm afraid it's completely unacceptable." In a flash, the gun was pointed straight at Smoke's head—

—but Pleasant's finger froze over the trigger.

Smoke sighed. "You think you're the first person to try that? Seriously? You can't and won't hurt me. Put the gun away."

"But of course," the skeleton said, holstering the weapon inside his jacket like it was his own idea. Cadaverous found that vaguely annoying. "Where were we?"

"I was about to suggest a *compromise*," Lethe said, "regarding this whole *killing Valkyrie* disagreement."

Cadaverous leaned forward. "No compromise," he said. "We had a deal."

Lethe held up a hand. "You both will *refrain* from killing her until, at the *earliest*, the resurrection of Abyssinia. The moment is *close*, but has yet to arrive, and who knows *what* will happen before then? If only *one* of you reaches the moment, you get to kill Miss Cain. If *both* of you survive until then, you'll *fight* for the honour."

Cadaverous frowned. "In a place of my choosing?"

"You were *first* to make the claim, so yes."

Cadaverous smiled. "Deal."

Pleasant shrugged. "I'm in," he said, and clapped his hands. "So, what's the next step?"

"First Wave," said Lethe. "This is a crucial juncture and they need *guidance*. They need *Parthenios Lilt*."

"He's being kept in a cell in the High Sanctuary," Pleasant said. "Do we break him out?"

"That won't be necessary," Lethe responded. "We have our *man on the inside* who can take care of this for us."

Pleasant tilted his head again. "Who?"

"A man on the *inside*," Lethe repeated. "You don't have to worry about *that*."

Pleasant shrugged. "If you have a secret you want to keep, then you keep your secret. Just tell me what you want me to do. How about the Soul Catcher that Melior's going to need for the resurrection? I happen to know where we could pick one up without too much trouble."

"Again," said Lethe, "that is *already* taken care of. We have one that Destrier is *adapting* to Doctor Melior's *specifications*. *Your* job, Skulduggery, will be to track down a *Neoteric*. The good doctor reckons he'll need the life force of two *sacrificial lambs* for the ritual to be successful, but I think *three*. It's better to *have* a sacrificial lamb and not *need* it, than *need* a sacrificial lamb and not *have* it. Memphis and Nero, you'll be going after the *first*. Smoke and I will go after the *second*. Skulduggery... you'll be teaming up with *Cadaverous* here, and you'll bring us back the *third*. Is that OK with you?"

Pleasant spread his arms wide. "I'm part of the team, Lethe. I'll do whatever I'm told."

"Wait a second," Razzia said, frowning. "How come I don't get to play?"

"Well," said Lethe, "*someone* has to stay here and make sure

Doctor Melior doesn't go anywhere and Destrier doesn't accidentally suck everyone's *souls* into a *snow globe*."

"You better not be assigning me babysitting duties because of my gender," Razzia said, getting to her feet slowly. "I may be a very nurturing person by nature, but I will kill every ratbag at this table if you think you can—"

"It's nothing to do with your *gender*, Razzia," Lethe said, hands up in a calming gesture. "And it's got nothing to do with your *nurturing nature*. It's your *murderous* nature that disqualifies you from this assignment. It's imperative that *each* of the sacrificial lambs is brought back *alive*."

Razzia paused. "Alive?"

"Yes."

"Not dead?"

"No."

She sat back down. "Not dead, not interested."

"And *that's* why you don't have to go."

"Sweet."

Pleasant rubbed his hands together. "I like this," he said. "The interplay. The camaraderie. It's almost like what I have with Valkyrie, except much, much less. Cadaverous, I know we're going to have our differences on this, but I want you all to know, from the bottom of the place where my heart used to be, that I'm really looking forward to killing Valkyrie." He clapped, once and happily. "This is going to be *fun*."

44

Valkyrie approached the Museum of Magical History from the east, walking quickly with her hands tucked into her pockets. It was another cold damn day in a cold damn week at the end of a cold damn month. She was tired of the cold. She was quite ready for it to be warm again. People were nicer when it was warm. Moods were lighter, and they lifted on the tides and eddies of warm air.

Her phone buzzed. A message from her mum. She opened it. A picture of her sister wielding lipstick and her father in the background, the lower half of his face smeared bright red. Her mum had written *Waiting for her next client* across the bottom of the image. It was funny. Cute. Valkyrie stared at the screen for half a minute, thinking up a reply. In the end, she sent off a *LOL* and put the phone away.

Militsa Gnosis was waiting for her at the entrance to the museum, shuffling from foot to foot in a feeble attempt to keep warm. She waved when she saw her, and Valkyrie gave an awkward wave back.

"Hi," Militsa said. "Thanks for coming. Isn't it freezing?"

"So cold," Valkyrie responded. "You didn't have to wait outside, you know."

"Ah, just wanted to make sure you found the place OK."

"Your directions did the job. So have you figured it out?"

"I'm sorry? Figured what out?"

"How to break Smoke's influence over Skulduggery."

"Oh," said Militsa. "Well, that's... Without being able to examine any of the..." She faltered. "That's not why I asked you here. I'm sorry."

The spark of hope, slight though it was, died in Valkyrie's chest. "OK," she said. "That's fine. So why are we here?"

Militsa's smile reappeared. "Come on in."

She took Valkyrie's hand and led her quickly up the steps and in through the door. Immediately, Valkyrie began to warm. The man behind the reception desk nodded to Militsa like he knew her well, but when his gaze flickered to Valkyrie he froze. Militsa missed it entirely, and Valkyrie ignored it.

"Would it be incredibly lame," Militsa asked as they followed the signs to the East Wing, "to admit that museums are some of my favourite places in the world? It probably would, wouldn't it? You don't even have to answer that. I know it is. I wish I hadn't said anything now. I mean, it's not *only* museums that I like. I like ordinary places, too, like libraries, and I'm quite partial to a good gallery. And ice-cream parlours."

"I like ice cream," offered Valkyrie, and Militsa beamed.

"See? We have something in common!"

"Are we here to look at an exhibition?"

"I'll get to that, I will. This way."

They took the doorway to their right.

"Isn't this wonderful?" Militsa asked. "Mementos of significant people and significant times in history all laid out for us, like knowledge waiting to be absorbed. Fair enough, it's not as impressive as the Repository at the High Sanctuary and all the powerful artefacts *that* contains, but it's still pretty mind-blowing, is it not?"

Valkyrie passed an old pair of eyeglasses that once belonged to Jorge Desesperación (1781 to 1918).

Militsa stopped suddenly, and turned. "Am I being awful? I'm being too chirpy, aren't I?"

Valkyrie took a moment to answer. "No," she said.

"It's just, I don't know what to say in situations like this. Not that I've been in many situations *exactly* like this. But you know what I mean? When I'm around people who are sad, I feel a ridiculous need to cheer them up, but I always make it worse. I think I'm just too obvious about it, and also I tend to tell people what it is I'm trying to do, like I did just there. The moment I do that it's game over, you know? Oh, God. I just did it, didn't I?"

"You're doing a good job," Valkyrie lied. "You're distracting me from my worries."

"I am?"

"Yes. Especially now at this moment."

"Oh, that's a major relief, I don't mind telling you. I was getting worried because you've barely said anything."

Valkyrie gave a small smile. "That's just me being me. I take a while to loosen up around new people."

"And are you loosened up yet?"

There was so much hope in Militsa's voice that Valkyrie just had to say, "Yes. Totally."

Militsa beamed again. "Then do you have any questions for me?"

Valkyrie nodded stiffly.

"Go ahead. Ask me anything."

"OK," said Valkyrie. "Right. I will. How, uh... How did a Necromancer end up as a teacher?"

"I went to university and got my degree."

Valkyrie nodded again. "I was actually expecting a more involved story."

Militsa made a face. "I know. It's pretty boring. I taught English at mortal schools and that was fine and all, but then I heard that there was an actual school for sorcerers being built at Roarhaven and I moved here immediately, started teaching Magic Theory. I suppose I've always wanted to be a teacher. Probably the same way you always wanted to be a detective."

"I, uh, I never wanted to be a detective."

"Really? Never?"

"Well, I didn't grow up wanting this. When I was a kid, I didn't know what I wanted to be. I wanted to ride horses, then for a whole summer I wanted to be an Olympic swimmer... Then Skulduggery came along and... ta-da."

"I keep forgetting you grew up mortal."

"You didn't?"

"My folks're both sorcerers. I knew about magic from the time I knew about shapes. Mum and Dad, they're nice people, so I was taught we're all equal. Though I did meet some sorcerers who held quite a different opinion."

"I suppose one group of people will always find reasons to complain about another."

"Aye, I suppose. But this new strain of hatred... that's only cropped up in the last ten or fifteen years. It's scary. Insidious."

"So the sorcerers hate the mortals," said Valkyrie, "and the mortals would hate the sorcerers if they knew we existed. This is a story that can only end well."

Militsa smiled. "As long as there are people like you and Skulduggery Pleasant fighting the good fight, we should be OK."

"Well, that's just it, isn't it? We don't have Skulduggery any more."

"I realised that just as the words were leaving my mouth. Really sorry. How are you doing?"

"I'm OK."

"It can't be easy."

"He's not an easy man to out-think."

"I actually meant that it can't be easy losing a friend in this way. How are you doing about that side of things?"

"Oh," said Valkyrie. "It's..."

"Yes?"

"Scary," Valkyrie said at last. "Not just having him as an enemy, but... not having him as a friend. Even when I was away, I knew

I could pick up the phone and he'd answer. I knew he'd always answer. I was never alone, you know? Never."

"This may be completely presumptuous," Militsa said, "but you're not alone now, either. I'll help however I can. I'm not the best at fighting, I really don't like hurting people and I have a serious aversion to being the one who's getting hurt, but if you need someone to stand there and lecture the enemy on Magic Theory then I am your girl."

"Thank you for volunteering," Valkyrie told her, "but don't worry, I'm not going to hurl you into a pit of danger or anything like that. Helping me out here will do fine... assuming this museum visit *will* help me out?"

"Hopefully," Militsa said. "Well, I don't know how helpful it will actually be, in any useful sense, but, as my old piano teacher used to say, knowledge is power."

"Was she a sorcerer?"

"No, just a piano teacher, back in Edinburgh. I'm really not sure what she was talking about, but it's a good motto to live by. When we were on the phone earlier, you described what one of the anti-Sanctuary people was wearing – the guy in the mask?"

"Lethe."

Militsa nodded. "Lethe, right. Now, I might be wrong, in which case this is a colossal waste of your time, but it sounded a lot like..."

They quickened their pace.

"It sounded a lot like...?" Valkyrie prompted.

"I thought it was closer," Militsa said apologetically. "Ah, here it is."

They came to a glass case, in which stood a mannequin dressed in a jumpsuit. The material on the outer layer, a deep grey, was tattered, burnt and slashed, barely held together in places. But beneath that was something that wasn't quite leather and wasn't quite rubber. It was black, and ribbed slightly. The boots were sturdy and the gloves were thin, and beneath the hood the mask was a shocking white against all that darkness – a stylised, angular skull with glass-covered eye sockets.

"That's it," Valkyrie breathed. "That's what he wears. The mask is different, it doesn't have the hood or the fabric over it... but that's it. What is it?"

"It's a necronaut suit," Militsa said proudly. "Necromancers used them for Deep Venturing. That's what they called it. It's when they would explore the realms of death."

"Solomon Wreath told me about that. Entirely dead dimensions, right? Where nothing could ever possibly live?"

"Not even Necromancers," Militsa said. "So they wore these when they went exploring. They're built to... I don't know the best way to describe it. They're built to *contain*, I guess. Like a Thermos flask keeping in the heat, although, when you're Deep Venturing, you want to keep in your *life*. When it's all done up like that, you don't need food or oxygen... you don't even need to take a pee. Which is simultaneously fascinating and gross."

"So Lethe's a Necromancer?"

"Maybe," Militsa said, "but not necessarily. I've seen necronaut suits repurposed for a whole range of different things. Apart from anything else, they're pretty durable. Bulletproof and fire-resistant, that kind of stuff."

"I'm guessing the answer is probably no, but do they have any glaring weaknesses to exploit? Like the way vampires are allergic to salt water?"

"They're not, actually."

"I'm sorry?"

"We've recently discovered that it's a certain amount of sea salt they're allergic to, not the actual salt water."

"Oh. Right. But... the suit?"

"No real weakness that I know about," Militsa said, "but it's not indestructible. It's bulletproof, though probably not as durable as the armoured clothing you used to wear." She frowned. "Why aren't you wearing those, by the way?"

"They were getting a bit snug."

"What's wrong with snug? I like snug. They looked really good on you."

"Thanks. So Lethe might not be using the suit for any specific purpose – he might just be using it as armour."

"It's a possibility."

Valkyrie nodded as they started walking back. "Well, every little bit of information we get is useful. And what about the reason I called? As the resident expert on Magic Theory, I was hoping you had some thoughts on how to break Smoke's hold."

Militsa sighed. "I'm sorry, no. I'll do more research into it, but from what you've told me about how it infects the aura... I don't know if there'd be anything you could do to cleanse it. We're not talking New Age hippies waving around cheap crystals here."

"But Skulduggery's different. His aura is unlike any I've seen."

"Valkyrie, that might not be a good thing. Yes, it might mean that he overcomes the infection quicker than the forty-eight hours – or it might mean the opposite, or it might make no difference at all. There's no way to tell. The fact is, we know very little about magic as it is. We've only just identified the gene that separates sorcerers from mortals, but we still don't understand how it leads to us being able to access magic. Not really."

"Is there anyone else we could talk to?"

Valkyrie could tell Militsa wanted to be able to give her hopeful news. It was in every helpless shrug and pained expression.

"Possibly," she said at last. "There's a team of some awesomely brilliant people running tests on the Source itself. They've located what they think is one of the fissures that allows magic to flow through into our reality. It's going to take them years of study, but they might have a theory about this. If I can get in touch with them. It's all very top secret."

"Could you try? I could ask China to help."

"That might not be the best thing to do," Militsa said. "The

Supreme Mage doesn't particularly trust Necromancers any more. It was hard enough getting her to accept me as a teacher. I'd probably be better off trying to get in touch with them myself."

"We don't have an awful lot of time, Militsa."

"I'll do my best. I promise."

Valkyrie's phone buzzed, and she glanced at the words on her screen. It was the address in San Francisco.

"Good news?" Militsa asked.

Valkyrie shrugged. "Depends on how many people I have to punch."

45

They emerged into the cold again and Militsa waved down a tram. "I'm heading back to the school," she said. "You?"

"High Sanctuary."

"That's where this line ends."

"Lead the way," Valkyrie said, and jumped on after Militsa.

The tram was, thankfully, well heated, and pretty empty. They chose the long seat down the back. A woman hugging her shopping bag to her chest glared at Valkyrie, who did her best to avoid her eyes.

"Excuse me," Militsa said loudly. "Can we help you?"

The woman muttered something under her breath, and looked away.

"I'll probably have to get used to that," Valkyrie said.

"You shouldn't have to," Militsa responded.

Valkyrie gave a half-shrug. "It's the least I deserve."

Militsa went quiet for a few minutes. The ride was smooth, the tram gliding through the streets, only stopping to let passengers alight.

"Was that a lead?" Militsa said at last.

"Sorry?"

"The message on your phone. Was it a lead?"

"Yes. An address I've been waiting for."

Militsa smiled. "See? Look at you, doing the detective stuff. You can't tell me you don't enjoy it."

"I enjoy it a lot more when I have Skulduggery with me. There's a very small group of people I like to spend time with, so I'm not looking forward to this next part at all. I don't even know if I'll be able to trust the Teleporter China sends me."

"Then use another."

"There aren't really any others, apart from Fletcher. I know one of his students can teleport, but we've already put one Corrival pupil in danger, and I don't want to do it again."

Militsa's friendly demeanour suddenly cooled. "I'm sorry?"

"Uh..."

Militsa turned in the seat to face her. "You put a Corrival Academy student in danger? Which one?"

"I, uh... I really shouldn't say..."

"Auger Darkly?"

"No," Valkyrie said, drawing the word out.

Militsa's eyes widened. "*Omen?*"

Valkyrie winced. "How did you know?"

"Omen's an easily distracted boy, but for the last few days he's not even been on the same planet as the rest of us. How much danger was he in?"

"Uh..."

"Oh, Valkyrie," Militsa said, wilting back into her seat. "You may have been able to handle a life of adventure at that age, but—"

"I know."

"Omen's a good boy. He's a gentle boy. And why go for him, why not his brother? I shouldn't be recommending any student for this kind of thing, but Auger is the Chosen One, after all. He's used to it."

"Auger was too well known. We needed someone to blend into the background. In our defence, and I accept that we don't have much of a defence, we honestly didn't think it would get dangerous."

"How dangerous did it get?"

Valkyrie hesitated. "Pretty."

"And what's that, on a scale of one to ten?"

"Like... two."

"Oh. OK. Well, that's not that bad."

"If ten is no danger at all and one is all the danger."

Militsa's hands went to her face. "Oh, Valkyrie... Omen's a kid."

"I know. If I could go back, I wouldn't do it. We had no right to involve him. It was a hideous, horrible thing to do, but we did it anyway because we needed it done. That's not an excuse, that's just a fact. But as awful as I feel about it, as much of a mistake as I think it was... Omen saved a life."

Militsa looked up. "He did?"

"A friend of ours. Well, a friend of Skulduggery's. Omen went into the enemy stronghold, found him and freed him."

"Omen Darkly did that?"

Valkyrie nodded. "It's the kind of thing that I did at his age. I think he'd surprise you. He sure as hell surprised me."

A smile was born, and grew across Militsa's face. "Well now, I guess it runs in the family. But that's it, isn't it? His involvement is now over?"

"That's what Skulduggery told him."

"Good."

"And Omen ignored it, which is something else I would have done at his age. He wants to be a part of this, Militsa. I don't agree with it – or at least I didn't. But am I really that hypocritical? I was doing this stuff when I was younger than him. When I was his age, I was fighting fully grown men. Yeah, I got my ass kicked. I got hurt. It was terrifying and dangerous and stupid... but I did it. I handled it."

"Omen isn't like you."

"He could be. Any kid could be. Who are we to say who would or would not rise to the challenge?"

"Valkyrie, I'm an educator. My job is to prepare these kids for life after school. My job is to keep them safe."

"Life after school isn't always safe, not for sorcerers. Keeping them protected from danger, not exposing them to the threats they'll have to face eventually... isn't *that* irresponsible?"

"No," Militsa said. "That's reasonable."

"But wouldn't you have loved it when you were fourteen?"

"That's... that's not the point. If the basis for all decision-making is what you would have liked to happen when you were a teenager, we'd be living in a pretty hedonistic world right now."

"And what a happier place that would be."

"You're not going to convince me, Valkyrie. Kids shouldn't be wrapped in cotton wool, but neither should they be dangled over the jaws of danger."

"But you're OK about Auger Darkly getting into danger all on his own?"

"Auger is... different. His family trained him from birth. He was brought up to do this kind of thing."

"Omen was there, too. He trained beside his brother, didn't he? Just because he hasn't had a chance to show it yet doesn't mean he hasn't got what it takes."

"I think you're probably biased."

"Maybe," Valkyrie said. "But I am who I am today because of doing stupid things in my teenage years."

"And how's that working out for you?"

Stunned, Valkyrie turned away.

"Oh, no," Militsa said. "No, I'm so sorry, I didn't mean that. I didn't mean it like that, Valkyrie, I'm so sorry."

"It's OK."

"It's really not." Militsa grabbed Valkyrie's hand in both of hers. "Please, I didn't mean it. It's just something I blurted out without thinking. It was meant to be smart and arch and it was just... it was cruel."

"It's fine," said Valkyrie. "And you're right."

"No, I'm not."

"I'm not exactly a well-adjusted adult, Militsa. I can't focus. I can barely use my magic. I don't even know what my magic is any more. And I'm scared. All the time, I'm scared."

"But you're a good person, doing good things."

"Debatable."

"You're a hero, Valkyrie. You were a hero to me when I was a kid, hearing about all those things you were doing. You can't imagine how much that meant to me, to know that there was someone my age out there, making the kind of difference you were making."

"It left scars."

"Everything leaves scars. You just can't see most of them. I'm really sorry I said what I said. Can you forgive me?"

"Of course."

"Thank you. And maybe... maybe you have a unique perspective because of everything you've been through. When it comes to Omen and what he can handle, maybe you know best."

"He only wants to be involved. I think it's the least I can do."

The tram stopped outside Corrival Academy, and Militsa stood. "Come on."

Valkyrie frowned. "I'm heading on to the High Sanctuary."

"To meet a Teleporter you don't know? No, no, you're getting off with me." Militsa pulled Valkyrie from the tram a moment before it started moving again. "Omen has a friend who is Fletcher's best student. If you need a Teleporter you know you can trust, Never is the one for you. Providing you can offer me some guarantee regarding the safety of my students...?"

"I can guarantee their safety," Valkyrie said, "up to a point."

"That... doesn't reassure me."

"They'll be fine," Valkyrie said. "I'll have another adult with me to supervise. We'll keep them as safe as we can and as far from danger as we can manage. Trust me."

46

"We're going to die," Never whispered.

"We're fine," Omen assured her. "Just act natural."

"Jenan knows we know. Is he looking over? He's looking over here."

"He's looking at the clock."

"What does he have in his hand? Is it a knife? Is it a gun?"

"It's a pen."

"What's he doing with a pen?"

"His homework, I think."

"Quiet down there," Mr Chou said, not even looking up from the papers he was marking. The study hall was only half full. Whispers carried.

Never lowered her head until her forehead was resting on the desk. "Why did you tell me?" she asked quietly. "Why did you even tell me about the anti-Sanctuary and people trying to kill you? I was happy being ignorant. Why did you tell me?"

"Because you said we shouldn't keep secrets from each other."

"I meant other secrets. Crushes on people, things like that. Regular secrets, Omen. Not *actual* secrets."

"I promise you, you're not in any danger."

She turned her head, glaring at him. "You don't know that. I might be putting myself in danger just by talking to you right now."

"None of the bad guys know who I am."

"But they saw you. They saw your face. What if one of them is a sketch artist? And he showed the drawing to Jenan, and Jenan said, yeah, I know that guy, he's an idiot, but he has a cute friend. Let's kill them both."

"Never," Mr Chou said, and Never sat up straight. "Omen. You may not think it, but my ears actually work, you know."

"Can you make out what we're saying?" Never asked.

Mr Chou sighed. "No. Your undoubtedly riveting conversation is lost to me. I will take that regret to my grave. But I can hear your murmurings and I can see your lips move. This is study hall. Either study, do homework, or at least work harder at disguising the fact that you're doing neither."

"Sorry, sir," said Omen, and made a point of looking like he was studying his textbook. Chou sighed, and went back to marking.

"There's so much I have yet to do in this world," Never whispered. "So much I have yet to experience. I've never opened a savings account. I've never studied for my driving test." Her head dropped forward again. "I've never filed a tax return."

"You're very strange."

"Don't judge me."

"Your life isn't in danger. I'm pretty sure they're not going to let me continue doing what I've been doing, so you can relax, OK? No one's going to come looking for us."

The door opened, and Miss Gnosis stepped in. "Excuse me, Mr Chou," she said in that distinctive Scottish accent, "could I borrow Omen and Never, please?"

Omen frowned while Never paled.

"Take them," Chou said, waving a hand. "You have my blessing."

Miss Gnosis smiled, and motioned them forward. "Come along," she said. "And bring your things."

Omen hesitated, then slid his textbook into his bag and stood. Taking great care not to even glance in Jenan's direction, he led

284

Never out of the classroom. When they were in the corridor and walking away, Miss Gnosis lowered her voice.

"You're in trouble," she said.

"I knew it," Never whispered.

Omen's mouth was dry. "What did we do?"

Miss Gnosis strode ahead, and it was all Omen and Never could do to keep up. "Don't play that game with me, Mr Darkly. I've had quite an afternoon, hearing about what you've been getting up to. And during school hours and everything."

"I... I don't know what you..."

"You're turning into as much of an adventurer as your brother, you know that?"

"Miss Gnosis," Omen said, choosing his words carefully, "are you going to kill us?"

She glared. "By the dead, no. What do you think of me, you silly boy?"

"Just checking, miss."

They stopped at their lockers. "Go on," she said. "Put your bags away. We don't have long."

They did as they were told, and moved on quickly to the science lab. Miss Gnosis nodded to the open door. "In you go," she said.

Never frowned. "You're not coming in with us?"

"I'm keeping watch," Miss Gnosis said. "And, before you go in there, remember: you don't have to agree to anything. No one will think any less of you. Go on now."

Puzzled, Omen and Never walked in, and Miss Gnosis shut the door after them. Valkyrie Cain stood up from the teacher's desk at the head of the room.

"Omen," she said. "And you must be Never. It's very good to meet you."

Never froze. Whether Valkyrie noticed or not, Omen didn't know, but she continued talking anyway.

"I'm not going to waste your time," she said. "I need your

help. Both of you. It won't be dangerous – at least, I don't think it will. I need to go to San Francisco. I need to talk to some people, maybe search a house. Then come right back. Never, Militsa tells me you're turning out to be a pretty good Teleporter."

Omen frowned. "Who?"

"Miss Gnosis," Valkyrie said. "Miss Gnosis told me, sorry. Never, are you OK?"

Omen put his hand on Never's back. A gesture of solidarity, he hoped. "There's something you should know," he said.

Valkyrie stood there, waiting, but Omen didn't quite know how to put it.

"Darquesse killed my brother," Never said, and Valkyrie's face went slack. "He wasn't fighting her, or anything. He was the age I am now. He didn't have a clue what was happening. A building fell on him."

"I'm... I'm sorry," Valkyrie said softly.

"Killed him instantly," Never said. "We'd just moved here. We'd been here a week. My brother was so excited about living in Roarhaven. We all were. We'd always wanted to live where we wouldn't have to hide who we were."

Valkyrie swayed slightly, like she was light-headed. "I'm... Do you mind if I sit?"

"I'd prefer that you stand, actually," Never said. "It's the least you can do, isn't it, when we're talking about my brother?"

"Never..." Omen said quietly.

"No, she's right," said Valkyrie. "Carry on, Never."

"Thank you, Valkyrie. I know Darquesse isn't you. We all know how it happened. Kind of. They teach us it here, did you know that? But they leave some bits out, such as exactly *how* your reflection malfunctioned so badly. I think they don't tell us that bit because they're afraid we might try something similar with our own reflections. Which is a bit of a laugh, to be honest. I mean, why would we want to copy something that murdered so many innocent people?"

"I never meant for any of it to happen," Valkyrie said.

Never nodded. "That bit they *do* tell us. They say that Darquesse became Darquesse because of a series of totally random circumstances that Valkyrie Cain had no control over. But I think you did have control – you just decided not to use it."

"That's not true."

"Wasn't there a prophecy, or something? Didn't the Sensitives have dreams about Darquesse, years before it all kicked off?"

Valkyrie stood up a little straighter, though it looked like something was twisting in her gut. "Yes," she said.

"But when you found out that Darquesse was your true name, that *you* were Darquesse, you didn't stop, did you? You didn't walk away and never use magic again – even though you'd had warnings that Darquesse would, at some stage, kill the world."

"I thought I could stop it from happening."

"But you didn't."

"No."

"You failed."

"Yes."

"You should have walked away, but you loved it too much. You loved being the hero. You loved hanging out with Skulduggery Pleasant and Tanith Low and the Dead Men... you loved hanging out with people like Billy-Ray Sanguine, a known murderer. You loved the adventure."

"I did."

Never nodded. "My mum met you once. You wouldn't remember – it was only for a few minutes. It was at the Requiem Ball. She says you were one of the most arrogant people she'd ever talked to. She said you were so young and full of confidence, and you looked at all the other sorcerers like you were so much better than them. She said she knew right then that you were trouble. Just trouble, waiting to happen."

"I'm not going to argue with you, Never."

"Could you argue, even if you wanted to?"

"Yes. Some of your points I would very much argue. But not the main point. The main point is that I'm responsible for what Darquesse did. That I failed to stop her in time. That haunts me. She haunts me. I'll never be able to forget that."

"You should just kill yourself."

"Never!" Omen said, shocked.

"I thought about it," Valkyrie said quietly. "When it would get too much for me, I'd think about it."

"I wish you'd done it," Never said.

"I hated myself too much. I needed to suffer. Ending my life would have ended my pain, and I couldn't allow that to happen."

"I hate you, too."

"I can see that. But I need your help."

Never laughed. "You really are as arrogant as my mum said."

"I'm trying to help people. I'm trying to save lives. I don't know if Omen has told you anything about what's going on, but Skulduggery Pleasant is no longer on our side."

"I heard."

"Then you know what's at stake."

"If you need a Teleporter, go to the High Sanctuary."

"I don't trust them."

"I don't trust you."

"Do you trust me, Never?" asked Omen. She looked at him and he saw the anger in her eyes. "I don't know what it's like to lose a brother. If I lost Auger, I don't know what I'd do. So I don't know what you've been through, or what you're going through now. But this isn't about Valkyrie. This is about saving people. If the anti-Sanctuary succeed here, they'll be one step closer to war with the mortals."

"You want me to help *her*?"

"I want you to help *me* help her."

"So you're going, even if I don't?"

"If Valkyrie will let me... yes."

"You can come," Valkyrie said, "and help me search. But, if anything goes wrong, you're out of there. No arguments."

Omen nodded, and looked at Never.

"Fine," she said. "I'll come. But only because she'll probably get you killed without me."

"Do you know San Francisco?" Valkyrie asked.

"Mr Renn has taken us to all the major American cities," she said. "I've been there before so I can get there again."

"We'll leave in ten minutes, if you want to change out of your uniforms."

Never shrugged, and walked out. When the door was swinging closed again, Omen spoke.

"She's a really good person," he said. "She's just angry."

Valkyrie gave a sad smile. "Thanks, Omen, but you don't have to explain. She's entitled to how she feels. Go on now, grab a change of clothes and I'll meet you back here."

Omen nodded, and left the room. He hurried to the dorms, got changed into jeans and a hoody, then swapped that for a shirt and pulled on a heavy jacket, and ran back.

He didn't get far before Jenan stepped out ahead of him.

"Where are you skipping off to?" he said, stepping closer.

Omen backed off. "Just... Just down there."

"Just down there? What's just down there? Eh? Why are you out of uniform? Where are you going, Darkly?"

Omen stopped backing away, and puffed his chest out. "None of your business, Ispolin."

Jenan charged, got a hand round Omen's throat and slammed him back against the wall.

"Get off me!" Omen gasped, trying to pull the hand away.

"I know it was you," Jenan said, right in his ear. Omen stopped struggling. "I should kill you. I really should. I don't know, I haven't killed anyone before. The idea... it's kinda scary. I'm just being honest with you here, Darkly. It's a big step to take. But I think killing you would be easier than killing someone that matters.

I mean, I doubt your folks would even notice. Your brother would be sad, so that's another reason to do it, to ruin the big shot's day. Killing you would be easy. How would you feel about that? How would you feel about being my first?"

Omen tried to bury his fear. "They're using you. Lilt and Lethe and the others. They're using all of you. They're telling you that you're special and they're making you feel like you belong, but they're lying to you."

"This is weird," Jenan said, his voice soft, almost dreamlike. "It feels... freeing. I've made the decision, you know? I'm going to kill someone. I'm going to kill you. I've been waiting my whole life to get to this point. I have, I don't mind saying, fantasised about what comes next. I have imagined so many scenarios, so many situations, so many faces... But, since the first time I met you, I think I've known it would be you. I think I always knew it'd be your face. I just want to thank you. I'm sorry I was so mean to you. I'm sorry I picked on you. I shouldn't have done it. It was wrong, and I'm sorry."

Both hands now, wrapped round Omen's throat. Squeezing.

"I should have tried being friends with you," Jenan whispered. Tears were in his eyes. "Thank you for doing this. Thank you for being the one."

Omen couldn't breathe. Jenan's grip was too strong.

"I love you for doing this, Omen. Thank you."

And then, just as the darkness was crowding in on Omen, there was space between them, and Jenan was being pulled backwards, a look of utter astonishment on his face.

"One of you had better tell me what's going on here," Miss Wicked said. "Omen, are you all right? Can you talk?"

Omen sucked in air and did his best to stay standing. It felt like someone was still strangling him.

Miss Wicked turned to Jenan. "This is it, Mr Ispolin. I don't care who your father is or how many strings he pulls, I will personally see to it that you are expelled from Corrival Academy."

But Jenan wasn't listening to her. Omen could tell. His eyes were clouded with disbelief. "How could you do that?" he asked. "How could you stop me?"

"Report to the Principal's Office immediately," Miss Wicked said.

"How could you stop me?" he shouted, and his fist cracked into Miss Wicked's cheek, sending her back a step.

From the look on his face, Jenan had expected her to go down, but after that single step Miss Wicked didn't even sway on her high heels. Jenan stepped in and swung again.

Miss Wicked barely moved and Jenan flew past her. Omen jumped clear as he spun. Jenan's next punch was redirected, his arm twisted, his face slammed into the wall. He lashed out and she guided him to the floor quite firmly. He landed and bounced slightly, the air knocked out of him.

"Omen, report to the nurse," Miss Wicked said, hauling Jenan to his feet. "Your throat looks like it will bruise."

"I'm OK," Omen said, his voice a whisper.

"The nurse, Omen," Miss Wicked said. "Now."

She didn't wait to see if he headed off in the right direction, she just twisted Jenan's wrist and he howled, and she led him away.

Omen doubted he'd ever seen anything as cool.

47

"My car is better," Pleasant said. "I don't mean to offend you. Your car is fine, and I admire the fact that you went to the trouble of transporting it across the Atlantic... but was that really the best use of anyone's time? A Cadillac is a fine car, but a Bentley... A Bentley has character."

"And where is your Bentley?" Cadaverous said, unlocking the Cadillac. "Is it back in Roarhaven? It is? Then I guess, all things considered, that my car is the superior vehicle."

He got in behind the wheel. A moment later, Pleasant curled his long frame into the passenger seat. He put his hat on his lap and buckled his belt.

"This is an odd sensation," he said. When Cadaverous didn't respond, he continued. "I'm used to driving, that's all. Of course, this is a left-hand drive car so I'm still sitting on my usual side, which alleviates the problem somewhat. But even so, I'm used to being in control. It's quite discomfiting to *not* be in control. It's not a feeling I'm used to. Maybe it would be a good idea if I drove?"

"Only I drive this car," Cadaverous said, pulling away from the kerb.

Pleasant nodded. "And I totally understand that. I do. However, I'm used to driving on this side of the road, so maybe it'd be safer for us both if I—"

"Only I drive this car."

Pleasant looked at him, then shrugged. "OK." He settled back into his seat. "Fine."

They turned left at the junction, joined the fast-moving traffic.

"If you tell me where Tanner Rut is living," Pleasant said, "I could just fly there. I can do that, you know. Fly. I could fly there, grab him, take him back, or fly there and wait for you, if you really want to be involved..."

"I'm not letting you out of my sight," Cadaverous said. "I don't trust you, skeleton."

"I am deeply offended by that, Cadaverous. I have been a loyal member of this team for almost twenty-three hours now. Does that bonding-time mean *nothing* to you?"

"Abyssinia doesn't trust you, either."

"Abyssinia and I have history. Did she tell you about that? No? Ah, so she's keeping something from her minions. That's interesting."

"I don't care."

"No? Are you sure? It's salacious. I stole her heart, you see. I stole it and I put it in that box. My point is, yes, she may have some trust issues with me, but time heals all wounds, Cadaverous. I have a feeling when we bring her back all will be forgiven, and, once that happens, you're really going to want to be on my good side. So what do you say? Will we be friends?"

"That will never happen."

"Do I detect a hint of growing admiration in your voice?"

"You're a ridiculous creature," Cadaverous said. "You're a bad vaudeville act. You belong on stage."

"That wasn't a no."

"I've known people like you my entire adult life," Cadaverous said. "Puffed up with their own sense of importance, inflated by their own so-called genius. Arrogant and pompous."

"You have formed an opinion of me."

"I have."

"I have formed one of you. Would you like to hear it?"

"I couldn't care less."

"I know you, Cadaverous. You think I don't, but I do."

"You know nothing about me."

"No?" Pleasant said. "But maybe I knew someone just like you. Except his name wasn't Cadaverous Gant – it was Charles Grantham, a retired professor of English at a semi-prestigious New England university. He'd written a few books of poetry, but nothing that set the world on fire. Truth be told, his poetry was lazy and uninspired. Hackneyed, I believe was the popular opinion among his peers."

Cadaverous's hands tightened on the wheel.

"At age seventy-eight, Charles apparently flew into a fit of rage after listening to a so-called 'street poet' reinterpret the works of Keats. Charles tried, unsuccessfully, to strangle this street poet, and suffered a heart attack as a result. While he was recovering in hospital, police raided his home. Interesting thing about his home – he'd had it built by three different builders. None of them knew what the others were doing, but Charles knew. There were corridors that went nowhere, doors that opened on to brick walls. There were secret passageways and pits. How many people did you kill in that house over the years, Cadaverous? Was it more than the police believed? Was it more than forty-seven? How many of them were your students?"

"You think you know it all," Cadaverous said.

"I know Charles Grantham disappeared," Pleasant replied. "The house had been searched illegally – everything in there was inadmissible in court. A few months later, Professor Grantham was gone. Is that when Abyssinia first spoke to you? Is that when Cadaverous Gant was born?"

Cadaverous slowed at the lights. A part of him, a significant part, had no desire to answer. Satisfying the skeleton's questions was not something that interested him. Another part, however, had been snagged, as if Pleasant's words were a hook cast into the still lake.

"It was the heart attack," he said, accelerating again. "When I woke up, I could feel magic. I could *feel* it. Do you have any idea what that's like, to get old, to watch your own body betray you, only to find out that you could have stopped it? That you could have stayed young forever?"

"I'd imagine that would have upset just about anyone, let alone a serial killer."

"You can't reduce my life down to a label like that."

"Why not? You reduced forty-seven lives down to nothing."

"They were cattle," Cadaverous said. "Each of them had a sad little existence that I ended. Each of them had stumbled through their lives with blinkers on. They didn't appreciate the world. They didn't appreciate art, or poetry, or the beauty in the everyday. Every single person I killed, every single one of them, deserved to die. They were small. They were meaningless."

"Unlike you."

Cadaverous nodded. "Unlike me."

"And then Abyssinia spoke to you, did she? And took you under her wing..."

"Is that what you did?" Cadaverous asked. "After we went after Valkyrie Cain, you investigated me?"

"After she sent you packing, yes, I did."

"You were coming after me, were you? For daring to harm your precious Valkyrie?"

"But I couldn't find you," said Pleasant. "So I waited. And finally here we are."

"Are you going to kill me now, skeleton?"

"I'm not sure," Pleasant said. "It would certainly be easy enough. According to Valkyrie, you're stronger and faster than you look, but outside your home, you're just as vulnerable as anyone else."

"You wouldn't last a minute in my home."

"I was there," Pleasant said. "Your house on Lombard Street. Valkyrie described it as a hellish inferno with metal catwalks and chains everywhere. She mentioned a bottomless pit of fire. And yet when I walked through it twelve hours later it was a nice, ordinary suburban house. Quite boring, actually. We demolished it."

"It doesn't matter," said Cadaverous. "My home is where I make it, and I am king of my domain."

"What an unusual power."

"Like I said, you wouldn't last a minute."

"So, if you invite me in, I'm to politely decline?"

"You wouldn't get an invitation."

"Even so, I'd just decline."

"You can't decline an offer you haven't received."

"I can pre-empt it, though."

"You can't pre-empt an offer you're never going to get."

"Not if I decline it before—"

"Stop it," Cadaverous said sharply. "Just stop it. Seriously. I'll drive us off a cliff if you continue this... this... whatever it is. We're not talking nonsense, do you understand me?"

"Sure," Pleasant said. "Of course. My apologies. I just get overly chatty when I feel like I'm not in control of the situation."

"You're not driving my car."

"Just a little bit."

"Stop asking me."

"Fine," said Pleasant, and sat back. "I'll try to enjoy the journey, then, shall I? Apparently it's not the destination that matters – especially when you travel with friends."

48

Never teleported them to the roof of the Golden Gate Bridge Welcome Center and immediately they ducked down. It wasn't a tall building, and a single glimpse would be all it took for the dozens of tourists to look up and point, and then for the cops to come investigating.

This was Omen's first time in America. Crouching down, with Valkyrie and Temper on one side and Never on the other, he focused on not being sick from the journey while he looked out at the suspension bridge that spanned the water. He was struck by how big it all was. The bridge. The skyline behind him. The sky.

"The bridge is one point seven miles long," said Never. He was wearing scuffed jeans, a hoody and a jacket. Omen should have worn his hoody under his jacket. It was cold up here. "It opened in 1937. That colour? It's called international orange."

"Why do you know so much about it?" Omen asked.

Never shrugged. "It's a bridge. I know stuff about bridges."

They teleported on to the grass behind some trees, and Omen threw up. He apologised profusely, and when he was done they walked to the roadside. Valkyrie hailed a cab and they climbed in, Valkyrie in front. The driver chatted and Temper chatted back, but Valkyrie stayed quiet and Never looked out of the window. Omen knew he was committing as much of their surroundings to memory as he could. That was one of Fletcher Renn's rules.

Omen had once wanted to be a Teleporter. The power to leave whenever he wanted appealed to him when he was growing up, watching all the attention being focused on his brother. Not in an entirely good way, of course. He knew, from the not quite disguised looks that would flash occasionally across Auger's face, that such attention was more burden than gift. All that training, all that testing, all those expectations... On someone weaker – Omen, for example – it would have proven too much. But Auger handled it the same way Auger handled everything, with charm and good humour.

But alas, teleportation was not to be for the younger Darkly twin. For a start, every competent Teleporter who'd ever lived had been born with the aptitude. To someone like Never, teleportation was instinct, albeit instinct he needed help channelling. Never's discipline – for there was no doubt in anyone's mind that Never would choose teleportation – was a part of who she was. Omen's was still a mystery. There was nothing yet that he could truly claim to excel at – even his Elemental skills were lagging behind those of his classmates. He liked the various languages of magic, he supposed, but that was mostly because he liked to read.

The drive to Haight Street only took a few minutes. Omen stepped out in front of a brightly coloured store brimming with psychedelic positivity, and Never nudged him, directing his attention to the multitude of exotic pipes in the window. Far out, man.

Valkyrie wasn't here to enjoy the scenery, and Temper was too busy adulting to show interest, so they walked ahead, going uphill, closing in on the address while Omen and Never followed along behind. An old guy with dreadlocks rocked by, moving to some internal rhythm only he could hear, and a small pack of street kids, lounging on someone's front steps, ignored them with such professional detachment that even Never had to raise an eyebrow in admiration. A dog sat beside a white and red fire hydrant, like it was considering whether or not to mark its territory. It watched them walk on.

They crossed the street and arrived at a fenced-off piece of flattened ground. Valkyrie looked at the map on her phone, checked all around, then stared at the empty space before them.

"Well, crap," she said.

"You're sure this is it?" Temper asked.

"I'm sure. Even if I wasn't sure, I'd know this is the place we're looking for simply because it's not here any more, and of course it wouldn't be here any more, because that's how life works. Just when you think it couldn't possibly suck any more than it already sucks, it burns down the goddamn house."

"Oh, that house didn't burn down," said an old woman, passing. "It was demolished years ago."

Temper gave the old woman a smile. "You live near here?"

"I live *right* here," the woman said, pointing a pale, knobbly finger at the house next door. "Do you know them, then?"

"Who, Richard and Savant?" Temper asked. "We do. In fact, we're trying to find them. You wouldn't happen to know where they moved on to, do you?"

"Maryland or Maine, somewhere like that, I think. After they were gone, squatters moved in and let the house fall into disrepair, and then the bulldozers came and flattened the whole thing. How are they doing, do you know? They were such lovely neighbours."

"They're fine," Temper assured her. "We just lost touch. We were hoping to find some clue as to where they might be living now, maybe track down some of their friends – but obviously that's not going to happen."

"I guess not," said the old woman. "But you could always check their things."

Valkyrie frowned. "What things?"

"Their possessions," the old woman said. "I went in there and packed up as much of their stuff as I could fit into their suitcases. The squatters were nice enough, I guess, but they didn't respect other people's property as much as they should have."

"Can we see it?" Valkyrie asked. "Can we look through the suitcases?"

"If you're friends of Richard and Savant, I don't see why not." She led the way to her house. "That's a nice accent you've got, by the way. Irish, is it? My grandmother was Irish. I was named after her. Bridget."

"I'm Valkyrie. This is Temper, Omen and Never."

Bridget beamed. "What delightful names! Your parents must have been hippies. We get that a lot around here. Come on in. Wipe your feet."

She took them into the back room of her warm house, which smelled of old people and cookies. Three suitcases were stacked in a wardrobe so big it could have opened up into Narnia. The case Temper searched contained nothing but clothes, but the cases that Valkyrie, Omen and Never looked through were full of papers and notebooks and pictures.

Never examined a framed photograph of two handsome, smiling men. "Which is which?" he asked.

Temper reached over, tapped the image of the slightly better-looking one. "Savant," he said.

"Lovely men," Bridget said, hands clasped over her bosom. "They'd do anything for you. I used to have terrible trouble with my pipes, and they'd come in here and fix it all up. Wouldn't even let me pay them for their trouble."

"Did you ever meet any of their friends?" Valkyrie asked, sifting through a handful of documents.

Bridget nodded. "All the time. They hosted the best dinner parties, and knew the most fabulously interesting people."

"I know some of those same people," Temper said.

"You do? You don't look half old enough."

Temper chuckled. "I remember them from when I was a kid.

300

A couple of them were a bit much, don't you think? They were a little – I don't know what the right word is... scary?"

Bridget gave a nod so quick she reminded Omen of a bird pecking at a crumb. "A few of them were," she confided, like she'd been given permission to gossip. "A few of them were downright weird – and I know weird. I grew up here. I was living in this house during the Summer of Love. I was a Deadhead. I thought I'd seen it all... but there were one or two of those friends who just gave me the heebie-jeebies."

"Do you remember any names?"

"I'm sorry, I don't. A lot of hippy names, though – that I do remember."

Omen pulled a small photo album from the case and flicked through it. The first third, or thereabouts, was filled with old pictures – black and white and sepia-tinged – of Melior and Vega. The first few were posed and stiff, the pair unsmiling, but gradually they eased, until their smiles were broad and their arms were around each other's shoulders. There was even a kiss here and there. Colour started seeping in as the decades brought their own advancements, and the hairstyles got progressively sillier. One photo, discoloured by age and sunlight, showed Melior and Vega standing with two other men and a woman. The men were all wearing bowling shirts and holding a trophy aloft, and the woman, who had a gigantic Afro and hoop earrings, was laughing. Omen frowned, and looked closer. The man standing to Savant's right was Parthenios Lilt.

"Found something," he said, and handed the album to Valkyrie. Her eyes widened.

"See something interesting?" Temper asked.

For a moment, Valkyrie didn't answer, then she flipped the album so he could see. "Recognise anyone?"

"That's Lilt," Never said, pointing.

Temper's own eyes narrowed. "The woman," he said. "She's an old friend. Her name's Tessa Mehrbano. You know her?"

"Not her," said Valkyrie, "and not Lilt." Her finger jabbed at the image of the small, smiling man next to Richard Melior. "Him."

Temper took a moment, and his eyebrows slowly rose. "Wow. Nice hair."

Omen and Never crowded round.

"Who is he?" Never asked.

Valkyrie pulled the photograph from the album, looking at Bridget as she did so. "Can I borrow this?"

"I guess so," the old woman said. "Is everything OK? You look ill."

"I'm fine," said Valkyrie. "Just eager to talk to some people. Thank you very much for your help."

"Of course," said Bridget. "If you track them down, please tell them I was asking after them. They were such lovely boys."

"We will," said Valkyrie, and led the way out. The moment they were out of Bridget's view – she stood in her doorway, waving as they walked – they dodged off the street, hurrying up the steps into the cover of Buena Vista Park.

Valkyrie spun to Temper. "This old friend of yours, what's her name again?"

"Tessa Mehrbano."

"You know where she lives?"

"Yeah. New York."

"Talk to her. We'll head back to Roarhaven, get things sorted out there. Maybe Mehrbano knows something that'll help us, maybe she doesn't, but it won't hurt to try."

Temper hesitated. "I haven't really been her favourite person for a few years now."

"I doubt you're anyone's favourite person except your own," Valkyrie said, "but you still have to go."

"OK, that was especially harsh."

"Sorry. Didn't mean it. Not thinking straight. Never, take him."

"I'm not a taxicab," Never snapped.

Valkyrie stiffened, and turned her gaze to him slowly. "Take Temper to New York," she said, "then come back for us. When I have time to ask nicely, I will ask nicely. But right now, do what I say or get out of my sight."

Never flushed. "Hey, you're the one who came to *me* for help."

"And if you're going to give that help then you're going to do it without sulking every time you look at me. *Now take him to New York.*"

Glaring, Never reached out and Temper took his hand, and they vanished.

Valkyrie deflated all of a sudden, sagging back against a tree. Omen got the feeling she'd forgotten he was there. A familiar sensation.

"Um," he said.

She looked up. "Yes?"

"I was... I was just going to ask. The guy in the picture. Who is he?"

"You really don't know? Have you ever been to the High Sanctuary?"

"No."

"If you had, you'd have seen him," Valkyrie said. She frowned, and looked around. "Huh," she said.

"What's wrong?"

She hesitated. "Nothing, I just..."

And that's when somebody punched Omen in the back of the head.

49

Valkyrie lunged, trying to catch Omen before he hit the ground, but he'd already face-planted in the dirt before she got anywhere close. He lay there, not moving, and Valkyrie looked around, trying to work out what the hell had happened.

"What's your name, then?"

She spun. The man standing there was a little taller than she was. He wore old jeans and dirty boots. No shirt. He was wiry, his muscles tight. His grey hair was long. Messy. He had a grinning mouth tattooed across the lower half of his jaw. Other tattoos decorated his torso and arms. He was painted like his skin was peeling back, revealing an army of swarming demons beneath the surface.

"Don't suppose it matters," he continued. His accent was New York. "You were asking about the gay guys, which automatically means you get put on the list. Which means I have to kill you." He shrugged. "Hope you don't take it personal." He reached into his waistband, and frowned. "Aw dammit," he muttered, and looked up. "Don't suppose you'd have the loan of a knife or a gun, would you?"

Valkyrie's hand lit up, but the tattooed man skipped forward and slapped her so hard she nearly blacked out. She stumbled sideways instead, went down on one knee, but forced herself up again, keeping distance between them, backing off as he closed in.

"Guess I'll just have to beat you to death," he said, and smiled.

She raised her hand, tried blasting him, but her body wasn't co-operating. By the time her fingertips finally started to tingle, he'd vanished. Teleporter.

She whirled, whirled again, then heard a boot stepping on dried twigs and she turned back to the spot where he'd vanished and there was no one there, but pain exploded across her face and her head snapped back and she staggered, both hands over her face while blood streamed through her fingers. Her nose was broken. The pain was excruciating. Through tear-filled eyes she watched his image solidify in front of her.

Not a Teleporter, then.

"I should have brought a gun," he said. "For the first month or two, I always had a gun on me. But they're pretty heavy, you know? And uncomfortable. So I stopped bringing it. Not very professional, I know, but this isn't a full-time gig for me. I'm being paid to keep an eye on that patch of land and, if anyone comes snooping, I have to kill them. To be honest, you're the first to come snooping. Until now, this has been the easiest money I ever made. Course, it's *still* pretty easy."

Never teleported in and his eyes widened immediately.

"Omen!" Valkyrie shouted, pointing.

Never ran to Omen's side, crouching beside him as he tried to sit up, and Valkyrie bolted towards them. The tattooed man ran to intercept, but Valkyrie's head start was more than enough to keep her out of his reach.

Never looked around, looked right at her with panic in his eyes, and just before Valkyrie could touch him he teleported, taking Omen with him.

Goddammit.

Valkyrie veered away and the tattooed man slammed into her.

They crashed through the undergrowth and tumbled down a small hill, Valkyrie managing to lash a kick into him as they rolled, and the moment she was able to she scrambled up, her right hand crackling.

The tattooed man froze in a half-crouch. "Ah," he said.

"That's a nice trick," she said, "turning invisible. You do it again and I'll fry you."

"Yeah," he said, "I got that."

Her left hand dipped into her pocket, pulled out a few leaves and crammed them into her mouth. The pain dulled, and went away. She used to be so much better at this. She'd snap out a line and be all ultra-cool and her voice wouldn't shake and her hands wouldn't tremble.

Or maybe her voice had shaken, even then. Maybe her hands had trembled. Maybe she had just been better at fooling herself.

"You're going to answer some questions," she said, wiping some of the blood away. "You're going to answer them or I'm going to light you up. My aim hasn't always been the best lately, but I doubt even I could miss at this range."

He gave a little shrug. "I believe in you."

"What's your name?"

"Shakespeare," he said. "Gleeman Shakespeare. Though most people in the press call me Mr Glee."

"Why do people in the press call you anything?"

Another shrug. "Oh, I like to kill people. As a hobby. I sign my name when I'm done."

"So you're a serial killer."

"I guess I am."

"You're not the first one I've met."

"I don't doubt it. Would you like a handkerchief? For the blood? It's clean, I promise."

"Yeah," said Valkyrie. "That'd be good."

Glee produced a spotless white handkerchief from his back pocket, and tossed it over.

She held it to her nose. "Abyssinia sent you to keep an eye on things here, did she?"

306

"Oh, I'm not one of the chosen few who are lucky enough to hear the voice of the telltale heart," Glee answered. "Naw, I get my orders the old-fashioned way, from people who aren't internal organs."

"So Lethe, then. Where are they keeping Savant Vega? Do they have him with them on Coldheart?"

Glee's smile spread beneath his tattoo. "That's on a need-to-know basis, and I am merely an underling, not privy to sensitive information such as that. Pardon me, can I stand? I'm not as young as I used to be and—"

"Stay right where you are."

He sighed.

"So you're saying you don't know anything useful? At all?"

"Pretty much," he replied. "You should probably just let me go."

"Or I could let the High Sanctuary's Sensitives poke through your thoughts."

Glee pulled a face. "Really? They'd have to wear wading boots and come armed with blacklights. It is *messy* in there."

It suddenly occurred to Valkyrie that she had neglected to bring any shackles with her. Yet another small, personal triumph for her to revel in later.

Glee frowned. "You OK, miss?"

"Shut up," she said. "I'm thinking."

"And you're sure I can't move? My legs are cramping something awful."

"Is this the face of someone who cares?"

"I did give you that handkerchief..."

"After you broke my nose."

He sighed again. "Then do you mind me asking what we're waiting for? I mean, are you going to arrest me or not?"

"You tried to kill me. Of course I'm arresting you."

"Right. It's just that you don't *look* like you're arresting me. You *look* like you're trying to remember what you had for

307

dinner yesterday. Or are you deciding if I'm worth the effort of hauling in? Maybe you're wondering if you should just kill me right here. Is that what you're doing? You want to kill me? Fry me?"

"You don't want to be tempting me right now, Mr Glee."

"Could you do it?" he asked, peering closer. "Hell, maybe you could, at that. You got a killer's eyes."

The crackling intensified. "Say one more word and you'll find out."

She heard Never calling her name.

"Down here!" she shouted, not taking her eyes off Glee.

A moment later, Never came half running, half skidding down the embankment, stopping beside her.

"I thought you'd abandoned me," Valkyrie said.

"I was scared," responded Never. "Fear is a magic inhibitor. Everyone knows that. Get over it."

"Should I step away?" Glee asked. "Let you two talk it over?"

"Not an inch," said Valkyrie.

"So what do we do with him?" Never asked.

"I haven't decided yet," said Valkyrie.

Glee smiled at them both, and the energy, which had been crackling so fiercely around Valkyrie's hand, started to fade. She focused, tried to pour more power into her fingertips, but she was overthinking, she was letting her doubts block her instincts, and Glee could see it. He straightened.

"Get us out of here," Valkyrie muttered.

"I... I'm trying," said Never, his hand on her shoulder.

As the energy in her hands crackled out and died, Glee started to whistle a tune, that 'Flowers in Your Hair' song from the 1970s, and then he turned invisible. Keeping Never beside her, Valkyrie backed away.

"Never..."

"I know, I'm trying..."

Valkyrie kept her eyes on the space where the whistling came from, trying to spot a telltale ripple in the air, but the only sign of his movement came from the grass that flattened under his feet. He was coming closer. Closer.

The whistling stopped.

She heard him, heard movement, a sudden exhalation of breath and he was running at her, and she grabbed Never, pulled him behind her and covered up, screwing her eyes shut and clenching her jaw and waiting for the impact, and then the cool breeze went away and no impact came, and she looked up and saw a wall.

"Oh my God, that was way too close," she said, the words tumbling out in one whispered sigh. She looked around. They were back at the school. "Where's Omen?"

"Nurse's Office," said Never.

"Is he OK?"

He shrugged. A couple of kids passed in the corridor intersecting theirs, but were too wrapped up in their conversation to notice them.

"Thanks," Valkyrie said. "I know first-hand how fear and adrenaline can affect your control over magic, so coming back for me took real guts." The handkerchief was sodden with blood. It dripped to the floor. "I need to get to the High Sanctuary as quickly as possible. Can you help me, just a little bit more?"

Never looked at her, and made a sound halfway between a grunt and a scoff. "I'm not a tram," he said, and walked away.

Teenagers.

Valkyrie turned and started running.

Startled students leaped out of her way as she ran, bloodstained and manic, for the street outside. She jumped into the first tram she saw and as it flowed towards Meritorious Square she probed her broken nose, hissing in pain. She did her best to wipe the blood from her face, but avoided her reflection in case she really did look as bad as she thought. When the tram slowed at the square, she threw herself off and sprinted to the steps of the

High Sanctuary. There was a line of Cleavers and City Guards outside, not letting anyone in or out, but when they saw her they let her through without even checking her badge.

She got a few worried looks as she bounded up the steps, but she ignored them and crashed through the doors. Immediately, she was hit by the wail of an alarm, and had to shoulder her way through the massing crowd. Someone's arm tipped against her face and it was like they'd swung a shovel into her nose.

"Move!" she shouted, in exquisite pain and sharp-edged anger. "Get out of my goddamn way!"

Her vision bleached like a washed-out photograph and the crowd parted suddenly, and she caught a glimpse of herself in the large mirror. The lower half of her face was indeed drenched in blood, just like she'd expected, and that blood was still dripping on to her T-shirt, turning it into a sodden mess. But the most startling thing about her appearance at that moment was the white energy crackling from her eyes.

Instinctively, she withdrew her anger, pulling her magic back into herself, and her eyes returned to normal.

She hurried on.

She found China two minutes later, striding through the corridor, surrounded by anxious mages and security.

"Let her through," China commanded, and pulled Valkyrie in beside her as she walked. "My word, you look dreadful."

"What's going on here?"

"Parthenios Lilt has escaped," China said bitterly. "We don't know how it happened yet – all our surveillance has been disabled. It would appear that we have a traitor in our midst. Your nose is broken, by the way."

"I know," said Valkyrie. "And I also know who freed Lilt."

"You do?"

Valkyrie reached out, grabbed the collar of the traitor and dragged him back towards her. Everyone stopped walking, and China leaned in and glared.

"You're going to suffer," she said quietly. "The rest of your life is going to be a catalogue of pain and darkness and suffering, you snivelling little *toad*."

Tipstaff paled.

50

"Some people are just not meant for this kind of life," Pleasant said. This was the thirteenth topic of conversation he'd broached since they'd set off, and it was all Cadaverous could do to not drive the Cadillac off this quiet coastal road. "I've known them, you've known them – it's plain to see. We can pretend it isn't. We can pretend they belong, that they fit... but the truth is like a good trap – inescapable. Take your friend Jeremiah, for instance."

Anger immediately started to flow through Cadaverous's veins. "Be careful what you say about him, skeleton."

Pleasant waved a gloved hand airily. "I have no wish to speak ill of the departed, even though that has never stopped anyone from speaking ill of me. I just wish to highlight the difference between your partner... and mine."

"Jeremiah was a burning light in the darkness."

"He rolled off a metal platform and fell into the fiery pit beneath. He was definitely a burning light somewhere. My point is, we each gave time and attention to someone else. Our positions could very easily be reversed right now – Jeremiah might be the one still living, and Valkyrie might be the one to have died. The difference between them is that Valkyrie was meant for this life. Jeremiah, sadly, was not."

Cadaverous braked. A car behind honked angrily and veered round.

"Jeremiah became my reason," Cadaverous said. "Before I took him under my wing, I was lost. I was despairing. And then I met him, and I recognised that he could be better than I ever was. He just needed the guidance. I know what you're thinking. I know what everyone thinks. Minds go to sordid places. But the bond between Jeremiah and myself was a thing of purity."

"Hey, I'm not judging," said Pleasant. "We have a lot in common, you and I. Especially now, with the overt murderous impulses. But I never took Valkyrie under my wing. She was never my protégée. She was always my partner. She made her own decisions and her own mistakes. Maybe that's where you went wrong with Jeremiah. Maybe you were so focused on teaching him that you never allowed him to find his own place in the world."

"The mistake I made with Jeremiah was not killing Valkyrie Cain the first moment I saw her."

Pleasant chuckled. "Yeah, she has that effect, all right."

Lights flashed behind, and a siren gave a short blare. As Pleasant's façade flowed up over his skull, Cadaverous glanced in the rear-view. Two cops were getting out of their car and approaching.

Pleasant got out first, then Cadaverous. Ignoring instructions to return to their vehicle, they approached the uniformed men. The cops raised their voices and backed away, pulling batons as they did so. Confidence renewed, they came forward now, furious that their authority had been so directly challenged.

The first one swung at Pleasant and Pleasant smashed his face into the bonnet of the patrol car.

"Hey!" the other cop cried, taking his eyes off Cadaverous. Cadaverous grabbed him, crushed his throat and let his body crumple.

"All I'm saying," Pleasant said, his false face slipping away as he got back in, "is that you got unlucky with Jeremiah. He just wasn't cut out for this. Maybe next time, you'll find someone who is."

Cadaverous put the car into gear and they moved off. "Luck

had nothing to do with Jeremiah's death, and you may try to convince me otherwise, but you will fail. Valkyrie Cain is mine to kill."

"That's not going to happen," Pleasant said, and they spoke no more until they found the small house on the very tip of the peninsula and got out of the car. Pleasant put his hat on. The stiff wind didn't even try to budge it. Cadaverous followed him to the front door.

It opened before they reached it, and a man with wild greying hair stepped out. The wind had fun with his hair.

"Tanner Rut?" Pleasant said, walking towards him with his hand extended. "Skulduggery Pleasant, very pleased to meet you."

"You can stop right there, Mr Pleasant," said Rut, and Pleasant duly stopped. "I haven't had any visitors in over thirteen years. I got used to the solitude. I liked it. Now you two. A skeleton and an old man. I've heard of the great Skeleton Detective, of course, but what about you, old-timer? Got a name?"

"Cadaverous Gant."

"Never heard of you."

"Nor should you have."

"What do you want?"

"We need you to come with us," said Pleasant.

"What if I don't want to?"

"We'll have to insist."

Rut shook his head. "I got nothing to do with the Sanctuaries," he said. "I stay out of their business, and they should stay out of mine. I'm a natural-born sorcerer."

"We're all natural-born sorcerers," said Pleasant. "The word you're looking for is Neoteric."

Rut laughed. "That's a stupid name. I just use magic differently from you Sanctuary types, that's all. Either of you want any tea? I'm making tea."

"I don't drink," said Pleasant.

"I'll have some tea," said Cadaverous.

Rut nodded, and walked into the house. Cadaverous and Pleasant followed. A small house, the kitchen part of the living room. Cold in here, despite the roaring fire. They watched him fill the kettle and put it on to boil.

"What are you going to do," Rut said, "if I resist?"

"We'll drag you," said Pleasant. "Or carry you. Politeness is not our primary concern."

"Yeah? Then what is?"

"You just have to be alive when we deliver you."

Rut looked at them both with narrowed eyes. "This isn't Sanctuary business, is it?"

"No," said Pleasant. "It is not. To be honest with you, the Sanctuaries don't even know you exist. I had to hear about you from a gentleman named Lethe, who claims you're something of a serial killer. Is that true?"

Rut shrugged. "Used to be."

"You gave it up, did you? Realised it wasn't for you?"

"It was a phase, I think. It passed."

"You killed eighteen people."

Rut shrugged again, didn't offer up an excuse. "Are you here to kill me?"

"Well," said Pleasant, "not *us*..."

Rut poured boiling water into twin mugs. "Milk?"

"No," said Cadaverous.

"Sugar?"

"I changed my mind. I don't want tea. I just want to get out of this decrepit shack before I start inhaling spores."

Rut dropped the mug, and dived behind the counter.

"This is ridiculous," Cadaverous muttered, going after him.

Rut emerged with a goddamn scimitar in his hand, a gigantic curved sword with an extravagant golden hilt, and he whirled that monster over his head like a madman and Cadaverous had to stumble gracelessly away to avoid being separated from his lower half.

For a heartbeat, Cadaverous thought Pleasant was just going

to watch, but at the last moment the skeleton stepped in, diverting Rut's attention. The blade swooped round and Pleasant ducked right then dodged left, barely keeping himself in one piece. He got some space between them and lobbed a fireball that Rut actually cut *through*.

Cadaverous straightened up. "I'm leaving!" he shouted.

Pleasant and Rut stopped fighting.

"I'm sorry?" Pleasant asked.

"I'm leaving," Cadaverous repeated in a more dignified tone. "I'm going to go. You can continue fighting."

"I'm not sure I get it," said Rut.

"There's no trick," said Cadaverous. "I'm just going to walk out of here."

Pleasant tilted his head. "What about our mission?"

"He's got a goddamn sword. Look at it. It's huge."

"But there are two of us."

"I'm not trained in this kind of thing," Cadaverous said. "I'm only good against untrained mortals, when I'm on home turf or when I can cheat. Look, this doesn't have to be a big deal. Keep on fighting, put him in shackles and I'll be in the car."

Cadaverous walked for the door, but Pleasant blocked his way.

Cadaverous sighed. "The unavoidable truth of the matter is that I'm an elderly man. The pair of you may technically be older, but I'm the one with the seventy-eight-year-old body. It hurts when I bend over. It hurts when I don't bend over. It just hurts."

"This is a very odd situation," Rut murmured.

"Quiet, you," said Pleasant, pulling out his gun and shooting Tanner Rut in the shoulder. Rut went down, screaming, his sword clattering to the floor.

The smell of gunpowder wafted through the small house, and the gun swung slowly until it was pointing straight at Cadaverous's belly.

Cadaverous regarded the skeleton without expression. "I was wondering when you were going to take your chance."

"Now seems like as good a time as any."

"Lethe won't like it. If you kill me, then he'll kill you."

"Lethe's not going to kill me," Pleasant said. "Abyssinia and I have a history. She won't let him."

"She has a history with me, too. She talks to me more than she does the others. In her eyes, I'm a favoured son. She's not going to look kindly on my murder."

"I know her better than you, Cadaverous. She'll get over it."

Cadaverous kept his voice even. "Are you quite sure about that, skeleton? Can you claim to know her plans? Can you claim to know her so well that nothing she does would surprise you?"

The gun stayed level. Tanner Rut stopped screaming. He'd passed out on the floor.

Pleasant put his gun away. "You can carry him to the car," he said. "Make yourself useful." He walked out.

Cadaverous exhaled, then took hold of Rut's ankles and dragged him out of the house.

51

"You look terrible," Auger said, sitting at the end of the bed. The school's Medical Wing was quiet. All the other beds were empty. Omen's head was still a bit fuzzy so he just lay there, waiting for Auger to say something else. Seconds limped by.

"Concussion," Auger said at last.

Omen tried a shrug.

"How did *you* get concussion?"

"Hit my head."

"How?"

"By accident."

"What did you do?"

"Hit my head by accident."

Auger watched him. "Mum and Dad called," he said.

Omen frowned. "You told them?"

"They knew. The school has to alert the parents if someone gets injured."

"It's just a concussion. You've had plenty."

"We're not talking about me. We're talking about you. They were wondering what you've been up to."

"Nothing."

"That's what I told them. I told them nothing. I said Omen hasn't been getting up to any mischief. That's not what Omen does. He leaves all that stuff to me."

"Because I do."

Auger nodded. "Because you do. That's right. You leave all the stupid stuff to me. That's kind of our deal, isn't it?"

"Is it?"

"Yes, it is. I'm the Chosen One, so I have the crazy life. You're the normal one, so you have the normal life. That's how we operate."

"I didn't know that."

"You didn't know that I have the crazy life?"

"I didn't know we'd divided it up. When did we do that?"

"When we were born."

"I mustn't have been paying attention."

"It's our system," said Auger. He pointed to himself. "Chosen One." He pointed to Omen. "Lucky one."

Omen raised an eyebrow. "Lucky one? Really?"

"Yeah. Aren't you? I mean... aren't you?"

"I suppose so," Omen said. "In a way."

Auger adjusted his position slightly. "So our system, our deal, is predicated on you staying out of trouble. It's predicated on you staying safe, and uninjured, and non-concussed. What part of that do you not understand?"

"The word 'predicated'."

Auger leaned closer. "What's going on with you? What's happening?"

"Nothing. I hit my head. It was an accident."

"Was it Ispolin?"

"Jenan had nothing to do with this," said Omen.

"I'll kick his ass."

"Please do, but he still had nothing to do with this."

"Then why has he gone?"

"What do you mean?"

"He's gone," said Auger, leaning back. "He and his buddies. All of the Arcanum's Scholars, they packed their things, left their schoolbooks and vanished. Nobody even saw them leave."

"Huh."

"That's all you've got to say? Because I heard that Jenan attacked you earlier. Like, seriously attacked you, and then attacked Miss Wicked when she got involved."

"Yeah," Omen said. "Yeah, that happened. He was slightly nuts at the time, though. He said he was going to kill me."

"They've expelled him."

"Probably a good policy."

"His dad's going ballistic, apparently. 'How dare you expel my son, don't you know who I am?' That kinda thing. The fact that Jenan's vanished with all the others hasn't helped calm him down. You think they're off sulking somewhere, or is it something else?"

"How would I know?"

Auger kept observing him. "Valkyrie Cain was here this afternoon," he said. "Nothing to say to that, either? That's interesting. Valkyrie Cain ran through the school, blood everywhere, at roughly the same time you had your accident."

"You think she did this to me?"

"No. Probably not. Still, it's a bit of a coincidence, wouldn't you say?"

"Suppose it is."

Auger sighed. "You're really not going to tell me, are you? OK, that's fine. We're allowed to keep secrets. But if you won't tell me what's going on now, then will you at least tell me if you need my help later on? Can you do that?"

"Of course," said Omen.

Auger nodded, and stood. "That's all I need to hear. Catch you later, dude."

He walked to the door.

"Hey, Auger? Did Mum and Dad... did they ask how I was?"

Auger hesitated just a moment too long before turning. "Of course," he said. "They told me to pass on their love. Said to get better soon."

"Right," said Omen. "Thanks."

*

The nurse dismissed him and Omen went back to his classes. Axelia Lukt passed him in the corridor and gave him a smile, and his heart turned into a million butterflies in his chest.

"Hey," Filament said, walking up. "I heard what happened with Jenan. Are you OK?"

"I am, yeah," Omen replied. "I'm fine."

"He should be arrested, not just expelled. You could have been brain-damaged. You might still be brain-damaged. How many fingers am I holding up?"

"You're not holding up any fingers."

Filament sagged. "Oh, you poor thing."

Omen had to laugh, which raised the corners of Filament's mouth.

"But Jenan didn't give me the concussion," Omen said. "That was my fault. I hit my head."

Filament frowned. "I heard he hit your head."

"Naw, he just choked me."

"The story going around the school is that he put you in the infirmary. Just to let you know, that story is getting you a lot of sympathy from the girls."

"It is? Really?"

"And it is the good kind of sympathy, not the other kind."

"Wow."

"I mean, not the kind you usually get."

"Yeah."

"The pitying kind."

"I got that, thanks."

Filament laughed. "I am joking. My apologies. My English is not so good."

"Your English is perfect and you know it."

"Ah, maybe. So what do you think about the Arcanum's Scholars running away? I think it is hilarious. I can imagine them

321

each packing some sandwiches into a little spotted handkerchief and tying it on to the end of a stick, like in the old cartoons. Then they walk off into the woods where no grown-ups will ever bother them again, *ever*."

"I wish they were that harmless."

"Did you hear? One of them fell from a balcony. I tried to help but I don't think I did any good. It didn't matter. Mr Peccant saved whoever it was."

"I'm sure they're grateful to you for trying," Omen said. "If they could thank you, I'm sure they would."

Filament shrugged. "Would I want any thanks from them? Probably not. They are a bunch of... what is it? The word? About the crying babies?"

"Crybabies?"

"Them, yes. They are a bunch of crybabies. No? You don't think so?"

"I don't know. Maybe."

Filament looked at him out of the corner of his eye. "You are hiding something."

"No, I'm not."

"You are. You know something I do not know."

"I swear, I don't. I know very little, in fact. Some might say I know *too* little."

Another smile. "You are a man of mystery, Omen. It is why we are friends."

Omen smiled with him, kind of surprised to learn this.

"Jenan and the rest of them, they are *idioti*. Oh, apologies. *Idioti* is Italian for idiots."

"Thanks," said Omen. "I worked that out myself."

Filament laughed. "I joke. About you, not about them being idiots. Only Byron has any intelligence."

"Why Byron?"

"Well, he is the only one who did not go."

Omen stared. "He's still here?"

"No, but he is not with them, either. I saw him arguing with Gall and Lapse – those two never go anywhere without the other, have you noticed that? – and then Byron walked off."

"And you're sure he didn't go back?"

"I'm not positive... But harsh words were exchanged. Names were called. Mothers were insulted." Filament shrugged. "Some things, there is no coming back from."

"And you don't know where he went? Where he might be?"

"I am sorry, I do not. I like Byron well enough, but we are not buddies. Is something wrong, Omen?"

"No," Omen said. "I just have... I have to go. Good talking to you, Filament. Thanks."

Omen left him looking puzzled, and walked quickly away.

52

Magic. Sorcerers. Freaks and weirdoes. So much of that stuff left Martin Flanery confused as all hell. He liked to think of himself as a simple man. The only son of a millionaire investment banker, he'd dragged himself up by his bootstraps and, aided only by his family name and wealth, built himself an empire. Now look at him. Thanks to his own dedication, hard work and super PACs, he had had himself elected President, for God's sake. A true rags-to-riches story. A tale to inspire the next generation, to show them that the American Dream can still come true.

He hadn't liked using the witch to win, but she was just another tool in the toolbox. And that's what winners did: they used every tool they had at their disposal. That's what his father had taught him, and Martin had learned the lesson well. Besides, it wasn't like he brought the witch into the White House or anything. She was kept at a safe distance. Plausible deniability, he guessed it could be called. He'd been learning a lot about that lately – he'd had to, in his dealings with the press.

Most of his interviews took place in the Oval Office these days. There were people – leftist journalists and other losers, a lot of them online – who complained that there were too many "meaningless" interviews conducted there lately. Flanery didn't pay much attention to liberal journalists, and paid even less attention to people on the Internet – apart from those who insulted him or challenged him or displeased him in some way – but his staff had convinced him to do this one interview live on air and in the studio. They had this wonderful plan to prep him for the questions ahead of time so that he could appear relaxed and confident. Flanery had sat still for a half-hour of prep before getting bored and telling everyone he was going to wing it. He was a smart person, after all. He could handle a few questions from a friendly interviewer.

While he waited in the green room, a hot blonde delivered him his sandwich. "You're exactly how I like my women," Flanery told her. "Beautiful, slinky and carrying food."

She seemed to freeze for a moment, eyes as big as a deer's, then she smiled at him and walked away.

"Is it my imagination," he said, watching her go, "or is she giving those hips an extra wiggle?"

Bradley Anderson chortled. "That's for you, Mr President!" he said, almost choking on his own spittle. "I don't know how you do it!"

Flanery shrugged. "You either have it or you don't. I have it. Always have. They can't resist me, I can't resist them. Being president just makes it easier. Women are drawn to power, Bradley. Like moths."

Bradley nodded. "Like moths to a flame."

Flanery took a bite. The sandwich was disappointingly dry. The hot blonde was suddenly losing her hotness. After his first bite, he'd rate her a six. "You either have it or you don't," he repeated. "And you, and I don't want to be cruel to you here, Bradley, you don't have it."

Bradley howled with laughter. "That's for sure! That's for damn sure, Mr President! Not like you! I see them flocking around you!"

Flanery shrugged again. Bradley may have been a sub-par anchor on a sub-par show, but, when he was right, he was right. "What's her name?" Flanery asked, chewing on another mouthful.

Bradley looked confused for a moment, then he brightened. "Oh!" he said. "The, uh, the—"

"The blonde, Bradley. What's her name?"

"Gabriela, I think."

"What is that? Latino?"

"I, uh, I think it's Latina if it's a woman."

"Whatever," said Flanery. "I don't mind a bit of exotic. I'm not racist. The Mexicans are a wonderful people. I know lots of Mexicans. They love me. I'm very good to the Mexican people. Make sure you mention that later when the cameras are on."

"Yes, sir. I don't know if she's Mexican, though."

"What's her last name?"

"Masterson, or something like that. But she's married, so..."

"I don't mind married women. I don't say no to married women. My wife's a married woman."

Bradley smirked. "Yes, sir. And she is a *beautiful* woman, if I may say so."

Flanery frowned. "Of course she is. I surround myself with beautiful women, Bradley. My wife, my daughter, every woman who works for me. You know the secret of a happy life, Bradley? It's beauty. You put beautiful women everywhere you're going to look, you only look at beautiful women, am I right?"

"Yes, you are."

"Yes, I am. Every wife of mine has been more beautiful than the one before." He put his plate down. "Send her over to me when this is done."

Bradley's smile dipped. "I'm sorry?"

"The blonde," Flanery said. "Whatever her name is. Send her over to me when this is done. She can take off my make-up."

"She's not a..."

Flanery looked at him.

"Yes, Mr President," Bradley said, quieter now. "I'll send her over."

"You do that," Flanery said, as Wilkes walked into the room.

He was followed by Dennis Conlon – just the man Flanery wanted to see. "Bradley, give us a minute alone, would you?"

"Yes," Bradley said, bouncing to his feet. "I should get back to the studio, actually. I'll see you there, sir, in—" he checked his watch "—just under eight minutes. It's gonna be a good one, I can tell!"

Flanery waved him away and Bradley left, grinning, and closed the door to the green room behind him.

Alone now, Wilkes and Conlon sat, and Flanery's good humour soured. "Tell me," he said.

Conlon tried smiling. "Tell you what, sir?"

"Tell me what you think," said Flanery. "As an expert. You are an expert, aren't you? I mean, that's why we hired you. That's what everyone told me you were. This last week. The mainstream media say it's been my worst week since I took office. What do you think?"

Conlon took a deep breath, and let it out. "There are positives we can draw from the past few days," he said. "We've seen a boost within your core demographic that is, quite frankly, astonishing, and something we should be keeping an eye on in the—"

"Are you a yes-man, Conlon?" Flanery interrupted.

"Sir?"

"A yes-man. Like Wilkes here. Isn't that right, Wilkes? You'd say yes to just about anything I suggested, wouldn't you? You wouldn't dare contradict me or tell me I'm wrong, would you?"

Wilkes sat there and went red, but Flanery wasn't letting him off that easy.

"Well?" he pressed.

"I'm here to give you the best advice I can—"

"Would you contradict me? Would you tell me I'm wrong?"

Wilkes licked his lips. "If... if I felt you were wrong, I would of course make it known."

"But you haven't yet."

"No, sir."

"Why not?"

"Because... because you haven't been wrong yet."

"Then how can I have just had the worst week of my presidency?" Flanery asked, leaning forward. "How can I have had a week so bad that I have to do a live interview to restore the public's trust in me?" Once he felt that Wilkes was suitably diminished, Flanery turned back to Conlon. "What about you? Are you a spineless yes-man like Wilkes?"

Conlon didn't move his eyes away from Flanery's. "No, sir. I am not."

"Then pretend for a moment that you're not working for my administration," Flanery said. "Pretend you'd been brought in to CNN as an analyst. After having seen the week I've had, what would your opinion be?"

Conlon wasted a moment looking pensive. "I would say the Flanery White House has made a series of missteps."

"For example?"

"The, uh, the singling out of the journalist at the press conference," Conlon said. "The revelations about your academic achievements in college. The alleged funding impropriety at the Foundation."

Flanery sat back. "So this is my fault."

"No, sir, that's not what I said."

"Yes, it is. You said my White House has made missteps, but what you mean is that *I* am making the missteps. Is that right? Am I understanding that right?"

"Mr President, the extra scrutiny that comes with—"

"Answer the question."

Conlon chewed his bottom lip.

"Answer!" Flanery exploded, thumping his fist on to the table between them. "You're wasting my time! Why does everyone waste my time? I ask a question and I expect an answer immediately! Let me tell you something, Mr Conlon. If you were better at your job, if you really were worth the money we're paying you, my approval ratings wouldn't be down. This past week is your fault. You didn't spin when you should've spun. I don't know what you've been doing, but it sure as hell hasn't been your job."

"Mr President—"

"Shut up. You know what? I can't stand the sight of you. You're fired."

Conlon paled. "What?"

"You heard me. Get out. Get the hell out."

Conlon looked at Wilkes, who didn't respond. Then he got up, buttoned his jacket and walked out of the room.

Flanery watched Wilkes. "We're going to need a new whatever-the-hell-he-was."

Wilkes nodded. "I'll have a list for you the moment you come off the air."

"The funding thing could hurt me. Fix it. Use the witch."

Doubt flickered across Wilkes's eyes. "Sir, using Magenta on a journalist... We agreed that might not be the wisest course of action."

"Did we?" Flanery sneered. "Did we agree? Who agreed? You and me? I'm the leader of the Free World – who are you? Who are you to agree anything with me? When you say *we agreed*, what you mean is *President Flanery decided*. That's what you mean. And yeah, I decided a while back not to use the witch when it comes to journalists. I decided it was risky. But that was before those loser reporters started poking around my Foundation. That was before they started questioning my college results. Now I'm changing my mind. I can do that, can't I? I can change my mind? Don't bother answering that, that was a... I don't need an answer for that. I have a problem, and I have someone who can solve that problem. Are we understanding each other, Wilkes?"

"Yes, sir."

"Then do it. Get it done."

"Yes, sir." Wilkes stood. "Uh, one more thing, sir."

Flanery flapped his arms, adopting a mocking tone. "*Uhh, one more thing, sir*. For God's sake, spit it out."

Was that anger that flickered across Wilkes's face? If it was, it vanished immediately. "It's Parthenios Lilt, sir. He's free. He escaped confinement this morning."

"Finally," said Flanery. "Finally, you deliver some good news to me. Today is indeed a momentous day. Now get out. I gotta prepare to be interviewed by a pipsqueak idiot and a fat pig in a dress – unless you've actually done your job? Unless you've actually arranged for me to be on camera with an *attractive* woman?"

"Uh... sorry, Mr President, they said she's the co-anchor and they can't... they can't really swap her out, especially at this late stage."

Flanery glowered. "Next time, make sure there's a beautiful woman in front of me, you hear? Next time I want the most beautiful woman in the world."

53

"Oh, I'm sorry," China said upon entering, "were you waiting for me?"

Tipstaff tried to stand, but the Cleaver pushed him back down. "Supreme Mage, please, I can explain—"

She interrupted like he wasn't even speaking. "I'm so sorry I'm late," she said, sitting at the table opposite him while he sweated in his chair. "I've just had a lot to do. It's all a bit of a mess without you, if I'm to be honest. You kept this place running like clockwork, you really did. Isn't it true that you never really miss a person until they're gone? I am really missing you, my friend. I really am."

The room was stark. Two chairs and a table to which Tipstaff was shackled. One Cleaver standing over him, another by the door. A mirrored window set into one wall. A single fluorescent light that hummed in the quiet moments.

"We have not had the best luck with Administrators in the various Irish Sanctuaries, have we?" she continued. "They either die, or they betray. And die anyway. But with you... I thought you were different. I thought I could trust you. Granted, this was only a recent thought. It took you well over four years to gain even the slightest modicum of my trust. But you earned it. *You earned it.* And now look where we are. Before we begin in earnest, I have one question for you, my friend. Why? Why did you betray me?"

Tipstaff licked his lips, and was about to answer when China waved her hand.

"Rhetorical question. I know why you betrayed me. Because you believe that mortals should be bowing and scraping at our feet. Honestly, once you've heard that monologue from one person, you've heard it from everyone."

"Our rightful place—" Tipstaff began, but China leaned across and cuffed him lightly over the head.

"I don't care to hear it," she said, spritzing her hand with antiseptic spray. "Do you understand me? If you've thought about this, planned what exactly you'd say to me if ever we were in this position, I'm afraid it was all a waste of your time. The only things I want to hear coming out of your mouth are names, locations and plans."

"I don't know any of that."

"I give credit where it's due, do I not? And you may be many deplorable things, but you are, above all else, organised. Are you trying to tell me that your friends at the anti-Sanctuary didn't make use of your attention to detail while they were forming their plans? Are you telling me you didn't furnish them with blueprints of Coldheart Prison? With its schedule?" She sighed. "I'm not angry, Tipstaff, really I'm not. I'm just disappointed." She stood.

"Supreme Mage, please—"

"Hush now. I have work to get back to. I still have to solve the problem of this city not having a working bank. You were going to help with that, weren't you? That's a big deal for the High Sanctuary. We're really going to change things, to make things better for sorcerers everywhere. And you could have been there beside me as we laid the foundations for a bright, prosperous, peaceful future. Instead... you're in here." She sighed. "When I leave this room, a gentleman will enter. He will ask you all sorts of questions. He will get to know you very well over a relatively short period. You will not enjoy the time you spend together.

You've met him, actually. He's the same man who interviewed Parthenios Lilt. Do you think you'll be able to resist him the way Mr Lilt resisted?"

Tipstaff's bottom lip was trembling, but he did his best to sit up straight.

"Look at this," China said. "Some backbone. I do so admire a man who can resist crying."

A tear rolled down his cheek.

"Ah," said China. She turned for the door.

"If I help you," Tipstaff blurted, "what do I get?"

She turned. "Sorry?"

He looked up at her. "If I tell you what I know, will my sentence be reduced? If my information is valuable enough, I mean? If... if you can offer me immunity, then I'll help you in whatever way I can."

China frowned at him, and then laughed. "Oh, no. No, no, no, you poor deluded fool. We'll find out everything you know anyway, though I can't imagine it's very much. You'll get no deal from me. You betrayed me, little man. I'm going to make sure that you regret that decision for every single moment of the rest of your cold, dark and lonely life. Starting now."

54

"She looks scary," said Omen.

"She's not," said Valkyrie. "She's very friendly. Pet her and see."

After a slight hesitation, Omen held out his hand. Xena sniffed it, then moved her head, allowing him to pet her. Valkyrie watched the smile that spread across the boy's face, as he hunkered down and the dog sat. It was her second time seeing him in civilian clothes – he wore jeans and trainers and a heavy coat – and she figured he suited it. As stylish as the Corrival uniform was, Omen somehow made it look untidy.

"She likes you," said Valkyrie.

Omen looked up, grinning. "Really?"

She smiled. Her nose no longer ached when she did that. It was back to its normal size and shape. She looked around as Omen continued to pet Xena. It was Saturday and the school was quiet.

"You have dogs?" she asked.

Omen shook his head. "Mum has never liked them. Me and Auger, we always wanted a pet, but..." He sighed. "Auger needed to focus. We kind of adopted a stray cat once, though, without our parents knowing. It was a tiny little thing and just the friendliest, and it wandered into the garden one day and we fed it and fixed it up with a bed made of blankets in one of the sheds nobody ever used. I'd spend hours in that shed, actually, and Auger would come by whenever he could. It went on for three days before Dad found us. He took the cat away and we never saw it again. My parents... they're not really animal people."

Xena rolled on to her back, and Omen rubbed her belly.

"What was it like," Valkyrie asked, "growing up knowing that all this stuff existed? I was twelve before I found out about magic."

Omen shrugged. "It was just part of my everyday life. I knew how to look both ways before crossing the road, I knew how to ride a bike, and I knew not to tell mortals that my family were sorcerers. Some of the people I go to class with were raised without knowing one thing about the mortal world, but most grew up just like normal people, with this little bit extra. As weird as it sounds, they didn't really miss out on having a normal life. Well, Auger and I did, of course, but that's just because our parents have been consumed by the prophecy since before we were born. It's not exactly easy raising the boy who's destined to save the world. They can't really make any mistakes with him."

"Or you."

"Ah, they're less concerned about that," he said, and laughed, not quite convincingly.

"So you'd watch normal TV and listen to normal songs and everything?"

Omen smiled again. "Yes. There's always been a channel you can only get if you know magic."

"The Global Link."

"Right, but I never watched it. They only broadcast the news and stuff, never cartoons."

"And you had mortal friends?"

"Yes. Well, no. I mean, I *could have* had, but we weren't really allowed any because my family's work with Auger was so important. That's why I like Corrival so much – I can actually have friends here." He stood and Xena scrambled up, her tail wagging madly and her tongue hanging out.

"How's your head?" Valkyrie asked.

"We went through this on the phone."

"Yeah. And now I'm asking in person."

"My head's fine," Omen said. "No headaches or anything. I'm perfectly healthy."

"I didn't mean for you to get hurt."

"I'm not hurt."

"But you were."

"So? I'm not hurt any more, and we have a job to do, don't we? So we should stop talking about this and go find Byron. He's the only one of the Scholars that didn't run, so maybe he'll actually tell us something."

She sighed. "Fine. So where do we find your friend?"

"Byron Grace isn't really a friend," said Omen. "But he used to date October Klein."

"Ah, and *October* is a friend?"

"I doubt October knows who I am. She's really popular. But the guy who tutors her in science is friends with the guy who sits across from me in French."

"And... and does *he* know you exist?"

"Of course."

"Right."

"But he doesn't like me."

"I see."

"He thinks I'm weird and have no friends."

"*Do* you have friends?"

"Yes, I do. I have one."

"One friend still counts," said Valkyrie. "One friend is all some people need. So we talk to this guy, who talks to his pal, who talks to October, who tells us where Byron is, right?"

"If she knows. She mightn't know."

"How long has it been since they went out?"

"About four years."

Valkyrie hesitated. "That's... that's a significantly long time, Omen. What age were they when they dated?"

"Like, ten."

"And how long did this relationship last?"

"I can't be sure but I think, maybe, a week."

"And why – dear God, *why* – would October know where Byron might be now?"

Omen blinked. "I just... I mean, she's our only lead."

"She's not a lead, Omen."

"Really?"

"Unless they stayed really good friends and she knows all his secrets. Is that what happened?"

"Not as far as I know."

"Then she's not a lead."

"Oh. I thought she was."

"Do you have any other bright ideas?"

"I don't. I'm really sorry."

"It's OK, Omen. Do you know where he lives?"

"Dublin. Somewhere in Dublin."

"Dublin's a big place."

"Yes."

"It's not as big as some places, I'll admit, but it's bigger than some others."

"I wish I could be more helpful."

"Me too, Omen. You being more helpful would be a big advantage to us right now. But it's fine. I'll ask Miss Gnosis to find Byron's home address, but I'll need you to come with me, just so Byron knows I'm someone he can trust. Unless... does he hate me, too?"

"No," Omen said quickly. "At least, I don't think so. And Never doesn't hate you, he just..."

"People are allowed to hate me. It's OK." She tapped her leg and Xena sprang up. "You stay here," she told Omen. "When I have Byron's address, I'll call you. Have you heard from Temper?"

Omen nodded, and glanced at his watch. "He should be talking to his old friend right about now."

55

Temper knocked on the door and a moment later it opened, and Tessa Mehrbano stood there, barefoot, in jeans and a T-shirt, and he gave her the look.

"Hey, baby," he said.

She returned the look with one of her own. Less friendly. "You've got some nerve," she said.

She walked back in and he followed her, closing the door behind him. The apartment hadn't changed much since he'd been here last. "I couldn't stay away," he said. "The rest of them, I'd happily leave in the dust. But you? I've always had a special place in my heart for you, Tessa."

"That right?" she asked, turning.

"It is."

"That's sweet."

"Me all over."

"You know what else is sweet?"

He smiled, walking closer. "I think I can remember."

He leaned down for a kiss, but her hand closed around his throat.

"This," she said. "This is going to be sweet."

Mehrbano lifted him, threw him over the table. He crashed into the side of the couch, sent it sliding while he hit the ground. He looked up in time to see her striding to him, but too late to stop the kick that blasted the air from his lungs.

"Awww, mann..." he wheezed, as she took hold of his shirt and hauled him up.

"You think you can walk back in here?" Mehrbano said, hurling him into the wall. "After what you did? After you betrayed us like that? You are full of it."

He held up a hand while he tried to breathe. "In... my defence..."

She hit him. She didn't use her full strength, but it still sent him careening off the wall like he was a stainless-steel ball in a pinball machine, sent him stumbling the length of the apartment. His knees buckled and he went down for a moment, but kept crawling until he was back up on his feet.

"In your defence *what*?" she asked, coming after him. "We were *tight*, Temper. We were *family*."

"Weird family," he mumbled, backing off.

"You were one of us," she said. "You were a believer."

"They tried to kill me, Tessa."

"Bull."

His head wouldn't stop spinning. "Now who's full of it? You know what they did to the others."

"They were blessed."

"That what you call it? When was the last you spoke to them, huh? When was the last time they held a conversation with anyone?"

Mehrbano didn't have an answer for that. Temper pressed on.

"Is that what you wanted to happen to me? You wanted me to be blessed like that? To be turned into one of those... things?"

"Not everyone gets chosen. You were lucky."

"And, if they had come for you, what would you have done?"

"For a chance to be closer to the gods?" Mehrbano asked. "I would have given up everything." Her posture changed. She wasn't going to hit him again.

"Well, I wouldn't have let you," he said. "I couldn't stand to watch you lose the parts of yourself that make you *you*. The

340

others, the ones they took, they aren't blessed, Tessa. They're not communing with the gods. They're standing somewhere, staring into space. Not moving, not talking. Not thinking. They're failed experiments. And I'd have been on that list. Just another failed experiment."

"Or you could have been the one to change everything," she responded. "There might have been something in your blood to unlock all the secrets."

"You can't justify it. I don't know why you're trying."

"It's the sacrifice, Temper. It's the sacrifice we all must be willing to make. It's not about us. We don't matter. We're insignificant."

"You were never insignificant to me."

"You're young," she said. "You don't know how the world works. Give yourself a hundred years. Talk to me then."

They looked at each other for another few moments, then she sighed. "What do you want?"

"Richard Melior. You know him, right?"

"Yeah. I first met him back in... I don't know, 1965 or something. I was living in San Francisco. Why?"

"You were friends?"

"At the time, sure. Why, Temper?"

"He's in trouble. I'm trying to help him."

Mehrbano turned away. She put a hand on the couch and pulled it easily back into place, then sat. "So it's true," she said. "You're working with the Skeleton Detective."

"We've worked together, yeah."

"Working with the enemy."

"Skulduggery was never any enemy of mine," Temper said. "I'm young, remember? The truce was seventy years old by the time I was even born. We live in a time of peace, Tessa."

"Yeah, yeah," she said. "So is this a case you're working on? You a private eye now? A detective?"

"I'm a something," he said. "Have you had any contact with Melior lately?"

"Can't say that I have."

"He's involved with some bad people, and his involvement could have consequences for the rest of us – your Church included."

"It's not *my* Church."

"Well, it's for damn sure not mine."

"The Church of the Faceless is a church for us all, Temper."

"Except the unworthy."

"You've been away for a while," Mehrbano said. "You haven't seen the changes that have been made. We've gone back to a more tolerant ethos – the true ethos of the Faceless Ones."

"Which is what, exactly?"

"Acceptance. Forgiveness. Love."

He laughed. "You expect people to buy into that? After a thousand years of hate?"

"Mevolent twisted the Church's teachings to reflect his own prejudices. Look at the original texts. There's nothing in there about sorcerers being the only ones to bask in the glory of the gods. The path is there for the mortals, too."

"That's interesting," Temper said. "Because when I was part of it, the mortals didn't get much in the way of consideration."

"That was under Eliza Scorn," said Mehrbano. "She's gone now, and so have the last traces of Mevolent's influence. It's a brand-new day. You'd probably be welcomed back into the fold."

"The same people who conducted those insane experiments are in charge, Tessa. *Creed's* in charge. The Church might be a different kind of crazy these days, but it's still crazy."

Mehrbano sat forward, elbows on her knees and head in her hands. "What do you want, Temper? Tell me what you want and then leave."

"I'm looking for Savant Vega," Temper said. "I'm trying to find out if he's alive or dead, and, if he's alive, I'm trying to find out where."

She looked up. "And then you'll go?"

342

"You know where he is?"

"No. No idea. Will you go now?"

"I need *something*, Tessa."

"What makes you think I know anything that could help you? There was a group of them. They used to go bowling, for the gods' sake. They even had the shirts. Man, I used to laugh my ass off at that, but I got along with Parthenios Lilt better than I got along with Melior and Vega."

"You were friends with him? Lilt?"

"Sure. We had similar views about mortals. Views I have since left behind me, by the way."

"I admire your new-found tolerance. You meet any of Lilt's other friends?"

"Sure. This chick named Quibble. Creepy guy called Smoke."

"Quibble's dead."

"I don't care."

"What do you know about Azzedine Smoke?"

Mehrbano shrugged. "Not much. I never paid attention to what any of them were saying. I remember one evening, over at Smoke's place, he just would not stop with the chatter. He was working on that freaky rubber suit the entire time and hours go by and I realise I have no idea what he's—"

"Wait," said Temper, "go back. What was he doing?"

"The suit," she replied. "The black suit. He was working on it. He'd been working on it for weeks."

"What was he doing with it?" Temper asked. "Think carefully now. This is important."

"What is?"

"The suit, Tessa. Tell me everything you remember about the suit."

56

The Brute was the biggest prison block in Coldheart. It had eighteen tiers of cells arranged around a wide-open space. Hanging over that space was the security hub/control room, a large, windowed cube that dangled on thick chains, accessible only via retractable walkways. Far beneath it, level with the block's second tier, was a large dais that hovered in place – no chains, ropes or struts necessary. Two tiers beneath that, a lake of energy rippled over the floor.

Cadaverous stood on the first tier, leaning against the rails. He flicked a silver dollar into the lake – it fried instantly.

The prisoners had stopped asking to be released. Every so often, one of them would mutter a curse, but they'd learned pretty fast that Cadaverous and the others were not here to free them, and they'd learned almost as quickly that continuous noise would result in their food privileges being taken away. For the most part, they just sat in their cells, sullen and bored and lucky they were being fed at all.

Cadaverous looked up towards the dais, following the sound of drills and welders. Working from Destrier's plans, three large metal Xs were being attached to hydraulic arms that would lift them high into the air. Doctor Melior was insisting that these things were absolutely necessary in order for Abyssinia to be resurrected. Cadaverous had his doubts. It all seemed needlessly theatrical.

Skulduggery Pleasant floated down from a higher tier, hands in his pockets. "Isn't it great?" he asked.

Cadaverous tried to ignore the intrusion, but Pleasant landed right beside him.

"It's very theatrical," he continued. "There's a wonderful sense of showmanship at work here. You don't get that any more. Not really. Very few people build elaborate sets in which to kill people. I think it's a lack of skilled labour as much as anything. Where have you been? Cadaverous?"

"What?"

"Where have you been?"

"Elsewhere."

Pleasant grunted. "I would have been elsewhere, too, but Smoke instructed me to stay in the prison. I don't much like taking orders, if I'm honest. At the first sign of his influence fading, I'm probably going to kill him."

"Why are you telling me this?"

"Because we've bonded, Cadaverous. We took a road trip together. We beat up some cops. You killed one. That brings people closer. Also, I've got no one else to talk to. I tried talking to some of the convicts, but I'm the reason a lot of them are in here, so conversation was awkward."

"That must have been awful for you."

Pleasant shrugged. "It's just so hard to make friends here. And, speaking of making friends, I was thinking about our earlier conversation."

"The one we finished, you mean?"

"Yeah, that one. I think it's time you got back out there, Cadaverous. You lost a partner. That's terrible. A few decades before Valkyrie came along I, too, lost a partner. The screaming, the flailing... It wasn't pretty, and I was helpless to do anything to save him. But do you want to know what I learned from that?"

"No."

"To employ a hideously overused idiom, I learned that you

must get back on the horse. Somewhere out there is another homicidal lunatic who needs guidance. Go to that homicidal lunatic, Cadaverous. Go to him."

"You mock me."

"I'm trying to help you."

"No. No, you're mocking me. You're mocking my pain. I only hope, skeleton, that when I do kill your precious Valkyrie you are no longer under Smoke's influence. I want to see you fall to your knees. I want to hear the despair in your voice as she dies."

"Cadaverous, Cadaverous," Pleasant said, shaking his head, "what am I going to do with you?"

Cadaverous snarled. "You're going to stay out of my way."

He went to push past, but Skulduggery grabbed and spun him and Cadaverous folded over the railing. The lake of energy crackled beneath him.

"Or I'm going to kill you," Skulduggery said.

Fully aware that all the skeleton had to do was apply a little pressure, Cadaverous kept his voice even. "You didn't do it earlier."

"If I'd killed you then, Lethe would have known it was me. But if I make it look like an accident..."

"You think this would look like an accident?"

"You're an old man, Cadaverous. Old men slip and fall all the time."

"You're not thinking clearly. Maybe it's Smoke's corruption, I don't know, but do you really think we're alone right now? She's watching. She's always watching."

"I take it you mean Abyssinia?"

"If you kill me, she'll tell the others what you've done. It won't be so difficult to kill you. All it'll take is a single word from Smoke and then you'll be the one diving into this magnificent lake."

"It *is* rather magnificent," Skulduggery said, and a moment later he pulled Cadaverous back. "Fine. I won't kill you, you decrepit old scamp. Not right now, at least. I'll probably end up killing you at some stage, though, so be warned."

346

There was a commotion up on the dais, and the skeleton lost interest in Cadaverous completely, and floated up to see what was going on.

Cadaverous wrapped his anger around a stone, deep in his chest, and when he was sure it wasn't going to rise to the surface he unclenched his fists and took the metal stairs, emerging on to the second tier. He jumped across to the dais, joining the skeleton and the others near the three metal Xs. No one had yet bothered to clear away the fallen Cleaver scythes. Cadaverous hated mess, but this was not his responsibility.

Nero and Memphis stood there like naughty schoolchildren.

"She's *dead?*" Lethe asked. "How did this *happen?* You were sent to *retrieve* the third sacrificial lamb. Retrieve does not mean *kill.*"

"I told him that," Nero said.

"It wasn't my fault," said Memphis.

"No killing!" Razzia whined. "Those were the rules! That's why I couldn't go! You cheater!"

"I didn't have a choice," said Memphis. "Lethe, I'm telling you, man, the woman was nuts. She figured out why we were there. Heck, she practically killed herself."

"Ah," said Lethe. "Yes. I've heard of that *happening.* Someone's attacked and, in a *startling* act of self-defence, they break their own *neck.*"

"She was struggling too much," Memphis said. "Itching like she was in a fuzzy tree. I told her to calm down, told her to be cool, but she was too busy arguing and crying and such, and she twisted the wrong way and... that's all she wrote."

"Smoke and I brought back our sacrificial lamb *unharmed,*" said Lethe. "Cadaverous and Skulduggery brought back *their* sacrificial lamb – *somewhat* unharmed. But you... you couldn't even *manage* to bring back your sacrificial lamb even *relatively* unharmed."

Memphis swallowed thickly. "We still have enough, though."

"Oh," said Lethe, "*do* we?"

347

"Yeah, man. The Doc said all he needed were two Neoterics. We have two. The third was just, y'know, a spare."

"The third lamb was *insurance*," Lethe said. "We only get *one shot* at this, Mr Memphis. One shot to bring Abyssinia *back to life*. Do you really want to risk running out of *life force*? The *third* lamb is as important as the *first two*." He looked around. "Where is the *good doctor*?"

"I'm here," said Melior, from the third tier. They looked up.

"We're *one* Neoteric *short*, Doctor Melior," said Lethe. "We need another *name* from you."

"I... I don't have one," said Melior. "The three names I gave you have very specific energy patterns. They're the only three I know of."

"I don't *believe* you, Doctor. You can find these people by *sight*. I don't believe you've only ever spotted three who possess this *specific* pattern."

"I'd need to search," said Melior. "I'd need time."

"Time is what we *do not* have. Time is what your husband *does not* have."

Melior shook his head. "You won't kill him. If you kill him, I won't help you."

"We don't have to *kill him*, Doctor. We can *blind* him. We can pull out his *teeth*. We can cut off his *hands* and hobble his *legs*. You'll still get him back. But he will not be the man you *knew*. So I ask you for the *last time* – give us the name of a new little *lamb*."

Cadaverous watched the emotions flickering across Melior's face, too many to keep track of. He'd never been that good at spotting emotions anyway. Apart from fear. He'd always been good at spotting fear.

"I... I know one," Melior said. "She's got the pattern we need. It's different from the others, but it'd do. I think it'd work."

"That is wonderful news," said Lethe. "A name, Doctor."

Melior wet his lips. "Valkyrie," he said softly. "Valkyrie Cain."

57

Valkyrie dropped Xena off at Grimwood. She fed her and locked up and on her way back she passed through Haggard. She had no intention of heading up towards the pier, but found herself indicating left at the traffic lights anyway. She dampened her thoughts. The light turned green and she followed the road past Gilmartin's Bar and Angelo's Takeaway, then a small pharmacy that hadn't been there five years ago. The row of houses on her left gave way to a wall, and the wall tracked the road and then opened up to the harbour. Gentle waves played with the small boats and the line of orange buoys on their approach to the crescent beach. She turned right, went up the slight hill, pulled in and looked across the road to the house she'd grown up in.

From here, she could see the window to her bedroom, the same window she had sneaked out of countless times, the same window Skulduggery would perch at. There were no cars in the drive and no lights on inside on this grey afternoon. She felt an urge to leave the car, to walk through the empty house, to stand in the kitchen, to sit in the living room surrounded by all those framed photographs of the family. She ached for the feeling she was only now realising she'd been missing – that feeling of belonging. Of being welcome somewhere. Of being loved.

She was about to step out of the car when her phone rang.

"Hello?"

"Valkyrie, hi." It was Militsa. "I have Byron's address. Naturally, I'm not supposed to give this out... but then again I'm not even allowed to access this information. Sorry it took so long. Anyway, his given name is Paul Matthews. He lives in Ballyfermot. Do you know it?"

"I do," Valkyrie said. She made a note of the exact address. "Thanks for this. Really. If it's all right with you, I was going to ask Omen to come with me on this."

"Will it be dangerous?"

"No," she said immediately. "I just want Byron to see a familiar face, that's all, and preferably not one that brings to mind the senseless slaughter of innocent people."

"Good point," Militsa said.

"Thank you, Militsa. Really. I know you could probably get into a lot of trouble for this."

"Don't worry about it. I'll, uh, I'll try and think of some way you can repay me. Take care of yourself, OK?"

Valkyrie texted Omen then swung round and headed back the way she'd come, leaving her family home to get smaller and smaller in the rear-view. The road curved and suddenly the house was gone, and tears came to her eyes.

She drove to Ballyfermot, and the world outside turned to concrete and cracked walls, interspersed every now and then with shocking green. She passed a pony grazing in someone's garden and an old man walking and did her best to ignore the cold feeling that was gnawing at her insides. Her hands felt numb on the wheel, like they weren't really connected to her. Her entire body felt heavy. It dragged her down, kept her anchored to her seat when all she wanted to do was rise up out of her shell, pass through the roof of the car and fly free and away. The car slowed, her foot clumsy on the brake. She pulled in, hopped the kerb slightly. Her stupid fingers turned off the engine. She sat there, head down, chin to her chest, staring at her lap. She could no longer tell if she was breathing. She could no longer tell if she was anything but a slab of meat.

The car was quiet. It was a tomb. She was a slab of meat and this was her tomb. She was dead. They were going to find her and bury her, close her up in a coffin and put the coffin into the cold, cold ground. The last thing she'd hear would be the shovels throwing dirt and she'd lie there in the cold and the dark forever.

She heard somebody call her name.

Her eyes were still open. She was still looking at her lap. She wasn't in a coffin. Wasn't in a grave. She was sitting in her car with her head down. Shadows moved over her jeans. Someone was at the window. Someone was knocking on the glass.

Her right hand. She could move the fingers of her right hand. She curled them, dug the nails into her palm. It hurt. She dug in deeper. It hurt more. When the pain was close enough, she took hold of it and let it drag her out, drag her up. The closer to the surface she got, the more she could feel. Her toes. She wriggled them, felt the socks she was wearing, the trainers. She moved her leg slightly, felt the jeans rub against her skin. She took a breath and her hand felt lighter. She lifted it, looked up, saw Omen looking in at her, a worried expression on his face.

Valkyrie fumbled for the button that unlocked the car doors, and motioned for him to get in.

"Everything OK?" Omen asked.

"Everything's fine," Valkyrie lied. "Did Never drop you off?"

"I took a taxi. Never's mad at me for letting myself get hurt."

"Sorry about that." She reached for her wallet. "How much was the taxi? I'll reimburse you."

"It's OK, Miss Gnosis pre-paid."

"Ah," Valkyrie said, taking her hand out of her pocket. "I'll reimburse her, then."

Omen shrugged. A moment passed. "Are you sure you're OK?"

"Don't I look OK?"

"You look fine now," he said. "I'm not being rude or anything, but a minute ago you looked... I don't know. You looked sad."

"I was just... I was thinking. I was a million miles away. But I'm fine. Really. You ready to do this?"

"Yep."

"You should probably knock," she said.

His face slackened. "Aw."

She raised an eyebrow. "Is that too much for you?"

"No," he said grudgingly. "I just hate knocking on doors. I'm the same with making phone calls when I don't know who's going to answer. I'm just not very good socially."

"Few people are. Most of us just pretend."

"Is that what you do?"

"Fake it till you make it," she said, getting out of the car. The fresh air, cold and sharp, filled her lungs and snapped her out of the last dregs of her morbidity. Omen joined her, and they searched for Byron's house, one in a thousand just like it.

"What'll I say?" Omen asked as they walked up the weed-spotted driveway.

"Say you're here to see Byron."

"That's his taken name, though, and I think only one of his parents knows about the whole magic thing, but I don't remember which one."

"Then ask if Paul can come out to play."

Valkyrie hung back while Omen continued on to the front door. He rang the bell and waited. A woman answered. Omen stood there. She stared at him.

"What?" she said brusquely.

Omen smiled back. "Hi. Hello. Is Paul in?"

"And who are you?"

"I'm Omen."

"You're a Mormon?"

"No. Omen. That's my name."

The woman frowned. "That's a funny name, that is. Is it foreign?"

"Not *too* foreign. I'm from Galway. Well, near Galway, a small town beside—"

"Paul!" the woman yelled, and then looked back at Omen. "He's coming."

"Thank you."

"He hasn't mentioned you. You a friend of his? You from that bleedin' school, are you?"

"I am, yes. We're in the same Year."

"Didn't think he had any friends. Always thought he was a bit touched, y'know? In the head, like. A bit strange."

Omen chuckled. "I think we're all a bit strange."

Her face hardened. "I'm not. What're you trying to say? You saying I'm weird?"

Omen visibly wilted, and Valkyrie walked over.

"Mrs Matthews?" she asked, extending her hand. "I'm Miss Cain, Paul's teacher. How do you do?"

Mrs Matthews shook Valkyrie's hand, her frown deepening. "Ah, what's he done? Is he getting expelled, is he? Nothing but a burden, that boy, since the day he burst outta me."

"We're just here to talk to him. I promise you, he's not in any trouble. I'm dreadfully sorry, what's your name?"

"My name?"

"Your name. Your first name. What is it, please?"

"Rose."

Valkyrie kept shaking her hand, kept eye contact. "Rose Matthews, so good to meet you. Rose Matthews, this is not a big deal. When you think about this later, you're going to skip over it. You're not going to dwell on it, are you, Rose Matthews?"

"I'm not going to dwell on it," Mrs Matthews responded.

"Of course you're not. There's no reason to. What were you doing before this?"

"Painting," Mrs Matthews said.

"A portrait? A wall?"

"The *Enterprise*."

"A *Star Trek* fan," Valkyrie said. "Well, you can go back to painting the *Enterprise*, Rose Matthews, and you don't have to give our conversation another thought. You can ignore us completely, in fact. You have a good day now."

"Have a good day," Mrs Matthews mumbled, and walked back into the house.

Omen glanced at Valkyrie. "I wish I could do that. They don't teach it in school."

"With good reason," Valkyrie said, stepping back as Byron Grace came down the stairs. He saw Omen and frowned, but when his gaze flickered to Valkyrie he froze.

"You don't have to worry," Omen said quickly. "We just want to talk. Byron, this is—"

"I know who she is," Byron said in an accent as thick as his mother's. "Am I... am I under arrest?"

Valkyrie shook her head. "Like Omen said, we just want to talk. Could you step outside?"

"I... I can't. They'll kill me."

"A lot of lives are in danger, Byron. There's a reason you didn't go with the rest of them, isn't there? It's because you don't want to see anyone hurt."

"Look, just leave me alone, OK? You shouldn't even be here. This is my home. You're not supposed to come to my home. My mam doesn't know about any of this stuff."

"And she still doesn't," Valkyrie said. "Step outside. Please."

Byron hesitated, then did as she asked, closing the door behind him. "Around here," he muttered, leading them away from the road to the side of the house. They passed two recycling bins and emerged in the back garden. Clothes hung limply on a rotary dryer, and a high wall blocked off the sun.

Byron turned to Omen. "You going to tell people?"

"About what?" Omen asked.

Byron laughed without humour, and spread his arms. "This. Where I live. About my mam. About how I really talk."

"No," said Omen. "God, no. I did the same thing when I joined Corrival, or at least I tried. I thought I could reinvent myself, but you... you've actually done it. I'm not going to tell anyone."

"I just... I prefer being, y'know... Byron." He stood up straighter, and his accent changed, though the look of hurt in his eyes remained. "I've always hated living here. I've hated living with them. My dad's OK – he organised for me to go to Corrival once he figured out what I was. But my mother... She doesn't care who I am or where I'm going. You know what I realised? She doesn't like it when I'm happy. Isn't that awful? My own mother doesn't like it when I'm happy."

"Is that why you joined up with Jenan and the others?" Omen asked.

"I thought they hated ordinary people as much as I did," Byron said. "But I was wrong. They hated them much, much more. I may not like my family, but I do still love them."

"So help us," said Valkyrie.

"I don't know anything," Byron said. "I don't know plans or schemes or anything. Lilt wouldn't tell us anything."

"You saw him? After he escaped?"

Byron nodded. "Jenan rounded us up, took us into the library and then Lilt appears from behind a curtain like a bloody stage magician, expecting applause and all that. Nobody clapped. I think the others were too stunned and too... too scared, I suppose. Lilt being back meant that some real orders would start coming in."

"What did he say?"

"He said the time is almost upon us. He said the anti-Sanctuary has big plans for First Wave. He said the mortal streets are going to run red with blood. Those were his exact words. We were told to pack some essentials because we were going to leave Corrival for good. I followed Lapse and Gall towards our dorm room, but..."

"You argued," said Omen.

"I told them I couldn't do it, I couldn't hurt anyone. I asked them to come with me, to just... quit. They said I was a coward and a traitor and to wait until Lethe got his hands on me."

"So you came home," Valkyrie said, "because you knew it'd be the last place they'd look?"

He frowned. "What? No. I just... I just wanted to spend some time with my family before they came after me. I can't hide from them, not when I have this." He pulled up his sleeve. A sigil was tattooed on the inside of his forearm.

Omen peered closer. "That's... that's a tracking sigil."

Valkyrie went cold. "They know where you are?"

"Yeah," said Byron. "Why?"

She looked around. "We have to get out of here."

Skulduggery's voice came from behind. "And why would you want to do *that*?"

58

Smoke and Nero grinned and Skulduggery stood between them, his hands in his pockets, his jacket unbuttoned, the chain of his pocket watch glinting against his waistcoat. Valkyrie altered her vision, just for a moment, just long enough to watch the tendrils of crackling grey that swirled around Skulduggery's aura. It was fading. She could see it fading.

"You can't leave," Skulduggery said. "We have so much to talk about. I've missed you, Valkyrie. I had just got you back and then we were pulled apart again."

"I've missed you, too," she said, making sure her voice stayed steady.

He tilted his head. "Thank you. Thank you for saying that. It means a lot. How's your leg, by the way?"

"It's fine."

"You're probably annoyed that I shot you."

She shrugged. "I could have done without it."

"You understand why, though, don't you? It's important to me that you understand."

"I do."

"Good," Skulduggery said. "Good. You've been busy, apparently. I heard about your encounter with this Shakespeare person. Did he hurt you?"

"No."

"You're sure? If he hurt you, tell me. I'll kill him."

Nero chuckled, and Skulduggery turned his head slightly.

"Why are you laughing?" he asked. "I'm quite serious. If anyone hurts Valkyrie, I will kill them. That includes you."

Nero's chuckle faded.

Skulduggery looked back to Valkyrie. "Cadaverous Gant wants to kill you, too, but don't worry about him. If he tries it, I'll shoot him in the head. You're safe. For the moment. Although we might have to kill you in order to resurrect Abyssinia. Melior's going to see if he can make do with the life forces of the two Neoterics we have shackled up back at the prison, but, if we need more, I'm afraid you're on the menu. Your magic is unique, after all. You draw your magic straight from the Source. You may not be Neoteric, but you qualify."

"Lucky me."

"Indeed. Or I might kill everyone before any of this moves forward one more step. I'm getting into that sort of mood."

Smoke placed a hand on Skulduggery's shoulder. "Behave, Skulduggery."

Skulduggery stiffened, and Valkyrie's heart plummeted. She activated her aura-vision just in time to watch the corruption overtake him once more.

Smoke took his hand away. "Stick to the plan. Understand?"

"Of course," said Skulduggery. "Apologies, Valkyrie. I had a brief moment of awakening. It was nice, but it's gone now."

Valkyrie's mouth was dry. She could have tapped the auxilium sigil on her hip there and then. She could have called in three dozen Cleavers, have them teleport in to the middle of Ballyfermot and engage in a battle in broad daylight. She could have put innocent lives in danger and risked exposing magic to the mortal world.

She could have done all these things with the tap of a finger. But her hands stayed where they were.

"So you're going to do it?" she asked. "You're going to be the one to kill me?"

Skulduggery nodded. "I think it's only right, don't you? After all we've been through together?"

She tried smiling. "I kinda wish you wouldn't."

"Don't do that," he said, and took a step forward. "Don't pretend. It's me, OK? It's still me. You can be yourself around me, Valkyrie. I've been trying to get you to be yourself since you came home. Nothing's worked, has it? You still won't come back to me."

"I'm doing my best."

"I don't think you are. I think you've given up."

She didn't say anything.

Skulduggery looked at Smoke. "You should have seen her, back in the good old days. She *sparked*. She met every challenge head-on. She was fearless."

"No," she said, "I wasn't."

"You were fearless in every way that mattered," he responded. "You were magnificent. You were funny, and tough, and confident, and amazing. You did things no one else could do. You survived what no one else could survive. Just being around you made me a better person. And now look at what you've become. This apologetic... shell. Meek. Timid." His head tilted up. "Ordinary."

"If I'm not worth your time," she said, "then go spend it somewhere else."

"I care for you too much to let your suffering continue," Skulduggery told her. "I thought you'd come back. I thought you'd wake up, find that old spark again... but now I don't think that's going to happen."

"So... what? Are you going to put me out of my misery?"

He looked at her and didn't answer for a moment. Then he said, "I think I'll have to."

She looked into his eye sockets to the shadows within and her gaze locked there, like he was pulling her towards him. She almost didn't notice Smoke passing her, reaching out to take Byron's arm.

"Come on, kid," he said. "Parthenios Lilt wants a word."

Byron shook his head. "I don't... I don't want to."

"Let him go," Omen said, trying to pull Smoke's hand away.

Smoke shoved Omen back and Valkyrie caught him before he fell.

"Screw this," Smoke muttered, tapping Byron's arm. Byron gasped, and Valkyrie didn't need her aura-vision to know he'd just been corrupted. "Let's go, kid."

Byron stared at him, and nodded, then stopped and glanced back at his house. "Can you give me a minute?" he asked. "I'll be real quick, I swear."

Smoke sighed. "What, you want to kiss your mommy goodbye?"

"No," Byron said. "I want to kill her. Please?"

"Fine," Smoke said. "But be quick about it."

Byron grinned, and Omen broke free from Valkyrie's hold and stood in front of him.

"Don't do it," he said.

"Out of my way," Byron snapped, trying to shove past.

Omen wrestled with him. "I can't let you. I can't. She's your mum, Byron. You just told us that you love her."

"Hey, Byron," Nero called. "Kick his ass."

Byron stopped wrestling and looked at Omen, and Omen's eyes widened. "Now, just wait a second..."

Byron hit him.

"Hey!" Valkyrie shouted, and went to pull Byron back, but Smoke was in her way.

"Let them scrap," he said, eyes on the fight, not even looking at Valkyrie, like they were in the playground or something. Like this was nothing more serious than a game.

Valkyrie turned sideways and slammed her foot down on to Smoke's knee with such force that she heard the sickening *snap-crunch* of bones breaking. Smoke screeched and fell, clutching his leg, rolling over and screeching some more.

Someone grabbed her hair, yanked her head back and she went stumbling. It was Nero, cursing at her, hissing in fury, and she twisted, took hold of his jacket with one hand and rammed the other into his throat. He staggered, gasping, his eyes wide, and her knee sank into his belly. She hammered a fist down on to the base of his skull when he folded over and he dropped, and she kicked him in the head.

Omen and Byron rolled across the ground, Omen trying to talk him out of it the whole time.

Valkyrie turned to Skulduggery as he hung his hat on the rotary dryer.

"I don't want to fight you," she said.

"Of course you don't," he replied.

He darted forward and she moved, absorbing the blow on her upper arm.

He circled her. "The fourth time we met, you fainted. Do you remember how I caught you? That's where our friendship began, with you in my arms. That's how it'll end."

"Third," she said.

"Sorry?"

"It was the third time we met. We'd only spoken twice up until that point, at the wake and the reading of the will."

He shook his head. "We had met years earlier, when you were just a baby. This was before things got strained between your parents and Gordon, and he was babysitting and I visited. You were adorable."

"I still am."

He laughed. "There you go," he said. "A flash of the old Valkyrie."

He tried to grab her and she swatted his hand away, moving to his right as she did so.

She could see Omen and Byron throwing punches, bloodying each other up.

"Remember that wig you used to wear?" she asked. "Before you got the façade?"

"I still have it."

"Seriously?"

"It's a good wig."

"It's a terrible wig. It's way too fuzzy."

"Fuzzy was in that year."

"Did Ghastly approve?"

"I can't recall."

"That's a no."

He laughed, reached for her, then whipped his hand up when she went to block, catching her with a backhand across the face. She stumbled, hand to her stinging cheek, blinking back sudden tears.

"Help!" Smoke roared. "Somebody help me! I need medical attention!"

"I think you've damaged my friend," said Skulduggery.

"He's not your friend," Valkyrie said. "I'm your friend. Dexter and Saracen, they're your friends. Ghastly was your friend. Smoke—"

"Smoke's a bad influence," Skulduggery said. "He's that child your mother always warned you about, the one who brings out your worst side."

"That's right," said Valkyrie. "And I can't believe you're letting it happen. I can't believe you're letting someone else dictate how you behave. I'm not the only one who's changed, you know. Back in the old days, your ego would never have allowed this."

"Are you saying I've become more humble?" he asked, amused.

"No," she said. "Just more ordinary."

A moment passed, slow and heavy.

She turned her head a millisecond before he struck her, and he was grabbing her jacket to make sure she didn't fall back out of range. His elbow jabbed into her shoulder, deadening her left arm. She didn't know what hit her then, a fist or another elbow, but her head snapped back and the world blurred and suddenly she was falling to her knees.

He retrieved his hat while he waited for her to recover.

Smoke was alternating now between screaming and sobbing. Nero gave out the occasional moan. Omen and Byron were back on their feet but not fighting. They panted for breath and glared at each other.

Slowly, Valkyrie stood up. Skulduggery punched her and she went down again, flattened on to the grass, the world growing mute and grey.

He crouched over her and snapped a pair of cuffs on to her wrists. She felt her magic drain.

"Goddammit!" Smoke shouted. "Skulduggery! Stop wasting time with her and help me!"

"But of course," Skulduggery said instantly. He walked over to Nero, hauled him to his feet. "Take us to Coldheart," he said. Nero tried to push him away and Skulduggery wrenched his arm behind him. "I'm under orders, remember. I will break you into bits if you do not teleport us all in the next five seconds."

"I can't!" Nero yelped. "I think I might have concussion! She kicked me in the head!"

"Then just the four of us." Skulduggery took out his gun, pressed it to Nero's temple. "Three. Two. One."

"OK!" Nero cried, and the grey sky turned into a grey ceiling. They were inside, in a cavernous room.

Skulduggery looked at her. "Welcome to Coldheart."

59

Skulduggery and Valkyrie and Smoke and Nero vanished, leaving Omen and Byron all by themselves.

"They left me behind," said Byron. He sounded disappointed.

"This is your chance," Omen said. "Get out of here. Run."

Byron frowned. "Why?"

"Mr Lilt wants you dead, Byron. You split from them. He's going to want to kill you."

"Lilt's not going to kill me," Byron said.

"He was going to kill you anyway, even before you split. I heard him say it."

Byron considered it for a moment. "Maybe," he said. "Maybe I'll run after I kill my mother."

"What? No. Come on." Omen stood in front of him. "You have a chance to get away. You don't want to kill her."

"Yes, I do," said Byron. "I hate her. I hate them both. They're small and weak and grubby and they hate me."

"No, they don't. They love you."

"They've never loved me," Byron said. "Why are you trying to help them? Your parents are the same."

"What? My parents don't hate me, Byron."

Byron sneered. "Yes, they do. Everyone in school knows it. Your parents love Auger. They love the Chosen One because they can be proud of him. When was the last time they were proud of you?"

"You're wrong. You don't know what you're talking about."

"You're so dumb," Byron said, and laughed. "You're so stupid. Axelia Lukt's parents know your parents. She told me ages ago that your folks go out of their way to avoid mentioning you in conversation. All they talk about is Auger. They're trying to forget you even exist."

Omen shook his head.

"Face it. They hate you, and you know it, and you'd kill them, too, if you had the chance. So let me pass, or I'll kill you first."

Slowly, Omen unclenched his fists and stood aside. Byron shouldered him out of the way. He'd almost made it to the trees when Omen wrapped an arm round his throat and pulled him back. They went down, but Omen had the choke on tight, and squeezed tighter. Byron struggled for a lot longer than he should have, and Omen knew he was doing something wrong, but he dared not let go. Eventually, Byron's struggles weakened, and Omen waited two seconds after he'd gone limp before releasing him.

Omen lay there, getting his breath back, keeping his eyes on the unconscious boy. He felt bad about what he'd had to do, but proud that he'd been able to do it. If only Axelia had been here to witness it. Or his parents.

He sat up slowly. His face was swollen and his ribs were sore. He got to his feet, groaning as he did so. His tongue probed each of his teeth, checking that none of them had been knocked loose during the fight. He checked his nose next. Byron had whacked it with his elbow as they were rolling around. It hurt like hell, but didn't appear to be broken.

He took out his phone, and didn't know who to call. When it suddenly buzzed to life, he almost dropped it.

"Hello?" he said, bringing it to his ear.

"Omen!" It was Temper. Thank God. "What's going on? Where is everyone?"

Omen puzzled over how to express this. "Things have happened," he said eventually.

"Valkyrie isn't answering."

"She's been taken prisoner by Skulduggery."

"Aw, man..."

Omen nodded. "I know. And I was in a fight."

"Who with?"

"A boy in my class."

"Did you win?"

"Well... he's unconscious and I'm not, so I suppose I didn't *lose*."

"Well done!"

"Thank you. What do we do now?"

"I'm still in New York, so I'm going to need Never to come get me. I have a way to stop all of this. I just need to talk to Richard Melior."

"But he's about to kill Valkyrie."

"Why's he going to do that?"

"To resurrect Abyssinia."

"How much did I *miss*?"

Omen looked around. "Like, a lot."

"Come get me, Omen."

"But they're all in Coldheart Prison, and we don't know where it is."

"I'll call the High Sanctuary, see if maybe they've managed to track it down. In the meantime, you call Never."

"I don't know if he'll answer," said Omen. "Last time I spoke to her, he was really mad with me."

Temper said, "Be your charming best, slick. Valkyrie's life depends on it."

60

Omen stepped off the bus just as his call was answered. "Never, thank God, you have to help us!"

"I can't," Never whispered. "I'm in the High Sanctuary. Surrounded by Cleavers."

"What?" said Omen, colliding with a crowd of people hurrying the other way. "Why?"

"The Supreme Mage brought me in." Never sounded nervous. Very nervous. "At first, I thought I was in trouble, y'know, for all of us going to San Francisco? And I thought, *I swear to God if Omen Darkly has got me expelled I'm going to kill him*. But it wasn't that. The Supreme Mage needs me to bring a bunch of Cleavers to help your friend."

Omen started walking. "What friend?"

"Your only other friend apart from me. The murderous one."

Omen's eyes widened. "Valkyrie? Do they know where she is?"

"I think they know how to find her, yeah. The Supreme Mage is going to draw a sigil on my arm to link me to an auxilium on Valkyrie, whatever that is, and then we wait around for her to activate it. Apparently, all I have to do is close my eyes and teleport and I'll end up right beside her. That's blind teleporting, Omen. I haven't done that before. I don't think anyone has. I'm terrified."

"Never, you're going to be fine. You can do this. You're a natural – Mr Renn is always saying that. I believe in you."

"Yeah," said Never. "Thanks, Omen. That actually... that actually helps."

"But I'm going to need you to not do it."

He could hear Never's scowl. "Why would I not do it, Omen?"

"Because arriving with a bunch of Cleavers might not be the best idea," Omen explained. "I was just talking to Temper. Apparently, he can fix everything – he just needs to talk to Doctor Melior, and Melior will probably be with Valkyrie. So, when the Supreme Mage draws that sigil on your arm, I'm going to need you to come get me, then pick up Temper in New York, and then we can all do the blind teleporting thing."

"No way. No way, Omen. The Supreme Mage *herself* asked me to do this."

"And I'm asking you to do something else."

"She's the Supreme Mage."

"And I'm your friend."

"She outranks you!"

"And *you're* my best friend, Never. I wouldn't ask you to do this unless I thought it was the best thing to do."

Never's voice was hushed but somehow loud. "You don't know the best thing to do! You don't know anything! Name me one class you're doing well in! Name me one piece of homework you didn't have to copy off me! You cannot ask me to do this, Omen, because you are an idiot and I can't trust that you'd know a good idea if it hit you with a brick!"

"I'll be on O'Connell Street," Omen said. "Outside Eason bookshop. I hope you'll come get me."

"I'm not going to do it, Omen. I'm not going to do it."

"I hope you do."

Omen hung up.

61

She hurt.

She was sitting up on the bunk, her back against the wall, her legs stretched out, and her mouth open. Her lips were burst. She'd washed some of the blood off at the sink, left the cracked porcelain stained with red handprints. Her jaw hurt like hell, but they'd removed her packet of leaves when they'd taken her phone.

She wasn't shackled any more, though her powers were still bound and the auxilium sigil, invisible upon her skin, was useless. The cell saw to that. Skulduggery stood outside, still as a statue, looking in at her. His hat cast a deep shadow, hiding his skull.

"They're going to kill me, are they?" she asked, her voice dull.

"Everyone dies," Skulduggery responded. "You might get lucky and come back as a skeleton like me. Wouldn't that be fun? We could have all sorts of adventures."

"We already have all sorts of adventures."

"Skeleton adventures are different. There's more room for puns."

She talked carefully with ruined lips. "You don't have to guard me, you know. I have no idea how to escape from a prison cell."

"I'm not guarding you," Skulduggery said. "I'm protecting you. Cadaverous Gant is eager to end your life."

"Why? Because Jeremiah Wallow fell when he tried to kill me? How is that my fault?"

"I mentioned this to Cadaverous. He didn't seem to care. Some people like revenge too much. It is a potent source of strength."

"Fair enough. Thanks for protecting me, though."

"Smoke told me to do it, in case you think my attitude towards you may be softening. I still very much want to kill you."

"You're not going to kill me."

"Is that so?"

"You're fighting back."

His head tilted, shifting the shadow slightly. "You can't see my aura."

"I don't need to. I can tell. You're fighting Smoke's influence."

"I'm not sure you're right, to be honest. You may be in for a disappointment. If you like, I could punch you to keep your expectations low. That way, if I do end up killing you, it won't come as too much of a surprise."

She smiled, but the smile made her lips hurt so she stopped, waited for the pain to pass. When they had returned to their former throb, she spoke again. "Do you think I've wasted my time?"

"On what?"

"On feeling sorry for myself. I've been back in Ireland for half a year and now it looks like I'm going to die, and I had all this time to spend with my family and I didn't. I didn't spend it with you, either."

"And you think you've been feeling sorry for yourself?"

"Haven't I?"

"I don't think so. Even if you were, so what? You do what is right for you, Valkyrie."

"I just think I've wasted so many opportunities to let the people I love know that I love them. And my folks have been so patient with me. They've given me all the space I needed without even knowing why I needed it. Every few days, Mum or Dad would send me a new message. Never to pressure me, just to... include me, I suppose. To keep me involved. If I die now, they'll never know how much I appreciate them." She looked away. "I've got something in my head. A recurring thought, or a... a belief. It resurfaces every once in a while. Sometimes I feel that I'm already dead, you know? Like I'm an actual corpse. That's weird, isn't it?"

"For anyone apart from me, that would be considered unusual, yes."

"I thought, maybe, because I have this belief, that I'd be used to it by now. The idea of death, I mean. But the prospect of real death, of actual death... It's still terrifying. I don't want to die, Skulduggery."

"You're probably not going to have a choice."

"I want to see my family."

"I'm going to kill you."

"Stop saying that."

"I'm sorry, I don't mean to upset you. Is there anything I can do to take your mind off your impending demise? A joke, perhaps? A witty anecdote?"

"I suppose you can tell me why you quit as Commander of the City Guard."

He tilted his head again, this time at an amused angle. She knew all his angles. "You're not going to give up, are you?"

"Hey, you offered."

"OK," he said, "I'll tell you. Do you remember China's little Council of Advisors?"

"Vespers, Praetor and Drang."

"All of whom are new additions," Skulduggery said. "Drang succeeded Warheit as German Grand Mage, Vespers replaced Graves as English Grand Mage and, most recently, Praetor took over from a man named—"

"Cypher."

"Yes. China had given Cypher control of the American

Sanctuary because he'd fed her information back when *his* predecessor was in charge. Cypher was ambitious and cunning, and that got him the job. But his ambition didn't stop there. He saw what China had and wanted it for himself, so he tried to have her assassinated."

"But you foiled it," said Valkyrie.

"Naturally. But, while in our custody, one of the members of the City Guard got a little carried away in the interrogation stage, and Cypher was killed."

"That Yonder guy, right? The one who doesn't like you?"

"That's the one. Some people called his actions overzealous. Some called it murder. China quite liked the rumour going around, that we'd executed Cypher in his cell for daring to oppose the Supreme Mage. She felt it set a healthy precedent, and Yonder was released with a reprimand. I resigned the next day."

Valkyrie picked some dried blood from beneath her fingernails. "So why wouldn't you tell me this? You quit because you didn't like the way things were going. What's so bad about that?"

"That was the straw, Valkyrie. The catalyst. But everything leading up to that point... that's the part of the story I didn't want to tell you. I didn't want to tell you about Somnolent."

She frowned. "Who's Somnolent?"

But he was already turning his head to the sound of an opening door, then footsteps, getting closer, and muttering. Skulduggery stepped back, clearing the way for Destrier to walk past. His head was down, his brow furrowed, his fingers moving like he was tapping a small, distorted keyboard.

"Destrier?" Skulduggery said.

Destrier spun suddenly, eyes wide, like he was shocked to find himself among people. "Yes," he said. "Yes, sorry, I... I got lost there. For a moment. In my head." He glanced into the cell. "You've got to bring her. The girl. The Valkyrie. Lethe is ready to begin."

"Excellent."

Destrier nodded. He went to move off, then stopped, turned, hesitated.

Skulduggery stepped into his line of sight. "And where are you going?"

"Work," Destrier said. "Going to continue my work. I'm not sure... I don't know where, though."

"Back through there is where Lethe is," Skulduggery said, pointing. "That's where we're going to resurrect Abyssinia. Is that where you want to go? I thought you'd finished working on that contraption."

"Finished, yes," Destrier said. "Other work to do. My work. Important work. Must be the other way." He turned again, hurried on.

Skulduggery watched him go. "What an odd, odd man." He took down a pair of shackles that had been hanging from the bars of the next cell over, and tossed them through. "Put those on," he said. "Your right wrist, then back up to the bars."

Moving slowly, painfully, she eased her legs off the bunk, scooped up the shackles and stood. "We can get out of here now," she said.

He took out his gun, aimed at her leg. "I'll shoot you again."

She clicked the cold metal over her right wrist.

"Come back to me," she said, walking up to the door. "Skulduggery, for God's sake, it's time to snap out of it. Please. For me."

He looked at her for a moment. "Valkyrie...?" he said, his voice soft.

"Yes! Skulduggery, yes!"

He laughed. "No, only joking, I wasn't snapping out of it, I was just being hilarious. You might not be in a laughing mood, though, which is understandable. You're probably going to die in a few minutes. Turn around."

She turned and he reached through the bars, clicked the shackles over her other wrist. When they were secure, he opened the cell door and motioned with the gun. She stepped out.

"How will you feel afterwards?" she asked, leading the way to her own execution. "When I'm dead and you're not under Smoke's influence any more? How are you going to feel when you're back to normal if you kill me today?"

"Pretty bad, I would imagine."

She looked back at him. "So don't kill me. Don't kill anyone."

"No... I see your point, but I'm still going to do it. I want to, you know? I want to kill you."

Right before they reached the door, she turned. "Skulduggery... please don't do this. Work with me. You've seen the vision. Some of it, at least. You've seen what happens if Abyssinia comes back. We can avoid all of that – *all of it* – if you come back to me. You just have to fight it. Fight them. I'm begging you."

"I thought you didn't beg."

"You're my exception," she said. "You always were."

Skulduggery reached for her slowly, brushing a strand of hair off her face with a gloved finger. Then he reached further, opening the door behind her.

"It'll be over soon," he said.

62

They emerged on to a tier of prison cells that circled a wide, empty space, and the volume of the world suddenly twisted up to 11. Convicts cheered, raged, cursed at her, shouted a thousand threats that competed against each other in their race to be heard. She glanced upwards. It was almost dizzying. Tier after tier of hatred and anger and barely contained violence. Skulduggery wrapped an arm round her waist and they floated over the railing and across the gap to the wide, flat disc that hovered above a crackling lake of energy.

They touched down on the dais. Three metal Xs, skilfully welded and attached to hydraulic arms, stood waiting. She didn't know what the curved metal plates were for, but, judging by the clasps on display, Valkyrie guessed that those Xs were reserved for her and the two other people on this platform who were wearing shackles. She didn't recognise the older men, but they looked terrified. Memphis, resplendent in a red jacket and black shirt, gripped the arm of one of them and Razzia, clad in her usual tuxedo, made sure the other stayed put. Nero was too busy holding his head to even glance her way, and Smoke sat on the ground amid all those fallen scythes, frantically chewing leaves and clutching his leg.

Lethe was examining a metal tripod that had been set up near a table. No, not a table – more like a mortuary slab. Upon that slab were two wooden boxes. The bigger one was plain, without any ornamentation. The smaller was carved with intricate symbols. That was the one containing the heart; Valkyrie would have bet her life on it, if her life had been hers to bet. She wondered if she'd be able to lunge for the box and toss it into the lake of energy before anyone stopped her, but Skulduggery's fingers tightened ever so slightly on her arm.

"Let's not, shall we?" he said softly.

Lethe looked up. "Finally," he said. "We are *ready* to proceed. Where is the good doctor?"

Melior appeared on the tier. He looked exhausted, and wouldn't meet Valkyrie's eyes. He peered down at the lake of energy below.

"Careful now," Lethe called.

Melior took a running jump on to the dais. He stumbled slightly as he landed, and Razzia cheered. Ignoring her, he hauled three thick, transparent hoses out of a large sack. He dropped the hoses between the Xs and the tripod, and walked up to Valkyrie. He didn't say anything, just raised his hand to her face. It started to glow, the warmth overcoming her pain, and when he took his hand away her lips were healed and her jaw didn't ache.

"Hey," Smoke said, getting up and hobbling over. "Do me. Fix my leg."

"And my head," said Nero. "I think I have concussion."

"I can't," said Melior. "I need my strength for the resurrection."

Nero sagged and Smoke stopped chewing leaves long enough to glare. "You fixed her mouth."

Melior nodded. "And now I need to conserve my energy."

Smoke grabbed his shirt.

"Hey now!" said Lethe. "Leave the good doctor *alone*, there's a good boy."

Reluctantly, Smoke released his hold. He turned his glare to Valkyrie.

"That feel good?" he asked. "It doesn't hurt any more? I don't think that's fair, do you? I think that mouth of yours should be punched all over again."

He drew back his fist and Valkyrie crunched her forehead into his face. Smoke staggered back, silent at first, hands covering his nose, but the howl grew and exploded as blood ran down to his chin. "She broke my nose!" he hollered. "She broke my knee *and* my nose!"

Lethe shrugged. "You probably shouldn't be so *careless*, then. Limp away, Mr Smoke. We don't have time for *silliness*. Memphis, Razzia, please move Mr *Collup* into position."

Collup tried gamely to struggle, but there was nothing he could do to prevent being pressed up against the first X. The clasps that snapped around his ankles were bound – Valkyrie could see the sigils carved into the metal. Memphis took the shackles from the old man's wrists, tossed them aside as Razzia secured his hands above his head.

Once all the clasps were closed, Razzia opened Collup's shirt, then swung the curved plate across his chest, locking it in place. The plate had a hole in its centre, as big as a drinks coaster. Satisfied, she stepped back and the hydraulic arm lifted the X off the dais. Melior stood nearby, calculating angles. When it was about seven metres overhead, level with the fourth tier, Melior gave a signal. The arm stopped moving, but the X whirred and slowly turned 180 degrees until Collup was hanging upside down.

"Mr *Rut* next," said Lethe.

Memphis reached out but Rut pulled away, scrambled back, ran for the edge of the dais. Right on the edge he froze, eyes widening when he saw the lake of energy below.

"You can't *escape*, Tanner," Lethe said. "This is a *prison*, remember? Let's just calm down and give our lives without *complaint*, what do you say?"

Memphis grabbed him, hauled him back. They clasped him to the X and secured the plate across his chest, then the arm lifted him high into the air and he, too, turned till he was upside down.

"And finally," Lethe said, "Miss *Cain*."

Valkyrie glanced at Skulduggery as Razzia and Memphis came forward, but she started walking before they reached her. They stepped aside, allowing her to position herself against the final X.

"Now that's what I like to see," Lethe said. "A little dignity in your final moments."

The clasps were tight around her ankles. Razzia removed the shackles and Valkyrie raised her arms, allowing her wrists to be clasped. Cadaverous watched her, irritation on his face. She knew he'd rather she struggle and beg. She let her eyes drift away from him, like he wasn't even there.

Razzia pulled Valkyrie's T-shirt down a little, then swung the curved plate across her chest. It was cold against her skin.

"Raise her up," Razzia said, and the hydraulic arm jerked a little, then lifted her relatively smoothly off the dais. With nothing to stand on, her full bodyweight hung from the cold, uncomfortable clasps. She looked down. Funny, it hadn't looked nearly as high from down there.

When she reached the other two Xs, the arm stopped. She could look straight into the cells of the fourth tier, and the convicts leered at her, shouted things that she ignored. The X started to turn. It was an unsettling sensation. She expected the clasps to break at any moment. Her hair got in her eyes. When she was finally upside down, coins spilled from her pockets and hit Smoke on the head.

He howled. She joined in the laughter. She couldn't help it.

"Let me do it!" Smoke yelled. "Let me kill her!"

The laughter died as Cadaverous took hold of Smoke's shoulder and leaned in. "You're not even on the waiting list, Mr Smoke. I'm the one who gets to end her life."

"Ah-ah," Skulduggery responded. "We had a deal. If we get to this point and we're both still alive, we square off."

"We don't have time for that," said Cadaverous.

The blood was rushing to Valkyrie's head. She felt woozy and ill.

"Cadaverous has a *point*," Lethe said. "We had an arrangement, this is *true*, but circumstances have *changed*. Events have *transpired*. We are now at a crucial juncture and I'm afraid we can't delay it for a *duel*."

"So," Cadaverous said, "I kill her."

"We, uh, we mightn't need to kill her," Melior said. "We might only need the life force of the first two. That could be enough. The only reason we even have a third is on the off chance we need extra."

"So *there* you go!" Lethe said, clapping his hands. "You might get the chance to duel over her *yet*! Memphis, attach the *hose* to Mr Collup, if you please."

Memphis took hold of one end of the first bit of hose and ran it up into the tripod from beneath, then went to the other end and picked up the nozzle. Slinging the hose over his shoulder, he climbed the hydraulic arm with ease. Collup watched him come. He tried to struggle. The prisoners loved it. They cheered.

Memphis reached the X and swung out of it with one hand. He took the nozzle and jammed it into the hole in the middle of the curved plate over Collup's chest, then twisted, locking it in place. He dropped then, tumbling elegantly in mid-air before landing.

Lethe went to the slab and stood there, hands over the carved box. He hesitated a moment, then opened it, and took out Abyssinia's heart.

Valkyrie couldn't see it that well, but it looked small and dry and pretty unimpressive. She didn't say anything, though. She was too busy not passing out.

Lethe turned to Melior. "*Richard*, if you would kindly get this *show* on the proverbial *road*..."

Melior appeared frozen to the spot. "I... I can't."

"We've made it *easy* on you, Richard. Our sacrificial lambs are *killers*. You'll do the world a *favour* by dispatching them."

Melior still didn't move. Lethe walked over to him, put a hand on his shoulder.

"I understand," he said. "You're *conflicted*. You don't *want* to release a centuries-old evil into the world, but then again you don't want to never see your *husband* again. That, Richard, is a *conflict*. That is a true *dilemma*. I only ask that you listen to your *conscience*. You do what is right for *you*, Richard. Forget about the three people dangling overhead – two of whom are self-confessed murderers of *perfectly* innocent people and the *third* being ultimately responsible for the senseless deaths of 1,351 poor unfortunate souls. Forget about that. Forget about their red faces. Forget about all the people who will *die* as a result of Abyssinia's return. That's not *on* you. That's on *us*. We are doing this *willingly*. But you? You have been *forced* into this position. You don't have a *choice*. If you choose not to resurrect Abyssinia, you will never, *ever* see Savant Vega again. You will condemn him to his *fate*. But, if you choose to do this, Savant will be *returned* to you, you have my word, and you will both be allowed to *leave*."

Melior didn't take his eyes from the heart. "And then what?"

"Then events will *unfold*," said Lethe. "Abyssinia will *succeed* in her plans, or she will *not*. That part of the tale has nothing to do with *you*. Do you want your husband back?"

"Yes."

"Then by all means... proceed."

Melior approached the slab. He raised his hands over the heart, but hesitated.

"No," he said, so softly Valkyrie barely heard him.

"*Sorry?*" Lethe asked. "What was that? You'd rather *never* see *Savant* again?"

Melior stepped away from the slab. "I can't be responsible for what Abyssinia will do."

"You *won't* be," said Lethe. "*We* will. I just *explained* this." He looked around. "Didn't I just *explain* this?"

Melior shook his head. "I won't do it. I won't be a part of something that will take innocent lives."

Razzia laughed. "Told you."

"Hush," Lethe said, and Razzia grinned. Valkyrie watched Lethe wrap an arm round Melior's shoulders. "Richard, I *understand*. I *do*. And I don't hold it against you. You're a *good man*. We tried making it *easy* on you by giving you dastardly villains, but you have *morals*. That is to be admired. However, I cannot allow *your* morals to get in the way of *our* plans." He looked up, and said loudly, "Mr Lilt."

Valkyrie turned her head. She watched, upside down, as a group of kids were shoved to the railings around her. She recognised one of the men doing the shoving from his photograph.

"Which one first, Doctor Melior?" Parthenios Lilt called down. The kids looked confused. Scared. Some of them wore Corrival Academy uniforms.

Melior had gone pale. "What are you doing? Let them go. They're children."

"But they're not totally *innocent*," Lethe told him. "These are the First Wave. They're on-board the *Abyssinia train*, Richard. They harbour *dark thoughts*. Bad apples to a one. And we will kill them *all*, every bad apple in the *barrel*, until you do what we want you to do."

Some of the kids started to struggle. Two of them were already crying.

"Mr Lilt," Lethe called, "who is your *favourite* student?"

Lilt pondered. "I think it would have to be Jenan Ispolin," he answered.

Lethe clapped. "Jenan Ispolin, Student of the *Year*! Throw him down *first*, Mr Lilt."

Lilt seized a lanky boy who started to panic, but could do nothing as he was tipped over the railing.

"Stop!" Melior shouted. "Stop! I'll do it!"

Lethe held up a hand, and Lilt pulled Jenan back. The kids

were led away. Valkyrie saw Lilt pat Jenan on the shoulder, like it had all been part of an act. She wondered if Jenan believed him.

Melior stood at the slab, and his hands began to glow.

Valkyrie didn't know what she had expected – beams of light, maybe, or some kind of weird chanting – but all Melior did was stand there with his glowing hands and his eyes closed, and the heart didn't do much of anything. It just lay there on the table.

Her head pounding, Valkyrie glanced across at Rut and Collup. They looked scared.

Melior opened the second box, and took out a glass globe, about the size of a bowling ball. The Soul Catcher. He lifted it on to the tripod where it settled, snug in its perfectly proportioned recess, and immediately a hundred sigils glowed along the transparent hose leading to Collup's X.

"Please," Collup called down. "I'm sorry for all the things I done. Please don't kill me. I'm sorry."

"I'm sorry, too," Melior said, and placed his right hand on the Soul Catcher.

Collup screamed so suddenly it made Valkyrie jerk in her clasps. Orange light spilled from the nozzle at his chest, filling the tube with its violent splendour, the sigils burning brightly now, straining to contain the power coursing through it. Collup's screams turned to a long, agonised howl as his skin dried and wrinkled while Valkyrie watched, and his body hollowed out and his bones snapped in their confinements. His life force flowed through the hose and filled the Soul Catcher and when it was done Melior lifted his hand and the hose went dark and Collup's head lolled forward.

His right hand trembling a few centimetres above the Soul Catcher, Melior moved his left to the heart on the table. With a look on his face like he was being forced to plunge his hand into boiling water, he took a deep breath and once again placed his hand on the churning sphere. He jerked upright as the energy passed through his body and out from his fingertips.

The heart soaked it up, soaked up every last bit of it, and when the Soul Catcher was empty Melior took his hands away. He stepped back, pale and exhausted, watching the heart.

The heart lay on the table.

Lethe looked at Melior. Melior kept looking at the heart.

And then it began to beat.

63

It was no longer small and dry. The heart was larger now, and it glistened, and it beat faster. Stronger.

It sprouted its first artery.

It happened quickly after that. The arteries grew, were joined by thickening veins, linked to capillaries that spread outwards, that grew pieces of meat, and from those pieces organs formed, lungs and kidneys and now bone, a spinal cord growing right there on the table, a nervous system being birthed, maturing, and Valkyrie saw nerve clusters and vertebrae and a mass of cells becoming a brain. Around that brain a skull was forming, while elsewhere there were ribs curling protectively around the organs and meat covering the ribs and she saw clavicles and a humerus and a pelvic bone and femurs, it was growing legs, and the meat was spreading and the veins were spreading and then it all slowed down.

"Well done, Richard," said Lethe, examining the half-thing that lay on the table. "Well done."

"I can hear her," Cadaverous said. "I can hear her louder than ever. Clearer."

Razzia giggled, tapping her head, listening to the voice. "She wants more," she said.

Memphis disconnected the first hose from the tripod and attached the second.

Tanner Rut looked at Valkyrie, but there was nothing either of them could say. They both stared at Collup's corpse as Memphis climbed the hydraulic arm. Rut closed his eyes as Memphis reached him.

"This won't hurt a bit," Memphis said, grinning, as he inserted the nozzle into the curved plate. He locked it.

Melior put his hand on the Soul Catcher and the hose sucked out Tanner Rut's life force. Valkyrie didn't watch him die. He tried not to scream, but that didn't last long. Thankfully, it was over in seconds, and then he was nothing but a dried-out husk and Melior was transferring his energy into Abyssinia.

The birth continued, spurred on with renewed vigour. Valkyrie became aware of the silence. The prisoners weren't cheering any more; they were staring. Whether in fascination or revulsion Valkyrie didn't know. On her part, it was a definite mixture of both.

Abyssinia was at her full height now. Her body was curled up like a foetus in the womb. Her internal structure complete, skin was beginning to form. It spread like paint. Silver hair sprouted and grew long.

Then the Soul Catcher emptied.

Lethe stood beside Razzia and Smoke, watching Melior as the doctor ran a glowing hand over Abyssinia's body.

"Well?" Lethe asked. "Is it done?"

"Almost," Melior said, his voice cracking with weariness. He looked up at Valkyrie. "I'm so sorry," he said. "We need just a little more."

The convicts cheered and hollered, rattling cups against the bars of their cells, and Memphis made to jump down.

"Stay where you are," Cadaverous said. "I'll do it." He grabbed the final hose, swapping it out for the one in the tripod. But as he reached for the nozzle it leaped into Skulduggery's hand.

"And how do you intend to get to her?" Skulduggery asked, lifting off his feet.

"Lethe!" said Cadaverous. "We had a deal!"

"I really don't *care*," Lethe admitted.

Cadaverous seethed, and glared upwards. "I'll kill you."

Skulduggery made an amused sound and came level with Valkyrie's eyes.

"Hello," he said.

"Hello," she said back.

"Your face is very red."

"I feel like I'm about to pass out – which would be a blessing, by the looks of things."

"*Kill her*," Lethe commanded.

Skulduggery ignored him. "I have hugely enjoyed our time together, Valkyrie. You are one of only two people I have ever known capable of surprising me on a nearly daily basis. You are extravagant and wonderful."

"You're not so bad yourself. Sorry I said what I said at Melior's place, by the way."

His head tilted. "What did you say?"

"When we were talking about resurrecting people. I said—"

"Ah," he said, "you asked how many people that I've lost would I love to see again. As I recall, you apologised at the time."

"Yeah, well, I'm apologising again, because I still feel bad about it."

"You're forgiven."

"Thank you," she said.

"And I apologise for calling your brain 'semi-remarkable'."

"That did hurt, but you're forgiven, too."

"That's very gracious of you. You don't seem daunted by the prospect of dying."

"I suppose I'm not," she said. "I think I've become a little immune to the idea. Is that weird?"

"Not for me," Skulduggery said. "For you... possibly."

"I think I might deserve it, though, don't you? Just a little? I don't know. I might be talking nonsense. Hanging upside down is doing weird things to my brain."

Below them, Lethe was prodding Smoke.

"Skulduggery!" Smoke said tightly. "Just kill her and be done with it!"

"In a moment," Skulduggery answered.

Valkyrie was in the perfect position to see the look on Smoke's face, as the surprise overtook the pain.

"Huh," Skulduggery said. "I disobeyed an order."

"Kill her!" Smoke shouted. "Do it now!"

Skulduggery brought up the nozzle, tapped it against the slot over her chest. "I feel the urge to do it," he said. "But I have to admit, there is some urgency lacking."

"Because you're fighting it," Valkyrie told him. "You're about to break free."

"Drain her!" Smoke yelled.

Skulduggery's hands jerked before he pulled them back.

"This is an odd sensation," Skulduggery murmured. "You're really not afraid?"

She gave him a sad smile. "I don't die like this," she said. "I die on my knees."

"Memphis!" Lethe shouted. "*You* do it!"

"Taking care of business," Memphis muttered, and jumped from Tanner Rut's X to Valkyrie's.

Before he reached it, Skulduggery waved his hand and he was knocked off course. He fell, screaming, into the lake of energy and was instantly vaporised.

"Well, that's torn it," Skulduggery said, dropping the nozzle while his hand went to the latches on her clasps. He freed her limbs and her magic came back to her, flooding her system.

Below them, Lethe shoved Nero. "Get him! Teleport him into the *lake!*"

"My head hurts..."

"Do it!"

Nero scowled and fixed his eyes on Skulduggery as Skulduggery thrust his left hand down, the air rippling, while at the same time his right fist spun behind him. Nero, focusing only on the attacking hand, teleported to a space above Skulduggery and dropped on to him, catching the right fist just behind the ear. Nero's head snapped back and he fell, too dazed to stop himself from crunching down on to the platform. He rolled over, clutching his left shoulder, screaming.

The curved plate swung away and Valkyrie immediately plummeted, but her fall was curtailed by cushions of air that rolled in beneath her. She found herself turned right way up and then she was drifting down by Skulduggery's side.

"I know what you're thinking," Skulduggery announced. "You outnumber us. You've got us trapped in a prison full of people who hate us. But I need you to understand something. When we're together, Valkyrie and I, there is nothing we cannot accomplish, and no number of enemies we cannot overcome."

They landed gently. Immediately, Valkyrie toppled over.

Skulduggery looked down at her. "You ruined that."

"My legs are asleep." She winced, and thumped her thighs. "Ah. God. Ow. Pins and needles."

Skulduggery looked up at their enemies. "You can ignore this part."

Cadaverous and Razzia ran at him. Skulduggery batted Razzia aside with a wall of air, but Cadaverous dived at him, took him backwards. Skulduggery spun, flipping the old man over his hip, but Cadaverous was a lot more durable than he looked. He grabbed Skulduggery and pulled him down, and they went rolling.

Valkyrie got to one knee, still wincing as the blood returned to her feet. She glanced up and Lethe was almost upon her. She jerked back, white lightning bursting from her fingertips. It caught him in the chest, sent him whirling to the ground. She stood up, stamped her feet a few times, turned to help Skulduggery.

Then someone whistled. That whistle was joined by another. And another. Suddenly the world was filled with whistling.

Valkyrie looked up. The cell doors were open. The convicts crowded the tiers.

And they started jumping down.

64

The first few convicts tore into Skulduggery with an unholy vengeance, but one of them landed right next to Valkyrie, stumbling slightly. She drove her knee into the point of his chin and he slumped backwards.

She turned to the sound of a maniac's battle cry. A long-haired prisoner made the leap down, her face contorted with hatred. But she missed the dais by a good arm's length and kept falling. This made some of the other prisoners rethink their plans.

Movement behind her and Valkyrie spun, but was too late to dodge Razzia's lunge. They went down, rolled, got up again, and Razzia punched Valkyrie and Valkyrie punched Razzia.

"I've been waiting for this," Razzia said, grinning.

Valkyrie didn't know what to say to that, so she said, "OK."

Razzia kicked at Valkyrie's leg and Valkyrie backed off, rubbing the spot where the kick had landed. The prison reverberated with the cheers of its inmates. She circled to her right, and Razzia stayed close, with that wide smile and those crazy eyes.

Valkyrie rushed her. Razzia tried stepping away and kicking, but Valkyrie was too close. She wrapped an arm round the kicking leg and swept the other one, landed on top. They wrestled there, rolling and tumbling, struggling for the dominant position. Whenever she could, Valkyrie fired a punch into Razzia's ribs. Whenever she could, Razzia returned the favour.

Suddenly Valkyrie was on top and wrenching Razzia's arm, turning her on to her side and kneeling on her head – but there was a flash of yellow and a prisoner dropped on to her. The world tilted and she was no longer holding Razzia. The prisoner had her. She could smell his hot breath. She could feel his clawing hands. She lashed out, got a lucky shot into the side of his neck. His eyes bulged and she pushed him off. Scrambled up.

Another prisoner landed. He stumbled and used his momentum to knock her off her feet. He fell on top of her, tried to pin her there. She dug her thumbs into his eyes and squirmed out from underneath as he screamed.

She stood and caught a fist in the jaw, tilted, went down, rolled, came to a stop with the left side of her body hanging over nothing but air. She rolled away from the platform's edge. A prisoner came at her, face alive with intent. White lightning danced between her fingertips.

She blasted him.

She blasted another.

Someone yanked her hair and pulled her into a headlock and she grabbed him between the legs and twisted, then blasted him off his feet.

She turned, panting. The platform was crawling with yellow jumpsuits. Skulduggery was dealing with a bunch of them. Another bunch were coming for her.

And Razzia was disappearing under another bunch.

Valkyrie leaped in, her knee crunching into the face of a convict who'd been raining down punches. Razzia kicked another away and Valkyrie grabbed her hand, hauled her up. Razzia elbowed and headbutted. Valkyrie stomped and hammered. They stood back to back and dealt viciousness to those who dared get close. When they'd cleared a space, they started using their magic.

Suddenly they had no more enemies left to fight. The convicts still on the platform were either unconscious or too injured to be a threat. The other convicts, still on the tiers, had quietened down considerably. Skulduggery extricated himself from a pile of beaten, moaning bodies. Cadaverous was still under there somewhere.

"This doesn't mean we're mates," Razzia said.

Valkyrie looked round. "Sorry?"

"This," said Razzia. "It doesn't mean we're mates, y'know."

"Oh. No, I... I didn't think it would."

"All right," Razzia said, nodding. "Just so we're clear." She walked for the edge. "Hey, skeleton man. Boost me to the other side, would you?"

Skulduggery looked at Valkyrie and she shrugged. He echoed the shrug, and used the air to carry Razzia to an empty tier, where she vanished into the corridor beyond.

"OK then," Skulduggery said, "is that everyone?"

"Not quite," said Lethe, slowly getting to his feet.

Skulduggery grunted, unimpressed by the turn of events. Valkyrie tapped a finger against the sigil on her hip, felt it glow warmly.

"I've never seen *anyone* break free of Smoke's influence before it wears off *naturally*," Lethe said. "I always knew you were *special*, Skulduggery. I gather it's why Abyssinia speaks so *highly* of you."

"You gather?" Skulduggery said, circling to Lethe's right while Valkyrie circled to his left. "She doesn't speak directly to you?"

"Sadly, *no*," Lethe answered. "The only voices in my head are my *own*."

"It must be lonely."

"Finally," Lethe said, "someone who *understands*."

Skulduggery hurled two fireballs that exploded against Lethe's chest. They didn't catch, but they forced him back a step and Valkyrie's hands lit up. Her lightning caught Lethe on the shoulder, spinning him as Skulduggery ran and jumped, his knee crashing into Lethe's sternum. Lethe ducked under Skulduggery's next attack and grabbed him, but Valkyrie wrapped an arm around his neck and pulled him away.

Lethe turned, reached for her and she rammed an elbow into his mask and dodged back before his fist could find her.

Skulduggery lashed a kick into the back of Lethe's leg and Lethe grunted, looked like he might go down for the briefest of moments... but he straightened up again.

"Ah, *teamwork*," he said as they continued to circle him. "It won't help you, you know."

Valkyrie looked around, expecting a battalion of Cleavers to teleport in at any moment.

Lethe picked up a fallen scythe, twirling it expertly before locking it in place by his side.

"I'm waiting," he said.

Another scythe rose into Skulduggery's hands. He didn't bother twirling it.

"When you see an opening," he said to Valkyrie, "blast him."

China's squad of Cleavers still hadn't teleported in, so Valkyrie picked up a scythe of her own, started casually twirling it as she circled. She twirled it one-handed, then two-handed, then finished the twirl one-handed again. Skulduggery and Lethe observed her silently and she raised an eyebrow at them both.

Lethe attacked Skulduggery so suddenly that he barely had time to block, barely had time to sidestep and parry and twist away. But that's how fights like these were fought – with barely enough time. Valkyrie took three quick steps and swiped low, then brought the scythe blade up high. Lethe dodged the first and blocked the second, responded with a swipe of his own like she knew he would. She countered, cracked her staff into his knee, rammed her shoulder into his chest and slashed at his head. The tip of her blade scraped a line in his mask, but didn't puncture through.

"Unusual *style*," Lethe said, backing away. His head turned fractionally to Skulduggery. "You didn't teach her."

"No, I didn't," Skulduggery said. "As ever, Valkyrie is full of surprises."

He used the air to nudge Lethe off balance and swung his scythe. The instant Lethe blocked, Skulduggery moved, changing up his angles, going low then high then low again. Staffs cracked and blades scraped. Valkyrie came in, tried a broad slash to mess with Lethe's rhythm, but he kept his tempo as well as any Cleaver she'd ever seen.

Lethe backed away and now Valkyrie and Skulduggery were fighting side by side, pursuing him across the disc, all three of them stepping carefully over the unconscious bodies at their feet while their weapons blurred and clashed. The exhilaration of that moment pumped through Valkyrie's veins, feeding strength into her muscles, sharpening her reflexes. Skulduggery's support allowed her to try things, to risk moves that drew Lethe out, opened up opportunities. Victory was mere seconds away.

And then it started to shift. The flow changed. Reversed. Now it was Valkyrie and Skulduggery who were stepping backwards and Lethe who was pressing the attack. His scythe moved impossibly fast. He blocked their strikes like he knew they were coming, batting aside their blades with something akin to contempt. He spun with a kick that sent Skulduggery stumbling and whacked his scythe's staff into the side of Valkyrie's face. She dropped her own scythe as she went to the ground. She lay there, too stunned to think, while Skulduggery plunged back into the fight.

Darquesse wandered into view. "Today is a good day," she said. "This morning I almost tasted an apple, and this afternoon I get to watch you die."

"Help us," Valkyrie muttered.

Darquesse laughed. "And why would I do something stupid

like that? If you really need help, though, maybe you should tap that sigil again. What's it called, an auxilium? The look on your face when nobody arrived to save you, a look of sad disappointment... I'll never forget it."

Valkyrie turned over, got to her hands and knees, waiting for her head to stop spinning. "If I die, you'll have no one to talk to."

The grin faded from Darquesse's face. "So I won't have to endure your whiny self-loathing. I think I'll be OK with that."

Valkyrie kept her voice low. "You hate me, right?"

"Obviously."

"And yet you still talk to me, because you know you'd go nuts otherwise. So either help us or say your goodbyes."

Valkyrie clambered up as Skulduggery crashed into her.

"You've got him on the ropes," Valkyrie assured him as they untangled themselves.

Skulduggery nodded. "That's just what I was thinking."

Lethe stood there, arms wide, awaiting their next attack.

"I have an idea," Skulduggery said.

"A strategy?" Valkyrie asked.

"More of a tactic."

"What's the difference?"

"A strategy is a plan. Tactics are the manoeuvres you employ to achieve that plan."

"He can hear us, though."

"That doesn't matter," Skulduggery said. "This tactic is so simple it doesn't matter if he knows it's coming."

"This should be *interesting*," said Lethe.

"We rush him," Skulduggery said.

Valkyrie frowned. "That's it?"

"It is."

"We run at him? That's the manoeuvre we're employing? Running?"

"And, when we get to him, we start hitting him," Skulduggery said. "That's the beauty of this whole thing. It ends with us hitting him. In the face."

"I do like that part," Valkyrie admitted. "But the rest sounds a bit iffy."

"He'll never expect it."

"I'm expecting it right *now*," Lethe said.

"He's lying," Skulduggery whispered.

Valkyrie thought for a moment, and shrugged. "OK. Let's do it."

"You're both *insane*," Lethe said. "I *love* it."

Skulduggery rolled his shoulders. "Ready?"

Valkyrie put a hand on his arm. "Wait a second. We'll go on my mark." She watched Darquesse walk up to Lethe, hesitate, and put a hand through his head. Lethe had no idea it was happening.

"Three..." Valkyrie said, "two... *one*."

Darquesse's hand crackled with energy and Lethe stiffened, and a moment later Skulduggery and Valkyrie slammed into him. They tumbled to the ground, Valkyrie falling through Darquesse, who sagged, drained by the effort. Skulduggery punched and Valkyrie dropped elbows, and then Skulduggery flipped Lethe on to his front and shackled his hands behind him.

"Will that do it?" Valkyrie asked, pressing her knee into the small of his back. "This is a necronaut suit. Do shackles work on these things?"

"They work," Skulduggery said, pressing Lethe's face into the ground. "Where did *you* hear about necronaut suits?"

"I'm not completely useless without you around, you know."

"I never said you were," he replied, amused.

"I can't believe that worked."

"There is genius in simplicity," Skulduggery reminded her.

Darquesse lifted off her feet. She'd gone gravely pale, her forehead covered with a light sheen of perspiration. She caught

Valkyrie looking at her and turned, drifted away from the dais and passed through the wall.

"Where is he?" Melior asked.

Valkyrie looked back, but Melior wasn't talking to her or to Skulduggery – he was talking to Lethe.

He came forward, fists bunched. "Where's Savant? Tell me where you've been keeping him."

Skulduggery straightened up and held him back. "We'll get all the answers you want, but give us space."

"Space?" Melior repeated, almost laughing. "He's had my husband for five years! For five years, he's walked around with that knowledge in his head and I couldn't say one thing about it because of what they might do. This is the first time I've ever seen this man beaten and this is my first chance to ask him and he *is* going to tell me what he knows. If he'd snatched someone you love, Mr Pleasant, would you be inclined to give him space?"

Skulduggery's head tilted. "I suppose I wouldn't. But I can't let you near him. Sorry."

Melior glared. "You really think you can stop me?"

Skulduggery didn't get a chance to answer.

He stepped within arm's reach of Azzedine Smoke, lying there half covered by unconscious convicts, and Smoke lunged, grabbed Skulduggery's leg with both hands and some internal switch flicked inside Valkyrie's mind and she saw the darkness swirl around Skulduggery's aura, faster than before, thicker and darker. Smoke was putting everything into this, everything into overpowering Skulduggery's essence, and then it was done.

Smoke looked back at Valkyrie. "Kill her," he snapped.

Skulduggery turned.

Valkyrie raised a hand, but he knocked it aside and hit her, a fist to the jaw that spun her, sent her to her knees. His gun flew into his hand, and he pressed it to Valkyrie's forehead.

The room stopped.

"Skulduggery," Valkyrie whispered.

65

On her knees, all strength having abandoned her, bruised and battered with her left eye swelling shut, Valkyrie could only whisper his name.

He stood over her, one hand holding a fistful of her hair, the other holding the gun that felt so cold against her forehead. He burned with darkness. Smoke's sickness wrapped around him, twisting and seething, infecting him until there was not one glimmer of his true self remaining.

She wasn't scared. That surprised her. She wasn't scared, she was just sad. So incredibly sad. This was what she deserved, of that she had no doubt. She was a killer who deserved to be killed, a murderer who deserved to be murdered. Her death, violent and bloody, was inevitable. If it hadn't been at his hands, it would have been at someone else's. If not today, then tomorrow, or next week, or a hundred years from now. But she could no more escape her fate than the Earth could escape its orbit of the sun.

He stood over her, his finger on the trigger. Time slowed. Not Destrier's doing. This was her perception of the moment of her own death, and time was generous in this instance, in order to allow her to fully appreciate the experience.

She thought of her sister, and her parents, and her dog, and she thought of Omen and Never and Militsa. She thought of Tanith, and wished she'd had a chance to say goodbye, and thought of Ghastly and Gordon, and wondered if she'd see them again. She thought of people and places and times, but only as sensations, memories of emotions that she recognised as clearly as faces. They flooded her mind, lingering both an eternity and an instant, and then she thought of Skulduggery, the man standing over her, and she hoped he'd never snap out of this.

"I love you," she said, and closed her eyes.

66

The shot filled the room.

67

"I love you, too," Skulduggery said, and Valkyrie opened her eyes, watching the fierce red of his aura bursting through the black like the sun through storm clouds. Her ears rang, the gun having gone off so close to her head. The red swirled, overcoming Smoke's darkness, burning so fiercely that she had to switch off her aura-vision before it blinded her.

"What are you doing?" Smoke demanded, hobbling on his good leg. "What the hell are you doing?"

Skulduggery turned and pushed at the air, and Azzedine Smoke flew backwards off the dais, and fell to the lake of energy below.

It was so incredibly surreal. Valkyrie was supposed to be dead, yet life seemed determined to continue.

She watched, dazed, as Lethe grabbed Melior and shoved him over to Abyssinia's body on the slab.

"Use me," Lethe said, attaching one of the hoses to the tripod and pressing the other end into his chest. "Use my life force. I'm a Neoteric. My life force will work, won't it?"

"I... I don't know," Melior said.

"It's over," Skulduggery said. "You've failed, Lethe. Let it go."

Lethe shook his head. "It's *not* over. It's *not*. Richard, kill me now, *right now*, and you get Savant back. I promise you. I *swear* to you. That's what you *want*, isn't it? Above all else?"

"I... I'm not going to kill you..."

"*Do it*," Lethe said. "I'm the one who's kept him *from* you. It was *me*. It was all *me*. Don't you understand? I did it. I ruined your *life*, and I have tortured Savant every day since then. *Every single day*. Have your *revenge*. Kill me."

Skulduggery raised his gun. "Don't do it, Richard."

"Kill me *now*," said Lethe.

Then Never teleported in, but, instead of bringing with her dozens of Cleavers, her hands were on the shoulders of Omen Darkly and Temper Fray.

"Stop!" Temper shouted, hands out towards Melior. "Don't do anything!"

"*Kill me* and you'll get Savant back," Lethe said.

"Kill him and you'll kill Savant!" Temper countered. "Richard, a few hours ago I spoke with a mutual friend of ours – Tessa Mehrbano."

Melior frowned. "So?"

"She knew Smoke. For weeks leading up to Savant's abduction, she saw Smoke pour his corruption into a black rubber suit – *Lethe's* black rubber suit."

"*Kill me*," Lethe growled.

"Lethe is Savant!" Omen blurted. "Lethe is your husband!"

Melior froze.

Skulduggery lowered his gun. "Smoke drenched the necronaut suit with his power," he murmured. "Once they sealed it, Savant was stuck. He had no escape."

"They're *lying* to you," Lethe said.

"The affectations," Skulduggery continued, "the vocal distortions, the deliberate speech patterns... it was all to disguise the man beneath."

Melior hesitated, then shook his head. "Savant is a pacifist," he said. "He couldn't hurt someone if he tried."

"He's a quick learner," said Skulduggery. "A *very* quick learner. That's his power, isn't it? That's why Lethe fights the way he does.

That's why he loses until he's learned your moves. Once he's seen you in action, once he's gone up against you, he uses your own skills against you."

Melior looked up. "Is that... is that true?"

When Lethe didn't answer, Melior's skin started to glow.

"You've been here the whole time?" Melior pressed. "The last five years, you've been right in front of me?"

Lethe dropped the hose and grabbed him. "*Kill me!*"

Melior's energy burst from him, flinging Lethe back.

Temper rushed over, but Lethe wasn't getting up. Temper knelt by him, started working at the fastenings around his throat.

Skulduggery helped Valkyrie to her feet. "Are you OK?" he asked gently.

"I'll live," she said.

Temper pulled the mask away, and Melior gave a strangled cry when he saw the face of his unconscious beloved beneath.

A tremendous feeling of déjà vu washed over Valkyrie and her skin prickled with the memory of fiery coals and swirling steam. An image, a single image from her vision, of a girl struck by a searing blast of energy, and she saw Never standing in front of her and she looked up, to the tier above, where the convicts roared and jostled. She saw a fierce light growing around a prisoner's hand, and the arm straightening, and she launched herself at Never, shoving her out of the way as pain exploded in her left shoulder.

The force of the blast twirled her, actually twirled her in place, and once she was done twirling she staggered, gasping and holding her arm, coming to a stop against the slab. Blood ran like a burst faucet. So much blood. So red. So warm. Dimly aware of Skulduggery waving his own arm, she watched as the convict with the glowing hand was plucked from his perch and tossed screaming into the lake of energy below them.

Valkyrie blinked. Temper was running over to her. Behind him, Omen helped Never back to her feet and Skulduggery was pointing. Pointing.

What was he pointing at?

She felt hands on her shoulders. Long fingers, weak but desperate. Hungry. She turned her head as Abyssinia sat up behind her, mouth open, inhaling Valkyrie's essence, her life force, her soul, and Valkyrie gasped, aware of the heat rushing from her body.

Abyssinia's eyes opened, locked on to Valkyrie's.

Someone else's hand, closing round her wrist, and the world speeded up and Temper was hauling her towards the others as Abyssinia swung her feet off the table. Abyssinia stood, gazing at her new hands, looking down at her new body, a smile spreading across her new face.

She was back. She was alive.

Abyssinia looked at them all and laughed, and Never teleported Valkyrie and the others away and suddenly they were outside, in a courtyard with Corrival Academy's South Tower looming over them, and Valkyrie's knees gave way and sent her tripping over Lethe and she went down in a tangle with Never and Melior.

She breathed, quick and shallow. Skulduggery crouched over her, pressing his hands against her wound. He was issuing orders. People were panicking. Valkyrie just kept her eyes on him.

68

It had been a rough few days.

Flanery was tired and cranky. He'd left the Oval Office by mid-afternoon, taking calls and holding meetings instead in the Executive Residence. He had the TV on in the background. Every few seconds, he'd look away from whoever was talking to flick to another news network. He knew he should stick to the friendly channels, the smart ones with smart journalists that understood him and what he was trying to do, but, like an itch he couldn't scratch, he always found himself going back to the ones who said mean things about him.

It wasn't that they didn't get it – he understood that now. It wasn't that they couldn't see the terrific things he was doing. It was that they had an agenda, and that agenda was to ruin him. They were stacked with liars and frauds and people who had it in for him.

Irritated, he started to cut meetings short, skipped phone calls and then cancelled briefings altogether. He wanted to be alone with the television. He wanted to stew in his own hatred.

His phone rang. The cellphone that only three people on the planet knew about.

He hesitated, and answered. "Hello?"

"Mr President," a man said, "it is an honour to finally talk to you, sir. My name is Parthenios Lilt. I think it's about time we met."

69

"Hello?"

Sebastian knocked again on the open door. Still no answer. He walked into the gloom, past the suitcases in the hall.

"Bennet? You home?"

He found him in the darkness of the kitchen, sitting at the table, half a mug of coffee left to go cold in his hand. Sebastian flicked on the light.

"It's my son," Bennet said without looking up. "Kase. He... he's staying. I'm moving but he's... not. He'll be living with his mother and... and Conrad. He says he'll see me in a couple of weeks when things have settled."

"I'm sorry to hear that," said Sebastian.

"I've lost my family. I've lost my job. The only thing I have left... is her."

"Darquesse."

Bennet didn't answer. He wiped a tear from his eye and sniffed loudly, then cleared his throat. He looked up. "What do you need?"

"Sorry?"

"You said if you helped me, then I'd help you. You helped me. It didn't work out the way I wanted, but you still helped me. So what do you need in return?"

Sebastian took off his hat, held it in both hands as he took a seat. His chin itched beneath his mask. "There are two types of people in this world," he said. "The type who fear Darquesse, and the type who worship her. I don't fear her."

Bennet nodded. "So you want to be part of our club, is that it? You didn't have to help me out to do that. You just have to turn up. Don't know if you've noticed, but there isn't exactly a line of people clamouring to join. We meet once a week. We pray. We share stories."

"Do you try to contact her?"

Bennet laughed.

"What's so funny?"

"She's gone, Mr Plague Doctor. She's not coming back. The Sanctuary people hit her with an illusion, made her think she'd killed everyone, and she left us for another dimension. She's not coming back because she doesn't think there's anything to come back to."

"So why do you pray to her?"

Bennet went quiet for a moment. "Because I saw first-hand what she can do, and when you witness something like that you... you understand what it's like to see God. You understand your own insignificance. Your place. And... and something else too. You... you..."

"You fall in love," said Sebastian.

Bennet looked up. "Yes. I suppose... I suppose, compared to that, Odetta didn't have a chance, did she? She was right to leave me. This is all my fault."

"Have you heard of Silas Nadir?" Sebastian asked. "Do you know what he did?"

"The serial killer?"

"That's him. He shunted Valkyrie Cain back and forth between this reality and the Leibniz Universe."

"The what?"

"The universe where Mevolent is still alive."

"Oh," said Bennet, "yes. So?"

"The pathway is open still. The Shunters here can now get over there relatively easily. And the Shunters there can come over here. More Shunters are being trained, probably in *both* realities."

"So? What does this have to do with Darquesse?"

"We'll need a Shunter and a way to track her," Sebastian said. "Getting a Shunter will be easy because of all this recent activity. That's our first step."

Bennet sat a little straighter. "You're telling me that there is an actual chance that we could communicate with Darquesse?"

"I haven't worked all of it out yet, and I'll need time and a lot of luck – but, if I'm right, we can do more than communicate with her. That's why I need your help, Bennet. I need your help to bring her back."

70

Omen sat on the edge of the fountain, facing the clock monument, listening to the splash of water and letting it overwhelm the distant sound of evening traffic. It was cold and dark, but the Circle was lit up prettily. The High Sanctuary looked majestic from this low angle, a cross between a fairytale palace and heaven's lobby.

The Dark Cathedral was also lit up, but this only served to accentuate its severe lines and intimidating splendour. If the High Sanctuary was the first step into heaven, the Dark Cathedral was surely the first step on the way to hell.

Someone sat beside him, and Omen shuffled over slightly.

"They're worried about you," Skulduggery Pleasant said.

Omen looked up in surprise. Skulduggery was wearing a façade. Omen had never actually seen one in real life. The clean-shaven face looked real.

"Your headmaster was about to send out a search party," Skulduggery continued. "I asked him to give me a little time, let me look for you. I told him you'd been through a lot in the last few days."

"Thank you," said Omen. "Can I, uh, ask you a question? About your façade?"

Skulduggery smiled. "Sure."

"When the Supreme Mage did it, when she carved the sigils

into your bones, what did she use? Was it her fingernail or a scalpel pen or one of those heat-knives?"

"A scalpel pen," he said. "You have an interest in the languages of magic?"

Omen nodded. "Though we don't really get to carve anything in class. It's mostly just working out angles and depths and stuff. Can she really carve sigils with her bare hands?"

"China? Yes, she can."

"Wow. I'll never be as good as her."

"Probably not," said Skulduggery, "but it won't be because you don't have the talent. You'll never be as good as her because she's over four hundred years older than you and she never stops learning how to be better. When she first gave me the façade, it could only be used for a half-hour each day, and it only covered my face. But she's been adding to it, improving it over the years."

"It changes each time, right?" Omen asked. "That's what I heard. Every time you activate the façade, it's a new face. Why don't you just get your old face, the one you had when you were alive?"

"I'm not that man any more," Skulduggery said. "Wearing his face would be no different to wearing the face I have on right now. They're all masks." His gloved fingers tapped his collarbones through his shirt, and the face flowed away, disappearing under his collar.

Now that his skull was on show, people glanced at him as they passed. They were probably wondering who Omen was, maybe thinking he was someone important. He felt that charge of pride and then, inevitably, the emptiness that followed. He was used to this. He was the Chosen One's brother, after all.

"Do you know if there's been any sign of Jenan and the others?" he asked. "It's been two days and the teachers won't tell us anything."

"Still missing," Skulduggery said. "Every Sanctuary around

the world is searching for them, and for Lilt, and we're all keeping a watch for Coldheart to reappear. We'll find them. Eventually."

"Why does she want them?" Omen asked. "Abyssinia, I mean. She has her gang of psychos and a prison full of convicts. What does she want with a bunch of schoolkids?"

"I don't know," Skulduggery said. "That is annoying, I'll grant you, and it's not a sensation I am either familiar or comfortable with. Do you mind if I ask you a question now? Why are you out here? It's cold and you're shivering."

Omen shrugged. "I kind of get the feeling that everyone's mad at me."

"Why would you think that?"

"Because everyone's mad at me."

"Not everyone, surely."

"The teachers are mad that Never disobeyed the Supreme Mage because of me. They see that as reflecting badly on the Academy, and they blame Never and Never blames me and they also blame me, I think."

"Well, yes," said Skulduggery, "I suppose that's true."

"And my parents are mad because of, well, all of it, and Auger's mad because I didn't tell him what was going on and I could have got myself killed."

"Fair enough."

"And then, even though none of the kids in school know I'm involved in any of this, they're still mad at me because they just don't like me."

Skulduggery nodded.

"And that's it, really," said Omen.

"That's not so bad!" Skulduggery said cheerfully. "I thought it'd be much worse! That's only a dozen or so people! Plenty more have been mad at me over the years. You'll be fine. Best thing to do is just not think about it."

"Right."

"See? Isn't that better?"

"I don't know. I'm still thinking about it."

"They'll forgive you," Skulduggery said. "You did a good thing. A brave thing. They're mad because they don't want you risking your life. They're mad because they care. Because they love you. Obviously, I'm not talking about your classmates or your headmaster here. They have legitimate reasons to be mad at you. But family, Omen... family forgives."

"Yeah. I hope so."

"If it makes any difference," Skulduggery said, "I'm proud of you."

"You are?"

"Absolutely. Although I sincerely thought you'd be a better fighter."

Omen smiled awkwardly. "Yeah."

"I was right to think you trained with your brother, wasn't I?"

"Oh, yes," Omen said, nodding quickly. "I was there, every single time. They brought in experts from loads of martial arts, loads of other combat systems... I was on the mat, same as Auger, for every one of them, and I'd leave the mat at the end of the day battered and bruised and exhausted."

"So you *were* taught to fight?"

Omen nodded again, then shook his head. "Well, no. You've got to understand that all of my parents' attention was on Auger, and everything was geared towards him. So, while I was there for every moment of his fight training, I was really only needed to... get hit."

Skulduggery tilted his head. "I'm sorry?"

"A few of the instructors, they called me the Human Punchbag. That's kinda what I did."

"You stood there and got hit?"

"Yes."

"For years?"

"Yes. Auger didn't like to do it, but the instructors always needed someone to demonstrate on, so..."

"That's quite an extraordinary way to be raised, Omen."

"Life in the Darkly household was pretty unconventional," Omen admitted. "Do you, uh, think I can get better?"

"At being hit? I'm not sure. You seem pretty good at it."

"And what about the other part? The hitting back?"

Skulduggery observed him for a moment. "I think you can improve," he said at last. "And I don't think it'd take you long. Even as the Human Punchbag, you'd have picked up on how to move, how to fall, how to absorb damage and keep going. I'd say the biggest obstacle to overcome would be a change in mindset."

He leaned in. "You think of yourself as the weak one, Omen. You think of yourself as unimportant. That's got to change. You need to figure out your own value. You need to face up to your own worth. The first step in winning a fight for survival is understanding why you deserve to survive. You haven't done that yet. Just because your brother is the Chosen One doesn't mean you're any less vital."

"OK."

"And saying OK does not mean you understand."

"Sorry."

"And stop apologising."

"OK."

"You've got some excellent combat instructors," Skulduggery said, "and some wonderful teachers in your school, but only you can decide who you want to be in life."

Omen nodded, and Skulduggery stood up. "You'd better get back to school, Omen. You're probably in a lot of trouble right now." He nodded, and walked away.

Omen jumped to his feet. "What do I do?" he blurted.

Skulduggery turned.

"I don't want to go back to being ordinary," Omen said. "I want to do *this*. I want to help *you*. I want to help people. I know I'm just fourteen, and I'm not like Valkyrie was, I'm not a warrior or whatever, but you wanted me to start valuing myself, so... so I was *not* useless."

"Of course you weren't," Skulduggery said. A woman walked by, gawking at him, and Skulduggery ignored her. "The fact is, we couldn't have done this without you. You identified Parthenios Lilt, you rescued Temper Fray, you brought us Lethe's true identity."

"Really?" said Omen. "I did all that?"

Skulduggery straightened his tie just a fraction. "You still have a lot to learn, you have classes to attend, and I'm not going to throw you head-first into danger like I did Valkyrie. But you're one of us now, Omen, and we'll call you when we need you."

Omen stood there and blinked, a big dumb smile growing across his face as he watched Skulduggery walk to his car. A City Guard was there, pointing at the car and then pointing at the sign that said NO PARKING. Omen heard Skulduggery laugh as he got behind the wheel.

You're one of us.

He was one of them. He was part of it all. He was part of the group. The gang. The team. He wasn't useless or pointless. He wasn't a waste of space or a waste of skin or a waste of perfectly good air. He may have been the Chosen One's brother, but he wasn't the Chosen One's Brother. Not any more.

He was Omen Darkly. He was whoever the hell he wanted to be.

71

Skulduggery pulled up outside Grimwood House. Valkyrie opened the front door, let Xena bound out into the cold night to greet him while she headed upstairs. Her phone buzzed when she reached the landing.

She stood still as she read the message, feeling the love and the warmth in every one of her mother's words. She thought carefully about her reply, started writing, then deleted it and started again.

She deleted that, then hesitated, fingers hovering over the keys. Finally, she just wrote *Looking forward to it!* and pressed SEND.

Skulduggery stumbled in, Xena doing figures of eight round his legs.

"Good God, dog," Valkyrie heard him say as he closed the door behind him. "Calm down. Calm down, I said. How can you expect us to have a cordial relationship if you can't stay still for one second? Sit. Xena, *sit.*"

Xena cocked her head at him, and sat.

Skulduggery brushed dog hair from his suit. Another glorious three-piece. "Good girl."

"I'm impressed," Valkyrie said, and both Skulduggery and Xena looked up. "She only ever obeys my instructions. She must have accepted you as some sort of authority figure."

"In much the same way that you have."

Valkyrie grinned. "Yeah. Totally."

"How are you feeling?"

"Grand," she said. "Fine. Shoulder's healed. Not even a scar."

"And your other injury?"

"Having some of my life force sucked out? I have no way to gauge my levels, but I feel fine."

"Good," Skulduggery said, and gestured to a small pot on the hall table. "Is that new?"

"I picked it up earlier today," she said. "I was thinking about what you said, y'know, regarding the whole redecorating the house idea, putting my own stamp on the place. So I visited a few furniture stores."

"You visited a few furniture stores, and all you bought was this pot?"

"Baby steps, Skulduggery."

"Indeed." He crouched beside Xena, scratched under her chin and then pointed up at Valkyrie. "Xena. Xena, *fetch*!"

Xena's ears pricked up and she stood on all fours, and Valkyrie gasped at her, locking eyes for a moment before breaking into a run. She heard Xena sprinting up the stairs after her, and made it to the bedroom before falling to the floor and curling up, hands over her head.

Xena charged in and climbed all over her, jabbing her snout underneath Valkyrie's arms, licking her face while Valkyrie laughed. Valkyrie wrapped her arms round the dog and dragged her to the floor, kissing and petting her, and Xena rolled on to her back, four paws in the air, waiting for her belly to be scratched.

Valkyrie dutifully scratched it as Skulduggery walked into the room.

"I've missed that sound," he said.

"What sound?"

"You. Laughing. I haven't heard you laugh in... a while."

"Maybe you should try being funnier."

"Oh, I sincerely doubt that it's my fault."

"Of course you do," Valkyrie said, smiling, and got up. Xena stayed exactly where she was.

"Am I keeping you from anything?" Skulduggery asked. "I just thought I'd fill you in on the latest goings-on in Roarhaven, but if you're busy..."

"You can fill me in while I get changed," said Valkyrie, walking to her wardrobe. "Did you speak with Omen?"

Skulduggery nodded. "I know you're not entirely convinced of the wisdom of his continued involvement, but I believe he'll surprise you."

"He's already surprised me," Valkyrie said, picking out her clothes and dropping them on to the bed. "As did Never. I don't mind involving them – I just don't think we should put them in any actual danger from here on out. Would you agree?"

"In theory."

She sighed. "Skulduggery..."

"You saw the Darkly boys in your vision, which means Omen has some trouble in store over the next few years, with or without us. I think the least we can do is help him prepare. Denied the proper guidance, he's not going to be ready. He needs us, Valkyrie."

She gave a reluctant murmur. "But we're going to *try* to keep him alive, aren't we? He's a really good kid. I don't want to see anything bad happen to him."

"We'll try our best."

"Fair enough. Turn round."

Skulduggery turned his back to her, and she started undressing.

"How's Savant?" she asked.

"Recovering," he said. "He only started to regain his independence this morning. He's got a lot of work ahead of him, a lot of rehabilitation. He's got to reconnect with who he was. Doctor Melior is helping him, as you would expect. It's going to be hard on both of them. Aside from the extraordinary circumstances of their situation, to lose somebody for that long and then to get them back..."

"You think they'll make it?"

"They love each other. Love conquers all."

"That's surprisingly upbeat of you."

"I have had my faith restored, Valkyrie. Humanity will do that to you, every once in a while. Beneath Lethe's mask was a good man clouded by other people's darkness. He'll step into the light again, I have no doubt."

"Love conquers all," she echoed. "Is that what's going to happen between you and Abyssinia? Next time we meet her, are you going to run into each other's arms in glorious slow motion while music swells in the background?"

"Seeing as how the last time we spoke I was cutting her heart out, I sincerely doubt it."

"How worried do we have to be, Skulduggery? Now that she's alive again?"

Skulduggery hesitated, then started to turn.

"Oi," she said. "Eyes front, Mr Pleasant."

He turned back. "Ah, yes, sorry. We'll deal with it, Valkyrie. We'll deal with Abyssinia and with her anti-Sanctuary the same way we deal with everything: with remarkable style and unerring good grace."

"That does sound like us," Valkyrie admitted, pulling on a fresh T-shirt. "I'm dropping in to see the family tomorrow, by the way."

"You are?" Skulduggery said, sounding pleased.

"Sent Mum a text before you arrived, just to check they'd all be home."

"And how are you feeling about that?"

She didn't answer for a moment. "Nervous," she said. "I don't know what I'll say. I know how it's going to go, though. Mum will be cool and Dad will be making stupid jokes and I'll be sitting there, trying to remember how I used to act when I was comfortable around them."

"It'll come to you," Skulduggery said. "You'll slip right back into place there. What about Alice?"

Valkyrie shimmied into her trousers. "What about her?"

"Do you think you'll be able to relax when she's around?"

"I don't know. I really don't."

"Do you want my advice? Give yourself a little time. And allow in the possibility that someday you might forgive yourself."

"Yeah," she said. "Tell you what – I'll forgive me when you forgive you. Deal?"

"Deal."

She sat on the bed, pulled on her boots. "Seriously, where is all this new-found optimism coming from?"

He shrugged again. "Even a pessimist can feel optimistic about certain things. I think that emerging from Smoke's influence has allowed me a little perspective. After you left for America, I took a wrong turn somewhere along the way. I let my priorities slip. Things happened. Mistakes were made."

"And now that I'm back?"

"You're back and so am I. Back to my old self. The person I like to be."

"Good," said Valkyrie, standing. "I'm quite fond of him, too, just so you know. You can turn round now."

He did so, and tilted his head as she slipped on her jacket. "You look good," he said.

She glanced at herself in the mirror. The black clung to her. "Yeah," she said.

"And you *are* back, aren't you?" he asked. "No more thoughts of leaving again?"

"Where would I go? Everything and everyone I care about is here. But... Skulduggery, you've got to understand that I'm not... I'm not the same person I was. There are times when I don't even recognise who I used to be. Then there are times when I glimpse her, you know? When I manage to forget everything that's happened and I just go back to being... normal."

"You were never normal."

She smiled. "Normal for me."

"Most people in the world walk nice, sunlit paths," Skulduggery said, "and when they look down they see their shadows clinging to their feet – attached but apart. Their shadows are not *them*. But you and I walk a different path. Our shadows are within us. We can't ignore them or forget them. They're a part of who we are, and they are vital to our survival.

"You may not like the darkness inside you, but it allows you to do things other people can't, or won't. And all those others – the good, the bad, the ordinary – they need people like us to protect them."

"And what about when we're the ones endangering them?"

"We'll just have to help each other find our way back to the light."

"I like that," she said, and walked over to him. Xena was still on her back, her paws in the air. Valkyrie put her hands on Skulduggery's chest. "Your tie's crooked," she said, adjusting it. "I can't have you looking dishevelled when you're out with me. I have a pretty terrible reputation to protect."

"We're going out, are we?"

"Of course," she said. "We have mysteries to solve, and adventures to undertake, and I need my partner looking dapper by my side."

"Are we taking the dog?"

"The dog is staying. Tonight it's just you and me." She gave the tie a slight adjustment, and nodded. "There. Perfect."

"Are you with me?" he asked.

She looked up at him. "Until the end," she said.

Glossary

Magical Disciplines

There are two main types of sorcerers – **Elementals**, who possess the ability to manipulate fire, earth, water and wind, and **Adepts**, whose wide variety of disciplines tend to be more aggressive.

The Three Names

You are born with three names. Your given name is what you were called upon birth, but this can be used to exert some rudimentary control over you. Your taken name is what you use to protect yourself from that control. Your true name is hidden from you, and is the source of all your magic.

Dramatis Personae

Alice Edgley: Valkyrie's six-year-old sister.

The Ancients: the first sorcerers. Exiled their gods, the Faceless Ones, from this reality. All dead now.

Baron Vengeous: One of the Mevolent's Three Generals. Fierce. Loyal. Deceased.

Cadaverous Gant: American. Dangerous.

China Sorrows: Intelligent. Beautiful. Not traditionally trustworthy.

Darquesse: Valkyrie's true name come to life. Mass-murderer. God. No longer in this reality.

The Dead Men: Skulduggery, Ghastly, Dexter Vex, Saracen Rue, Anton Shudder, Erskine Ravel, Hopeless (later replaced by Larrikin).

The Faceless Ones: A race of super-powered gods. Insane.

Fletcher Renn: English Teleporter. Young. Ridiculous hair.

Ghastly Bespoke: Elemental. Tailor. Made Valkyrie's armoured black clothes. Deceased.

Gordon Edgley: Valkyrie's uncle. Skulduggery's friend. Believed the Edgleys were descendants from the Last of the Ancients. Deceased.

Lord Vile: One of Mevolent's Three Generals. Necromancer. Merciless. Skulduggery's dark side.

Mevolent: Elemental. Disciple of the Faceless Ones. Worst of the worst. Waged a war against the Sanctuaries. Deceased.

Mevolent: Alternate-reality version of our universe's Mevolent. Very much alive.

Nefarian Serpine: One of Melovent's Three Generals. Murdered Skulduggery's family and Skulduggery himself. Deceased.

Skulduggery Pleasant: The Skeleton Detective. Wears exquisite suits exquisitely.

Tanith Low: English. Wall-walker. Carries a sword.

Tipstaff: Administrator at the Sanctuary.

Valkyrie Cain: A young lady with a lot on her mind.

MIDNIGHT

For years, Valkyrie Cain has struggled to keep her loved ones safe from harm, plunging into battle – time and time again – by Skulduggery Pleasant's side, and always emerging triumphant.

But now the very thing that Valkyrie fights for is in danger, as a ruthless killer snatches her little sister in order to lure Valkyrie into a final confrontation. With Skulduggery racing to catch up and young sorcerer Omen scrambling along behind, Valkyrie only has twelve hours to find Alice before it's too late.

The clock is ticking . . .

Read on for a taste of the next Skulduggery Pleasant adventure.

1

The old castle stood dark against the star-filled sky, its tall windows empty, its battlements jutting like teeth. Upon those battlements, and indifferent to the cold winds that scoured the mountaintops, stood Wretchlings, monstrous things of scabs and sores whose insides boiled with poisoned blood and decaying meat.

Lying on a blanket on a snow-covered perch 809 metres west and 193 metres up, Skulduggery Pleasant put his right eye socket to the scope of his rifle and adjusted the dial.

He wriggled slightly, settling deeper into the blanket, then went perfectly still. His gloved finger began to slowly squeeze the trigger, and Valkyrie raised her binoculars, training them on the closest Wretchling.

The gun went off with a loud crack that the wind snatched away, but they were so far from the target that it took a few seconds for the bullet to hit.

The Wretchling jerked slightly, and looked down at its chest. A moment later, it started to tremble. The stitches that held it together unravelled, and the Wretchling came undone, its body parts falling, its stolen entrails spilling out, and it collapsed on top of itself, a pile of meat steaming in the cold air.

Skulduggery moved on to the next target and adjusted the scope once more.

"You think they feel pain?" Valkyrie asked.

Skulduggery paused for a moment, and looked at her. "I'm sorry?"

"The Wretchlings," she said. "Do you think they feel pain?"

"Not really," he answered, and went back to aiming his rifle.

"But they have brains, right? Fair enough, they might not be thinking great thoughts, but they do still think. And, if they think, they might be able to feel. And, if their body can feel physically, can't their minds feel emotionally?"

Skulduggery fired again. Valkyrie didn't bother looking to see if the bullet had hit its target. Of course it had.

"They do have brains," Skulduggery said. "They're stolen from the dead, along with the limbs and the internal organs, and they're twisted and warped and attached to the Wretchling like the parts of a machine – because that's what they are. They look alive, but it's all artificial. Are you feeling guilty about what we're doing?"

"No." She watched him acquire his next target. "Kind of."

"They're just like Hollow Men." He put his eye socket to the scope.

"But Hollow Men don't have brains."

"I don't have a brain."

"But Hollow Men can't think."

"Believe me, the only thing on a Wretchling's mind is the messiest way to kill someone."

Valkyrie looked through the binoculars. "So we kill them first? That's hardly enlightened, is it?"

"We're not killing them," Skulduggery said. "These clever little bullets are designed to dismantle, not destroy."

He fired, and she watched as the next Wretchling was dismantled. Black blood gushed.

Skulduggery stood. "That's the last of them," he said, taking Valkyrie's hand and pulling her to her feet. He left the sniper rifle on the blanket and she handed him his hat. It was black, like his three-piece suit, like his shirt and tie. Valkyrie was dressed all in black, too – in the armoured clothes made for her years ago by Ghastly Bespoke and the heavy coat with the fur-lined hood she wore over them.

Clouds were moving in from the east, scraping over the jagged peaks of the mountains, blocking out the stars. Below where they stood, the drop disappeared into gloom. The wind nudged Valkyrie, like it wanted to tip her over the edge, send her spinning downwards into the cold emptiness. She felt an almost irresistible urge to take a big step forward.

"Are you OK?" Skulduggery asked.

Her face, numb though it was, had gone quite slack. She fixed it into a smile. "Peachy," she said, taking off her coat. "Let's go."

He wrapped an arm round her waist. "Are you sure you don't want to try this alone?"

"If I knew I'd be able to fly, no problem," she said. "But I told my folks I'd be there for roast dinner, and if I plunge to my death before that they'll just think it's rude, so..."

They lifted up and drifted beyond the ledge, the world opening up beneath them. Skulduggery redirected the freezing winds so that not a single hair was disturbed on Valkyrie's head. It was strangely quiet as they flew, surrounded by the howls and shrieks of the mountains, but tucked away from it all.

"The thought has occurred to me that maybe you'll only start flying when you absolutely need to," Skulduggery said.

"Do not drop me."

"Indulge me for a moment. The range of your powers is still largely unknown to us, yes? You can fire lightning from your fingertips, you certainly have destructive potential and you have the burgeoning psychic abilities of at least a Level 4 Sensitive. Plus, you have flown before."

"Hovering is not flying."

"I bet if I were to drop you, you'd fly."

"I'm not sure if I can emphasise this enough, but *do not* drop me."

"The promise of imminent death could release you from the mental barriers that are holding you back."

"It wouldn't be imminent death, though, would it? You'd catch me. There's no threat there. You'd save me because saving me is what you do, just like saving you is what I do. The only thing that dropping me would accomplish is to annoy the hell out of me."

Skulduggery was quiet for a moment.

"*Do not drop me*," Valkyrie repeated.

He sighed, and they continued over to the castle, landing beside a pile of Wretchling remains. A sudden gust surrounded them with the stench of putrid meat and human waste. It filled Valkyrie's nose and mouth, and she gagged. As Skulduggery sent the foul air away with a wave of his hand, Valkyrie lunged for the battlements, sure she was going to puke over the side – but she swallowed, managed to keep it down.

"Sometimes I miss having a sense of smell," Skulduggery said. "Tonight is not one of those times."

Valkyrie spat, wiped her mouth, and stayed where she was for a moment to recover. She felt sure that she'd once been told the proper names for the different sections of the battlements, but couldn't for the life of her remember what they were.

The wind whipped her hair in front of her face, so she tied it back into a ponytail, then took a wooden sphere, roughly the size of a golf ball, from her pocket. She gripped the sphere in both hands and twisted in opposite directions, and a transparent bubble rippled outwards, enveloped her and stabilised. The personal cloaking spheres didn't have nearly the range of their regular-sized versions, but they were just as effective, and a lot handier to carry around.

Skulduggery took out his own cloaking sphere, did the same and vanished from her sight.

She slipped the sphere back in her pocket and stepped closer to him. Her cloaking bubble mingled with his and suddenly she could see him again.

Sticking by each other's side, they set off down a set of stone steps, a flurry of snow chasing them into the gloom. Skulduggery held up his hand just before they reached the bottom. A tripwire glinted on the final step.

"Sneaky," Valkyrie said.

They jumped the last few steps, and the moment before they landed Skulduggery caught her and kept them hovering off the ground.

"Pressure plates," he said.

"Even sneakier."

They drifted along the corridor, stopping at the end so that Valkyrie could push open the door. They touched down on the other side and took the next set of stone steps that spiralled downwards, Skulduggery leading the way.

Two guards with sickles on their backs stood at the open windows in the next corridor, their heads covered by black helmets. Rippers. It was freezing in there, but they stood with their arms by their sides, as though the cold didn't bother them, keeping watch on the road leading to the castle.

"Which one do you want?" Skulduggery asked.

Nodding to the nearest Ripper, Valkyrie said, "This one," in a soft voice, even though she knew that her words wouldn't travel beyond the bubble that surrounded them.

"Count to ten," Skulduggery responded, and walked away, vanishing from sight.

Valkyrie moved up behind the Ripper, finished the count and stepped closer. Out of the corner of her eye, the second Ripper disappeared as Skulduggery did the same.

She wrapped her right arm round the Ripper's throat, grabbed the bicep of her left arm and hooked her hand behind the Ripper's helmet. His hands came up, trying to free himself. He put a foot to the wall and pushed out, shoving them both backwards. Valkyrie held on, her head down, her eyes closed. She kicked at his leg and dragged him backwards, laying him on the ground as his struggles weakened.

She looked up, watched as the second Ripper fell into view. He hit the floor and stayed there.

When her Ripper was unconscious, she released him and walked to the other end of the corridor. Her cloaking bubble intersected with Skulduggery's and he appeared before her so suddenly she jumped.

"Sorry," he said.

She waved his apology away. "I'm sure I scared you just as much as you scared me."

"Not really."

Valkyrie took his hat and threw it out of the window, and was totally unsurprised when a moment later it floated in again and settled back on his head.

"Are you quite finished?" he asked, adjusting it slightly.

"It wouldn't kill you to admit to being a little startled every now and then," she said.

"I don't get startled," he responded, walking off again. She caught up to him before he left her bubble, and fell into step beside him. "I anticipate and adjust accordingly."

"You don't anticipate everything."

"Of course not. Where would be the fun in that?"

"I'm just saying you shouldn't feel like you have to keep up this unflappable demeanour around me."

"Has it occurred to you, after all these years together, that I just might not be flappable?"

"Everyone is flappable, Skulduggery."

"Not me."

They came to a door that took them to a tunnel that took them to a room, and in this room they chose an archway that took them to more stairs. Down they went, and down again, until the torches in brackets were replaced by bulbs and the steady thrum of power reverberated through the floor. They avoided large groups of Rippers, passed rooms where white-coated scientists murmured to one another, and kept going until they came to a Perspex window overlooking a large laboratory packed with machines that blinked with volatile energy.

Doctor Nye sat on a stool, its back stooped, working on the intricate insides of a rusted device. Nye's thin limbs looked smaller than when Valkyrie had seen it last, when it had towered over her, its head nearly brushing the ceiling, but she wasn't altogether surprised. Crengarrions shrank as they got older, and their skin colour tended to lighten. Now it looked, at most, about ten feet tall, and its skin was a delicate ash.

"It looks old," she murmured. "Good."

They found the stairs, followed them down, arriving at the double doors that led into Nye's lab. Two Rippers stood guard.

"I've got this one," Valkyrie said, walking towards the Ripper on the right. She was halfway there when the cloaking sphere started to vibrate in her pocket.

Alarmed, she pulled it out. The two hemispheres were ticking towards each other quickly – much quicker than they should have been – counting down to the bubble's collapse. She tried to twist them back, then struggled to keep them in place, but it was no good.

The bubble contracted. Not all the way, just enough to reveal her feet and the top of her head. She crouched, before either of the Rippers caught sight of her. There were sigils on the wall – Valkyrie could see them now. She recognised one of them: a security sigil that attacked Teleporters. She was pretty sure the other one was forcing her cloaking sphere to malfunction.

Keeping low, she pocketed the sphere and hurried over to the Ripper. The bubble contracted again. He heard her footsteps and his hands went to his weapons.

Valkyrie pulled her own weapons – shock sticks held in place on her back – and launched herself at him. The first stick cracked against his helmet, but he ducked the second, spinning away. Valkyrie's bubble collapsed completely now, as did Skulduggery's, and she glimpsed him throwing fire even as her Ripper attacked, sickles blurring.

Valkyrie knew the pattern and countered, slipped to the side and struck the Ripper's knee, then spun and caught him in the ribs. His clothes absorbed the electrical charge, and he didn't seem to mind the pain.

He left her an opening and she fell for it, committing herself to a swing that she regretted instantly. A sickle blade raked across her belly, would have torn her open were it not for her armoured jacket. He kicked at her ankle, swept her leg, and she hit the ground and somersaulted backwards to her feet, defending all the while. His knee thudded into her cheek and the world tilted.

He leaped at her. She dropped the stick in her right hand and white lightning burst from her fingers, striking him in the chest and blasting him head over heels. He rolled and came up, his jacket smoking.

Valkyrie picked up the fallen stick, placed it end to end with the other one. They attached and she twisted, the staff lengthening, and when the Ripper ran at her she whacked it into his leg, then spun and cracked it against his head. He fell back and she followed, the staff striking him once, twice, and then a twirling third time. He dropped one of his sickles.

She went to finish him off and he dodged, dodged again, dodged faster than she could strike. He jumped over to the wall and rebounded, flipping over her head. She whirled, but he was too close, and he grabbed the staff and pulled her into a headbutt that would have broken her nose had she not lowered her head. Even so, bright lights flashed, and she felt the staff being wrenched from her grip as she went staggering.

The Ripper let the staff drop, and swung his remaining sickle towards her neck. She raised an arm, her armoured clothes saving her once again, and snatched the weapon away. It fell, clattering against the stones.

Valkyrie ducked low and powered forward, grabbing him round the waist. Snarling, she lifted him off his feet and slammed him against the wall, then seized his helmet, searching for the twin releases, and then tore it from his head. The Ripper fell back, blinking, and she swung the helmet into his jaw and he went down, and she hit him again and again until she figured that was probably enough.

She dropped the helmet and got her breath back.

"You got his helmet off," Skulduggery said, standing over the motionless form of the second Ripper. "How did you manage that?"

She shrugged. "I adapted accordingly. Come on. We have a doctor's appointment."

2

She pushed the double doors open and Doctor Nye waved a long-fingered hand.

"Do not disturb me," it said in that familiar high whisper. "I left strict orders not to be—"

It looked up then, and its small eyes widened and its wide mouth opened as it got to its feet, the stool crashing to the ground behind it.

Skulduggery held his gun low, by his hip. "The moment you set off an alarm, I will shoot you. I feel we ought to be clear on that from the very beginning."

Nye stopped moving backwards, and raised its arms. "I have no weapons."

Up close, Valkyrie could see that the threads that had once sewn Nye's mouth and eyes shut were still there, poking out of its skin. She walked forward. "You act like you're not pleased to see us, Doctor. That hurts my feelings. I thought we'd bonded that time you autopsied me."

"The years have been good to you," Skulduggery said, coming round the table. "I mean, you've obviously shrunk, but apart from that you look great. How have you been spending your time? The last I heard, you'd escaped from Ironpoint Gaol. Who was it that broke you out? Eliza Scorn?"

"How is Eliza?" Valkyrie asked. "Any word?"

"I haven't seen Eliza Scorn in years," Nye said. "I was not the only one she freed. There were others."

"But she set you up here," said Skulduggery. "You'd lost everything when we imprisoned you. We made sure of it. She helped you."

Nye licked its lips. Its tongue was small and pink. "She could see the importance of my work."

Valkyrie picked up a scalpel and walked over slowly. "Excavating the soul," she said. "How's that going for you? Found it yet?"

"I believe I have," said Nye.

"So what next? Now that you've found where it hides, what are you going to do with it?"

"Finding the soul was only the first step. Now I follow it to where it leads. I'm not hurting anyone. I'm not experimenting on anyone. You can search the castle. I have no patients here."

"No?" Valkyrie asked. "You don't have anyone strapped to a table somewhere, their ribcage open, their organs on a nearby tray while they look around, hallucinating friends and family come to rescue them? No? Well, I have to say that's an improvement. You're practically reformed. Skulduggery?"

"You're quite sure there is no one being tortured, Doctor?" Skulduggery asked. "Maybe having their skin peeled off? I heard about one experiment you ran during the war where you decapitated prisoners and then kept their heads alive in jars."

Nye backed up. "What do you want?"

"You're under arrest," Skulduggery said. "You're going back to Ironpoint."

"We'll be sure to request a smaller cell this time," Valkyrie said. "Something snug."

"Or you can make it easy on yourself," Skulduggery said. "You can tell us where Abyssinia is."

Incredibly, Nye paled even further.

"Wow," said Valkyrie, "your poker face sucks, dude. That means we get to bypass the bit where you tell us you don't know what we're talking about – and we threaten you and you eventually break – and go straight to the part where you answer our questions. So where is she?"

"I do not know."

"I'm just going to warn you that we've been looking for Abyssinia for almost six months. Do you hear me? Six months. And we haven't found her, or the floating prison she's commandeered, or any of her little anti-Sanctuary friends. We're both extremely annoyed about this. Our patience has worn thin, Doctor. When we found out that she paid a visit to this charming castle no less than two days ago... Well, I'm not going to lie: I cried a little. Tears of happiness. And when we learned that you were working here? It was like all my birthdays had come at once. Not only do I get to see my old friend Doctor Nye, but Doctor Nye gets to help us in our search, and tell us where Abyssinia has gone."

"I promise you, I do not know."

"Then why was she here?" Skulduggery asked.

"If... if I tell you, you must let me go."

"OK."

"I think you are lying."

"Of course I'm lying. You're going back to prison, Doctor. The only choice you've got is the size of your cell."

Nye hesitated, then sagged. "It was not a thing she was looking for. It was a person. His name is Caisson."

"And who is Caisson?"

"Abyssinia said he is her son."

"I see," Skulduggery said, taking a moment. "Does he work here? Is he a scientist or manual labour?"

Nye hesitated.

Valkyrie folded her arms. "He was a patient, wasn't he? You may not be experimenting on anyone right now, but up until two days ago you were."

"When I came here, this facility had already been running for decades," Nye said. "I was brought in to replace a scientist who had gone missing. My instructions were clear: I was to continue the work of my predecessor. On my initial tour, I was shown the room in which Caisson was being kept – but I was not the one who worked on him."

"How long had the experiments been going on for?"

"As far as I am aware, for as long as this facility has been operational."

"Which is?"

"Sixty years."

Valkyrie frowned. "He's been experimented on for sixty years?"

"No," said Nye. "He was experimented on *here* for sixty years. I do not know where he was before this."

"What else do you know about him?" Skulduggery asked.

"Nothing. Experimenting on Caisson was not my job."

"So who did the work?"

"An associate. Doctor Quidnunc."

"Is he in today?" Valkyrie asked.

"I have not seen him in a week, since Caisson was removed from this facility."

"Caisson was removed a *week* ago?" Valkyrie said. "So, when Abyssinia came for him, he was already gone? Why was he moved?"

"I do not know for certain," said Nye, "but I imagine somebody learned that Abyssinia was drawing close and we were told to evacuate as a result. Caisson was the first to be moved."

"Then why are you still here?"

"I, and a handful of other scientists, refused to leave. I can only speak for myself, but my work had reached a critical stage and I could not possibly depart."

"Abyssinia wouldn't have been happy that her son wasn't here," Skulduggery said.

"She was not," said Nye. "She killed many Rippers."

"Did you tell her where he was moved to?"

"I did not, and do not, possess that information."

"Who took him?"

"I do not know. A small team of people. The owner of this facility sent them."

"Which brings us back to Eliza Scorn."

Nye shook its head. "Eliza Scorn does not own this facility. As far as I know, she was merely obeying orders when she delivered me here."

"Then who's your employer?"

"I am afraid I do not know."

"You're working for someone and you don't even know who it is?"

"What does it matter?" Nye asked. "My work is important and needs resources. I do not care who provides them."

Valkyrie sighed. "What about Abyssinia? Did she say anything that could lead us to her? Remember, you really want to make us happy."

"She provided no such information."

"Did you tell her about Quidnunc and his experiments?" Skulduggery asked.

"Yes."

"Did you tell her where she could find the good doctor?"

"I do not know where he is."

"Then how are you still alive?" Skulduggery asked. "You don't know anything helpful; you worked in the same facility where her son was being experimented on... Why didn't she kill you, Doctor?"

"Because I did to her the same thing as I am doing to you," Nye responded.

"And what is that?"

"Delaying you."

The shadows converged and twisted and from the darkness stepped a woman in a black cloak, her face covered by a cloth mask so that only her eyes were visible.

Skulduggery raised his gun and the woman's cloak lashed out, and Skulduggery ducked and fired. The cloak absorbed the bullets and whipped again, slicing through the table to get to him. Skulduggery jerked to the side, his hand filling with flame, but the cloak twisted back, covering him – and, when it whipped away, Skulduggery was gone.

The woman turned to Valkyrie, but Valkyrie had already moved behind Nye and was buckling its legs. It dropped to its knees and she gripped its throat, keeping her eyes on the newcomer.

"Have to admit," Valkyrie said, "that was pretty cool, even for a Necromancer. But, if you try anything like that on me, I will fry the stick insect here."

The woman in black didn't respond. Her cloak coiled around her.

"You would not kill me," said Nye, its voice a little garbled. Its skin felt oily in her grip.

"I wouldn't *want* to kill you," Valkyrie corrected him. "I wouldn't want to kill anyone. But, if your awesome bodyguard tries to kill me, I'll kill you faster than your beady little eyes can blink."

Nye made a small sound, like a laugh. "Then it seems that we have reached an impasse."

"Not at all," said Valkyrie. "An impasse implies that we're evenly matched. But we all know that's not true." She glanced at the woman in black. "I dabbled with Necromancy. Did you know that? Solomon Wreath taught me a few things. So I know that you can shadow-walk. That's what you did with Skulduggery, right? But I also know that the range for shadow-walking is limited – so he's already on his way back here and he's coming mighty fast. We only have a few seconds before he bursts through these doors, and when that happens... it's not going to be pretty. All I have to do is wait, because time is on my side. But for you the clock is ticking. Can you hear that? The tick-tock in your head?"

"I am not going back to Ironpoint," said Nye. "I only have a few years left in my life. I will not spend them in a cell. Whisper – kill her."

"Whisper – wait," Valkyrie said, tightening her grip. "Why is it always killing, huh? Why is it always fighting? Why is violence always the default position?"

Nye held up a hand to Whisper, even though the woman had not moved. "You offer an alternative?" it asked.

"Give me Quidnunc, and I'll let you go before Skulduggery gets back."

"I do not know where Quidnunc is," Nye said. "But I do know one thing that could possibly lead you to him."

"Did you tell this one thing to Abyssinia?"

"I did."

"So we'd be playing catch-up."

"Yes."

Valkyrie considered her options, of which there were none. "OK," she said. "Deal."

"First, you must release me."

"I don't trust you enough to release you, Doctor."

"Then you had better make a decision before the Skeleton Detective gets here, Miss Cain. Time is ticking away."

Valkyrie almost smiled. She took her hand from Nye's throat and stepped back as it stood. It turned, looking down at her, as Whisper came up behind it. Her cloak swirled around them both.

"Quidnunc suffers from liquefactive necrosis," Nye said, and the shadows convulsed and Valkyrie was left alone.

"Huh," she said.

The doors burst open and Skulduggery stormed in, gun in one hand and fire in the other. "Where are they?" he demanded.

"Gone," said Valkyrie. "You just missed them."

Skulduggery stood there for a moment, then shook the flames from his hand and slipped the gun back under his jacket. "That's annoying," he said. "Are you OK?"

She shrugged. "Grand. Quidnunc has, um, liquid active necrosis."

"Do you mean liquefactive necrosis?"

"Let's say that I do. What is it?"

"A form of organic rot that Mevolent had weaponised during the war."

"That the same thing Tesseract had? So Quidnunc wears a mask, like him?"

"Perhaps," Skulduggery said. "In any case, he will need the same serums that kept Tesseract alive, and those serums are hard to come by. If we find who makes them, we'll find Quidnunc."

"Cool. Although Nye told Abyssinia, y'know, about the liquid factor thing."

"Liquefactive necrosis."

"He told her about that, too."

"Then we have no time to waste," Skulduggery said, stalking to the door. He spun round. "Unless you're hungry. Are you hungry? You haven't eaten since noon."

"I'm pretty hungry, yeah."

"Then we'll stop for pizza," Skulduggery said, and marched out.